Books by Nancy Springer

The Sable Moon
The Silver Sun
The White Hart

Published by TIMESCAPE

Nancy Springer

THE SABLE MOON

A TIMESCAPE BOOK
PUBLISHED BY POCKET BOOKS NEW YORK

Another *Original* publication of TIMESCAPE

 A Timescape Book published by
POCKET BOOKS, a Simon & Schuster division of
GULF & WESTERN CORPORATION
1230 Avenue of the Americas, New York, N Y 10020

ISBN. 0-671-44378-X

First Pocket Books printing February, 1981

10 9 8 7 6 5 4 3

POCKET and colophon are registered trademarks
of Simon & Schuster

Use of the trademark TIMESCAPE is by exclusive license
from Gregory Benford, the trademark owner

Printed in the U S.A.

I am a crescent moon.
I am a rustle of padded paws,
I am a seed in the earth,
I am a dewdrop.
I am a hidden jewel,
I am a dream,
I am a silver harp.

I am a fruit on the Tree,
I am a beast of curving horn,
I am a swollen breast,
I am the argent moon.
I am soft rain,
I am rivers of thought,
I am sea tides,
I am a turning wheel.

I am the waning moon.
I am the mare who rides men mad,
I am the sable moon.
I am the howl of the wolf,
I am the hag,
I am the flood of destruction.
I am the ship that rides the flood,
I am the crescent moon.
I am the dark, bright, changing moon.

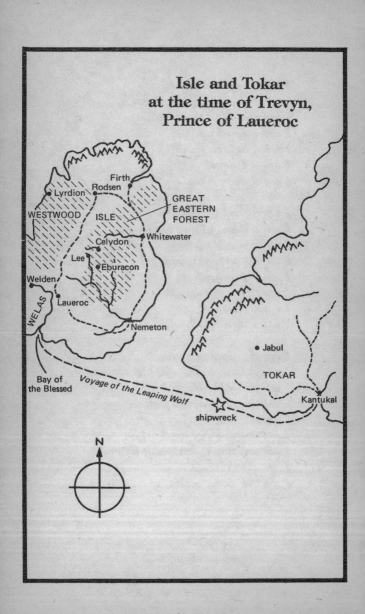

Isle and Tokar at the time of Trevyn, Prince of Laueroc

Firth
Rodsen
Lyrdion
WESTWOOD
ISLE
GREAT EASTERN FOREST
Whitewater
Celydon
Lee
Eburacon
Welden
WELAS
Laueroc
Nemeton

Jabul
TOKAR
Kantukal

Bay of the Blessed
Voyage of the Leaping Wolf
shipwreck

N

Book One

FATE AND THE MAIDEN

Chapter One

Prince Trevyn was seventeen years old, and still struggling out of childhood like an eaglet out of the shell, when he first met Gwern. It was not a happy meeting.

Trevyn had galloped far ahead of the others, because his half-fledged falcon had led him a crazy course over the grassy downs. Muttering to himself and whistling at the bird, he topped a rise and saw a herd of yearling colts in the dingle below. Small heads, arched necks, level backs, and high-set, windswept tails—young though they were, everything about them marked them unmistakably as steeds of the royal breed. A stranger stood with them, stroking a chestnut filly on the nose.

"You, there!" Trevyn shouted hotly. "Let the horses alone!"

The fellow glanced at him without moving. Trevyn sent his mount plunging down the slope toward him.

"Let the horses alone, I say!" he called again as he approached.

The stranger, a youth of about his own age, met his angry eyes coolly. "Why so?"

3

Trevyn almost sputtered at the calm question. Did the dolt not know that he was Trevyn son of Alan of Laueroc, that he was Prince of Isle and Welas, sole heir of the Sun Kings? The *elwedeyn* horses had been the special pride of the Crown ever since his kindred the elves had presented them, before his birth. No uninstructed hand was permitted to touch them. Indeed, they would not lightly suffer the touch of any hand. The royal family commanded their love through the use of the Old Language that had come down to them from the Beginning. . . . Quietly, Trevyn ordered the chestnut filly away from the stranger. It unnerved him that she permitted that hand upon her at all.

The stranger looked up at him with eyes like pebbles, expressionless. "Why did you do that? Are these horses yours?"

"Ay, they are mine," replied Trevyn, trying to keep the edge out of his voice. Perhaps the yokel was a half-wit. There was something odd about his face.

"You are a fool to say so." The fellow turned away indifferently and stroked another horse, a cream-colored one. "These horses belong to no one."

Trevyn's temper flared, all the more so because the other was right, in a sense. Galled, he sprang down from his mount and jerked the stranger by the arm. "Get away, I say!"

Still expressionless, the youth pulled from his grasp and lashed back with a closed fist. In an instant, both of them were flailing at each other, then rolling in a tussle on the grass. Trevyn wore a sword, and after a bit he wished he could honorably use it. The stranger was as hard and resilient as an axe haft, and his blows hurt.

Before the fight reached a conclusion, however, the combatants found themselves hauled apart. "Now *what*," inquired a quiet voice, "is the cause of this?"

Trevyn blinked out of a blackened eye. It was his uncle, Hal, the King of the Silver Sun; and though he did not look angry, Trevyn hated to cause him sorrow. Trevyn's father, King Alan, faced him as well, and he looked angry enough for two.

"Surely," Hal remarked, "this row must have had a beginning?"

"He was bothering the horses," Trevyn accused, and pointed, childlike, at the stranger.

"The horses don't look bothered," Alan scoffed harshly.

The horses, apparently pleased by the excitement, had formed a circle of curious heads. The chestnut filly stretched her neck and nuzzled the stranger youth's hand.

Hal and Alan exchanged a surprised glance. "Fellow," Alan addressed the stranger, "what is your name?"

"Gwern." The youth spoke flatly.

"And who are your parents?"

"I have none." Gwern did not seem to find this the least bit remarkable.

"Who were you born of?" asked Alan with more patience than was his wont. "Who was your mother?"

For the first time Gwern hesitated, seeming at a loss. "Earth," he said at last.

Alan frowned and tried another tack. "Where is your home?"

"Earth," Gwern replied.

They all stared at him, not sure whether or not he was deliberately courting Alan's anger. He stared back at them with eyes like stream-washed stones, indeterminately brown. He was brown all over, his skin a curious dun, his hair like hazel tips. He was barefoot, and his clothing was of coarse unbleached wool, when most folk of these peaceful times could afford better. What was he doing in the middle of the downs, with the nearest dwelling miles away?

"Take him along home," Hal suggested mildly, "and I'll look him up in the census."

When he was king, Trevyn promised himself, he would set such nuisances in a dungeon for a week or so, to teach them some respect. Take him along home indeed!

Alan shrugged and turned back to his son, less angry at Trevyn now. "Who struck first?"

"I pulled him away from a horse, and he struck me."

"Pulled him away from a horse? And why? If an *elwedeyn* horse sees fit to bear him company, lad, you also had better learn to abide him. The horses are well able to defend themselves, and they're better judges of men than most chamberlains. Think before you fight, Trevyn." Alan was disgusted. "So now you have a black eye, and you have lost your hawk. Get on home."

They all rode silently back to the walled city of Laueroc, with Gwern behind Hal on his *elwedeyn* stallion, over rolling meadows where the larks sang through the days. For miles before they came to it they could see the castle anchored on the billowing softness of the downs like a tall ship on a shimmering, grassy sea. Atop the highest swell its ramparts vaulted skyward, and from its slender turrets floated flags of every holding in Isle. In every window, even the servants' windows, swung a circle of cut and faceted glass to catch the sun and send colors flitting about the rooms.

Centuries before, Cuin the Falconer King had raised the fortress at Laueroc with pearly, gold-veined stone brought all the way from the mountains of Welas. He had not wanted to mar his new demesne with diggings. The land at Laueroc, in Trevyn's time, was still nearly as scarless as the day it was born. The castle lay on its bosom like a crystal brooch, and two roads wound away like flat bronze chains. There were no buildings outside the walls. In the topmost chamber of the westernmost tall tower, athwart the battlements, King Hal made his study and solitary retreat.

Trevyn climbed up there after him when they had stabled the horses, and to his dismay Gwern followed. It troubled him that the dirt-colored stranger should come so familiarly to his uncle's room. Hal was more than Sunset King; he was a bard, a visionary and a seer. In all the kingdom, only three persons approached him with the love of equals: Queen Rosemary, his beloved; his brother Alan; and Lysse, the Elf-Queen, Trevyn's mother and Alan's wife. Trevyn held him in awe. When he entered the tower chamber he silently took his seat, knees loaded down with tomes of history, awaiting Hal's leisure. But Gwern poked and prowled around the circular room, disturbing Hal's scholarly clutter. And Hal stood gazing out of his high, barred window, seeming not to mind.

"What do you see?" Gwern asked suddenly. Trevyn winced at his effrontery. The King of the Silver Sun had always looked to the west, toward Welas and the reaches of the sunset stars, and Trevyn had never dared to ask him why. But Hal turned around courteously.

"I see Elwestrand, what else?" he replied, the sheen of his gray eyes going smoky dark. "And a fair sight it is."

"Where is Elwestrand?" Gwern craned his neck, peering.

"Nay, nay," Hal explained eagerly, "you must look with your inner eye. Elwestrand is beyond the western sea." His voice yearned like singing. "I have seen a tree with golden fruit, and a great white stag, and bright birds, and sleek, romping beasts. I have seen unicorns."

"Elwestrand is the grove of the dead," Trevyn told Gwern sharply, jealous that Hal would speak to him so equably.

"Grove of the dead?" Hal turned to regard his nephew with a tiny smile on his angular face. "Elwestrand is but another step on the way to the One, for all that it lies beyond the sunlit lands."

"It must be dark," Gwern said doubtfully.

"Nay, indeed!" Hal cried. "It shines like—like the fair flower of Veran used to shine, here in Isle, before the Easterners blighted it. . . . Elwestrand is lilac and celadon and pearly gray-gold and every subtle glow of the summer stars. And glow of dragons from the indigo sea, every shade of damson and quince and dusky rose. The elves remembered it all in their bright stitchery—all that this world was, and this Isle, before the Eastern invasion, before man's evil shadowed and spread." Hal turned back to his window on the west, pressing his forehead against the bars.

"My kindred the elves sailed to Elwestrand," Trevyn told Gwern more softly. "All of them except my mother."

"Now they live amidst the stuff of their dreams," Hal said from his window.

"But does no one return from Elwestrand?" Gwern asked.

"Who would wish to return?"

"Veran came from Elwestrand, did he not?" Trevyn spoke up suddenly.

"Who is Veran?" Gwern pounced on the name.

Hal turned to answer with patience Trevyn could not understand. "He from whom I derive my lineage and my crown, the first Blessed King of Welas. He sailed hither out of

the west; perhaps he came from Elwestrand." Hal looked
away again. "But when I go, I will not return."

"Elwestrand," Gwern sang in a rich, husky voice.

> "Elwestrand! Elwestrand!
> Be you realm but of my mind,
> Yet you've lived ten thousand lines
> Of soaring song,
> Elwestrand. Is the soul more sooth
> Than that for which it pines?
> Are there ties that closer bind
> Than call so strong?"

Hal wheeled on him sharply. "How did you know that
song?" he demanded. "I made it, years ago."

"Elwestrand," Gwern chanted, and without answering he
darted out of the door and skipped down the tower steps, still
singing. Hal silently watched him go. Trevyn watched also,
hot with jealous anger. For he, too, had felt the dream and
the call, and it seemed to him as if Gwern had stolen it from
him.

"Why do you abide him so tamely?" he burst out at Hal,
startled by his own daring. "He is—he is uncouth!"

Hal shifted his gaze to his nephew, and as always that
detached, appraising look made Trevyn shrink, inwardly
cursing. Hal threatened nothing, but he saw everything, and
Trevyn had dark places inside that he wanted to hide. . . .
Hal frowned faintly, then turned his eyes away from the
Prince to answer his question, seeming to see the answer in
the air.

"He is magical," Hal said. "He is like a late shoot of those
who were lost to Isle centuries ago when the star-son Bevan
led his people out of the hollow hills. Magic left Isle then, and
I believe nothing has been quite right since—though I have
sometimes thought that Veran brought some back to Welas—
and your mother's people, in their own clearheaded way—"

"Magic!" Trevyn blurted, astonished to hear longing in
Hal's voice. He knew how his uncle had always avoided the
touch of magic. The Easterners had made magic the horror of
Isle. At Nemeton their sorcerers had performed barbaric

sacrifice to the Sacred Son and the horned god from whom they drew their powers. Hal had been reared in the shadow of that cult, and he and Alan had worked for years to stamp out such black sorcery.

"I know I have taught you not to meddle with magic." Hal sat by his nephew. "It is perilous. But all fair things are perilous. Dragons breathe fire, and the horn of the unicorn is sharp. Even this Gwern might be perilous, in his own rude way." The Sunset King smiled dreamily. "But it must bode well, I think, that he has come to us. Who or what can he be, I wonder? I don't really expect to find him in the census."

As, in fact, he could not. So Gwern stayed on at the castle; the Lauerocs kept him there for want of anything better to do with him. The peculiar youth did not seem suited for any work, but Alan claimed he was no more useless than most of the other courtiers. He was fey, sometimes shouting and singing with barbaric abandon, sometimes brooding. He always went barefoot, even in the chill of late autumn, and often he slept outdoors, beyond the city walls, on the ground. He generally looked dirty and uncombed. He observed few niceties. If he spoke at all, he spoke with consummate accuracy and no tact. But he was handsome, in his earthy way, and the castle folk seemed to find him amusing, even attractive. Trevyn fervently disliked him. Striving as he was for adolescent poise, he found Gwern's very existence an affront.

Yet, with no malice that Trevyn could prove, Gwern attached himself to the Prince, following him everywhere. Often they would fight—only with fists, since Gwern knew nothing of swordplay. Trevyn could hold his own, but he never succeeded in driving Gwern away from him. The mud-colored youth confronted him like an embodied force, inscrutable and haphazard as wind or rainclouds, leaving only by his own unpredictable whim.

"Father," Trevyn begged, "make him stop hounding me. Please."

"You'll see worse troubles before you die," Alan replied. "Find your own cure for it, Trevyn." He loved his son to the point of heartache, but Trevyn would be King. Above all, he must not become soft or spoiled. Alan had seen to his training

in statesmanship, swordsmanship, horsemanship. . . . The
discipline was no more than Alan expected of himself, his
own body trim and tough, his days given over to royal duty,
early and late. So when Trevyn saluted, soldierlike, and
silently left the room, Alan could not fault his conduct. Great
of heart that he was, it did not occur to him that Trevyn
showed too little of the heart, that he concealed too much.

Trevyn was almost able to hide his anger even from
himself, minding his manners and tending to his lessons as
Gwern dogged him through the crisp days of early winter. But
frustration swirled and seethed through his thoughts like a
buried torrent. In time Trevyn found Gwern obstinately
intruding even into his dreams at night. Gwern and a unicorn;
Gwern standing at the prow of an elf-ship, with the sea wind
in his face. . . .

"I!" Trevyn shouted in his sleep.

He felt sure that Gwern longed to go to Elwestrand, as he
did. But he swore that it was he, Prince Trevyn, who would
go, and alone, and to return, as no one had done before him.
Someday he would do that. But he could not possibly take
ship before spring. The winter stretched endlessly ahead.

Trevyn did not stay for winter. When the first snowstorm
loomed, he slipped from his bed by night and made his way to
the stable. He loaded food and blankets onto Arundel, Hal's
elwedeyn charger, the oldest and wisest of the royal steeds.
The walls and gates were lightly guarded, for it was peace-
time, and who would look for trouble in the teeth of a storm?
Warmly dressed, Trevyn rode out of a postern gate into the
dark and the freezing wind. By morning even Gwern would
not be able to follow him.

It was so. Dawn showed snow almost a foot deep, and more
still falling, blindingly thick, in the air. Folk struggled even to
cross the courtyard. It was nearly midday before Alan could
believe that Trevyn was missing, and then he could not eat for
anger and consternation. He paced the battlements for hours.
But Gwern had known as soon as he awoke what Trevyn had
done, and he had run to the walls screaming in rage.

"Alan, don't fret so." Hal came up beside his brother,
encircled his shoulders with a comforting arm. "Arundel will
see the lad through."

"Trevyn has gall," Alan fumed, "taking the old steed out in such weather. Are you not worried, Hal, or angry?"

"Why, I suppose I am," Hal admitted. "But I like Trevyn's spirit, Alan. He plans his folly with sense and subtlety. You'll have to keep a looser rein on him after this."

Alan snorted. "Worse than folly; it's lunacy! What sort of idiocy must possess the boy? I thought he was my son!" Alan paused in his pacing long enough to glare at his lovely green-eyed wife.

"He is your son, right enough." Lysse smiled. "Look at Gwern for your answers."

"Gwern!" Alan glanced down from the battlements to where the dun-faced youth stood in the courtyard pommeling the air in helpless rage. "Gwern is the nuisance that drove him away, you mean? That is no excuse."

"Nay, I mean that Gwern's passion matches Trevyn's own. The boy is no boy, Alan, but nearly a man, and he left in anger. What would Gwern do if you shackled him with lessons and books?"

"I do not understand." Alan stood scowling at his golden-haired Elf-Queen. "Are you speaking from the Sight?"

"From elf-sight and mother-sight." Her misty gray-green eyes widened in proof. "Trevyn hides his feelings from us constantly, Alan, but he cannot hide them from Gwern. Read Gwern like a weathercock for your son. Remember how surly he has been these weeks past?"

"What," Alan asked slowly, "does Gwern have to do with Trevyn?"

Lysse shrugged helplessly. "Gwern is Trevyn's wyrd," said Hal.

"Weird enough," grumbled Alan, choosing for the moment to ignore the esoteric word. Lysse was staring into nothingness, her eyes as deep as oceans. "Even now Trevyn hides his mind from me," she murmured. "I can tell that he is alive, nothing more. But Gwern knows more. All morning he has faced east."

Alan wheeled to look at the youth again; it was true. Lysse went back into her trance, her eyes like springtime pools in her delicate face.

"Lee!" she exclaimed at last with satisfaction. "He goes

toward Lee, and Arundel knows that way well. There will be a messenger from Rafe, mark my words. But do not tell Gwern."

"Lee!" Alan protested, astonished. "But how can you be so sure? Celydon also lies eastward, and Whitewater, and Nemeton. Not to speak of the whole Great Eastern Forest."

"Something awaits him at Lee," Lysse stated with quiet certainty. "Do not tell Gwern! I want to see what happens."

Chapter Two

Meg had never, not even in her silliest daydreams, fancied herself to be pretty. She knew that she had a comical, pointy face and a sharp nose like a benevolent witch. Indeed, witch was what some folk called her, all because the birds would alight on her hands. She did not mind being different, and it pleased her that the dappled deer did not fear her touch. But she minded being skinny. Some girls could make do with comeliness that bloomed below the neck, but not her, she told herself. Her skirts fell straight from her waistless middle, and she always had to sew ruffles inside the front of her blouses to give some fullness—though not fullness enough.

Still, she had never, not even in her grimmest nightmares, imagined herself looking such a fright as now. Slogging along through the snow in her old pair of men's boots, skirt torn and draggled, shawl clutched from her shoulders by the lowering Forest trees. Hatless, with her hair frazzled by the wind, eyes red and weepy, sharp nose running from cold and exertion and emotion. Flushed and panting, she struggled along, knowing it would be lunacy to stay out after dark, but too stubborn to give up.

She found her cow at last and stood frozen a moment in

astonishment that overcame her hurry. Mud! A gooshy, oozing, undulating pool of mud filled a hollow of the frost-bound Forest. From the center of the expanse, round brown eyes looked back at her. Only the cow's head showed above the surface. Wisps of steam rose around her.

"Come on, then, Molly," Meg called gently.

The cow did not budge.

Meg coaxed, pleaded, extended a bribe of oats. Molly did not even twitch an ear. The day was moving on apace. Meg rolled her eyes heavenward and went in after her.

"What is even more appealing than yer plain, everyday Meg?" she muttered viciously to herself. "Why, a Meg covered with mud, that is what! World, are ye watching?"

As she had hoped, the bottom of the mud hole was solid. She forced her way through the twenty feet of brown pudding that separated Molly from the shore and took her by the halter. Molly would not move. Meg could hardly blame her, for the mud was deliciously warm and the air increasingly cold.

"Come on, Molly, we can't stay here all night!" she cried helplessly, tugging at the cow. Then she jumped, and screamed.

Where before there had been only snow and the dark trunks of trees, now there was a rider on a beautiful silver horse—a young man, blond and very handsome. As Meg's eyes met his of stormy green, she felt an instant of utter abeyance, as if heart and soul had stopped to gaze with her. Then she came back to self with a pang, feeling how ill-prepared she was to meet him, up to her elbows in mud. Still, she saw no amusement in his face. . . . She could not know that, for his part, he had felt an odd leap of heart on seeing her. He could hardly account for it himself, and irritably shrugged off thought of it.

"I'm sorry I frightened you," he told the girl.

Meg tossed her head at that. She did not consider that she had been frightened, only—well, startled. Perhaps he had been frightened himself.

"Are you all right?" he asked. "Can you get out?"

"Ay, to be sure!" she snapped. "But I'll not leave without this cow."

Trevyn rolled his eyes at her tone. "Humor me," he urged with exaggerated courtesy, "and come out. *Please.*"

She fought her way toward the edge, retracing her steps. It was harder than she had expected. The ooze clung to her skirt as she inched along, panting. Trevyn dismounted and glanced around for a stout stick to offer her. "None strong enough," he muttered.

"Give me a hand," Meg gasped.

She meant that literally. Trevyn had not wanted to touch her. Grimacing, he grasped her by her muddy wrist and hauled her out, splattering himself with chunks of goo. She stood on the verge, breathing hard, rubbing her face and peering at him. "I've never seen anything like it," she declared.

"The mud? I've heard about these holes in the southern Forest. Some are clear water, steaming hot. Too bad your cow couldn't have chosen one of those." He unpinned his cloak as he spoke, evidently steeling himself for action.

"Ye're going to go in after her?"

"I suppose I'm going to have to," he replied ungraciously. "Arundel—" He spoke to the horse in the Old Language.

"What?" asked Meg, straining to understand the peculiar words. But then she cried out in protest as the young man took off his cloak and sliced into it with his sword. It was a thick wool cloak lined with crimson satin, more beautiful than anything she had ever owned. Trevyn stopped at her cry, looked at her quizzically.

"Is the cloak worth more than your cow?"

"That is not fair!" she answered hotly. "Molly is—is—she's family! I dare say she is not a great worth, but—" Meg fell silent and regarded Trevyn curiously. His tunic was of linen, and his sword was inlaid with gold. It was not that which gave her pause; she had seen finery before. But this youth had a proud air about him, though he had not yet reached his full growth. He was not in her lord's service; she would have noticed him if he were. Perhaps he was some lord's bard or herald, or even a lord's son? "What's yer name?" Meg asked.

Cutting strips from his cloak, he answered her without looking up. "Trevyn."

"Oh," she replied. "Are ye from Laueroc, then? I have

heard that many young men there are named after the Prince."

"I am not named after the Prince," Trevyn stated, quite truthfully. "But ay, I am from Laueroc."

"Are ye in the Kings' service, then? What are ye doing in the Forest?"

"Will you ask one question at a time!" He smiled at her as he knotted his makeshift rope. "Indeed, I am at the Kings' service, but I am here on my own business. What is your name?"

"Meg."

"Margaret?"

"Nay. Megan."

"Ah." Trevyn slipped off his tunic and folded it as a pad for Arundel's neck. The girl stared at him. She had not thought that a man could be muscular and graceful at the same time. Trevyn laid his sword belt aside, fastened the rope around Arundel's shoulders, took the other end, and started into the pool of mud. Meg aroused herself. "What must I do?" she called after him.

"Help Arundel pull."

Trevyn reached the cow and looped the rope around her horns. Then he grasped Molly around her heavy shoulders, braced his feet, and started to lift. As he wrestled the cow from her mucky bed, he called to Arundel in that strange tongue Meg had heard him use before. The horse threw his weight against the rope, and Meg tugged with all her might. Molly lurched forward, and Trevyn moved with her, lifting, shoving. Within moments she was out. Meg ran to her, kissing her broad, pink nose and feeling for injuries. Then she turned to Trevyn, who was gingerly putting on his tunic, scowling at the brown blobs on the fine white cloth.

"Thank ye so much."

He smiled sourly, scraping mud, and suddenly she laughed, a sweet, healthy laugh. "Are we not pretty, though!" she cried, so infectiously that he gave in to good humor and grinned at her. But then he buckled on his sword and frowned, glancing around at the trees that stood, black and silent, on every side.

"What's to be done now?" he asked flatly. "Dark is scarcely an hour away."

Meg stopped laughing with a sigh. "I must get home, dark or no dark. My mother will be frantic with worry even now."

"There's more to think of." Trevyn leaned against a tree, judiciously. "Have you considered how Molly came to be here?"

"I have not had time to consider!" Meg bristled at his tone. "I've been hours and hours after her. She has never come this far before."

"She was chased." Trevyn pointed at the snow all around the margin of the pool. "Wolves. See their tracks?"

"Ay, those prints look fresh," Meg agreed reluctantly, "but why would wolves hunt Molly? It has been a mild autumn, and there are rabbits enough about."

"The wolves have been singing of larger game today," Trevyn said evenly. "Their voices have filled the Forest." Meg looked into his shadowy green eyes and saw foreboding there that she could not understand.

"What're ye saying?" she demanded, half frightened, half angry. "That the beasts are of a mind to attack? There is nothing in the Forest that will harm me."

"I would have said the same of myself," Trevyn muttered.

They stood eyeing each other in perplexity. Meg started to shiver as her clothes dried in the winter wind.

"Wolves or no wolves," Trevyn broke silence, "you need a fire."

"We should camp here, then," she agreed heavily. "If they come, we can get into the mud hole—"

"It's too small for all of us. Come on." Trevyn strode back the way he had come without even a glance at his horse. It followed him unled, and the cow, Molly, lowed softly and followed him as well.

Meg stared in disbelief. "The poor thing must be addled," she murmured, and trotted after.

"Gather wood," Trevyn called.

He filled his arms as he walked. After a few hundred feet he found the campsite he had noted earlier, a jumbled pile of rock protruding from a steep forest slope. Such formations were not uncommon in those parts, but this one had a jutting shelf of granite overhead. The dirt beneath was trampled clear of undergrowth, black with ashes. Many travelers had camped here—perhaps even Hal and Alan in years gone by.

Trevyn made the fire, then collected firewood feverishly until full dark stopped him. The girl tended the animals and the blaze. Arundel stamped restlessly where he stood against a wall of rock. Molly stood beside him, swaying.

"She's quite exhausted," Trevyn remarked.

"Hadn't ye better put the rope on her all the same?" Meg asked. "She'll run off if—if anything should go wrong."

Trevyn shook his head. "She will not run."

"Humor me," Meg told him pointedly. It was a phrase she had recently learned.

So he tethered the cow and came to sit by the fire. He and Meg stared silently over the flames at a wall of darkness beyond. Trevyn felt satisfied with the sizable pile of wood he had brought in, and the rock that half surrounded them retained the fire's heat almost as well as a house. Still, he had to admit that their situation lacked a certain comfort.

"Nothing to eat," Meg sighed.

"Ay." Trevyn grinned at the hint. "You're right, Meg, I've nothing."

"Drat." She shifted her position, trying to ease the contact of her bones with the hard ground. "Well, there's no use sitting here like dummies all night, waiting for shadows. Let's have a story."

"Certainly," he said agreeably. "Go ahead."

"Nay, nay, I mean a story of Laueroc! Something about courage, something to speed our blood, give us heart—a story of the Sun Kings!"

"Oh," he remarked.

"You're from Laueroc," she prodded impatiently. "Surely you know what I mean."

He did indeed. But it was not their courage that he valued most in his uncle and father.

"It's not quite what you have in mind," he said slowly, "but it's a beautiful tale. Have you ever heard about the Sun Kings and the proud lord of Caerronan?"

"Nay!" She clapped delightedly.

"Nay?" he exclaimed with mock surprise; he knew that the story was not told outside his family. "Well, it took place only a few months after King Hal and King Alan were crowned. . . ."

He felt strange, speaking of them so impersonally. As if his mind had been disjointed, bent to a new angle, he saw them differently, envisioning them as he had never actually known them, when they were nearly as young as he.

Here is the tale Trevyn told:

The young Sun Kings missed their wandering life, and they got tired of courtly ceremony. So sometimes, when they could, they would put on old clothes and slip away for a week or two. They would ride at random around Isle, camping in the open or staying at a cottage. Perhaps people humored them and were not really fooled. Hal and Alan could not bring themselves to ride any horses but their own, and the beasts were far too beautiful for ordinary wanderers. Of course, the Kings were beautiful as well.

Their wives humored them, too, but Lysse and Rosemary also got tired of staying at Laueroc. At the time of the trouble with Caerronan, Rosemary had put her foot down, with the result that she and Hal were riding court through Isle in cavalcade. Alan and Lysse were left to manage affairs at Laueroc. But after a few weeks of councils and hearings, Alan got restless and took a notion to ride by himself to Caerronan. Old Einon, the lord there, had failed to send tribute to Laueroc, give homage or take his oath of fealty. He held a small, isolated manor in the foothills of Welas, and his spurning of the Sun Kings meant practically nothing aside from insult. But Alan needed an excuse to get away.

So he rode across Welas, all alone, through the last bright days of autumn, and went to see some friends he knew from his outlaw days. They said that Einon was a hard, rough old rascal, fair within the letter of the law but entirely lacking in generosity to his tenants, his family, or anyone else. There was no hospitality to be got at his hall.

Hearing that, Alan left his horse and walked toward Caerronan. When he had reached the lord's woodlot, he found a large stone—the heaviest one he could lift—and heaved it up and dropped it squarely on his own right foot. He gasped, and barely kept himself from howling. Then he took a stick and hobbled over to Einon's fortress, limping pitifully, to request shelter and care.

Even Einon did not have the gall to turn away an injured man. Customary law decreed that he was obliged to maintain Alan for a reasonable length of time, as long as Alan had need. So he had to take him in. But old Einon grudged every bite of food that went into his guest's mouth; Alan could tell by the way the lord eyed him over the table. Einon went about in a velvet cap with a glittering pin, and jeweled rings, and golden bracelets stacked halfway up his skinny arms, and a broad gold collar that dangled jewels over his velvet jerkin. But the old lord didn't eat much, and he seemed to think that no one else should either.

For three days Alan lounged by Einon's warmthless hearth, his sore foot up on a bench or soaking in a medicinal bath, chatting with every servant who passed, winning the sympathy of every woman in the keep, and eating night and day. Then, for another week or so, he hobbled around with a stick, conferring with the kitchen folk and flirting with Einon's young wife, just to gall him. Alan spoke the Welandais tongue brokenly, with a terrible accent, but he had always had a knack for making friends. He was not able to befriend Einon. Still, he found out nothing untoward about the lord except that he was stingy.

His leisure ended abruptly one night at dinnertime. Einon had seated himself early and was watching with a sour eye as his household arrived for the meal. As Alan entered, the old miser went rigid, then stood up, leaning on the table and shaking with rage, stretching out a long, trembling finger of judgment. Alan felt as if that finger jabbed him, though he stood half the length of the hall away.

"You cursed Islender!" Einon shrieked. "You cursed Islendais spy! You're limping on the wrong foot!"

Fairly caught, Alan felt like a royal dolt. His foot was healed, of course, and Einon knew it. Einon shrilled for his guards, wanting the impostor thrown in a cell at once. Somehow Alan didn't care to mention that he was the Islendais King. He made some humble protestations, suitably flattering to Einon's hospitality, and finally the two of them agreed that Alan should work off his debt of freeloading, as the old lord saw it. So Alan went to help in the kitchen, and a couple of weeks later, when Winterfest came, he was still at it.

There was not much giving of gifts in that pinched household, but there was a feast of sorts. Alan was appointed to carry the dishes to the lord's table, since he made such a fine, golden sight, and since the lord took some pleasure in seeing him kneel. And just as he presented the roast pork, a minstrel rode into the hall. He sent his horse right up to the foot of the dais, in the best old bardic tradition, and in his arms he carried a finely carved plinset, the stringed instrument esteemed by the Blessed Kings. The silver horse was so beautiful that everyone blinked, and somehow the minstrel shone, too, though he was dressed plainly enough. It was Hal, of course, back from his courtly rounds and checking on his comrade. Alan had to duck his head so that no one would see him smile.

"Greetings, Einon, son of Eread, lord of Caerronan," the minstrel proclaimed in the purest speech of the old court of Welas, without a trace of Isle in his voice or of mischief on his face. Hal was a master of sober statesmanship.

"Greetings," Einon snapped. "Are you a minstrel or a thief? Where did you get that horse?"

"It was given to me by the King of Isle, for my surpassing excellence in the tuneful arts."

"The more fool, he," the old lord growled. "I've always said those Kings of Isle must be fools, the two of them halving a throne between them, and never any gold of mine they'd see to spend on horses! You'll get no horse from me, minstrel. If you sing here, you must sing for your supper."

"Willingly," Hal replied, and dismounted, and sent Arundel to the stable, and tuned his plinset. After a while he plucked it, and sang, and the whole clattering hall quieted at the sound of his voice. He sang the great lays of Welas first, the stories of Veran and Claefe, and their twins Brand and Brenna who flew with the ravens for a season, and the story of an Islender, Alf Longshanks, who won the fair and willful Deona away from the royal court at Welden. All old songs, but he sang them into springtime newness, sending bright notes flying like birds through the hall. Servants set food before Hal, then, from the lord's own table, but he took no time to eat. He sang songs that no one had heard before, his own songs, of love and the Lady, and the white, foaming horses of the sea, and Elwestrand. Einon never moved, but Alan saw tears slide down the grooves of the old lord's face.

Finally Hal stopped singing. Lord Einon spoke a single word. "More." But Hal shook his head and reached for his wine.

"More!" Einon urged, and undid the jeweled pin from his velvet cap, tossed it to the minstrel. So Hal flexed his fingers and played again. He sang about the lost fountains of Eburacon. He sang of valiant Bevan, the star-son, who strove with Pel Blagden, the Mantled God. He sang of Ylim, the seeress, weaving prophecy in her hidden valley. He sang of Queen Gwynllian. All the food sat cooling on the tables, and no one ate. The servants had gathered in the shadows, not moving. After a while, Hal stopped again, and Einon exclaimed, "More!" and tossed him a golden ring.

All that night Hal played and sang, and no one left the hall. The servants settled to seats on the floor after a while, but no one slept. Alan had often heard Hal sing to the tune of his plinset, in manor halls or alehouses or by a lonely campfire; but he had never known him to cast such a spell as he did that night. Hearing him, or even looking at him, Alan wept. It was as if a silver magic flew on the notes of the music, moved in his face with the mood of the song, flickered in his gleaming eyes. By daybreak, old Einon's arms lay bare of gold, his jerkin stripped of jewels. He moved at last, stepped down from his dais, took off his golden collar, and fastened it around the Sunset King's neck.

"More," he begged softly.

But Hal silently held up his fingers; the tips were bleeding. Einon's face crumpled.

"Minstrel," he whispered, "I have given to you as you have given to me. But now my wealth is spent. What can I give you to sing for me?"

"For the sake of that blond-haired fellow there beside you," Hal answered quietly, "one more song."

"Him!" Einon burst out. "He is a lazy, useless, conniving Islender. What do you want with him? I'd rather give you a horse."

"I already have a horse," Hal replied, and played his last lay. It was the story of Leuin of Laueroc, who had died of torment in the Dark Tower at Nemeton, and even Einon sensed that Hal had given his all in giving that. The day brightened. Hal packed his instrument, gathered up his rewards, and rose to leave.

"Will you go with him, fellow?" Einon asked Alan roughly.

"Go with him!" Alan retorted. "I'd follow him into the sea! Good health to you, my lord." The two of them walked out into daylight with Einon blinking after.

They rode off, both of them on Arundel. "I hope you're satisfied, Alan," Hal croaked when they were a good distance away. "My throat will be sore for a week, my fingers are raw to the bone, and I never did get my supper." So Alan brought out a packet of food he had stolen from the table.

"That's how they were," Trevyn concluded. "Faithful comrades . . ." He fell silent, frowning.

"What did they do about Einon?" Meg asked after a while.

"What? Oh, nothing. They had the worth of ten years' tribute in gold and jewels, and what would have been the use of telling him so? They let him alone, and when he died at an irascible old age, they found him a more amiable heir."

"They are marvels, the Sun Kings," Meg said softly. Though she, like Trevyn, had never known the bad times before Hal's reign.

"Faithful comrades," Trevyn muttered, still scowling at the ground. It had been many months, he realized, since he had heard Hal sing. The Sunset King hardly stirred from his tower; he looked more often than ever toward the west. An uneasy ache filled Trevyn at that thought.

The moon sent prickles of light through the tangled trees, and on the north wind rose the hunting cry of the wolves.

Chapter Three

It began far off at first—eerie, almost beautiful. To the east one would yelp, and far away to north or west or south another would answer him. But Arundel snorted at the sound, and Trevyn felt his fear-sweat run, for he sensed that these were cries of blood such as no animal ought to voice. With clever ease the wolves drew closer on all sides, exulting to each other over the echoing distances of the Forest. Trevyn could no longer hope that he was not the quarry. Arundel's quivering ears bore him out. Tensely he rose, fingering his sword hilt. Meg piled wood on the fire, then stared soundlessly over the flames. In the firelight the grinning teeth of the wolves shone spectrally bright.

"You'll not fend us off with fire, Princeling," they jeered. "We are not ordinary wolves, you know."

"So you have been telling me all day," he answered them in the Ancient Tongue. He drew his sword with a flourish. "But even if you are gods, steel will separate your souls from your bodies quite effectively."

They laughed, yapping with open mouths and lolling tongues. "But there will be more, Princeling; always there will be more. We do not care if we die; blood is life to us, even our own. And after your guts are spilled on the snow and your brains fill our bellies, what then? What then for your muddy cow and your skinny maid and your fine war horse quaking against the stone?"

"Arundel is too old to fight," Trevyn excused him. But his heart turned to water, for he knew that a steed of the elfin blood should fight to the death, no matter what his age. And Arundel, of all such steeds, to be so filled with terror! He who had seen Hal through a hundred combats. . . .

"Trevyn," Meg whispered, "what is happening?"

"Just exchanging insults." He kept his eyes on the ring of leering eyes that shone scarlet in the firelight. "They would like to bait me out there beyond the ledge. I'll wager you anything you like that a score of them are up there waiting to jump me."

"Bet me a new cloak!" she demanded with comic eagerness. Trevyn grinned, and some of the sickness faded from him.

"Keep some long sticks ready for torches," he told her. "When it comes to fighting, light my way as best you can. But stay back!"

"Never fear!" she retorted.

A bit farther away sat a wolf half again larger than the rest, shining ghostly gray in a patch of moonlight. The others yelled taunts, jumping in place as if restrained by invisible leashes, quivering and whining with eagerness for the scuffle and the kill and the warm human blood. But the big wolf squatted at his ease. He barked once, and the wolves froze to a silence that screamed like the silence of a bad dream. Trevyn could not ignore the challenge in the leader's yellow eyes. He met them, and his head swirled in nightmare, a nightmare imposed on him by an alien will.

Laueroc, its green meadows overrun, its high walls breached, the people ugly with panic. The proud *elwedeyn* steeds fleeing, their flanks dappled with blood drawn by tearing teeth, bursting their great hearts and falling dead with shame and despair. His father, a giant gray form at his throat—

"Trevyn!" Meg cried. "Beware!"

The vision vanished as Trevyn shook his head, dazed,

realizing that he had moved steps nearer to the seated leader. "He almost had me," he murmured. "Talk to me, Meg." But before she could say a word the big wolf barked and the others sprang. Trevyn swung his sword like a reaper cutting a swath, and the fight was joined.

The fine points of swordsmanship were of little use to Trevyn against tooth and claw. But quickness and a long reach served him well. Though the wolves lunged at him in unison, none came nearer to him than the length of his sword. Many fell back, yelping, and three toppled dead. At Trevyn's back, Meg held the torch high. The wolves could not come at him from behind without treading in the fire. Yet they pressed the fight like things possessed. Even the wounded attacked him. Half a dozen furry bodies now lay scattered, and the living clawed over them in their frenzy to reach Trevyn. His flashing sword held them off.

In his patch of moonlight, the wolf leader sat watching, but no longer at his ease. He growled with displeasure and rose from his haunches, padding toward the fray. Trevyn noted the movement, and for an instant his strength ebbed from him. That instant of hesitation nearly caused his doom. He felt jaws close around his legs, striving to bring him down. He beat at the wolves with his sword, but they kept their hold. They dragged him out from the fire, and he reeled as heavy bodies hit his back from above, teeth and claws tore at his shoulders. He knew that if he went down he was finished. The gray leader's face was before his, with bristly hair and long, snarling snout but something strangely human in the jaundiced eyes. . . . What name of evil to put to this? It was over now, they were pulling his legs from under him. . . .

A yell as fierce as any warrior's rang in Trevyn's ears, a comet of light flew past his cheek, and unbelievably the grip on his legs was released. Entranced, he watched a howling wolf run madly by with the fur of its back on fire. Meg stood before him, swinging a torch in either hand. She thrust the leaping wolves in their gaping mouths, and they screamed and fell aside. Two circled around and came at her from behind. Trevyn blinked and skewered them with his sword.

"Back!" he shouted, vaulting to her side. "Get back, Meg!" They edged back until they could feel the warmth of the fire behind them. Still the wolves lunged to the attack like mindless things, and still the bright sword drew their life's blood. Then the leader barked, and they stopped, forming a ring just at the rim of the firelight. The big wolf sat behind them, grinning with long white teeth.

Trevyn blazed into thoughtless fury at this thing he feared and did not understand. He threw his sword to the earth at his feet. "Come out, you!" he shouted. "Fight like other things of flesh! Rend me though you will, I will wrestle you to the ground and break your foul neck with my unaided hands!"

The wolf raised his head and laughed, a high, sinister sound. "Not yet, Princeling," he cried gaily. "Let us play yet a while. The time for us to meet will come soon enough, and it will be sweet, so sweet. . . ."

Then they were gone, and the sound of weird wolfish laughter floated on the Forest air. Behind the fire, Arundel trembled and huddled against the sheltering rock.

"So!" Meg softly exclaimed. "Ye're the Prince of Laueroc."

Sunk to earth and trembling in his turn, he couldn't answer her. She tore strips from her muddy skirt, kneeled beside him, bound his hurts as best as she could before she spoke again. "I should've known it long since. But I never dreamed yer folks'd let ye go gadding about alone."

"They don't, as a rule," he muttered. "Are you all right, Meg?"

"To be sure, I'm fine!" She smiled tightly. "They didn't want *me*, those wolves."

He glanced up at her, wincing. "Is that what made you guess?"

"Everything. Yer outlandish talk, yer lovely horse, yer lovely self . . ." She teased him, not being willing to say that she had seen his eyes blaze like green fire. But he did not seem able to smile.

"You saved my life," he mumbled. "Meg, I'm sorry. . . ."

"What?" she protested. "Ye'd rather be dead?"

"Nay, nay!" He had to laugh at her, though the movement brought tears of pain to his eyes. "Sorry I didn't tell you more truth. . . . It's hard."

"I can imagine," she said wryly.

The wolves still sang, sending echoes scudding like shadows between the trees. Trevyn could not talk anymore. He sat by the fire till dawn, shivering in spite of the warmth of the flames, and Meg kept him silent company. The wolves made the whole Forest wail, but they did not return.

At daybreak, Meg and Trevyn quitted their comfortless campsite. The girl lived just beyond the Forest's edge, near Lee. They headed that way, both on Arundel, with Molly trailing along behind. Trevyn felt tense, almost too shaky to ride. He wished that they could speed out of the Forest, but they had to travel slowly because of the cow. He found himself jerking to attention at every sound or stir. But before midday he smiled and sighed with relief. A search party thundered toward them, a dozen grim, armed men, headed by Rafe, the fiery lord of Lee. The troop hurtled up to them and pulled to a jarring halt. Rafe grabbed at Trevyn and missed. He nearly fell from his horse in his excitement.

"Trevyn! Are you all right?" he shouted, and gave the youth no chance to answer. "By thunder, is that Meg?" He peered at the grimy girl. "Your father's been bellowing for you since yesterday, lass. Trev, you young rascal, what have you been up to? Rescuing fair maidens?"

Meg snorted; she had never felt less fair. Trevyn scarcely heard. "Wolves," he muttered, and felt horror ripple through him, the horror of a nightmare not his own, the horror of a shadow not understood. Wolf and stag were both in Aene, he had been taught, like hawk and hare, water and fire, and all of these part of the old order that only man sometimes leaves—so how could the wolves turn against him? They had attacked him like brigands. . . . Pale and sweating, he closed his eyes, laid his head on Arundel's neck. He felt Meg's thin arms around his shoulders, trying to steady him, but he knew he would slip away. . . . He heard a cry from Rafe, then nothing more.

He awoke hours later to find himself tucked into a monstrous sickbed. At Rafe's stronghold, he knew, because he saw that same lord seated beside him. "Have you nothing better to do?" he mumbled.

Rafe smiled. "How do you feel?"

Burns stung him, seemingly to the bone, even before he

moved. He hoisted himself painfully. "Confounded. Not long ago I hated snow. Now I could go out and roll in the stuff. I take it you've cauterized the wounds."

"Ay, we've had to brand you, lad." Rafe pulled back the sheet, reached into a bucket at his feet, and piled mounds of snow on Trevyn's legs and shoulders. "You've slept for five hours or so. Could you manage more?"

"Hardly!" Trevyn supported himself gingerly on one elbow. "I don't remember much. Did I make a fool of myself?"

"Nay, indeed! You were in a dead faint—lay like a felled tree. By my troth, I don't think I could have done it otherwise."

Startled, Trevyn glanced up to see tears sliding silently down Rafe's rugged face. He reached out to touch the older man's hand.

"Rafe, you must be spent. Get some rest. I don't need a nursemaid."

"I'm sorry, Trev," said Rafe wretchedly. "But how am I to feel? Meg told us about those wolves, and they must have been mad, rabid. What if—" Rafe gulped to a stop.

"They were not rabid."

"If you die," Rafe blurted, "it will mean more than the loss of one that I love."

"They were not rabid. You are worrying for nothing, Rafe. I am not likely to die from a few bites." Trevyn felt the touch of a shadow and lay back wearily. Still, he spoke with assurance. Rafe studied him, mindful of the visionary powers of the Lauerocs.

"You are not just saying that. You are quite certain."

"Of course." But Trevyn did not tell Rafe why he knew he would take no harm from his wounds. The big wolf, it seemed, had plans that they should meet again. Unpleasant as the thought was, it afforded some solace. Luck, in the form of Meg, had seen him through the first encounter. And the next time he would somehow be better prepared.

Chapter Four

A few days later, as soon as he felt well enough, Trevyn rode out to see Meg.

The cottage stood at the Forest's fringe. The goodman, Brock Woodsby, Meg's father, took his name from that fact. Working in the yard, he was the first to see the visitor approach, and he stumped over to the rickety gate to meet him. Watching from within the cottage, Meg put her hands to her mouth in consternation. She could not hear her father's words, but she recognized the stubborn set of his back.

"Who might it be?" Brock gruffly addressed his visitor.

Perhaps the man was a trifle dense, Trevyn thought. He introduced himself by name and title, still sitting on his horse, waiting for the gate to open. But Brock Woodsby did not move.

"I thought as much," he stated. "I thank ye for the sake of the lass, Prince. She says she'd have been lost without ye. But ye're mistaken to come gallanting hereabouts. Ye'll be the ruin of the girl. Already folk are saying ye've had yer way with her. I think not, if I know my lass, but that's the talk. And what else might ye want with her indeed?"

What indeed? But Trevyn was too young to be amused or

intrigued by the aptness of Brock's question. He bristled and fixed the goodman with an icy green glare. "What, are you denying me admittance, then?" he demanded.

"Mothers defend us!" Meg whispered. The small cry brought her own mother to her side. Glancing out the window, the goodwife fluttered like a partridge. The youth outside the gate wore a bright sword, and he looked tempted to use it on her husband.

"I deny hospitality to no one," Brock replied stiffly. "I only ask you to *think*. Think of the girl." As he spoke, the maiden in question came out of the cottage and approached him, walking serenely. He rounded on her. "Get back i' the house!"

"What? Stay out of the Forest, ye tell me, and is it stay out of the yard now? Ye'll be keeping me in the chimney corner next." Meg faced her father sunnily, and Trevyn grinned at her, all his chagrin suddenly forgotten. He slipped down from Arundel and opened the gate for himself, though a moment before he had been determined to make Brock do it. The quarrel no longer seemed worth pursuing.

"Rafe's not allowing me in the Forest, either," he remarked to Meg. "Small fear I shall disobey him in that regard."

"Nay?" she said slowly. She missed the Forest; she missed the foxes that would come and follow by her feet, the wild doves that would light on her shoulders. She felt hurt by her Forest, betrayed, that any of its creatures could turn against her as the wolves had done. But she could not explain this, and especially not to Trevyn. She didn't want him to think her queer, as so many others did.

Her mother saved her from further response. The goodwife came bustling out, having settled her hair and flung on a shawl. "Come in, young master, have some fresh, hot scones!" she beseeched Trevyn. She did not take it the least bit amiss that Meg had found a prince in the Forest. And Brock, having had his say and been ignored, led his guest to the cottage with dour courtesy.

The scones were very good. Trevyn sampled them that day and many a day to come. He stayed a month at Lee, riding out nearly every day to see Megan. His motive was only partly to gall Brock Woodsby. He would greet the goodman distantly, but he always met the girl with honest delight. Meg chatted with him like a longtime friend, and she was full of questions.

"What's yer name mean, Trevyn?"

"Beloved traveler, or some such." The youth gestured impatiently. "It's just a baby name. I shall have a sooth-name someday."

"Ay?" Meg wondered cheerfully. "How so?"

"That is as it comes," Trevyn countered. "What does your name mean, Megan?"

"Not a thing." She grinned wickedly. "We're common folk here."

Trevyn almost flushed, feeling a hint of reproach, but Meg went on unconcernedly. "What brings ye to Lee, Trevyn?"

He laughed. "Arundel! He brought me through the snow straight to the manor gates, and very surprised Rafe was to see me! I would have perished in the storm if it weren't for him. He is a marvelous horse. Twenty years ago he carried my uncle through far stranger perils in this same Great Forest and beyond."

Bemused, Meg let it pass that he had not really answered her question. "Then was yer uncle an outlaw as well?"

"He joined with the outlaws of the southern Forest after they had saved his life. Arundel brought him to them nearly dead from tortures in the Dark Tower of the evil kings."

Meg shuddered. "And he met yer father then?"

"A bit later. They did not know that they were brothers. Hal had been raised as King Iscovar's heir, but really his father was the lord of Laueroc."

"Folk say that King Iscovar killed Leuin of Laueroc and the Queen."

"Ay, and he would have liked to bend my uncle to his will. Hal roamed the land constantly to elude him, with my father as his blood brother and companion. Your lord Rafe was their friend, too, in those times; they met him and Queen Rosemary at Celydon. And they traveled to the Northern Barrens, and into Welas, the west land, and even to Veran's Mountain, where they met my kindred, the elves."

"Elves!" Megan bounced excitedly. "I thought that was just—singing, y'know."

"Nay, the elves are real. But all of them except my mother have sailed to Elwestrand, a land beyond the western sea." A faraway look filled Trevyn's eyes. "Hal sang of Elwestrand long before he knew it existed anywhere but in his mind."

Meg grappled in vain for an answer to this. Trevyn had that look sometimes that can make a woman weep, sad eyes and a smiling mouth. . . . But other times he had the look of eagles. After a moment he went on.

"When Iscovar died, Hal and his followers ousted the evil lords, and my mother gave up her immortality to marry my father. Those were strange times for him; he had never expected to be a King. But when Hal found out they were brothers, he found Father his crown. Hal had never wanted power anyway, though it was fated on him."

"How so?" Meg sat agape at this matter-of-fact talk of elves and destinies.

"It was written in *The Book of Suns,* the prophecies of the One. The Book made their kinship clear, and told them that Hal would have no heir."

"I saw him once, and Queen Rosemary, as they rode to Celydon," Meg remarked. " 'Tis a shame they've no children. But ye're lucky ye've no cousins or brothers to fight ye for the throne."

"I wish I had a dozen," Trevyn grumbled. "And they could have the throne, and welcome."

"Why?" asked Meg, not at all disconcerted.

"Never mind." Trevyn smiled in spite of himself. "Save your breath to cool your porridge, Meg."

"And let ye spend yers to swell yer wings of fancy? Ye're so bursting with portents and mysteries, how is a poor girl to know the way of it?"

He had to laugh at her. It was a relief to see his forebodings as nonsense, even for a moment. Meg's teasing was a balm on spirits too often darkened since the fight with the wolves.

Meg had long since learned that fellows liked her best if she jested with them. When she did it well, they could forget that she was a skinny, plain-faced maid and treat her simply as a friend. So she had no sweethearts, but at least she had male company at the occasional social affairs of the countryside. Her brave show fooled no one, not even herself. But she made the best of what she had: a quick mind and a droll wit. And when the Prince came, she bantered with him as was her wont.

He had known no such easy companionship from the youths and maidens of Laueroc. They had shied from his rank and his elfin strangeness. So he found it a relief and a delight to be treated with something less than royal respect. Meg's shafts of wit were never cruel, and she aimed them most often at herself. Trevyn had seen her with the wolves; he knew her courage. Her merciless honesty concerning her own short-comings was a different kind of courage, he thought, and he admired her for it.

"No doubt the bards will sing of how ye pulled the fair maiden from the mud hole," Meg mused. "They hold forth about everything ye Lauerocs do."

"No doubt," Trevyn gravely agreed.

"'Twill be known, of course, that they speak of Molly," Meg added. "As she is young, and has not yet calved."

Trevyn never tired of listening to her. He had met many kinds of women in his young life: high-scented foreign princesses, chilly court maidens, flirtatious servant girls. None of them had tempted him to more than a quick conquest. But this fine-boned, birdlike creature, bright and cheeky as a sparrow, drew him back to her again and again. He had felt for her small breast once, wondering what she kept beneath her shapeless peasant blouse, and she had pushed his hand away. "Nay, Trev," she had told him, not even angrily, only with a certainty he could not question. He did not try again, but he came to see her even more often than before. All his life he had dreamed of finding a friendship such as Hal and Alan shared, or of finding a true love. . . . But he told himself that this Megan, this homely, comical maid, was nothing more than a diversion to him. He liked to be diverted, and certainly the girl did not mind.

He was thoughtless, as Brock had feared. Otherwise he might have known how his face floated before her inward eye day and night. He should have known how he inspired her love, he who was the talk of every lass in the countryside. But it must be said that Megan hid her love well. Once she had showed fondness for a youth, and it had driven him away. Brave though he thought her to be, she would not risk showing her heart to the Prince. She fed her soul merely on the sight of him and the memory of his lighthearted words. Sometimes, lying in her bed at night, she silently wept.

"When must you be going, lad?" Rafe asked Trevyn one evening at the manor keep.

"Trying to rid yourself of me?" Trevyn retorted. Though he would talk to Meg for hours, he found little enough to say to his kindly host.

"You know that you're welcome to stay the rest of your life." Coming from Rafe, this was not hollow courtesy. "But surely you must be back to Laueroc by Winterfest."

"There will be ill cheer at my home this feast-tide," Trevyn responded sourly. "Nay. I'll stay a while longer."

Rafe gaped, for Trevyn had told him nothing about his troubles with Gwern, or about Hal's strange behavior, or even about the wolves. But the lord of Lee rose to the occasion with the enthusiasm for which he was famous. "Why, we'll make a royal festival of it, then!" He rubbed his hands in delight, for Rafe was as eager as a boy when it came to a frolic. "We'll have a regular carole, with musicians and everything, O Prince, in your honor. It will be just what this poor country place needs for some waking up."

Trevyn smiled, knowing quite well that the manor already buzzed with his presence. "I will invite Meg," he decided.

Rafe cocked a quizzical eye at him, not knowing what to make of the youth's friendship with Meg. The girl was odd, folk said, talked with animals as if they were human. . . . Of course, the Lauerocs spoke with animals, too, and possessed many stranger powers, and no one spoke ill of them.

"No harm to little Meg, lad," Rafe asked cautiously, "but why? You could have your pick of many a lass who would do you better credit as a partner."

"But Meg makes me laugh," Trevyn replied.

When he made his request of Meg she answered as

seriously as she had ever spoken to him. "I'd love to, Trev. But I have no dress, and I wouldn't know how to behave. Ye'd better ask a girl who is better prepared."

"Act like yourself, and you'll please me well enough. And as for the dress—" He frowned. Rafe was unmarried, so there was no woman to help him. "It's not quite proper, I dare say, but will you not let me take care of it?"

"What? Make it yerself? Ye'll prick yer fingers and cry. . . ."

"Nay, nay, little jester, I'll pay for it! Humor me?"

"I must ask my parents," Meg said.

They consented, though not without some argument from the goodman. It took the determined persuasion of both females to get him to agree to the plan. Rafe did not like it much better than Brock.

"Half the country will say you are betrothed!" he sputtered when Trevyn asked him the name of a dressmaker.

"I dare say worse things could happen."

"Ay! They could say she is your mistress!"

The dressmaker was a terse, tight-skinned old woman, straight and proud. The manor folk stood in awe of her, saying she had Gypsy blood. When Meg shyly presented herself in her baggy frock and heavy peasant boots, the old seamstress looked her up and down without smile or comment.

"What does the Prince like best in you?" she asked. And, although Trevyn had never told her, Meg knew the answer at once. "I make him laugh," she replied. There was a trace of bitterness in her voice, and the old woman glanced into her eyes. In an instant the Gypsy saw what Megan had so carefully hidden from everyone else.

Without a word she got her tape and carefully measured every part of Megan's slender body. Trevyn had already chosen the goods: a soft silk, dusky rose with a thread of gold, well fit to bring out the color of Meg's thin cheeks and the lights in her muted hair. The old woman held it up, and Meg stroked it speechlessly. "What sort of dress do ye want out of this, now?" the seamstress asked her.

"I know nothing of it," Meg faltered. "I have never had such a dress."

"Will ye leave it to me, then?"

"Ay, surely." It did not matter, Meg thought, what sort of dress she wore. She had never known a dress to flatter her.

"Ye will trust me in this." There was something gentle in the Gypsy's voice, and Meg looked at her and smiled.

"Ay, indeed I will. But you will have to work hard, Grandmother, to have it done in time."

"Ay, even so. But 'twill be done, little daughter."

The evening of the dance, Trevyn rode Arundel out through the frosty night to fetch Meg. The stars glowed clear as a thousand candles, and the night was full of whispering, jostling light. Over the snow the square of the cottage window shone like a beacon, near even from afar. At long last Trevyn reached it, and beams from within picked out Arundel's form, silver as a spirit of the night. Trevyn found the door and stepped inside. Then he stopped, thunderstruck. A shining sprite awaited him.

Meg's dress made no effort to conceal her thinness; quite the opposite. Tiny tucks drew the fabric snug over her small round breasts, then released it to fall in soft, clinging folds over her waist and hips. Her skirt swept the floor, and long sleeves embraced her slender arms nearly to her fingers. Only her neck was bared, and the tender curve of her collarbone below. Somewhere she had got delicate slippers to peep from under her skirt. She was lovely, and she knew it. Her eyes glowed as warm as the firelight. She met Trevyn's stare almost merrily, then turned to fetch her old brown mantle. He stopped her and took off his bright cloak of royal blue, putting it around her shoulders and fastening it with his golden brooch that bore the Sun Kings' emblem.

"Ye must be the hard one to keep in cloaks!" whispered Meg. Trevyn restrained his smile.

"I will have her back to you before midnight," he told Brock Woodsby, and they departed.

Meg moved through the evening in a happy trance. Any girl in Lee would gladly have taken her place, but their envy could not taint her with foolish triumph; it was Trevyn himself who lit the flame of her joy. He watched her, talked with her, danced only with her, guiding her through the circling patterns of the courtly carole. Megan could not hide her love this night. It glowed in her wide eyes, misty brown as a forest vista. Trevyn looked, and saw, and Megan felt quite certain that something answered her gaze in his. They drifted away from the dancers to the dim reaches of the great hall, and they scarcely noticed at first when the stately notes of lute and viol faltered to a stop.

"What bard is that?" Trevyn murmured.

A dark, feral voice was singing, chanting out a harsh ballad that rang like a blast of wintry air through the warm room.

> "Out of shadowed Lyrdion
> The sword Hau Ferddas came;
> By Cuin the heir Dacaerin won
> For Bevan of Eburacon,
> To win him crown and fame.
>
> And won him fame, and won his land,
> And nearly dealt Cuin doom;
> And Bevan of the Silver Hand
> Went over sea to Elwestrand,
> Where golden apples bloom.
>
> So Cuin Dacaerin seized the cares
> To which his sword gave claim,
> High King in Laueroc, and his heirs
> Held sway for half a thousand years,
> Until the warships came.
>
> *Mighty sword of Lyrdion,*
> *Golden blade of Lyrdion,*
> *Bloody brand of Lyrdion,*
> *Long your shadow falls."*

"What tale is that?" Meg wondered. "I have never heard it."

"Few people have," Trevyn exclaimed under his breath. "The magical sword of the High Kings still lies where my uncle Hal left it; he would not use its tainted power. But only he and my father knew of it, I thought!" The Prince moved closer to see the singer's face, but the crowd stood in his way, held rapt by the strange song.

> "Claryon was the High King's name
> Who died without a wound;
> Culean, his son of warlike fame
> Who took Hau Ferddas, bright as flame,
> Where fortune importuned.
>
> It won him woe, it won him shame,
> And cozened him to slay him,
> By his own hand himself to maim
> To keep the sword by his own blame,
> And in a barrow lay him.
>
> And in a barrow of the Waste
> Hau Ferddas still lay gleaming,
> And Isle, her land by war disgraced,
> Lay at the feet of foes abased,
> Hope lost beyond all dreaming.
>
> *Mighty sword of Lyrdion,*
> *Golden blade of Lyrdion,*
> *Bloody brand of Lyrdion,*
> *Long your shadow falls."*

Rafe made his way to Trevyn, parting the crowd in his wake. At last Trevyn and Meg were able to see the husky-voiced singer, looking like a ruffian in his brownish wrappings. "Do you know that fellow?" Rafe asked the Prince in a low voice. "He walked straight in and started his song, and I haven't the heart to stop him, though he sounds like branches in a wind. There's an elfin look about him in a way."

"Son of a—" Trevyn groaned. It was Gwern, meeting his eyes without a hint of expression as he finished his ballad.

> "Till, half ten hundred turnings done,
> A Very King returned,
> And Alan of the Rising Sun

And Hal, the heir of Bevan, won
The crowns their mercy earned.

And scorned Hau Ferddas, spurned her calls,
And still the sword lies gleaming,
And long and fair her shadow falls,
And sweet her golden song enthralls
When warrior blood falls streaming;

And seers have said that, years to dawn,
If hand can bear to loose her,
The mighty sword of Lyrdion
Must to the western sea begone,
Or stay our fair seducer.

Mighty sword of Lyrdion,
Golden blade of Lyrdion,
Bloody brand of Lyrdion,
Still your shadow falls."

The listeners applauded, bemused, but heartened by the names of their Kings. Gwern turned away indifferently and headed toward the dainty foodstuffs arranged on long tables by the walls. He started to eat ravenously, grabbing sweetmeats with his grimy fingers. Meg stared at him in wonder.

"Yer brother?" she blurted to Trevyn. "But I know ye've got none."

"My brother!" Trevyn cried. "I should hope not!" He strode over to the newcomer. "Gwern, you are making a mess."

Gwern said nothing; being Gwern, he did not care. It had taken him days of frustration to leave Laueroc, for Alan had doubled the guard since Trevyn's escapade. At last he had made his break, bareback on Trevyn's golden charger Rhyssiart, but it had been painfully slow going through the snow. And a nameless, peculiar illness had struck him as suddenly as a blow, sent him reeling to a shelter to lie for days like one wounded. At last he reached Lee, starving, dirty, ragged. Now, gazing at Meg, he forgot to eat.

Grudgingly, Trevyn made the introduction. "Meg, this is

Gwern, my—my acquaintance. Gwern, this is Megan By-the-woods."

Gwern only stared. Meg did not mind his gaze, or even think him impolite. It was like the wordless, thoughtful look a badger might have given her.

"Gwern, you're an eyesore," Trevyn said impatiently. "Get to my room, will you, and I'll have them bring you some things."

Somewhat to his surprise, Gwern did as he had said, and he sent up a servant with food and instructions for a bath. Trevyn and Meg saw no more of Gwern that night, nor did they speak of him. Megan felt Trevyn's agitation, and she was glad to feel it subside. They danced, and walked the room together, and ate fine foods that she was never able to remember to her satisfaction, and danced again. By the time the lutes and viols finished playing, she felt music moving through her even when her feet were still.

Taking her home through the frosty night, Trevyn held her before him on Arundel and felt the warmth of her slender body against his. Why should he want her, this skinny, sharp-nosed little maid? Yet something rose in him. To release it, he stopped Arundel where all the thousand stars could see, turned her to him, held her, and kissed her long and deep. He trembled, but not with cold, and felt her body quiver in answer. Then he felt tears on her face. He nestled her against his shoulder, stroking her hair and kissing her eyes until she was calm. She did not speak as he took her home. He saw her within doors and kissed her once, lightly, in the dark of the cottage; then he went without a word. Only as his hoofbeats faded away did Meg realize that she still wore his cloak and brooch.

He will come for them on the morrow, she thought, and the thought made her glad to overflowing. She undressed in the dark and lay awake on her narrow bed, feeling the touch of his kiss still on her lips. It was the first kiss she had ever known.

All the way back to the manor, Trevyn berated himself. It was mad and cruel, he scolded, to give the girl hopes. For surely he could have no serious thoughts of her! She was a commoner, without education, dower, or social grace. And she was homely, or at least so he had once thought. . . . But he was the Prince of the realm, gifted with knowledge, power, and beauty. Surely there would be a princess for him, a woman worthy of his regard—perhaps an elfin princess in fair Elwestrand across the sea! He must not see Meg again, he decided, not even for parting. He did not care to cause a scene.

When he reached his chamber, he found Gwern lounging on his bed, looking more presentable since his bath. The fey youth sat up to greet Trevyn with a perfectly unreadable face. Trevyn meant to ask him how he knew about the ancient sword of Lyrdion, why he had sung his eerie song. But Gwern spoke first.

"Meg is a beautiful girl," he said. There was no trace of mockery in his voice, and Trevyn knew by now that Gwern only spoke the most straightforward truth. Such truth sent a pang through him.

"What of it?" he retorted gruffly.

"I would like to know her better. Where does she live?"

"You!" Trevyn flared in sudden anger. "You are only fit to consort with pigs! Stay away from her!"

Gwern gravely rose from the bed. "Why, she is only a commoner, and you think she is homely," he replied without heat. "And you have decided to cast her aside. Do you grudge me your castoffs?"

"I grudge you life and breath," grated Trevyn between clenched teeth. He was white with rage; he had never felt such rage. "Stay away from her, I say!"

"Why, you need not worry," Gwern remarked reasonably. "She is the Maiden, you know. Where she would not have you, she will not have me."

Trevyn sprang at him, knocking him to the floor with one smashing fist. Blood trickled from Gwern's nose. But this time he did not punch back. Trevyn stood panting, helpless to vent his wrath, and vaguely ashamed.

Gwern got up, taking no notice of his gory nose. He went to the door. "I will tender her your parting regards," he told Trevyn levelly, "since you will not face her." There was no fight in his words, only fact. Desperately, Trevyn hit him again, hard enough to split his own knuckles. Gwern staggered and shrugged off the blow.

"If you go near her," Trevyn gasped wildly, "I will kill you!"

"You can't," Gwern stated, and ambled away down the stairs. Trevyn sensed that he was right, and in sheerest chagrin he wept.

"How was the carole?" Megan's mother asked her the next morning.

"Wonderful," her daughter answered. "There were marvelous ices. And I believe Trevyn liked my dress." She smiled in a way that made her mother's heart ache, for the goodwife hated to see the girl disappointed.

Confidently Megan waited for Trevyn to come to her. But instead came Gwern, with his bare brown feet hanging down, bareback and bridleless on Trevyn's golden stallion. The big horse obeyed him at a touch. Filled with sudden foreboding, Meg went out to the fence to meet him, and he vaulted down from his steed to speak to her.

"Prince Trevyn started back to Laueroc early this morning," he told her. "I have come to take his leave of you, since he would not."

Meg regarded him steadily, her sharp face only a little tauter than usual, for she was practiced in hiding her feelings. "And which of us has frightened him away," she asked at last, "ye or me?"

"You," Gwern said promptly. "He bears no love for me."

Her face twitched at that. "And how does it come to be," she wondered aloud, "that ye're Trevyn, and yet ye're not Trevyn?"

"I don't know," he grumbled, then looked at her with something like alarm. "Did you speak to him of that?"

"Nay! He is not ready; he is terrified." Meg was the wise woodland Maiden, as Gwern knew, but she knew herself only as a hurt and bewildered girl. Tears trickled from her eyes. "Will he ever come back to me?" she murmured.

Gwern came to her, finding his way around the rough rail fence. "Megan, I love you," he said flatly. "Let me stay with you, since Trevyn would not."

She quirked a wry smile at him, amused in spite of her misery. "I don't know much," she retorted, "but I know wild, and ye're as wild as wind. And ye cannot bear to be long away from him. How long would ye stay?"

"A few days," Gwern admitted. "But if he goes over ocean, I must learn to bear that pang. I cannot leave earth. My sustenance is in the soil beneath my feet."

"And he longs to go to Elwestrand," Meg mused. "The tides wash in his eyes. . . . Go now, Gwern. I don't need yer comfort. But if ye need mine someday, come to me."

She spoke bravely. But that night, after the fire was banked and she went to her bed, despair struck her that went too deep even for tears. She had let herself show a woman's heart, and the showing had driven Trevyn from her. For who would want to be loved by a skinny thing like her? To think it of him, and he the Prince! And yet, what of that kiss. . . .

In months to come, when she had driven from her all other hope of his regard, the memory of that kiss was still to linger in the heart of her heart, like a glowing coal in the ashes of a benighted fire.

Chapter Five

The winter holidays had nearly ended when Trevyn returned to his home—to Laueroc, fair city of meadowlarks. No birds sang now over the meadows that ringed the town, but the towers shone golden in the wintry sunlight. In the fairest tower, Trevyn knew, King Hal dreamed his visionary dreams. Below, artists of all sorts wrought their own dreams within his protecting walls. The countless concerns of the court city of Isle hummed on, and Alan saw to them all, frowning.

King Alan heard the shout go up when Trevyn rode in, and he met his son at the gates to the keep. Time was when he would have been waiting with a stick in his hand, to thrash the Prince for going out-of-bounds. Trevyn was expecting a mighty roaring at the very least. But Alan surprised him. "I am glad to see you, lad," he remarked quietly. "I ought to knock your head, but I haven't the inclination. Come get your supper."

Trevyn stood still and peered at him. "What is the matter?" he asked.

"It's Hal," Alan told him candidly. "He's been sulking in his tower for weeks now, scarcely eating, scarcely speaking. . . . I have known him for a long time, Trevyn, and borne with his moods as he bears with mine, but this—it harrows me. I don't want to speak of it. Come get your supper."

Preoccupied, Alan had not noticed Trevyn's borrowed cloak or his missing brooch, and Trevyn gave private thanks for that. He flung the cloak aside and followed his father to the huge, cobbled kitchen. None of the Lauerocs had much patience with the prerogatives of rank; they usually helped themselves rather than eating in great-hall style. Trevyn's mother and his Aunt Rosemary sat at a big plank table near the hearth, slicing bread. Rosemary smiled wanly as Trevyn entered, but Lysse jumped up to hug him, gauging his well-being with her elfin eyes.

"You have been in danger, Beloved!" she exclaimed. "What was it?"

"The snowstorm perhaps?" he hedged. He had left Rafe with the understanding that he would carry report to the Kings concerning the peculiar behavior of the wolves. But now, guiltily, he realized that he had no intention of doing so. He could not risk his newly won independence by telling his parents he had come to woe. Childishly, he felt that they would never let him out alone again, never let him sail to Elwestrand! Shaking off thoughts of duty, he turned the talk. "What is the matter with my uncle?"

"He is fey." Queen Rosemary proudly raised her lovely auburn head.

"He is Mireldeyn." Lysse spoke the name neither in agreement nor in denial. She sat down with effortless, fluid grace. "His ways are not the ways of men. He has withdrawn from men now."

Trevyn dipped himself a bowlful of stew, for he was hungry from his ride. No one else ate much; they all sat watching him. "But Uncle Hal has always been a recluse," he ventured between bites of bread and meat.

Alan distractedly shook his head. "Not like this. He was only a recluse in body, Trevyn; his mind and vision were focused on Isle and on me; I could feel his love even from afar. But now—his dreams have pulled away, like a sea pulling away from shore. He scarcely speaks to me; it is as if he is already gone. How will I rule without him? How will I live? He is Very King."

"But where—how—" Trevyn faltered. Alan looked as if he might weep, and Trevyn had never seen his father weep, even over the tiny bodies of his stillborn sisters. "I don't understand. I know you were close, but I thought—"

"You thought I ruled," Alan snapped, suddenly burying his grief in asperity. "Hal has suffered and labored for Isle, and men think I rule. He longs only for peace, and yet he was the greatest war leader this land has ever seen. Men rallied around his dreams. Likely his dreams will last longer than all my busy devices. And his wisdom in the court of law deserves to be legend. And yet, because I am the one who counts the gold, men think I rule."

"You suffered too," Trevyn protested.

"We both bear scars," Alan grumbled. "What of it? Let suffering go, Trevyn."

"Hal has never been able to let go of his pain," Rosemary whispered to her hands. "It has driven him mad."

"Nay, Ro," Lysse said gently, "the truth is cleaner and harder, I think. There will be a ship for him, at the Bay of the Blessed, to take him where the others have already gone. Aene has called him, and he goes as he has lived, in his own solitary way." Lysse shifted her gaze to include her husband. "You seem to have forgotten the days when he led and you followed."

"Why follow where there is no love?" Rosemary asked bitterly, and began to weep. Lysse turned to comfort her. Trevyn was grateful that his mother's eyes were not on him. She had said, *there will be a ship,* and his heart had leaped in his chest; it pounded still. *We will both set sail,* he thought, and strove to hide the thought. Without speaking he stumbled from the room. Then he stopped in the corridor, groping at a wall for support, blinded and dizzied by vision.

The others who had gone before, taking their magic from Isle . . . The star-son Bevan, with lustrous hands and lustrous brow, black hair parted like raven's wings, facing the sea breeze. The long line of Bevan's brethren the gods riding down to the Blessed Bay, leaving the hollow hills forever . . . Ylim, the ageless seeress, had lived and finally died in her own peaceful valley, Trevyn knew, but he envisioned her on a white ship beneath a changing moon. And the elves, his mother's people, setting sail on the swanlike boats Veran had prepared for them with his own magical hands—boats like Bevan's that went without sails. And now Hal, a Very King like Bevan of a thousand years before . . .

"All right, lad?" Alan had come out and stood before him anxiously. Trevyn blinked and nodded, shaking shreds of legend from his head.

"It's a hard thing to come home to," Alan added gruffly.

Trevyn lowered his eyes to hide a gleam of joy and wonder. Let Alan think he had been sorrowing. But he was learning the elfin Sight at last, it seemed. It had never caught him up so strongly before, except that horrible time when a wolf had given him bad dreams, false dreams. . . . But these just now had been his own dreams; he felt sure of it.

"I had better go to see my uncle," he muttered.

He climbed the long, spiraling tower stairs, his breath quickened by more than exertion. Hal did not answer the rap on his door, so the Prince pushed it open. King Hal stood staring westward through his window bars, his face haggard, his skin drawn into taut folds over the straight lines of his cheekbones. He did not stir for Trevyn's presence.

"Mireldeyn!" Trevyn called him by the sooth-name, and in a moment he trembled at his own boldness. Hal turned slowly and fixed his nephew with a silvery stare. In all the seven ages there had been no one quite like Mireldeyn, and even Trevyn, who had bounced on his lap not too many years before, could not fail to feel his greatness.

"Trevyn," Hal remarked. "I am bound for Elwestrand at last. You'll not try to sway me from my destiny, lad? You are too young for that, I think—and also, in your own foolish way, too wise."

Trevyn did not know how to react. "Elwestrand is fair, you have told me," he said at last. "But my father is saddened, my aunt angry and sad."

"I grieve that Alan must grieve." Hal turned away to his window again, his voice cold and tight. "But the ways of men are strange to me now, and I do not understand his sorrow. Nor can I see any longer what may be in store for him. But as for your aunt—she will find fulfillment that I could never give her. It was not by her fault that we have been childless,

Trevyn. Ket can better serve her, he who has loved her all these years."

"Ket!" Trevyn's astonishment left him open-mouthed, and for a moment he wondered if Hal was really mad. Ket, the former outlaw who had never learned to properly ride a horse! He had once been valiant, Trevyn knew, but now he was only the stooping, gravely courteous countryman who taught archery and served Alan as seneschal. That he should so regard the Queen!

"Do you think he has stayed in Laueroc for want of choice? He could have had any manor or town in Isle." Hal skewered Trevyn again with his icy stare. "Nay, do not mistake me, young man. Rosemary has always been faithful to me. Indeed, I believe she does not know of Ket's devotion; she is too modest to credit herself with such devotion. And Ket is a man of honor, and my friend."

"But you—has he told you?" Trevyn gasped.

"He knows there is no need to tell me. I saw his love twenty-some years ago, when he and my lady first met. But she was a lass of sixteen, my betrothed, and he was thirty, with a price on his red head. So he guarded her well, for my sake as well as her own, and he has cherished her all these years." Hal sighed, still staring into the reaches of the west. "I should have let him have her."

Trevyn could think of no answer, and left the tower room, shaken. He had thought himself adult, but in the face of adult trouble he felt very much the child. The more so because his own thoughts would cause his father pain, he knew. In days that followed he tried to give up such thoughts of sailing to Elwestrand. But vision replaced his conscious dreams, taking him at its will, day or night, flooding him like water and leaving him shaking. A silver ship, a silver harp, a winged white steed circling above the highest mountaintop. . . .

One vision came often. A woman with skin white as sea foam, hair like living gold, claret lips, and azure eyes—a woman as lovely as any elf, and yet not of elfin kind, for passion moved in her white breasts and wine mouth; Trevyn had felt it, lying limply in his bed at night. Around her hands flew ruddy robins and little gold-crested wrens; at her feet nestled leopards and deer, graceful swans—all manner of creature loveliness, even a kingly silver wolf. Hal had once said that the eagle and the serpent were friends in Elwestrand. Surely this woman was a princess in Elwestrand; could there be another place so fair? Trevyn grew certain that she awaited him there. There would be a ship for him, too, a sign to help his parents see that his destiny lay with the sea. His mother, at least, would understand if there was a sign. But Alan might never understand.

Trevyn avoided thought of Alan, let himself become lost in the dreams. He no longer worried about the wolves, or about Meg, or his uncle. And when Gwern returned from Lee, several days after himself, he scarcely minded his dogged presence. He moved through his days of lessons and training serenely, almost indifferently, with his mind's eye on the white-breasted sea.

Lysse frowned at him. "Vision is a chancy thing, Trevyn," she said to him abruptly one day. "Love or pride or sorrow—any one of them will send you astray like a strong wind. It will be years before you can read the Sight aright."

But Trevyn would not be lessoned by her, and soon her attention was demanded elsewhere. Before the winter was over, Hal left his window and took to his bed. He lay there day and night, restless at first, but later unmoving, uneating, unsleeping. Alan came to him often, to shout at him sometimes, but also to reason, and plead, and, Trevyn suspected, to weep. Rosemary came often, to sit silently by with averted eyes. Trevyn came uneasily, and as seldom as he could. But the only person to have any speech from Hal those days was Lysse. She sat by his bedside like the others who tried to care for him, but she did not lower her eyes.

"That son of yours is dreaming of glory," Hal said once. She could scarcely hear his voice, but the elves do not always need the words of the voice to hear.

"I know it," she answered. "Alan and I have expected it for years, and guarded against it, perhaps too well. . . . Surely you have not forgotten the portent that attended his birth?"

On Trevyn's natal morning, great golden eagles had circled the towers of Laueroc, mighty-pinioned eagles from Veran's Mountain by the faraway western sea. Green-clad Lysse had watched them from her window as she gave her baby his first milk.

"I have forgotten nothing," Hal told her sharply.

"So he is fated to travel ways far and solitary and strange to us," she said, ignoring the tone. "He will leave the mother-hood of earth, at least for a while; sea and sky will claim him. But I hope not yet. He dreams because he is young, and he shrinks from the grief that drapes his life these days. Alan is of no help to him. He is so fogged with bitterness that he scarcely sees beyond his own pain."

"I cannot help him," Hal whispered.

"I know it." Lysse spoke with mindful understanding.

"But the lad," Hal continued. "He flees from more than sorrow, I think."

"You think he flees? From Gwern?"

"Ah, the wyrd," Hal murmured. "There is a portent for you, of great weight. I tell you, Trevyn will be more important than any of us, more than King, more than Very King. Of all the Kings of Isle and Welas, I know of none that have had a wyrd."

"Why, what is a wyrd?" Lysse asked curiously.

"More than comrade, more than brother or blood brother, more than second self. Alan was all of those to me. . . ." Hal floundered. "How I wish I knew. I can only sense dimly that the wyrd is one who will be sacrificed when the time comes." Hal closed his eyes. "Suffering and sacrifice—they are required of any true king. How much more, then, of Trevyn. . . . He will blunder into the teeth of suffering soon."

"I believe he has already begun. But I don't understand." Lysse creased her fair brow. "Who will sacrifice Gwern? And why?"

"Aene. Or the goddess. For greatness." He stirred slightly, faced her again. "There are marvels to come, a quickening, new magic, or old magic made new. . . . There are things I could never do, and they will be done. That mystic sword I found will be thrown in the sea at last; I have seen that. An elfin King must hurl it away, to end the long shadow of Lyrdion on our land. I was never able to do it; 'twas all I could do to touch that weapon once, then walk away."

Lysse leaned forward with as much excitement as he had ever known her to show. "What else?"

"Something about unicorns, and the shape where two circles meet, the spindle shape. And the seeress . . . Trevyn mounted on a cat-eyed steed. Virgins and dragons . . . Do you think it might be a girl he's running from?"

"It has occurred to me," Lysse snapped. "What was Trevyn doing on such a peculiar horse?"

"Bringing the legends back to Isle, from Elwestrand. To travel to Elwestrand and return—I could never do that. It has never been done. But he shall do it. Trevyn shall, the young fool. I have seen."

"Mother of mercy," she murmured, stunned. "You haven't told him!"

"I am not a half-wit," he retorted frostily. "What is the good of a prophecy told? He must work it out himself, or make a hash of it, as the case may be. I've written it down among my things, for some scholar to grub up years hence. Then Trevyn shall have his glory, if glory is due."

"Mother of mercy," she said again. "Unicorns stand for wholeness. . . . What are the two circles that meet?"

"Gold and silver, sun and moon . . ." Hal's voice faded dreamily away. He was tired, and spoke no more, then or in the weeks that followed. He lay in deep stillness. Alan stopped trying to talk him out of his strange trance, though he was full of anger that had no vent. Sometimes he climbed the tower stairs to Hal's door and looked silently in for a while, then turned and went away. He would not sit by his brother's side.

Hal faded into brightness. Though he did not eat or move, his body remained beautiful—frail, scarred from old wounds, but glowing with spirit life. During the first days of spring, when a hint of green began to tinge the hillsides, Hal gradually, carefully ceased to breathe. Power and vision still shone from his open eyes.

Alan could not grieve anymore; how was he to grieve for one who had not truly died? But Rosemary wept, for she was a woman and she knew her loss. Trevyn clung to his dream. When the trees began to bud and Hal still did not stir, his loved ones prepared to take him to the Bay, where, Lysse's

Sight told her, an elf-ship awaited him. Alan dressed him in the bright, soft raiment of the elves and laid him in a horse litter. Beside him Rosemary placed the antique plinset that had always been his comfort. Alan brought the mighty silver crown that had come with Veran to Isle.

"Hal does not want the heavy crown," Lysse said. "He told me so. He will be no king in Elwestrand."

Alan looked at the great crown that was rayed like a silver sun. The sheen of it was the same as the tide-washed gray of Hal's eyes. Alan blinked and turned away.

"It has no place here without him," he said roughly. "He is the last of that line. I will throw it into the sea whence it came. Lysse, get him the circlet I made him, at least. . . ."

Trevyn came out, leading Rhyssiart, his golden steed, ready to ride with the others. But Alan turned on him brusquely. "Put that horse away. You are to stay here."

Trevyn's jaw dropped in astonished protest, and hot anger stirred in him; he quickly squeezed it down. He watched, motionless, as Alan and the Queens rode off with the horse litter between them. Arundel followed behind, riderless. Meadowlarks sang high overhead as the little procession moved slowly toward the Bay of the Blessed, a seven days' journey away. Trevyn stood with his disobedience already forming in his mind.

Chapter Six

"I am going, too," Gwern stated.

Trevyn sighed, gloomily accepting that Gwern knew of his plans even though he had not told him. He scarcely ever spoke to Gwern, though he had not fought with him since the row over Meg. His dislike had not abated, but he had become somewhat ashamed of it. He had decided to be dignified.

"Very well," he replied coolly, then smiled grimly to himself. He judged that Gwern would not ride with him more than a few days. Gwern would not be able to pass the haunt that guarded the Blessed Bay.

After nightfall they were off, with heavy packs of food stolen from the kitchen. Trevyn knew the sentries would be wary of him now, so they had to do some climbing with a rope. The Prince barely bothered to wonder why he trusted Gwern as his companion. Once well beyond the walls, far out on the downs, the mismatched pair called up some horses and set their course by the summer stars that hung low on the western horizon.

Trevyn had never been to the Bay of the Blessed, but he felt sure he could find the way. He would show his parents whether he was a child, to be so lightly left behind! He rode hard, to be certain of arriving before the slow horse litter. Once he had passed the haunt, the abode of bodiless spirits, he need not fear any pursuit. No mortal could withstand terror of those unresting dead except a few who still remembered the mysteries of the old order, the sound of the Old Language. Among which few, as a Laueroc, Trevyn numbered himself.

Within three days Trevyn and Gwern came to the end of the green meadows and tilled land, to the haunt, where the shades of the dead thickly clustered. Trevyn could feel their eerie presence chill the air. Smugly, he turned to watch Gwern shriek and flee. At last he would be rid of the muddy-hued upstart who hounded him! But Gwern only straightened to attention on his horse.

"Dead people!" he exclaimed, with something like delight. "But why do they not rest? Whence do they come?"

"How should I know?" Trevyn sputtered, fighting off his astonishment and the conclusions he did not wish to reach. Irrationally fleeing, he spun his mount and sent it springing into the haunt. Gwern followed without hesitation, and the wild terrain soon slowed Trevyn's pace. He and Gwern picked their way silently between looming gray rocks and dark firs. Once through the invisible barrier, Trevyn breathed easier, knowing he would not be ingloriously escorted back to Laueroc. But Gwern still rode at his side.

"I think they were gods," Gwern said with the unreasoning certainty of a child.

"Gods!" Trevyn snorted. "Only peasants talk of gods, Gwern!"

"They were little gods, such as can be killed, and they tried hard to cheat death; they still try. But the great gods cannot be killed. There is the goddess my mother; her sooth-name is Alys."

Trevyn gaped at him, staggered anew. Gwern had spoken in the Ancient Tongue, which Trevyn had never heard him use before or expected to hear from him. He hazily sensed that Gwern could not have said "Alys" in the language of Isle or any language of men. But he thought more of his earthy companion than of the goddess. There was no escaping the conclusion now: Gwern moved in the old order. He should have known it the first time he saw him touch an *elwedeyn* horse.

Gwern took no pause for his astonishment. "She answers to many names, but that is the most puissant," he continued soberly. "Call on her when you have need."

Trevyn regarded his dun-faced companion in mingled wonder and suspicion. What was this Gwern, and why should he offer aid when Trevyn had never showed him anything but hostility? "I have been taught to call only on the nameless One, and that seldom," he said at last.

Gwern shrugged. "And what is this Aene?" he asked, again in the Ancient Tongue.

"Dawn and dusk, the hawk and the hunted, sun and sable moon." Trevyn impatiently parroted the words Hal had taught him; already he had tired of riddles. "What of it? Come on, Gwern, let us be moving!"

The brown youth obeyed with a strange smile. Trevyn had just spoken the name of destiny, and in his ignorance he rushed to leave it behind.

For another three days the two rode through a wilderness of jumbled stone and giant, lowering trees. They saw no living creatures except birds and deer and the *elwedeyn* horses that also liked to explore these parts. In time they came to the Gleaming River and followed it south, down to the Bay through which Veran had entered Welas. They reached that quiet expanse without a sight of Alan and the Queens. Signaling their horses to a stop, they looked out over the shimmering water.

"There it is," Trevyn said.

Through the perpetual shadows of that dusky, brooding place moved a slim, gray elf-ship—a living thing, restless as a blooded steed between the confines of the shingle shores. Great evergreens towered overhead, the silvery water glimmered between, and the elf-boat circled like a swan, waiting. Trevyn moved closer.

"Mireldeyn is coming," he told the vessel in the Old Language. Then he gulped. "What in the name of—of my fathers is that?"

Another ship floated close to shore near the mouth of the

Bay, wallowing sullenly in the gleaming water. It was no elf-craft. It was broad, heavy, and high-headed, and it glittered all over with gold, shining like a miser's dream. The railings were riotous with gold filigree. At the bow leaped a figurehead—a golden wolf with bared teeth of mother-of-pearl. Trevyn felt sick. This could be no mere chance.

Slowly he rode along the verge of the Bay until he came to the glittering ship. There was no anchor or line holding it in place, no captain or any living being on board. The gilded wolf glared balefully, daring Trevyn to come closer. Grudgingly, he found a boarding plank, left at that sacred place from times long past, and he laid it to the polished deck.

"Don't!" Gwern whispered.

Trevyn had never seen him so frightened. Gwern's fear gave him a perverse triumph. Goaded, he stalked onto the golden boat.

The very boards of the deck were gilt. Trevyn edged across them and looked below, every muscle tense with caution. He half expected an ambush of wolves or of wolfish men. Instead, he found casks of water and provisions for a long voyage. Then he felt the ship shudder beneath him, heard the boarding plank fall away. He sprang to the deck and leaped off at once, landing over his head in icy water. He fought his way to shore, sputtering. Gwern reached out to help him, and Trevyn did not scorn to take his hand. As he stood dripping, the wolf-boat clumsily circled and came back to its place.

"In good time!" he shouted at it angrily. "I must say farewell to my father!"

All his dreams of Elwestrand had been shocked out of him by the danger he had tried too long to ignore. He would be voyaging, but not to Elwestrand, he knew now. He might have let Gwern say his farewells for him, he reflected, but he had done that once too often already. Shivering, he rode into the shelter of the trees, and Gwern helped him build a fire. There he sat and warmed himself through the rest of the day and the night. The sleek elf-ship swam impatiently about the

Bay; Trevyn could glimpse it in the moonlight. But the gaudy wolf-ship lurked stodgily in the shadows near the shore, flickering like marsh-lights in a darkened swamp. Already Trevyn hated its squalid splendor. He slept little and was glad to see the dawn.

Rosemary, Alan, and Lysse came late the next day. Gwern and Trevyn watched from the shadow of a giant fir as the elf-boat sped gladly to meet them and nestled close to shore near their feet. Arundel gave a joyful whinny, the greeting of an *elwedeyn* steed to the elfin ship that was like kindred to him. But Alan exclaimed in consternation, "Look yonder! What is that chunk of metal floating there?"

"Perhaps that boat does not concern us," Rosemary murmured.

"It does not concern Hal," Lysse agreed.

So Alan put the boarding plank to the elf-boat and lifted Hal's still body from the horse litter, cradling him like a baby. He carried him on board his boat and settled him gently on the open deck. Hal would lie under wheeling sun and stars on his long voyage; his gray eyes gazed up serenely. Alan laid his plinset beside him, in the sturdy leather case Rosemary had made years before. Then he took the great silver crown of Veran and flung it with all his strength far out into the Bay. With a sigh that Trevyn felt even from afar, Alan knelt to kiss Hal's quiet face, then left him there and stepped to shore. He looked at Rosemary, and she nodded.

Alan slid the plank away. Instantly, the swan-ship glided off, over the bright water, straight toward the golden light of the setting sun. Gulls flew low, calling, and water rippled. There was no other sound.

Trevyn watched it go. He thought he had put desire from him, but he had not yet felt true desire. He had never felt a force such as the mystic longing that took hold on him now. Scarcely knowing what he did, he started from his hiding place, running down the stony beach until his feet met the waves. He stared after the elf-ship, yearning. The sun reached out to him. The ship was a shape of marvel in its embrace. It swam swiftly away, at one with the wash of waves and the circling sea currents. Then it was gone, engulfed in

the golden horizon, and Trevyn realized that the wash of
water was in his own eyes. Still he stared westward. Not until
the sun slipped from view did he realize that his father stood
beside him, holding him. Alan, the great of heart. Trevyn had
not yet learned the depths of his love.

"You are quivering like a harp string," Alan said.

Trevyn shook his head to clear the haze of his trance.
"Father," he muttered. "I have grieved you, and I must
grieve you more."

"Why, Trevyn?" Lysse and Rosemary drew closer to listen.
Gwern quietly emerged from the trees.

"I must go on that golden ship," he told them.

Gwern was expressionless, Rosemary too sunk in her own
sorrow to care. Lysse looked at the wolf-ship with quiet eyes,
seeking to pierce its secret. But Alan exploded.

"If you had not been here, you would not have seen it!" he
cried. "The elf blood is strong in you. I knew that if you came
to the Bay you would yearn to sail, as Hal did. . . ." Alan
choked and subsided. "From the moment he saw your
mother's folk taking ship to the west, he dreamed of the
sea."

"I dreamed before I came to the Bay," Trevyn answered in
a low voice. "But the elf-ship is gone, Father. That gaudy
boat will not take me to Elwestrand."

Alan stared at his son, truly seeing him for the first time in
months. There was no glory lust in Trevyn's eyes, no youthful
impulsiveness. White-faced, the Prince looked as frightened
as Alan had ever seen him, but still set in his resolve.
"Where, then?" Alan whispered. But Trevyn had no answer
to offer.

Lysse turned from her study of the strange vessel, looked at
her son instead, and he did not elude her gaze. "It is true, my
husband," she said to Alan. "He must go. There is a destiny
on him."

Alan staggered as if he had been struck. "How can I know
that?" he gasped wildly. "Suppose I defy this—this so-called
destiny of yours, young man, and bid you stay. What
then?"

"Then I would defy you, and I would fight you, if it came to that." Trevyn did not try to hide his misery. "Short of my killing you, nothing worse can befall us both than my biding here. No good can come to anyone who shirks a destiny, you have told me. No good can come to us if I stay."

"It will not come to that," Alan muttered. For Trevyn's sake he would yield, though in all his life he had never surrendered with good grace. "Still, I do not understand," he added bitterly, perhaps to the One. "On any other day or hour I could have borne this better."

"I can wait a few hours, or even a day," Trevyn said quietly.

"Nay, go if you must go! Are there provisions on that sickly ship?"

Trevyn only nodded.

"Confound it, let us be on with it, then!"

They put the boarding plank to the gaudy wolf-boat. Trevyn strode off and fetched a bundle of clothing from his horse. Lysse stood probing the strange, glittering craft with smoky gray-green eyes. Only when Trevyn approached did she stir from her trance.

"Your cloak," she urged, motherlike. "It will be chilly on the open sea."

Trevyn got out the garment and flung it around his shoulders. Alan watched him intently, trying to seize the moment with his mind. Trevyn fastened his cloak, not with his golden brooch, but with a simple pin.

"Your brooch," Alan said. "What has become of it?"

"I lost it somewhere along the road." But Trevyn was taken by surprise, and the lie showed plainly in his eyes. Alan stared at him, stunned. Falsehood, and at this, the last moment they had to share! Trevyn returned his father's gaze with anguish in his own. Then Alan removed the jeweled brooch from his own shoulder, the rayed emblem of the royal crown that he had worn since Hal had given it to him on the day of Trevyn's birth.

"That is yours!" Trevyn exclaimed. "Keep it. I can't take it from you!"

"Borrow it, then. Bring it back," said Alan tightly. He pinned it over his son's heart, wordlessly handed him a purse of gold.

"I will. I swear to you I will return." Trevyn's voice shook. "Father, I am sorry—"

"Hush." Alan gripped his shoulders. "There is no need for speeches. Go with all blessing. . . ." He hugged his son hard and kissed him fiercely before he released him.

"Farewell, Mother," Trevyn murmured, and embraced her hastily. Rosemary stood among the horses, her russet head bowed to Arundel's neck; Trevyn knew she was hardly aware of his departure. But Gwern stood silently by. Trevyn froze with one foot on the boarding plank, feeling suddenly, absurdly, naked and incomplete. Gwern, whom he had wanted so badly to begone—Gwern had not moved from his place.

"Nay, I cannot leave earth. You must sail alone." Gwern stolidly answered the unspoken question. A hint of pain shadowed the claylike mask of his face, and Trevyn found himself utterly taken aback, astounded by that pain, astounded by the answering pang that put its grip on him.

"I didn't know," he whispered.

"Stay, then," urged Alan.

"Nay, I must go." Hesitantly, Trevyn offered Gwern his hand, and the barefoot, brown-haired youth gripped it without comment. Trevyn turned and strode onto the gilded ship.

He kept his head low, but Alan saw the tears that streaked his face. The ship started from its place like a hound unleashed, churned away from the shore. Alan put his arm around Lysse—to give comfort or to receive? He raised his hand in salute to his son. Gwern stood like a stump.

"All good come to you, Beloved!" Lysse called.

Trevyn straightened and waved to them. They watched after him until the ship turned the headland and was lost to view, vanishing like spook lamps into the dusk.

"A wolf is an animal that roams the night and sings to the moon," Lysse said softly. "There is no great harm to it."

"East!" Alan muttered. "The wolf-boat goes east. No good lies that way."

* * *

It was not until weeks later that the goodwife found Trevyn's brooch among Meg's belongings. Fluttering, she summoned her husband. They hated to scold Megan, for she had turned silent and moody since the Prince had gone away. But the brooch was valuable, and they were frightened.

"Ye cannot keep this, Meg!" the goodman cried. "Likely 'tis solid gold!"

"'Tis mine. He gave it to me."

"He only lent it t'ye! Did he say for ye to keep it?"

"If he wanted it back, he could have come for it."

"Who are ye to say where he must come or go? He is the Prince! Why would he give ye such a thing? Folk will say ye stole it!"

Meg had looked sullenly down, but now she straightened and flared back at her father. "What was I to do? Run to his castle, peradventure, and beg an audience?"

"Ay, daughter, 'twas a hard spot, that I'll not deny." Brock's voice was softer. "Still, ye should not have hid it away. We must take it to the lord; 'twill be safer with him."

Rafe regarded Meg with compassion while Brock told the tale. He had last seen her in a dress fit for a princess, glowing with the beauty that only love gives. Now she silently stared at the floor, and Rafe could see that her cheeks were pale. The pallor of love withheld, he judged.

Goodman Brock could not be less than honest. "And there is the cloak, my lord, as well," he concluded. The girl's eyes flashed up, and Rafe quickly hid the pity in his own, for he knew she would not welcome it.

"I think there is no need to say anything of the cloak." Rafe saw, without appearing to see, Meg's relief; this remembrance at least would be left to her. "I know my liege, and I am certain he would not begrudge it to you. But this brooch"—Rafe turned it delicately in his hands—"bears the emblem of the Sun Crowns. The King must know of its whereabouts." Rafe climbed down from his audience chair and headed toward a table where lay parchment, pen and ink, sand, and sealing wax. "Come, Meg, let us write a letter to Trevyn's father."

Within a week, a messenger came to Laueroc and presented to the King the following curious missive:

On this, the ides of May, in the Nineteenth year of his reign, to Alan, Heir of Laueroc, and Rightful and Most Gracious Ruler of Isle, Greeting.

It being that a thing I hold may not be mine in truth, I hereby state my willingness to relinquish it, obedient to the word of my Liege and King.

It being that my lord the Prince graciously lent me his brooch to fasten a cloak thereby, and his returning not therefor, I have cherished the brooch on his account until this time.

It being that this brooch is of precious substance and molded in the likeness of the Royal Emblem, I have rendered it into the safe keeping of my lord Rafe of Lee until my Liege the King has seen fit to judge the ownership thereof.

With many thanks to my lord the Prince for his gracious favors on my behalf, and especially for the sake of the cow Molly.

Your humble servant, Megan By-the-woods.

By the hand of her good lord, Rafe of Lee.

Alan read this three times, then stumped off to find Lysse. "What do you make of this?"

She read it and handed it back with a wistful smile. "Poor lass. I wonder what she is like."

"Either very honest, or else commending herself to our attention. Can he have got her with child, do you think?"

"I think—I would have felt such a child."

"Perhaps." Alan sighed. "Well, Rafe can tell us if anything is amiss. I will have him send the brooch to us."

"Nay." Lysse laid her hand on his arm. "Let the girl keep it."

He looked at her in surprise. "Whatever for?"

"There will be hard times ahead for all of us." She faced him steadily. "Hard enough for you and me, my love, but we have much to sustain us. It may be that—she does not have so much."

Alan cupped her chin in his hand and regarded her closely. "Have you seen something?"

"Nay, nothing clearly. It is only feeling."

He knew that feeling. His life had been a long battle with such heavy feeling since Hal and Trevyn had left. Call it foreboding, but not yet so dark that it benighted his thoughtful curiosity. He penned a reply to Rafe, commending the girl to his watchful care, then placed Meg's letter in his files. Months later, he still remembered her name.

Book Two

MOTHER OF MERCY

Chapter One

This gaudy craft was a dead thing, Trevyn decided, with no power of its own. Certainly it was not a living, swimming being like the elf-ship he had seen. He felt no vitality in its timbers, as often as he lay and lost himself in study of the mystery of its motion. He could discern no surge from behind or below, no gathering of heart at the bottom of the billow or of breath at the top. As the weeks went by, Trevyn became certain that the source of the power lay far ahead. He was in a bright bauble drawn by invisible wires, smacking crudely against the waves, for all the world like a child's toy being dragged across a vast watery yard. He thanked the One that the sea remained calm.

As yet, Trevyn had known nothing of the nausea that makes sea crossings a misery. To pass the time, and to keep from growing weak with the long voyage, he exercised for hours every day. Then he paced the deck as he studied the sky and sea. His course was to the south and east. Every morning at daybreak the rays of the rising sun haloed the hulking form of the wolfish figurehead. To Trevyn it seemed unfair, even treasonous, that the emblem of his father's royal greatness should bedeck the wolf, which to him had become a symbol of lowest evil. Since he could command neither the ship nor the sun, he learned to turn his back on this moment.

Trevyn had examined the figurehead closely on his first day out and had found it to be nothing more than gilded wood with glass eyes and pearly teeth. But at night it seemed to him that the lupine form was lit with more than reflected sheen. Amid the gleaming of the starry sea, he could not be certain. Yet the thing gnawed him with slow fear, even colored his dreams with its frozen leap, and he went near it no more. Another thing troubled Trevyn: that Meg from time to time would intrude her thin face before his inward eye. He strove to forget her, and turned his back on her image as on the wolf. Yet, had he noticed, where Meg's image was the dread of the wolf was not.

By the sixth week of the voyage, Trevyn began to see birds hunting the sea, wheeling ahead and to the left. He looked that way eagerly, searching the horizon for land. In the seventh week he spied it, a low, dark smudge where sky met sea. Trevyn judged that the land was no more than a day's voyage away, though the ship's course lay counter to the sighting.

But the sun next day came up in a sultry, coppery glow. The wolf loomed against it featureless and terrible, like a faceless specter in a dream. Trevyn stared at it in spite of himself, this thing that he could neither fight nor flee, and he paced the deck in unrest. The sky was filled with omen, a clamor heard with inner ears. Soon dark gray clouds blotted out the murky sun, and the storm clamored in truth. Rain fell, hiding the land like a molten curtain. Wind harried the rain, and the swell grew. The glittering ship plunged on stupidly, like a fish hauled in by a heavy hand, smashing through the heaving water. Spray flew as constantly as the rain; Trevyn wondered where he still found air to breathe. The ship did not swamp, for it rode very high, but it spun and teetered dizzily. Trevyn could not stand on the deck, and he did not want to be trapped below. He crawled to the filigree rail, and there he clung.

When night came, scarcely to be distinguished from the dark day, Trevyn knew that the ship would break. He did not care how soon. Nausea had long since purged him of any desire and left him limp. When the shock came and timbers flew like the spray, Trevyn was torn away from the rail and hurled through a confusion of water and rubble. Feebly he fought and thrashed, clawing at illusion, gulping at water and air. His gear hampered him. He rid himself of boots, sword, purse—even his father's brooch. He seemed to be sinking into a dark and alien place. Then he was quite naked, and found that he could breathe again, and opened his eyes.

Unaccountably, the sea was calm. Not far away, the wolfish figurehead glinted, its gilded form eerily etched on the dark water by the flickering lightning of the retreating storm. Trevyn shied away from it, but it did not come at him. Straight as an arrow it made off, dragging through the water like a stick through sand, and Trevyn knew that it laid a line toward the rising sun. He wheeled a quarter turn northeastward and swam toward the remembered sight of land.

He paddled through blackness unlit even by a star. The sea was warm in these southern parts, far warmer than the day of soaking rain and chilling wind. Trevyn relaxed in its embrace, surrendered to its flow, scarcely feeling the effort of his motions. The sea was a mother, a lover for whom he yearned. He laid his face upon her bosom as on a pillow, and more than once he breathed her watery essence into his lungs. He stirred in her at random, kicking out like an infant in the womb, cushioned by warm liquid from any harm, so it seemed, for all eternity. How cruel it was, then, how unfathomably harsh, when a pounding rhythm took hold of him and forced him away from this deepest haven, rushed and battered him, tossed and shoved him through a weary stretch of time and space, abandoning him at last in a strange place from which he might never return.

Trevyn crawled up the beach, just out of reach of the grasping sea surf, and collapsed onto the cold, hard sand.

He awoke with a shock to full daylight and the sound of rough voices. Four muscular, sun-scorched men stood around him, seized him as soon as he opened his eyes. He struggled to throw them off, but he was weak and dazed; a hard cuff to the side of his head stunned him. The men bound his wrists behind him with thongs and jerked him to his feet, prodding him to make him walk. Trevyn stumbled and fell to his knees, then sprang up as a lash bit his shoulders. His captors roared with laughter. "It works every time," one said.

They walked along the seaside, driving him before them. He would bring a fine price, they said, by the goddess of many names! Some lord would pay well to have such a handsome, yellow-headed oddity in his household. If he had been shipwrecked, there should be more. They would search the beaches well.

It did not surprise Trevyn that he could understand them, for he had studied many languages. He knew now that he was in the country called Tokar—a villainous place. Though he had expected nothing more, he felt desolate, like an abandoned child. Corruption flourished in Tokar; the rulers were sunk in greed. Isle had endured such eastern rulers for seven generations, until Hal and Alan had shed their blood to free her. . . . And now he, a Prince of Isle, had come to the realm of Herne's sorcery and Gwern's goddess, it seemed. Well, he was freeborn, with a freedom dearly bought, and he would not yield it easily, Trevyn silently vowed. Not to slavers or to any god or goddess that bore a name.

Throughout the day the slave traders tramped the beaches, prodding Trevyn before them or tugging him along behind. He gave them as much trouble as he could, dragging and blundering along. Even making allowances for his weakened state, they soon found it necessary to discipline him with the lash. They felt no particular desire to put welts on their merchandise, but a balky slave would be no bargain to anyone. By nightfall, when they had gained nothing for their day of searching except growling stomachs, they were mightily tired of Trevyn. They hurried him through the dark, flogging him to his feet when he fell, giving up finally and half carrying him to the slave pen. Sick as he felt, Trevyn thrashed when he heard the noise of bolts and bars being undone, nearly struggled free. Cursing, the slavers quieted him with dizzying blows. They seized him by the arms, cut his bonds, and flung him forward. Trevyn fell through emptiness, hit the bottom limply, and lay still. Above him he heard the bars slide into place and the bolts clang to. He turned his face to the dirt, letting despair take him.

From the hushed silence rose a murmur of voices; there were other people in this place. A hand touched Trevyn, feeling him over blindly. He did not stir.

"Better move aside, lad." It was an old man's voice. "They're liable to send something down on top of ye."

Trevyn moved, crawling forward, and hands guided him to a stony wall. There he huddled. The night was filled with voices and noises; he did not heed them. Dimly he sensed bodies pressed close beside him, as naked as his own. They stank, as did everything in this den, but he did not recoil. The night air was chill, and his companions, whoever they might be, were warm. Trevyn settled himself on dank earth and slept.

He awoke the next day to shouts and scramblings. Chunks of bread were falling through the high, barred trapdoor. Below it, the slaves sprang and shoved for a share. Trevyn blinked, but before he could stir his stiffened limbs the bread was all taken. He sat up slowly to watch the others eat. An old man approached him, picking his way carefully over the uneven floor. He stood before Trevyn and spoke with dignity. "I am old and have small need of this. Eat."

Trevyn took the bread and broke off a mouthful. The rest he gave back. He chewed his morsel very slowly; it was heavy stuff and sank in lumps to his stomach. When he had finished, the old man still stood before him, offering the bread. "Eat."

Trevyn shook his head, but the old man did not move. A few paces away, a big slave stirred dangerously. "If ye'll not eat it yerself, graybeard," he growled, "then give it to one who will." Yet the old man scarcely glanced at him. Turning his back contemptuously on the other, he squatted beside Trevyn and poised the bread under his nose.

"Eat!"

Trevyn ate. Bit by slow bit, the bread disappeared. The other slaves watched in silence, but no one made a move to hinder. When the bread was gone, Trevyn sank back and lay very still, afraid he might retch. But he kept it down, and toward evening he felt strength coming of it. He sat up and looked around.

"Whence d'ye come?" a slave asked him, but he only smiled and shook his head. There were about dozen men in

the pit, of all ages and sizes. Some had black hair, some
brown or russet, but none were as blond as he. They stared at
him curiously. "Were ye shipwrecked?" another ventured,
but again Trevyn gave no spoken reply. Almost insensibly he
had resolved to be a mute in this land, so that he would not
betray himself. And also in silent, inward rebellion. . . .
Throughout the long day on the beaches he had uttered no
sound. That had been his father's stubbornness in him; they
could enslave him, but, by blood, they could not make him
cry out. Now Trevyn realized that his bravado might stand
him in good stead. Better even to be a mute slave than a
dishonored prince held for ransom, or dead, or worse.

The slavers kept Trevyn in the pit with the others for a
week. The food was only bread in the morning, raw turnips or
carrots at night, and dirty water that seeped down the walls
into shallow stone cups. But even on this diet Trevyn gained
strength, for he was allowed to rest. Indeed, he paced the
stony floor with boredom and restless rage. Every once in a
while some wretch was hurled down from above as he had
been. Many had been slaves all their lives and picked
themselves up almost as if they were used to it. Others looked
as miserable as he had been. But none, Trevyn noticed, had
been beaten as cruelly as he.

The morning of Trevyn's eighth day in the pit, a narrow
ladder dropped through the trapdoor and a slave merchant
shouted at the slaves to come up. They went docilely, almost
numbly, took their places, and were roped into a line as if
they were indeed nothing more than trade goods. Hatred and
pride would not let Trevyn go so tamely. Let them come get
him, he grimly thought. Heart pounding, he waited.

"That towheaded lout must be deaf as well as mute," he
heard one slaver say.

"If he has eyes, he knows well enough what he's to do,"
another snapped. "If he weren't so good-looking, I'd kill him
now and save someone else the trouble."

Three of them came down after him. He crouched, hands
at the ready; by any god, they had better beware of him now
that he had the use of his hands! They came at him from three
sides. He lunged at one . . . and then they pinned him more
deftly than he would have believed possible, tied his wrists

with cutting force. One of them glared angrily, a bruise forming on his swarthy face.

"Give me that whip," he said, reaching for it.

"We're already late starting," the other replied testily. He turned on Trevyn. "Get up the ladder, you, or we'll leave you here to starve!"

He wanted to make them hoist him up by main force. But he sensed that the threat was not idle; the slavers seemed to have reached the last stages of exasperation. Reluctantly, slowly enough to make them lash at him from behind, he went up and took his place in line. He had never felt less willing to yield; his helplessness would not let him yield, his lost self cried out for recognition like an infant screaming in the night. But the body wished to survive.

The slavers placed him just behind the old man in the string, and Trevyn was glad of it. Even to the unspeaking, the old man provided more decent company than most. They all set out toward the distant market. The four slave traders rode shaggy ponies and led pack animals. With their whips they kept their human merchandise to a shambling trot over wild, rocky terrain. Most of the slaves went along readily enough on thickly callused feet, but Trevyn's feet, long accustomed to boots of soft leather, had not had a chance to toughen. Before the first day's journey was half over they had started to bleed. Trevyn's pace slowed, and the slavers had run out of patience with him. They kept him going with the lash.

At dusk they stopped at last, and the slaves dropped where they stood while the slavers pitched camp and built fires for themselves. After a while one moved down the line of slaves tossing each a chunk of bread and, for a wonder, a bit of cheese. But when the slave trader came to Trevyn, he only paused with a hard smile. "None for ye, bully," he said. "By the goddess, ye're too full of sauce to bear feeding. Bow when ye face me, sirrah!"

He passed on, laughing aloud, while Trevyn stared. When his back was well down the line, the old man halved his portion and passed Trevyn a share. "Pride makes a thin porridge, lad," he remarked. Trevyn was thankful that his muteness saved him the necessity of replying.

The slaves huddled their naked bodies together through the

night while their masters dozed blanket-wrapped by the fire, taking guard by turns. The next morning Trevyn's feet were oozing pus. The slaver who brought bread noticed it and came back with a bucket of brine. He grasped at his slave, but Trevyn stepped in with high head and a level look, though the pain took his breath. The man scowled and went away, bringing no bandaging for the feet.

That day was a nightmare for Trevyn. He could not keep the pace, stumbling and limping despite himself, and the slavers flogged him until his back was as raw as his feet. Pain and hunger made him reel lightheadedly. More than once he would have fallen if the old man had not caught him with the rope. Nearly hallucinating, he imagined that none of this was happening to him, that he was not himself at all, but Hal, facing the torturers in Nemeton's dark and hellish Tower. . . . Had Hal cried out? But he was Trevyn, after all. He would not cry out.

"If ye'd only yelp once in a while, or even lower yer head a bit," the old man whispered to him in honest concern, "I believe they'd treat ye less cruelly."

Trevyn answered him only with a wry smile, wishing in a way that he could take the advice, knowing that, being what he was, he could not.

Chapter Two

In a small chamber of the royal palace at Kantukal sat the king of Tokar, Rheged by name, and his counselor Wael. Rheged was a lean, long-armed man of middle age. Sparse, flabby flesh draped his loose frame; his look was hungry. He hungered insatiably, though not for food, and he could be as dangerous as a starving wolf. Wael, his advisor, was a shrunken wizard of incalculable years, a scholar of intrigue and the arts of influence as well as a sorcerer. The two men found little to like in each other and less to trust, but their mutual greed for power bound them almost as securely as love, for the time. They hunched in council over a figurehead in form of a leaping, gilded wooden wolf.

"It seemed faultless," Wael breathed in his soft old voice, hypnotic as the hissing of a serpent. "A young prince must perforce fancy a fairy boat of gold, and once he was on it, all was easy. I drew him here more surely than if I held him by a rope in my hand. Who would have thought it would ship-wreck? Never has such a storm been seen in the spring of the year. In autumn, perhaps—"

"Ay, ay," Rheged interrupted impatiently, "no one can fault your scheme, laugh though they might that we took

75

armed men to the harbor to await a swimming wolf! They do not smile to my face, not unless they wish to die quite slowly, but I cannot stop the snickers behind my back. But that is past; the question now is, what to do about Isle? It is small use to us that the heir is dead, if his body cannot be found."

"Perhaps he is not yet dead," Wael mused. "If he got ashore, he could be anywhere by now; it has been almost two weeks. But we should hear news of him, for he would cut a strange figure in these parts. Perhaps he has been enslaved. It would be wise to check the markets."

Rheged nodded sardonically and made a note.

"If I could only have something that belonged to him, a piece of clothing or a knife or even a coin," Wael went on intensely, "I could draw him to me, dead or alive, as surely as if—"

"As if you held him by a rope in your hand," Rheged finished sourly. "What of it? Am I to send to Isle, now, for an article of his apparel?"

"Nay, nay, Majesty, send men to search the beaches! Offer rewards enough to render them honest. And send spies throughout the realm to find news of him. Offer rewards for that, also."

"You make plentifully free with my gold," muttered Rheged. "Even so, it shall be done. It will be worth much gold if I can hold that prince my hostage."

"Or even," whispered Wael, "your sacrifice at the altar of the Wolf."

"As you will," Rheged growled. "But how is that to help my invasion of Isle?"

"That upstart little country, Isle!" Wael laughed softly, a wheezing, murky sound. "King, I could have given you that victory a dozen times by now. But it is the game itself that brings more joy, and the game has just begun, do you see? Just begun!" Wael lurched forward in his intensity. "And you know wolves belong to the winter. We will strike then."

"If you say so, wizard," the monarch wearily assented. "As you say."

The slave market was nothing more than a large cobbled clearing set amid the houses and shops of a place called Jabul.

Here the traders came with their wares at the dawn of the market day, and even before the arrival of the buyers the place was crowded. Thousands of human beings filled it—an eerie gathering, Trevyn thought, for the slaves hardly moved or spoke. The silence of despair hung over them all. About half of the slaves were women, bound in their own strings apart from the men, many with babes at their breasts. Trevyn stared, gaped indeed, for they were as naked as himself. The sight did not thrill him so much as dismay him; they were as beaten, as filthy, and as bereft of dignity as he. Suddenly he thought of Meg, imagining her in such company, and his face turned hard as stone. He stood like rage immobilized while the buyers arrived and looked him over, feeling his limbs for soundness as if he were a draft animal.

"Here is a man looking for a mute!" one of the traders cried to another, leading a buyer through the lines of slaves.

"Then here is his mute!" shouted the other, striding to Trevyn and jerking him forward. "Right here, sir, a fine, strong fellow!"

"Are you quite sure he is unable to speak?" the buyer asked, addressing the slave trader with distaste he made no effort to conceal. He was a slender young man, a bit shorter than Trevyn, with a high, pale forehead over eloquent eyes. The noisy slave merchant did not seem to mind his evident distrust.

"Why, he's not made a sound these two weeks past," the slaver blustered, "not even in pain. Here, let me show ye." He grabbed Trevyn's finger and wrenched it back, but the young man gasped and struck his hand away.

"That will not be necessary," he said imperiously. "I take it, then, that he has not lost his tongue?"

"Nay," answered the slaver, crestfallen. Then he brightened. "But if ye want him, sir, I'll take the tongue out of him for ye, right enough—"

"Great goddess, nay!" The man was emphatic, and Trevyn allowed himself a sigh of relief. "Mischance enough if it was born in him." The young man turned to Trevyn, studying him, not poking at him as the others had done, but looking into his eyes. Trevyn met his gaze steadily, and the man nodded, satisfied. "How much?" he asked.

"Softly, sir, he's a handsome piece; if I put him on the block he'll bring me a pretty price."

"I cannot wait for the bidding; I have business at home. Name your price."

The slave trader named a price. It was high, but the young man doled out the gold without demur. The slaver undid Trevyn from the string, leaving his hands tied.

"He is mine now," the young man said.

"Ay."

"To do with as I like."

"Ay, to be sure!" The slave merchant laughed and cracked his whip.

"Good." The young man brought out a slender knife, such as scholars use to sharpen their pens with, and began carefully to cut Trevyn's bonds.

The slaver shouted, and his face went white. "Nay, young master! He's a wild 'un—he'll go to kill me!" But the thongs were cut, and the young man stepped back without comment. Trevyn rubbed his chafed wrists and studied the shaking slaver, who was backing cautiously away. No courage in the man without his fellows, it seemed! He would gladly have settled his score with this tormenter, and it was no cold caution that restrained him. He could not say why he stayed his hand, unless it was somehow because of the young man who stood quietly beside him. He could have leveled him with a single blow, by the looks of him, but the fellow had freed him fearlessly. . . . Trevyn turned and nodded farewell to the old man who had befriended him. Then he looked to his new master.

"Here," the young man said, handing him a sort of loincloth; hardly the raiment of a prince, but Trevyn put it on gladly. His feet were healed by now and his back mostly healed. The traders had been obliged to tend to him, not wanting to bring him to market looking like a scandal. Still, the young man winced and muttered to himself when he saw the stripes.

"This way," he said when they were both ready. They walked together through the marketplace. "My name is Emrist," he told Trevyn. "Not that it matters, I suppose," he added vaguely. "Though, of course, you can hear. . . ."

They turned out of the marketplace into a crooked alleyway that wound up terraced slopes between houses perched precariously on their foundations. At the top of the steep hill they paused for breath. If Trevyn had looked back, and if he had known, he could have seen Rheged's men entering the marketplace to search for him.

He and his new master traversed a ragged country cut by rocky ridges into patchwork gardens, vineyards, and orchards. They stopped often to rest, for Emrist was not strong. Toward noon they shared bread and cheese and a flask of weak wine. It seemed to Trevyn that Emrist was not a rich man. He went afoot, though easily tired, and his tunic and sandals looked plain and worn. Trevyn wondered how he had got the gold to buy him, and, indeed, why he had bought him at all. For his manner was gentle, and he did not seem to be the sort of person who would lightly own another.

By early afternoon they had moved into wilder country, where habitations were fewer and growth cluttered the meadows until they were really young forests. The look of the land made Trevyn wary, and he was not entirely surprised when robbers ran at them, screeching, out of the brush. There were four of the rustic brigands, each armed with a wicked-looking sword. If Trevyn had been by himself he might have run; his fray with the slavers had taught him caution. But there was Emrist to be thought of. . . . Trevyn lunged under a whistling sword, wrested the weapon from its owner, aware that Emrist had already fallen. He killed the robber with a swift stroke to the throat and turned on the other three, frantically beating them back from Emrist's prostrate form. In a moment they rallied and circled him; he took some cuts then. But he had been trained to use the sword against odds and soon felled them. Though it sickened him to do so, he made certain that each robber was dead before he turned his back on them.

Emrist was sitting in the roadway, holding his head and looking pale as a wraith. "What are you?" he whispered. "You fought like a King's man."

Trevyn laid down the bloody sword before he went near him, not wishing to alarm him. He kneeled and probed his master with careful fingers. A welt was rising on Emrist's head, but nothing else was wrong that Trevyn could find. Yet Emrist reeled and went limp under his touch. Though he hated the thought of staying any longer in these unfriendly parts, Trevyn could see nothing for it but to make camp. He slung Emrist over his shoulders and carried him into the woods, looking for shelter.

If it had not been for fear, the night would have seemed luxurious to Trevyn. He found everything he needed on the bodies of the slain robbers. In the shelter of a rocky scar he made a fire with their flint and steel. He set rabbit snares with the lacings of their sandals. Later he warmed himself against the night chill in a looted cloak while he carved his dinner with a looted knife. It was the first fresh meat he had eaten in over two months. Bits of bread, too, had been in the robbers' pockets. Trevyn saved them for the morrow.

Throughout the night he sat by the fire with naked sword in hand, starting at every shadow. Strange chance, he mused, that he, a king's son, should have become a robber of robbers. At his side lay Emrist, also wrapped in "borrowed" cloaks. From time to time the young man moaned and gazed half fearfully until Trevyn soothed him with a glance and a touch of cooling water. Strangest of chance that bound him to this slaveholding Tokarian! Not that he could ever desert a helpless man, but—was a courteous word so rare in this eastern land, a friendly glance so precious, that Emrist had sent such a flood of comfort to his heart?

Emrist awoke fully in the morning, and though he sat up painfully, the dazed look was gone from his eyes. Trevyn gave him the bread and the little wine that remained. He ate slowly, but finished it all. "Did you not sleep at all?" he asked.

Trevyn cast a wry glance at the woods all around them.

"Ay, it is an evil place," Emrist agreed. "I would rather be far away from here." He hesitated. "Good friend, it should be no more than a half-day's journey—do you think you could help me home?"

Trevyn nodded his willingness, then pointed inquiringly. Emrist laughed.

"Of course, you do not know the way! Or you would have

taken me yesterday, hah?" Trevyn grinned and nodded. "Well, it's not hard," Emrist continued. "We just follow the road. It turns to a track, then to a trail, then at last to a little path through the forest, and it ends at the house, in the clearing atop the hill. My sister will welcome us. She must be frightened by now, though she is a strong-hearted woman. There are no neighbors to comfort her. Even the robbers do not come near the haunt—" Emrist stopped short. He had spoken with dreamy happiness about his sister and his home, but now he believed that he had said too much. He stared at Trevyn in open terror.

"I beg you, do not leave me," he whispered.

Trevyn shook his head and laid a hand on his master's arm in assurance. He filled their flask at a nearby stream, and he cut Emrist a staff to lean on. Trevyn still wore his looted cloak, and he belted his captured sword to his waist, but the rest of the robbers' gear they left behind. Trevyn helped Emrist pick his way back to the road and strode beside him restively as he slowly moved away from the scene of carnage. They could not leave this place soon enough to suit him. After a while they had put it well behind them, and Trevyn's impatience quieted. But Emrist's pace grew slower yet, and soon Trevyn had to support him with a hand under his elbow. It was not yet midday when Emrist began to topple. Trevyn caught him easily and did what he had expected to have to do before then: rolled his cloak as a pillow for Emrist's head and slung the man upon his back.

Even carrying his master, Trevyn could now move far more quickly. He strode along, sharpening all his senses for any sign of danger. That his new master lived in a haunted place had been the best of good news to him. No evil would trouble him there. Only people versed in the mysteries of the Beginning could brave the haunt, and only those of good heart. But what sort of man, then, must this Emrist be that he lived among the shades?

At long last he felt the heaviness of Otherness around him and passed through the haunt to a feeling of warm welcome, even a sense of coming home. Everything was just as Emrist had said. The track had long since dwindled to a trail, and now a mere path wound up a steep hill amid tall, silent trees.

Trevyn followed it until he saw light ahead and the gables of a building. Bent under Emrist's weight, he entered the clearing. An old man looked up from his gardening, stared, and scuttled inside. A moment later a dark-clad woman came running out.

"What has happened? Oh, Em!" she was crying, but as Trevyn only stared at her she took control. "This way," she gestured, and he followed her inside, up a narrow flight of stairs. At the top, she indicated a room furnished only with a table, a cot, and a sturdy wooden chest. Trevyn laid Emrist on the shabby bed and gently turned the man's limp head to show the bruise. The woman nodded. "I shall care for him."

In the doorway stood the old man and an equally ancient woman, both shaky and gaping. Their mistress spoke to them firmly. "Dorcas, pray find our friend something to eat. Jare, prepare a room for our guest. I shall see you later." She almost shooed them all from the room. As Trevyn turned to leave, he saw Emrist's sister reach to unlock the wooden chest at the bedside.

In the kitchen old Dorcas set about heating Trevyn some dinner. She was obviously frightened of him, so he kept away from her, sitting still and looking about him. The house was simply but strongly built of stone and timbers, with a low roof and small windows—not a rich man's home, by any means. Emrist's bed had been hard enough, his chamber bare of comforts, and Trevyn saw nothing downstairs either that betokened ease. No rugs or draperies softened the floor or walls. Instead, traces of mice lay about, and cobwebs covered the windows and rafters. On the table sat some greens and a few onions. Little food for much labor, especially for the old ones. Trevyn could understand why the cleaning was neglected. And Emrist was sickly, it seemed. . . . But had he come all this way, then, just to serve such as these?

The old woman brought him a bowl of thick bean soup, setting it hastily before him and backing away as if wary of his reaction. But Trevyn was eager enough to eat it, and Dorcas watched him with less alarm; a hungry man was something she could deal with. Presently her husband, old Jare, came downstairs with a bundle of clothing, offering it to Trevyn as hesitantly as his wife had offered the soup. Trevyn took a tunic and tried to slip it over his head, but it was too small and threatened to tear. Smiling, he shook his head and handed it back. The old man retreated back up the stairs. His wife busied herself banging pots in the scullery. Suddenly, achingly, Trevyn felt the limitations of his muteness. These two would welcome no help from him for a while yet. He wandered to where a rude bench stood against the wall and draped himself over it, only for a moment, to rest. . . .

Hours later, Trevyn awoke with a start to a gentle touch. Dark had fallen, and flickering oil lamps cast a dim light. Over him stood Emrist's dark-haired sister, rendered mysterious by the night. "He wishes to speak with you," she said, and Trevyn rose swiftly to follow her.

Emrist sat propped up by pillows, with flasks and tumblers on the table near his bed. He looked much stronger, though pale. Trevyn knelt at his bedside, so that their eyes met.

"I never expected to see you here," Emrist said in tones low with wonder. "I thought perhaps you would bring me as far as the—barrier—and then drop me and bolt. If chance had favored, Maeve here might have found me. For that I would have owed you thanks enough. But this—it stuns me."

Trevyn gestured deprecation. Emrist regarded him long and thoughtfully.

"Surely you have a name, but I do not know it," he said. "I will call you Freca, if I may, for you are a brave youth."

Keen interest sprang up in Tervyn's mind. It was an *elwedeyn* name—that is to say, in the Old Language. Even as he nodded his consent, Trevyn looked on Emrist with new eyes. Emrist returned his gaze, and puzzlement creased his brown.

"I cannot believe you cannot speak!" he exclaimed. "There is song in your movements and epic in your glance. What are you, Brave One?" Trevyn stiffened in consternation; he had shown too much. But Emrist went on. "It does not matter, you know, that I have bought you. You are no slave. You are a free man. Fill your stomach with us as long as you will, or go where you will." He turned to his sister. "Is it not so, Maeve?"

"Even so," she answered.

Something let go inside Trevyn. Shackles he had not known

were gripping his spirit melted away. He forgot his muteness, but his thankfulness was too great for words; this man had just healed the deepest hurt he had ever known. He seized Emrist's hand and clung to it like a child, felt tears fall. He hid his face in the sheet. Frail fingers touched his hair.

"Ay, they were foul enough to you," Emrist said, and his voice held a sharp edge of wrath. "All because you would not hang your head and play the dog. But you stood like a caged eagle. You were free before I met you, Freca."

"He is spent, Em," said Maeve in her cool woman's voice, "and so are you. Let me show him to his room, and then I will come to fix you a draught."

Trevyn was more dazed than tired, but he followed her willingly. She led him to a room even barer than Emrist's. Still, the bed beckoned with pillows and blankets. Trevyn settled himself swiftly and lay puzzling while his tears of relief dried on his face. What was he to do? He did not know where to go. Surely he had come to this place for some reason other than to leave. . . . There was something special about Emrist. Also, the man needed him; for some secret reason, he needed a mute slave. Well, he would have a mute servant, Trevyn decided, at least for a while. There was the price of his redemption to be considered—much gold from a man who was not rich. He would like to make it up to him somehow. For the time, Trevyn wanted nothing better than to serve this Emrist in whatever way he could.

Chapter Three

For the next several days Trevyn worked feverishly, heaving rocks out of the garden for old Jare, snaring rabbits and quail for Dorcas. After a few days, Maeve gave him a plain tunic of coarse cloth, and knee breeches, and crude sandals of leather and wood. Scarcely finery, but it made him feel the more indebted. Only at mid of day, when the sun beat down, would he cease from his voluntary labors to bathe in a dark, mirrorlike pool that lay in a hollow amidst the towering forest trees.

By the time Emrist got up from his bed, a week after his injury, Trevyn had made his mark on the household. The cobwebs were gone from the rafters. Old Jare whistled tunelessly under his breath. Dorcas set more food on the table, and even the stoical Maeve moved about her tasks humming contentedly. Emrist was still weak; for a few days he came downstairs only to sit and watch. But on a rainy day, seeing Trevyn restlessly rubbing the grime from the small window panes, he spoke to him.

"It seems you will stay with us yet a while, Freca."

Trevyn was almost startled into speech, but he merely shrugged his shoulders.

"You are a very beaver for industry," remarked Emrist. "It is not necessary, you know. We won't turn you out."

Trevyn only grinned at him. Emrist sighed.

"Well, since you have decided to be of use, come help me today. It's time I was getting back to work."

With considerable curiosity as to what that work might be, Trevyn followed him up the stairs. They entered Emrist's chamber, and Trevyn waited for him to go, perhaps, to the locked chest. But instead Emrist strode to a corner and wrestled a moment with a rough wooden plank of the wall. Reluctantly, a panel slid, and another narrow staircase was revealed.

Eagerly, Trevyn followed his master up to the dusty garret. The place was close and windowless, though some light seeped in through the leaky wallboards. Emrist lit a pungent oil lamp that sent soot streaking toward the already blackened rafters. In its yellowish glow, Trevyn could see great numbers of parchments and leather-bound books ranked on splintery shelving. Fans of dried plants rustled overhead, and all kinds of formless rubble lay on the floor. Under the low peak of the roof stood a worktable cluttered with pots and urns and little jars, a brazier, and some metal caldrons. Trevyn recognized a scholarly disorder similar to Hal's, but somehow warmer and more secret. Emrist poked at some of his earthenware jugs.

"Potions for my interminable illnesses," he grumbled, "old now, and weak. And dried-up paints and dyes, and spoiled perfumes, and messes I have forgotten the meaning of." He rumaged through the containers, picking out a score or more and heaping them in Trevyn's arms. "Take them out among the trees and let the rain have them. Wash the jars and bring them back. But do not put your fingers to your mouth, hah?"

For many weeks thereafter Trevyn worked with Emrist in the cramped garret. Sometimes he ground minerals or dried plants in the mortar, taxing work that Emrist was glad to leave to him. Emrist was too easily tired to go roaming in the woods, so Trevyn would search out the plants he needed. Trevyn often wondered what to think of his master, who seemed to have knowledge of every kind of magical lore. Day after day the frail man compounded potions with long labor and greatest care. But no one came to buy his charms from him, not in this haunt, and Trevyn had found none of the strange trappings of sorcery among his things such as Hal had described from his days in Nemeton. No censers and ceremonial robes, no black-handled swords or talismans of bright metal. In fact, Trevyn doubted if high magic could be performed in the littered garret, which Emrist refused to let him clean. Spirits of ancient might would only come to surroundings suitable to their greatness.

Still, Trevyn wondered. Sometimes the two of them made candles in many subtle colors, delicately-scented tapers molded from the rare and precious beeswax no ordinary person could afford. He found traces of chalk on the floor sometimes, in strange star and circle designs. And always on the worktable a kettle of salt stood—big, stone-white crystals. Salt could never be used in any evil spell and was essential to any good one.

In time Trevyn became convinced that Emrist was not merely a dabbler in hidden lore but a master working cautiously toward some definite goal. One day, when supper was late because of a balky kitchen fire, Trevyn observed Emrist surreptitiously prodding the sodden wood into flame with a mere flick of his fingertips. Another time, Trevyn awoke in the dark of night to see his master padding down the corridor with only his raised forefinger, glowing eerily, for a light. After that, seeming to intuit that Trevyn knew his secret, Emrist showed his power more openly. He would set a streamer of nonconsuming fire in midair to read by or send objects scooting across the garret into his servant's startled hands. He could bring forth miniature whirlwinds out of stagnant air and showers of rain from clouds of arid smoke. He could make rocks split, make dirt heave and roil like bubbling broth. These were his simpler magics; to command any of them, he spoke no word, but only gestured with his graceful hands. Trevyn felt sure that Emrist was not practicing, that he did not need practice, such was the ease of his power. He had observed his master eyeing him in the light of strange, leaping flames, and he felt that Emrist must be testing his fortitude for the next step toward the hidden goal.

Apparently, Emrist was satisfied. One day he began to

summon the spirits of the elements, speaking to them in words of the Elder Tongue. Trevyn felt the ancient call and power of that language go through him like a tide of fire; all his heart must have leaped to his eyes. Emrist froze in midspell, staring at him. *"Selte a ir,"* he whispered, still in the same tongue. "Speak to me."

Trevyn only answered his stare. So long had he shackled his tongue, not speaking even to the little creatures of the forest, that his own will constrained him to silence like a brank. Even as his heart went out to Emrist, he felt that constraint stubbornly strain against the command his master had spoken. Command or plea? Hurt was in Emrist's eyes.

"Do you not yet trust me, Freca?"

Brave one, he had named him. Trevyn felt himself plentifully brave to fight, to endure, to strive, but not to love. At that moment he would far sooner have faced the fiercest of warlocks than the gentle sorcerer before him. His cowardice bound him helpless, sickened him. He lowered his eyes and sank his head in his hands. Emrist's face, had he seen, went bleak with disappointment and pity, but his voice was calm.

"Ay, they served you ill enough," he said softly, more to himself than to Trevyn. "No wonder you clench yourself against them still. Bide easy, Freca. Time will have the healing of you."

But time only locked Trevyn more into his muteness; time and Maeve, in a way. Emrist's sister was a sturdy woman who moved impassively about the never-ending work of her household. Trevyn could not guess her age; her face was unlined, but hardened with years and toil and some quality he could not name. Her body was always hidden in folds of dark cloth, even in the heat. She spoke seldom. Trevyn paid her little mind after the first few days, and he never expected to see her naked in the light of a waxing moon.

She came to him in his bedchamber, with her dark hair falling softly around her shoulders. Trevyn woke with a start and gaped, unable for a moment to think who she was. Moonlight and her nakedness had changed her; she was all sheen and surface, pearly and unfathomable, her breasts like argent globes, full and high. Her face was as blank as

Gwern's, her eyes pools of purple shadow. She sat on the bed by his side and wordlessly ran questing fingers along the smooth skin of his neck. He trembled under her touch, gulping and scarcely moving as she drew back the covers and fitted the alabaster curves of her hips onto his. Her body was thick and firm, supple from her labors. He sighed and shifted his hands to her breasts, letting her take him.

In no way could Trevyn consider Maeve his conquest. She cradled his body as a harper cradles his harp, played upon him expertly, played against him with catlike warmth and grace, and both of them as mute as the watching moon. Later she left him with catlike indifference, drifting out without a backward glance. After she was gone, Trevyn's thoughts turned unaccountably to Meg. What was she like under her baggy blouses and full peasant skirts? Fleetingly, he envisioned rosebuds and dew; he remembered the butterfly tremor of her lips when he had kissed her. Maeve's lips had been as firm as her competent hands. Suddenly, Trevyn was fiercely glad that he would not or could not speak. He wanted never to whisper endearments to Emrist's white-breasted sister.

In the days that followed, Maeve moved about the house as serenely as ever, with no change in her manner or her sober face. Trevyn found it difficult to think of her as the same woman who came to him, palely shimmering, at night. She came for the seven nights of the swelling moon; Trevyn found himself longing for Meg whenever he embraced her. When the moon had reached the full, she left him to come no more. He did not expect her or seek her out in nights that followed. She had pleasured him to satiety. He wondered guiltily how much Emrist knew, for he had sometimes suspected that the sorcerer had uncommon means of knowledge, and he had constrained himself to keep even his thoughts buried deep. But Emrist showed no sign of knowledge or displeasure.

The two of them still spent their days in the garret, invoking the disembodied essences of the elements. Trevyn practiced walking through their focus of being in the room. He found that the moistness of water did not wet him or blasts of air so much as ruffle his hair, just as he had long since learned that he would not be slain by the spirits of the dead. The invocation of fire pained him, terribly; he bore it, and found that his flesh did not shrivel. In a way, earth was more difficult to withstand. Dense, alien, crushing, an almost hostile presence choked him. Trevyn struggled for breath, but he felt Emrist's eyes upon him even through his heavy covering of insubstantial soil, and shame stiffened his spine.

After that day, Emrist sat for a week in the garret staring at nothing that Trevyn could see, waving him away when he came near. Trevyn was used to such trances. Hal had been accustomed to lose himself in visions of Elwestrand or the loveliness that had once been Isle. So Trevyn judged that Emrist was also refreshing himself in some such private retreat, gathering himself for the next drive at the hidden goal. He had seen how spell-saying sapped the magician's small physical strength.

In fact, Emrist was visiting a less pleasant place than he imagined. But Trevyn was glad enough to leave him alone, to escape the stifling garret and work in the outer air. It was the height of summer. Though cool breezes were still to be found beneath the trees, the sun beat down fiercely on the garden. Old Jare suffered from it and kept to the shade, but Trevyn gloried in the sunlight. He stripped to his loincloth as he carried water for the wilting squash and beans. His skin turned golden brown and shone with his sweat; his hair, long uncut, lay startlingly bright against his bronzed neck.

Maeve stood at the upper windows sometimes and looked on. She did not stir when one day Emrist came up and stood beside her.

"So you take your pleasure in watching these days," he remarked placidly.

"Ay," Maeve replied. "It's far enough away here that I cannot see the scars. They hurt me even to look at. Praise be, they didn't show in the moonlight."

"Have you noticed the scars of his legs and shoulders?" Emrist asked. "Not the whip welts—"

"I know the ones you mean. The vermin branded him also, it seems."

"Nay, it was not the slavers who did that. The whip stripes lie over the brands, and you know the odd, jagged shapes of them—do you think perhaps some animal attacked him and the wounds were seared for safety?"

Maeve was not listening. "Yet he moves with grace and joy in spite of it all," she murmured. As her eyes followed Trevyn, her brother was startled by the softness, almost the beauty, that transformed her time-tempered face to that of the girl he scarcely remembered. Emrist frowned in consternation.

"Do not place your contentment too much on him, Maeve," he admonished her softly. "Only the One knows what may happen in the next few days."

Her face hardened, and she turned from the window to face him. "I always knew that he came but to go," she answered. "You are ready, then?"

"Ay, but I have decided I must do that alone. Freca would stand me in good stead; he is like a lion for bravery. But his soul has been bruised, and I think he is younger than he seems—" Emrist spoke with fumbling haste. "I will not risk scarring him anew."

"But, Em," Maeve protested in exasperation, "have you forgotten why you bought him, a mute? To help you, no matter what the risk? The stakes are too high to think of one soul overmuch."

"Using him would make the stakes higher yet. Have you not sensed that he is of the old order? His eyes speak the Elder Tongue, though his mouth cannot. That is why I say he will be leaving us. He has some destiny to fulfill; I think he came here only to heal."

"Of course I know he is a special one," Maeve flared. "More special than you imagine. But what of your own special destiny? You must not spend yourself without support. Let me stand by you."

"You know Wael scorns and hates womankind," Emrist replied grimly. "Fear, perhaps, in scornful guise, for woman's love is a strong magic. . . . But most likely he would not come before you. Or if he did, your presence would only add fuel to his fire."

"Ay, the more cursed he," answered Maeve impatiently. "Well, then, send Freca on his way and get another mute! Only a few months will have been lost."

Emrist shook his head. "I must invoke Wael tonight."

"Why, in the name of the One?" She was ashen.

"Because I have seen—they have found the brooch of the Islendais Prince."

That day, when Trevyn entered the garret, he found Emrist reading from a parchment dark with age. Trevyn made shift, as he had often done before, to glance at the title, and what he saw shook him like a blow. "On the Transferring of the Living Soul." The crabbed old letters seemed to sear themselves on his eyes, for at their head leered the emblem of a leaping wolf.

"I need nothing, Freca," Emrist said without looking up, and Trevyn turned and went in a daze. He wandered out of the house and into the forest, stopping when he reached a quiet place to sit and compose his reeling thoughts. It did not occur to him to break his silence, to speak to Emrist and ask his help. His long silence had made him a spy in this household, and now his shame guarded the secret.

Trevyn's curiosity had often been piqued by his snatched moments with Emrist's lore. The properties of wingless flight. . . . The seeking of sprites. . . . The science of griffins and firedrakes. . . . Any of these things, and many more, he would gladly have studied. But he had not let Emrist know that he could read, for a mute who can read and write is a mute in tongue only. Trevyn had refrained from reading in secret; he clung at least to some shreds of his honor. But in this matter of the wolf, where life and kingdom might someday be at stake, he found his honor to be of smaller concern. He returned to the house with a calm face and a plan.

He lay awake that night until all sound in the household had long since ceased. Then he arose and made his way stealthily to Emrist's chamber. He was not too afraid of awakening Emrist; he knew that the magician took draughts to sleep, to counter the pains of his frail body. Trevyn crept into the room, heading for the garret and the ancient parchment. But surprise tingled through him. Emrist was not in his bed, nor had the coverings been disturbed. The bright moon showed that plainly. The forbidden chest stood open, nearly empty. Trevyn ran up to the garret. Emrist was not there; nor did Trevyn's hasty search find him the parchment he needed.

For all Trevyn knew, Emrist might venture out every night. Sorcerers were supposed to be partial to moonlight and stars. Yet Trevyn's very sinews sang of danger, and he descended the stairs hastily to the kitchen. Emrist was not there. Trevyn went outside and studied the night with all his senses, searching for a sign. Then he set off rapidly into the woods.

At some distance from the house, just when Trevyn was doubting the direction he had chosen, his night-sharpened eyes glimpsed a ghost of murky light somewhere ahead. He hurried on, sometimes wondering if he really saw it, so faint was the yellowish glimmer amid the white moonlight. Then he reached the brown woodland pool, which lay in the shadow of a steep rise, and his way was made clear to him. The light seeped from behind a tangle of vines and bushes halfway up the wooded scar; it streaked its pale shadow across the mirrorlike surface of the water and mingled with the reflected moon like an arrow piercing a swan. Trevyn skirted the pool and silently climbed up the rise, came to the entrance of a concealed cave that was curtained by living greenery.

Within, the air looked thick with sultry light. A malodorous smoke seeped out with the light and almost set Trevyn to coughing. Once he had caught his breath and accustomed his stinging eyes to the sulfurous gloom, he could see Emrist within. The magician wore a flowing, shimmering black robe that must have come out of his mysterious chest, for Trevyn had never seen it before. He had a rude stump of wood for a table, and on it stood black, flaring candles, smoldering saffron-colored bits of incense, an earthenware mug of water, and a tarnished metal dish of salt. Emrist held the parchment with the lupine seal, reading it, the lines of his face taut with strain. It seemed he was preparing for the summoning of some particularly difficult spirit.

As Trevyn watched, full of foreboding but uncertain what to do, Emrist began his incantation. He raised his mobile hands and half closed his eyes in concentration, chanting words in some tongue unknown to Trevyn, words even harsher than the unlovely language of Tokar: *"Zaichos kargen—Roch un hrozig—ib grocchus—"* On the parchment before him, the emblem of the leaping wolf glowed eerily bright.

Trevyn felt something coming through the air from the south and east, something of such darkness that he thought it would blot out the moon. It smote him with fear, terrible fear such as no spirit had ever caused in him, fear even beyond screaming. He silently trembled against the unfeeling earth as the focus of evil passed beside him and into the cave. Then he heard Emrist catch his breath, and, moving with leaden reluctance, he forced himself to look within. A shape of nightmare was growing in the shadows of the cave, a being of obscurest gloom that displaced the haze of Emrist's making. Trevyn felt its terror as a crushing weight that robbed him of breath or movement. It was a spectral wolf, substance only of blackness, huge, looming, floating forward, with eyes and bared teeth of flame. Emrist snatched up a handful of salt and flung it at the thing, spoke to it in the Ancient Tongue, words of exorcism: *"Este nillen, gurn olet, kenne Aene."* ["Be no more, evil thing, in the name of the One."] But his words were a trembling whisper, and had no effect. With a wrenching effort, Trevyn glanced at his master and saw him sway on his feet. The shape of shadow and fire was nearly on him, and his words stopped with a choke as he caught at the cave wall for support.

Sudden fury swept up Trevyn like a gale tearing a ship from its moorings. By the One, he would not again be unmanned by some wolfish apparition! He leaped into the inner thickness, to Emrist's side, and words long pent burst from him with a power he had not known he possessed: "Begone, vile phantom, and trouble him no more! Begone, dark thing!" In his passion, Trevyn lunged at the grinning specter to throttle it, but he blinked; his hand passed through emptiness, and his enemy vanished.

Beside him, Emrist leaned against earth with lidded eyes. Trevyn lifted him and, grasping a candle in his free hand, supported him out of the cave and down the slope to lay him by the pool. Emrist gasped painfully at the clean night air. Trevyn cradled his head in silence, dabbing water on his face and rubbing his bony chest. Presently, Emrist's breathing eased, and he opened his eyes. Wonder grew in them.

"Alberic!" he exclaimed in the Old Language. "No wonder Maeve went to you! I should have known it long ago."

Though he had never heard the name before, Trevyn understood its meaning: elf ruler, spirit ruler, eagle King and unicorn King. But he did not know why Emrist should call him by that name.

"Nay," he replied gently in the same tongue, "my name is Trevyn."

"Your sooth-name is Alberic," Emrist murmured, gazing up at him.

Trevyn could not doubt him. Though Emrist was not much older than himself, he seemed old as Isle just then, and wise as any seer. A warm ache of gratitude filled Trevyn, making him blink and tighten his arms around the frail man. Once again Emrist had given him back to himself and like a father had named him.

"Blood, what am I thinking of!" Suddenly urgent, Emrist struggled to sit up. "My lord, you are in great peril."

"Ay," Trevyn agreed regretfully, "that wolfish thing will tell its master of my whereabouts. I must leave, and quickly."

"Worse than that. They have got your brooch!"

Trevyn frowned in puzzlement, knowing he had left his brooch with Meg. "Who?"

"Rheged and that warlock Wael. They have had men hunting you these many weeks, and yesterday I saw that they had found it—" Emrist lost coherence in his earnestness. "And I, the dolt, not to realize it was you! Haven't you felt it tug, my lord? He can draw a soul to him from any such belonging, and the body of necessity with it, just as he drew the wolf-boat by a splinter of the figurehead—"

Trevyn's brow creased anew. "I have felt nothing. Can the Sight have misled you, Emrist?"

He mused. "Perhaps it was sight of future, not of present— but the peril is the same. I heard them gloating, and I saw the brooch in their hands. It was in the half-sun shape of Veran's fame, golden, with jeweled rays, a kingly thing. There was no mistaking it."

Trevyn struck his forehead with his palm. "They are mistaken even so," he exclaimed hoarsely. "It's my father's! He only lent it to me. . . . Tides and tempests, Emrist, I must get it back at once! What could happen to him?"

Emrist's eyes, full of horror, gave him answer enough. "I will come with you," he said.

Trevyn bit his lip in dismay, for he knew Emrist's traveling pace. Though he was reluctant to hurt one to whom he owed every thanks, his fear for Alan firmed his answer. "Nay. I must go with all speed."

"Then you will go with all speed into disaster!" cried an unexpected voice. "What will you do when you come to Kantukal, indeed?" Trevyn and Emrist stared as Maeve entered their little circle of light, but she ignored their discomfiture in her concern. "If your father the King is of such stuff as you, it will be many days before Wael's spell can have much effect. Perhaps it has not yet even begun. After you two come to Kantukal, there should still be time enough for Em to thwart Wael's scheming."

"Maeve," her brother interposed mildly, "how do you come to be here?"

"Did you think I would sleep through this night? I heard Freca leave and followed as soon as I could. I was loath to interrupt, loath to spy, and yet loath to steal away; so I hovered near, like a moth at the lamp."

Trevyn laughed shakily. "I know what you mean. I have been such a moth these many weeks past, afraid to singe my wings. . . . But Maeve, would you not rather have Emrist by you here and safe?"

"There was little safety for him here tonight." She met his eyes quite candidly. "And though he is frail of body, Freca, his power is a giant in him."

"His name is Trevyn," Emrist corrected her. "He who shall rule as Alberic, son of Alan, of the line of Laueroc—"

"'Freca' will do well. If we are to go a-courting to Kantukal, you cannot be my-lording me." Trevyn could not say what had changed his mind, unless it was the wisdom he had seen in Maeve's eyes. But he felt assurance at once that what he did was right for Alan as well as for Emrist.

"—of Isle," went on Emrist, unperturbed. "Heir also of Hal, of the line of Veran of Welas, King of the Setting Sun—"

"Spare me." Trevyn got to his feet. "I'll go fetch your things from the cave."

"Leave them there till they rot," Emrist replied bitterly. "I'll use them no more."

"The parchment? I would like to read it, if I may."

The magician hesitated. "It is a very evil thing," he answered slowly. "But it may yet be of use, I dare say."

Trevyn made his way up to the cave in the dark, leaving them the candle. He found the entrance mostly by the smell of pungent smoke. The other candles had drowned in their wax, and the incense had subsided to ashes, but still there was light within the cave—a small, spectral light. It had been no trick of Trevyn's mind that the emblem of the leaping wolf shone with the same warmthless shimmer as the death-lights flickering over a marsh. It almost seemed to move before his eyes, and the mouth gaped, glinting with ranked teeth. Trevyn stared at the thing awhile before he took hold of the parchment by a far corner. He rolled it so that the emblem disappeared inside, and, grateful for the darkness, made his way back to the others.

"What is her name?" Maeve asked as she and Trevyn worked in the kitchen later that night.

"Who?"

"Your sweetheart. The one you dreamed about sometimes as you lay with me." There was no bitterness in her voice, and she glanced with some surprise at his burning face. "There is no need for shame!"

"Her name is Meg," Trevyn replied slowly. "She is a little peasant who lives by the Forest near Lee. . . . I don't know why she cozens my mind so."

"There is no need for a reason." She was packing food for their journey, and Emrist was asleep; his adventure had left him exhausted. On the morrow, he and Trevyn would start toward Kantukal. But Trevyn hardly knew how to take leave of Maeve.

"It is true, I have loved you in my way," she remarked, reading his thoughts again. "But my way is only the way of the wild things that know their seasons. I am bound by nothing, and no one owns me, or is owned. . . . Go from here in all peace, Alberic."

She had made him her king, now. So, since he had nothing to say, he nodded and left her there.

Chapter Four

With first light, Trevyn and Emrist took to the road. Trevyn wore the sword he had won from the robbers, and he carried the wolfish parchment in a fold of leather, gingerly, as if it might burn. As they walked, Emrist explained to him about the cult of the Wolf.

"Wael is chief priest; he speaks for the Wolf." Trevyn nodded in understanding; Hal and Alan had banished such powerful sorcerers from Isle. "So folk raise idols in its honor in Kantukal, and the coffers of its temples grow rich. That is nothing new; there are many such gods. But this one is vile even in the reckoning of Tokarians; its rituals are unspeakable. Human sacrifice is not the worst of it. People live utterly in fear of the Wolf. I have known for months that I must try to—destroy it—"

Emrist faltered to a stop, conscious of the contrast between his slight physique and his brave talk. But Trevyn soberly waited for him to go on. He knew the power and stature of his master.

"So I went to buy a mute," Emrist said at last, "I, who have never bought a slave. I needed someone to stand by me in case my body failed me, someone who could not ever utter the spells, for they are perilous."

"And yet you did not use me?"

"Nay. . . . You had bled, Freca. . . ." Emrist grimaced, mocking himself. "Of course, Maeve offered to help. Truth is, I could not bear to risk either of you. And I wanted to face Wael myself."

"Wael? But you summoned the Wolf."

"Nay, I summoned Wael," Emrist corrected grimly. "There is no Wolf without Wael."

"But what was that black phantom—"

"A thing of smoke and fire. Your hand passed through it unharmed. Any sorcerer could make one as fine—though I confess I was not expecting it last night." Emrist glanced at Trevyn, half laughing, half angry. "Wael has made a fool of me."

"Wael was there?" Trevyn breathed.

"He was there. You felt the fear?"

"Ay, terrible fear." He shuddered at the memory.

"That was the fear of his living spirit, which I summoned. Without its mask of flesh, the evil of his soul overwhelmed us. That and the shock of something not understood." Emrist shook his head ruefully. "How stupid I was to be so taken in!"

"Well, you will have your chance for revenge," Trevyn muttered. He tripped over a twisting root and scarcely noticed the bump, thinking. "Then that was Wael, too, in the laughing wolf in Isle," he finally said.

"I thought teeth made the occasion for those brands!" Emrist exclaimed. "Ay, I do not doubt it."

"How are we to get the brooch back from him, Emrist? What do you know of Wael?"

The magician sat down on a shady bank to answer. Trevyn sat beside him, restraining his impatience at their slow progress.

"I have often watched him by the power of my inner eye," Emrist said when he was settled. "I have seen him with the king, or in court, or at his vile rites, or alone in his chamber. Rheged places much dependence on him, and his days are full of consultation."

Trevyn peered. "And where does he keep the brooch during all this consultation?"

Emrist had to smile at his eagerness. "Why, on him, of course," he answered gently. "Or else the spell would not take."

"On him?" echoed Trevyn numbly.

"Ay, even when he sleeps. It must always touch his skin, you see, to draw. He wears it pinned inside his shirt, facing his stony heart. I saw him pin it there."

"Mother of mercy!" Trevyn swore morosely. "I am likely to need this bloody hacking sword."

"Unless it is a magical sword, it will be of small avail against Wael. Nay, we can only face him with our own poor powers. . . . And what an ass he has made of me!" Emrist sighed hugely. "I might have been slain by sheer, foolish fright last night if it had not been for you. I owe you my thanks, Freca." He spoke the name with warm affection.

Trevyn reddened at the words. "You owe me nothing," he said roughly. "The debt is all mine. What about the gold you gave for me?"

Emrist smiled sheepishly. "That was only sorcerer's gold. I would not use it with honest folk. . . ."

"Why, what becomes of such gold?"

"It vanishes after a little while. . . ." Trevyn threw back his head and laughed, and Emrist joined in, a laugh from the heart that shook his small frame. "Ay, I would like to have seen those slave merchants drubbing each other for the theft of it!" he gasped.

"Is there any chance you could conjure up some horses for us?" Trevyn asked wistfully. "Or even a donkey for yourself?"

"Nay, that would be dishonor." Emrist rose to his feet with dignity. "I can do what I must without such devices. Come, let us be moving."

They traveled more east than south for the time, working their way through a maze of small valleys between wooded slopes. Eventually, following that direction, they would find the broad Way that ran due south to Kantukal. It would make traveling easier, if no less dangerous. Trevyn carried a quarterstaff of green oak as well as his sword, in case they were beset. Though he distrusted these wilds, he knew they must sleep that night, for they had scarcely rested the night before. At dusk he found them a camp within a thicket of cypress, and they watched by turns.

Nothing happened that night. But the next day Emrist's pace was slower, and pain clenched his face. Trevyn gave him the staff to lean on, but he grew weaker hour by hour. Trevyn rubbed his legs for him that evening and prepared him a draught to ease his rest. Sunk in a haze of weariness, Emrist drank what Trevyn gave him without thought or question. In a few minutes he was deeply asleep. Trevyn slung their packs onto his waist, then carefully lifted Emrist, blanket and all, to his back. The moon, nearly at the full, lit his way. Trevyn went softly, hearkening to every sound, for he would have been hard put to protect himself and Emrist if he had been taken unawares. Still, he made good speed, and by morning he found himself in a tamer country, with cottages and garden plots to be seen from time to time.

The sun was high before Emrist stiffened on his back and spoke. "By thunder, what is happening here?" Trevyn set him down and grinned at him.

"Did you rest well?"

"Like a babe in the cradle, being rocked." Emrist looked around in bewilderment. "We must be nearly to the Way! Did you not sleep at all?"

"I'll sleep tonight. Come, let us eat!" They had reached a deserted stretch, where the path wound between dirt banks topped by beech and oak; homesteads showed only in the distance. Trevyn swiftly settled himself on the ground. He was very hungry after his night's journey, already breaking the last of their bread as Emrist sat, but his hand stopped midway to his mouth as he saw the shadow on Emrist's face. "What is it?" he asked.

"Nothing." Emrist forced a smile. "Eat."

Trevyn put the bread down. "Not until you tell me what is wrong."

Emrist gestured irritably. "A foolish thing. It vexes me that once again you bear my weight for me. A fine adventurer I make, who must be carried to the fray!"

"You are man enough, Emrist," Trevyn replied quietly. "You do not need strength of the body for that. I thought you knew."

"Most of me knows." Emrist smiled, warmly this time. "But there is no such thing as a man without foolish pride. . . . Never mind me, Freca. You did what you must."

"Just as you shall, when the time comes."

Trevyn gulped his portion of food. Emrist ate more slowly, picking his way through the meager meal as if it were a puzzle he had to solve. Trevyn watched him, brooding. He couldn't really carry Emrist to Kantukal; he knew he was going to have to find him a horse somehow or they would never reach the court city in time. They were out of food now, and they had no money to buy any with. The journey seemed impossible, the quest itself impossible. He wondered if Emrist dreaded the confrontation with Wael as much as he did.

"Emrist," he asked suddenly, "can you teach me magic to face Wael with?"

Emrist looked up with thoughtful amber eyes. "You can learn magic, perhaps," he said slowly, "but I cannot teach you. Magic cannot be taught. It must always be learned anew."

"But why?" Trevyn raised his brows in bewilderment. "Are there not schools for magic, where spells are taught, and rituals, and symbols—"

"Schools!" Emrist's scorn burst from him. "Schools where the riches of the whole world and beyond are boxed into tidy charts—'a' is for *alembic,* and ten is the perfect number. Bah! Don't they know that an emerald is not just the stone of the Lady? Everything of here or Other connects, and not in neat little boxes, either—or circles, or spirals, or any design a man can understand. Not even the mighty mandorla." Emrist subsided a bit. "Really, more than two circles must join. . . . Nay, it's only Wael's kind of magic that you'll learn in such schools, Freca. Even a villain can memorize certain ancient words, the puissant words of the Elder Tongue, and if power of self-will is in him. . . ."

"So that is how a man such as Wael comes to be a

sorcerer." Trevyn glanced at Emrist mischievously, prodding him toward further asperity. "I dare say he has a black-handled sword—"

"Ay, an athane, and robes of every color, gloriously embroidered, and gongs and censers without number. All that is good for show. But I have always scorned even to make the ceremonial circle; why should I need to protect myself? And to do any magic, either good or ill, only one thing is necessary: to call upon the dusky goddess of the Sable Moon."

"The great goddess?" Trevyn yelped, shocked. ·He had expected Emrist to call on Aene.

"Nay, nay, only Menwy of the Sable Moon. She is only one phase of the moon, and one of the Many Names, though all are in her, nevertheless. But if one knew the true-name of the goddess, that power would encompass every pattern and power and peril."

"But someone has told me that name," Trevyn protested. "It is Alys—"

A tremendous crash and rending noise engulfed them with its vibrations, washed over them from every side. Earth moved under them and split around them; rocks slid from the slopes above and mighty trees toppled with a roar. Trevyn crouched over Emrist, shielding him with his arms, as stones and branches hailed around. A huge oak thundered to rest beside them, lifting a canopy over them with its trembling, upraised limbs. Then gradually the clamor subsided, and earth trickled to a standstill. Utter silence fell.

Trevyn and Emrist got cautiously to their feet, gazing wide-eyed at the destruction all around them. Only the little plot of land on which they sat was untouched, as if they had been at the vortex of a mighty storm.

"Where did you ever hear that name?" Emrist gasped. "Don't say it!" he added frantically.

"Gwern told me," Trevyn murmured. "But he said it without any such scene as this."

"Then he, whoever he is, must himself be of godly sort," Emrist declared.

It took them the rest of the day to fight their way out of the devastated patch of woodland. They wondered, at times, whether the wreckage stopped with the woods. But they got clear of it at last, and Trevyn was relieved to see that no households had been touched. He and Emrist went hungry that night, for they had found nothing to forage and, oddly, no animals killed by the uproar they had weathered. Trevyn's snares, set in the underbrush around their camp, netted them nothing. The situation put Emrist in a bad humor.

"You knew that name," he grumbled, "a name of incomparable power, and you let yourself by flogged half to death. . . . And played at being mute, forsooth! Who is your enemy, Prince of Isle?"

Trevyn creased his brow at him. "Why, Wael, of course!"

"Wael is just a silly old man," Emrist snapped. "He could have slain you in Isle or on shipboard, but he plays at power as some people play at dice, reluctant to consummate the game. Who is your more worthy enemy?"

"Fate, then. The goddess, if you will."

"She is friend or enemy to no man; she is above such dalliance. Guess again."

"Gwern," Trevyn hazarded.

Emrist snorted. "You want to face Wael with magic, and you do not yet even know your own enemy! Prince, what did this—Gwern—tell you about that name?"

"To use it when I had need."

"And when could you have more need than when you were enslaved? You had only to make a proper appeal, and the whips would have turned against their wielders. It is because you mentioned her so offhandedly that she threw things at us earlier. And that is but a taste of her power. We might feel more."

"So she is sending us to bed without our supper," Trevyn retorted. "I'll say 'please' to no such goddess. We Lauerocs call only on the One, and not to turn weapons at our command."

"You are your own enemy, Prince," stated Emrist softly. "Do you really think Aene is not the goddess?"

Trevyn sputtered. "Indeed, ay! Aene can have no name—"

"But all things you can name are in Aene, and Aene is in them. How can you set yourself against any of them? They are part of you as well." Emrist sighed, having vented his spleen, and lapsed into a gentler tone. "Nay, Freca, you are like a mighty castle for endurance, but you will never do true magic until you have learned the wisdom of surrender, the joy of swimming with the tides of your selfhood and your life. Women, many of them, come by that knowledge instinctively, and do not feel the need of chants and charms; they have their own spells. No wonder Wael hates and fears them so."

"Does he call on the goddess to do his kind of magic?" Trevyn asked curiously.

"Only to make her a whore for his own lusts' sake. . . . Nay, Freca, no such thing!" Emrist made startled protest against Trevyn's thought, which he had heard like speech. "You cannot use that name against him. You could bring the castle down on top of us, but, what is worse, if Wael learned that name and survived to use it, he would become invincible. Do not even think of it in his presence." Emrist quirked a wry smile. "I know you are practiced at hiding your thoughts."

"Then how are we to face him?" Trevyn demanded.

"That is as it comes. For your part, I hope that endurance is all that will be necessary, for the time."

The next morning Trevyn awoke to find himself looking into the long, mournful countenance of a horse. Its whiskery nostrils were poised within inches of his face. He reached up to grasp the halter, then scrambled to his feet and looked the beast over. It appeared to be a pack horse that had escaped from some trader's train—hardly a luxury animal, but suitable enough to carry Emrist to Kantukal. And the pack on its back contained a quantity of very barterable goods.

"I think the goddess is over her pique," Trevyn called.

Emrist sat up painfully and stared at the horse with distaste. "Don't press her," he said finally. "We're likely to find ourselves in trouble on that beast's account."

"Nay, I think the Lady has made us a gift of it. Food, Emrist, we shall have food! Come on, get up!"

He badgered Emrist onto the horse's back and traded for bread and cheese with the first cottage wife he could find, making a very bad bargain of it; he didn't care. That day, with Emrist mounted, they went along steadily, reached the Way, and turned south at last, keeping an eye out for kingsmen who might recognize Trevyn. And he was hardly inconspicuous: a golden-haired youth with sword at side leading a mouse-colored, plodding nag on which sat a companion perched atop a packsaddle! Some changes had to be made, and that evening at their campsite they attended to it.

"If you are going to ride," Trevyn decided, "you must look like a horseman."

So Emrist had to wear the sword and a cloak, for rank. He would sit on a gaily patterned blanket. Trevyn attached reins to the horse's halter, hackamore style, and brushed the animal up a bit. In these warm lands, even men of rank went bare-legged and sandal-shod during the summer. Mounted on his nag, Emrist might be able to look the part of a very minor noble.

"And, if it is not too outrageous to be endured," Emrist suggested tartly, "might we sully that crowning glory of yours?"

A more humble servitor went forth the next morning, a sun-browned fellow with flattened, grimy hair of an indeterminate muddy hue. Trevyn would not have appreciated knowing how much, except for his eyes, he looked like Gwern. There was nothing to be done about the sea-green eyes, startlingly bright in his tanned face. He cast them down, as befits a mannerly slave, and took care to lag a step or two behind his master. A horseman traveling with a slave in attendance was no rarity. Kingsmen passed them with a nod.

In a few days they came out of the jagged hill country and onto the great plain that stretched all the way to Kantukal, a flat, dusty expanse planted with famished beans and vines. They traveled it for over a week. Now and then the road crossed streams trickling deep in baked beds, each with a fringe of bright green grass. Everything else looked faded and worn, like a poor woman's dress. The occasional kingsmen on the Way seemed interested only in putting this comfortless region behind them. The sun beat down without surcease. Trevyn and Emrist moved steadily through the days, camped gratefully in the cool of evening, and sometimes talked late into the night. The journey had become an interlude for them, an entity in itself; they did not think too much about the end of it. They clung quietly to the fellowship of the road.

It must have been their tenth day on the plain, walking through the sweltering heat of southern Tokar, that Trevyn felt a breeze and smelled salt in the air. Gulls wheeled far ahead. With one accord he and Emrist stopped a moment in the road, staring at the birds and then at each other.

"We are nearing our journey's end," Trevyn said. Emrist wordlessly nodded.

By evening they could see the towers of Kantukal rising hazily out of the flat horizon. Beyond the town, more sensed than seen, lay the glimmer of the southern sea.

Trevyn and Emrist camped in a grove of acacia that night. The lamps of Kantukal colored their sky, tree trunks loomed darkly all around, and dread weighted their hearts.

Chapter Five

"We must have a plan," Trevyn insisted.

With childlike obstinacy, he desperately believed that something could be done to improve their chances of defeating Wael. Emrist sighed wearily, for they had been through this discussion before. Moreover, he had his own reasons for melancholy.

"How can we plan for such idiocy?" he grumbled. "Trust the tide, Freca."

"I'd rather depend on something I can control. This parchment, for instance."

"Control?" parried Emrist dryly. "Leave control to Wael, and perhaps he will manage to destroy himself, and perhaps not us."

Trevyn did not answer, but pulled out the parchment with silent stubbornness and unfurled it in the firelight. He could not be sure, in that orange glow, whether the emblem of the wolf was shining with its own spectral light. He took care not to touch it. He read the heading again, "On the Transferring of the Living Soul," and the text, and found that it made no more sense to him than ever. Most of it was in a harsh language that neither he nor Emrist understood. Emrist used it as Wael would use the Old Language, without comprehension.

"This is a property of Wael's cult," Trevyn said.

"Ay, to be sure. I took it—well, no matter how I come to have it. I have never been sure how to use it. I believe it is not merely a document, but a magical thing, a talisman. Note the sheen of the device."

"I've noted it," Trevyn replied sourly. "Perhaps Wael wants this parchment back. We could trade it to him for the brooch."

Emrist gravely sucked his cheeks. "Only as a last resort. It is sure to increase his power. But it saps ours; such an evil thing cannot be used for good without a dire struggle."

"Ay, I can feel it draw." Trevyn put it away and sat back with a sigh. "If only I knew Wael's sooth-name. . . ."

"Ah," the magician mocked gently. "If."

"Who was he born of, Emrist? Where is he from?"

Emrist shrugged. "Who knows? He seems to have some connection with Isle. I think he is probably Waverly, Iscovar's old sorcerer. But he could have been Marrok, who tried to win the magical sword Hau Ferddas by a spell. Or even old Pel Blagden himself, he who was vanquished in the dragon lairs of inner earth. . . . Sorcerers are like the mighty folk of legend. Gods fight and are slain, goddesses sorrow and pass away, but in a sense they never really die."

Trevyn sat up in sudden abeyance, open-mouthed and breathless, utterly forgetting Wael. Something had moved deep in Emrist's gold-flecked eyes, something that filled him with a pang of loss and longing and, nearly, recognition. "And you, Emrist," he gulped at last. "What legend from out of the past are you?"

"I am myself, young, spent, and sickly!" Indeed, Emrist looked like no legend just then. He sat huddled by the fire, hunched in pain and perhaps in despair. But after a moment he looked up, caught Trevyn with a clear glance, determined to give the Prince what he could. All he could.

"Do you know the legend of the star-son, Alberic?"

"I know what Hal has told me of Bevan," Trevyn stammered, shaken anew that Emrist had called him by his true-name. "His comrade Cuin won him Hau Ferddas from the dragons of Lyrdion. Bevan lighted it with the power of his argent hand, defeated Pel Blagden, the Mantled God. . . . Later he left the sword with Cuin and sailed to Elwestrand. That was over a thousand years ago."

"Ay, he was a star-son, and Hal, too. But the legend is older than either. Patience a moment." Emrist settled himself tenderly against a tree, watching the ebb and flow of the fire. Presently he spoke, his eyes still on the iridescent shimmer just above the restless flames.

"The story begins so long ago that the sky was still sea, the sun not yet thought of, and the moon was a pearly island on the tides. In those days the moon-mother gave birth to a star-son, for that Lady is by nature a bearer of sons and needs no help to conceive. But this was her first and best beloved son, though she has had many since. The baby grew quickly to a boy and a young man. But, except for his mother, he lived all alone on the island. So one day, when she found him sad, his mother gave him a silver harp that sang by itself to amuse him and keep him company. And the harp sang of a place where all his unborn brothers lived, the faraway dancing ground of souls, where all selves are part of one. Inconsolable longing took hold of the moon-mother's son.

" 'All of life is but a decay unto death,' he exclaimed. 'Let me go to that marvelous place, Mother, quickly, before I start to wane.'

" 'Death is only a journey and a change,' his mother protested. 'Stay! Look, I can give you powers to make your own marvels, and your own fair light to adorn you.' And she gave the gifts.

" 'Still I must sail,' said the youth, and left the pearly land. Some say he went on a swan, or on a silver boat like a hollow crescent moon. Others say he sailed on the silver harp itself. Whatever the means, he left to wander, glowing with his own white light, across the midnight deeps like the wandering stars.

"Then the moon-mother faded and went dark. And in her despair, and not recognizing the nature of her own change, she went to the great dragon that girded the deep, the one that Sun drove down later. And she lay with the dragon and conceived. So she waxed again, great with child. But her new babe was born as dark as the unlit lands and grew into a serpent with coils so huge that they forced her to the fringes of her domain.

"One day, as she was walking along the waves, she found her first son's bones lying among the seashells, his skeletal hand clutching the silver harp. Hungry to take him back into herself, she ate a single finger and conceived. She hid the harp in a cave by the sea. And her child was born as fair as the first, and grew rapidly, and killed the serpent when he was grown. Then heart sickness took hold of him. He cried, 'I have slain my brother!' and lay without eating until it looked as if he would die. Then, in despair, his mother went to the sea and fetched the silver harp."

"Don't tell me," Trevyn interrupted. "He went—"

"He set sail, wandering like the evening star that leads in the mother moon." Emrist stirred the fire, prodding old embers into new flame. "There are many such tales. Sometimes the star-son weds his mother, and her love destroys him. Or sometimes he has a dark twin with whom he quarrels. But he always leaves, and only his seed returns.

"Bevan was one who left Isle. He was born of a goddess, Celonwy of the Argent Moon, sister of Menwy, of whom we have spoken, and also of the maiden Melidwen. His father was Byve, once High King in ancient Eburacon, where fountains flowed and golden apples grew. His hands could command any element, bend steel, open locked doors, scale smooth towers. . . . Sometimes they shone with pale fire. People stood in awe of him. He never learned to be entirely at home in the sunlit world. He would roam the night like the chatoyant moon every night, singing across the reaches of the dark; it was said to be good luck if one heard him. The loveliness of his voice has become legend. When Hal sang so beautifully at Caerronan, that was Bevan's legacy in him, that silver voice of mystery and the moon."

Trevyn started. How could Emrist have known of that night at Caerronan? But Emrist, eyes focused on depths of time, seemed not to notice his discomfiture.

"Cuin left his legacy to your father. A warrior by blood, he traced his lineage to the ancient Mothers of Lyrdion. He loved sunlight and sport and the sweep of a good sword. He knew a fine horse and a fine hawk. And he loved a golden maiden to whom Bevan was betrothed. Still, he followed Bevan into Pel's Pit. . . ."

"Why are you telling me this?" Trevyn whispered. The tale dismayed him, though he could hardly say why, and Emrist brooded strangely over the flames.

"I must show you the pattern," Emrist murmured, "if I can."

"What pattern?"

"The one that leads back to Veran, the seed of Bevan, and to Bevan himself and beyond. A pattern of strange binding between two distant islands, and between men. . . . Think, Alberic. Cuin could not follow his comrade across the western sea." An odd catch had taken hold of Emrist's voice.

"You are leaving," Trevyn breathed. He saw the flash of foreboding in Emrist's eyes and scrambled to his feet in alarm. "Emrist, what—"

Emrist rose quietly to face him, placed a light hand on his shoulder. "More likely it is you who will sail away from me. It seems to me that you are needed to round out the pattern, and the larger pattern, the greater tide. An age of ages may come to end and beginning if you fulfill prophecy—Ylim's prophecy—and rid Isle of the magical sword."

"I have always known I must return to Isle someday," said Trevyn shakily. "Bindings of rank on me . . . but I'd hoped to serve you yet a while. I'd follow you to world's end, if that were your pleasure. I wish we could always be together. You are my friend. . . ."

Emrist met his eyes, unsurprised, accepting. "Who is following whom, Alberic?" he asked whimsically.

"You are he," Trevyn whispered. His throat ached, as if something fluttered in it, caught. "You are the one I have yearned for . . . and now our journey's done." Bewildered, he sank to the ground, hid his face in his cupped hands. He felt Emrist's warm touch follow him. The magician settled beside him.

"Freca, I have been happy traveling with you, happier than I have been since I was a child. I know you have felt it too, good friend—and there was little enough time left to me for happiness, wherever I spent my days. I am truly grateful to have known you and to be of use to you. Can you understand?"

"Ay." Trevyn forced out the words. "You have foreseen your death. And you have journeyed to your death, and you would not tell me. . . . Why have you told me now?"

"Because I need your promise, Prince."

Emrist's tone had turned calm and faintly challenging. Steadied in spite of himself, Trevyn lifted his head to face him, puzzled. "All right. What?"

"In regard to a certain power of Wael's, the cruelest trick of the Wolf. Wael loves to drive out the soul and replace it with that of a criminal, in the same body. He has done it to the wolves in Isle, and he is likely to try to do it to us. And I am frail, as you know. . . . So if he should change me in that way, Freca, please use the sword on me, and quickly. It will not be myself that you kill. Do you understand?"

"Nay!" Trevyn swayed as if he had himself been struck; swords of fear ran through him.

"You will understand tomorrow. But you must promise me now, if I am to rest tonight."

"Is that all I can do, then?" Trevyn asked bitterly. "Endure, and be a slayer with the sword?"

"Times to come, you shall be worth ten of me. There is sky in you, and also deeps where dragons dwell; bring them to light, and you shall master us all. You shall be Sun King, Moon King, Star-Son, and Son of Earth. . . . But for now you must trust me in this. Promise."

Trevyn only nodded, for unshed tears swelled his throat. Emrist saw him bite his lip to contain them.

"Grieve later," he said gently. "I can't be sure even of doom."

"What of Maeve? She knows?"

"She knows I have need to be a man. She is strong." Emrist's face went bleak at the thought of her, and he turned away, toward his blanket. "Let us get some rest."

"Wait," cried Trevyn, clutching at hope. "We could go now, take him in his sleep—"

"With the city closed and the castle guard doubled? Nay, it must be in the morning. Courage, Prince." But Emrist faced toward the dark, not meeting his comrade's eyes. Trevyn longed to go to him and embrace him, but he could not bear to weep, or to make Emrist weep, just then. Instead, he spoke numbly.

"Let me prepare you a draught."

"Nay. I must not be slow-witted in the morning."

"Then let me rub your legs to ease you."

Emrist lay on his makeshift bed, still hiding his face, his whole body tense and aching. Trevyn rubbed until the knotted muscles relaxed, until Emrist lay quiet and deeply breathing under his hands, shoulders sagging into sleep. Then he covered him with his ragged blanket and sat beside him with all that they had said turning and turning in his mind. His father. . . . He could not have let Emrist face Wael if it were not for Alan's sake. A heart's love, newly found, to be as quickly lost. . . . Suddenly, like a stab, Meg entered his whirling thoughts. Trevyn knew that her sunny bantering would have lifted the leaden weight from his heart, but the memory afforded him no comfort—he had cut himself off from her. Anguish struck him. He longed for Meg more passionately than he had ever wanted anything, far more than he yearned for life itself. Pain twisted his face and bowed his head. By his own doing she was lost to him, even if he survived the morrow.

Chapter Six

"Did you not sleep at all?" Emrist asked in the morning.

"I'll sleep tonight," Trevyn answered. "Perhaps."

They could not eat. They took their horse and went. The city gates were just opening when they reached them, and they entered Kantukal amid a throng of farmers bringing their wares to the morning market. The towers of Rheged's court rose above the shops and temples, so they found it easily. They paused at a distance and looked in through the iron bars of the gate. Slaves scurried about the courtyard tending to early morning chores. Burly guards watched, lounging. Emrist squared his narrow shoulders, straightened his spine, and sent his nag forward at a fast walk, with Trevyn trotting at his side.

"Who goes?" inquired the gatekeeper lazily.

"Sol of Jabul, on the king's business. Open up."

"Come back after midday." The fellow began to turn away, but he was seized by Emrist's glance, held motionless like a pinned insect. Emrist's eyes flashed like jewel stones in a face turned diamond hard.

"Open up," he ordered softly, "or I will skewer your head for a present to your king, and he will thank me. . . ."

Emrist's hand went to the sword he wore and slid it in the scabbard. He had no need to show that he did not know how to use it. At the sword sound, the gatekeeper jumped to let them enter. They passed in without a word or a glance. Emrist urged his horse across the courtyard and flung himself down from him as Trevyn tethered him. Then he strode off headlong, with Trevyn trotting after. But once within doors he stopped, and Trevyn came up to him.

"Well done, my lord!" Trevyn whispered, with mischief edging at the awe in his eyes.

Emrist grimaced. But before he could speak, Trevyn's eyes narrowed in warning. A guard was studying them from the shadows at the far end of the corridor.

Emrist tightened his lips. Then, as suddenly as lightning, he smote Trevyn across the face with the back of his hand. For love of him, Trevyn did what the whips of the slavers had never made him do: yelped and flinched from the blow.

"Churl!" Emrist grated. "You shall bow when you speak to me, sirrah!" He beckoned imperiously and strode off again with Tervyn at his heels. The guard let them pass without comment.

"Again, well done, my lord!" Trevyn whispered when they came to a large open hall.

"I am sorry," Emrist murmured.

"No need; I've taken worse in sport. Which way?"

Emrist shrugged in vexation. "I can't tell. The Sight doesn't work that way; it's not a map! Just keep moving. . . . You tied the horse?"

"Only loosely. He can free himself with a jerk and go where he will. But he will wait for us yet a while."

They moved through the labyrinth of the palace purposefully but at random. The council halls stood empty, for the court officials were still in their rooms. Slaves sped by with breakfast trays, taking no notice of the strangers. Presently Emrist and Trevyn reached a rear courtyard serving the kitchen and slave quarters. They stopped, for they could not expect to find Wael there.

"We must go back," Trevyn said, "and try to find some stairs. I should think a sorcerer would be lodged in one of the towers; that is customary, is it not?"

Emrist had no chance to answer. From behind them came a startled exclamation and a clatter of pottery. Trevyn whirled. An old man sat with scrub rag in hand, his mouth agape and suds dripping unheeded down his arm. Trevyn went to him swiftly and knelt beside him.

"Peace, Grandfather," he warned softly, "for my life's sake."

"What is it, Freca?" Emrist came up beside them.

"He was a slave with me in the pit and in the string where you found me, and he was a good friend to me."

"All that flogging," the old man gasped, "and ye never spoke or squeaked—"

Trevyn pulled a wry face at the memory. "Ay, for I am a king's son, Grandfather. I could not let them master me."

"Ye're the one they seek!" the old man breathed.

"Ay, and come to beard Wael for it, if we can. Where is he to be found?"

"In the tower, as ye said. The farthest one. But ye're mad to face him. He is terrible!" The old man spoke with trembling earnestness.

"I have no choice," Trevyn told him quietly. "You'll not betray us?"

He wordlessly shook his head.

"Freca," asked Emrist worriedly, "can we trust him?"

"Ay, I think so. Anyway, what else can we do? Do you have a way to silence him?"

"I'll quiet yer fears yet a while," said the old man with dignity, rising stiffly to his feet. "I'll come with ye, to show ye the way."

"You're likely to get a drubbing, if you're missed," Emrist said.

He shrugged. "I am an old man and thick of hide; I do not mind."

"Then, many thanks. And let us go quickly."

The old slave took them up the back stairs that the servants used. They met no guards. They climbed up flight after spiraling flight, till Trevyn lost count. Their guide stopped at last at a landing leading to a corridor.

"He's within," he murmured. "I can feel it. The first door. I'll go no farther."

"Get yourself to safety," Trevyn told him. "A thousand thanks for your help."

"May yer gods defend you," the old man breathed, and hurriedly stumped down and away. Emrist and Trevyn looked at each other.

"Rest a moment, gather your strength," Trevyn whispered. He reached for the sword that hung at Emrist's side, drew it silently from its scabbard. The two steadied themselves for the count of a hundred. Then they wordlessly touched hands and walked to the fateful door. Emrist reached out, and it swung open beneath his fingertips. They entered Wael's chamber.

The room, in the properest tradition of the sorcerer's tower, surrounded and confounded them and hemmed them in with shadows and shadowy apparatus. Amid all the confusion, Trevyn's glance picked out one thing at once: the gilded form of a wooden figurehead, a wolf leaping with bared teeth of pearl. The shaggy object beside it, however, he was slower to recognize. He blinked as the grayish form turned and rose to a meager height to face them. A bent old man stood before him; yellow eyes stared at him out of a face covered with bristly gray beard. Trevyn had seen those eyes before.

"Greetings, Wael." Emrist spoke sedately.

"Little Emrist the Magician!" Wael made the name into a yelp of triumph. "Well met! And you also, Prince of Isle." His voice turned crooning. "How fortunate for you that you have come to me at last! I can make you the most powerful of Kings, King of Sun and Moon, if you let me."

Trevyn felt his heart jump at the echo of Emrist's words. But he took a tighter grip on his sword. "Is that how Rheged comes to be under your thumb? A promise of power?"

"Rheged!" Wael let out a single harsh bark of laughter. "Rheged is leaden of nature. Nay, worse than leaden; he is dross, and you could be pure gold. What, Prince, have you not yet learned the first quality of magic? I should think even Emrist might have taught you that." Wael shuffled closer, hunched and glaring with what was meant to be sincerity. "It is power, the power of perfection. Just as sorcery can raise the nature of metals, it can raise the nature of men, firing away what is base, freeing the rest to fly like the eagles, lending power like a god's. You are young and beautiful, and you could be anything your power and vision can encompass." Wael had crept to within three feet of Trevyn's staring face. "Think of it, Prince of Isle."

"He knows you well," Emrist remarked.

"Too well for honesty. He has been spying on my dreams. Picking at my thoughts with his soiled hands—" Trevyn slowly swung his sword up until it rested against Wael's gray-robed chest. "Your words sound fair, old man, but your face is the color of vomit. Get away."

Wael sprang back with surprising agility, his face ugly with rage. He abandoned his caressing tone. "That was discourtesy," he snapped, "and I will punish it as I am accustomed to punish those who cross me." A clawlike hand left his sleeve with serpent speed, and power snapped across the room. The sword fell to pieces, clattering to the floor. Pain shot up Trevyn's arm; he dropped the hilt with a gasp. "Thus," Wael added. "You see?"

Trevyn did not glance at the useless weapon. "You have a brooch of mine," he said flatly. "This causes me some discomfort. We have come to get it back."

"Indeed?" Wael mocked. "I am the master here." He fixed his jaundiced gaze on Trevyn. "I am the master here," he whispered in dreamy, hypnotic cadence. "Come to me, Trevyn of Laueroc."

Trevyn matched his stare and did not move.

"Come to me, Trevyn of Laueroc." Wael recited a spell in the same silky whisper, ill suited to the guttural language of his magic. He thinks the brooch pulls me, Trevyn thought, and ached inwardly for Alan. But Wael's efforts were ludicrous, just the same, and Trevyn felt his thoughts swerve to Meg, her teasing, her smile. He could almost hear her exclaim, "Silly old man!" Hugging memory to himself like a talisman, Trevyn threw back his head and laughed the sweet, healthy laugh she had taught him. Wael stopped his chanting abruptly, and a faint frown shadowed his eyes.

Emrist quickly pressed the advantage. "Let us see that brooch, Wael!" he cried, and power flickered through him. Wael's coarse gray garments parted like wings, and Trevyn glimpsed the sparkle of Alan's brooch within them. Excitedly he stepped forward. But in an instant Wael clapped his arms down over his robe, and Emrist was jolted as his spell was severed. Wrath crawled across Wael's face.

"Fool," he hissed, "you shall pay for that." He snapped both hands forward like spitting snakes, and Trevyn saw Emrist reel from an unseen force. "Stop that!" Trevyn shouted, and once again started toward Wael. But then the blow struck him in his turn, blinding him with the magnitude of its malice. He stopped where he was, clenching himself in helpless wonder that anything could hurt so hard and yet continue without abatement.

"Take no notice, Prince." Emrist's voice, though labored, was composed. "It's only pain."

"Very true." Trevyn forced his sluggish tongue to move, trying to match Emrist's tone.

"He drains himself of power with the making of it," Emrist went on. "When he stops, he will be the weaker."

"Still strong enough to deal with a dozen such as you!" shrieked Wael. Nevertheless, the pain stopped. Trevyn shook his head to clear the haze from his eyes. Then he stiffened. The leaping figurehead leered into his face, scarcely a foot away.

"Ay, you remember him well, do you not, Islendais Prince?" Wael gloated. "You will be his, you who have spurned me!"

Trevyn could not move or speak. Some inexplicable horror of the thing bound him immobile. Its glass eyes took on a saffron sheen from the gilded wood and held his sickened gaze. Beyond them, shielded from his reach by the wooden wolf, another pair of yellowish eyes entered his narrowed view. "Look at me, Trevyn of Laueroc," Wael whispered.

Behind Trevyn, Emrist spoke tightly, forcing words from his frail, anguished body. "Do not heed him, Prince!"

"A fine wolf, is it not?" Wael went on. "But this is only a toy. Since you will not join me, you and all yours shall be a sacrifice at the altar of the Very Wolf. Would you care to see him? Look at me!" Wael's voice rose to a hiss. "Can a Prince such as yourself not withstand the gaze of an old man?"

Trevyn looked, whether from stung pride or sheerest

compulsion he could not say. In a moment his world had faded into nightmare. Laueroc had fallen, his father lay dead, his mother torn and dishonored; the wolves surrounded him in his turn, frenzied for his blood, worrying at his legs to pull him down. The largest wolf came at him, huge, looming, dark enough to blot out sun and day and sky. . . . Falsehood, he knew it to be, and he pressed his mind against the vision, struggling to see with present sight. For an instant, he thought he had succeeded. The sorcerer's shadowy chamber was again before him. But a giant black wolf with teeth of flame was coming at him, leaping for his throat. . . . Trevyn could not, or would not, scream. He closed his eyes.

"A thing of smoke and fire," said Emrist in a strong voice. "You shall not gull us so easily again, Wael." Trevyn's eyes snapped open. The specter had vanished. Only old Wael faced him over a carved figurehead, his wrinkled face twisted in fury. Emrist stood with hand raised in command, straight as a young tree, his russet hair flying, though there was no wind. Trevyn went swiftly to his side.

"Hold fast," Emrist murmured to him. "The worst is yet to come." Wael was muttering a spell in the harsh language of his cult, and Trevyn recognized some of the words; it was the spell for the transferring of the living soul. But not until he felt grinding misery fill his veriest being did he fully realize what Wael was doing.

"Hold fast!" Emrist charged him again.

The new torment was not so much pain as pressure, a straining within and a battering, hostile presence without. Though he breathed, Trevyn felt crushed, as if he held his breath under water, under something heavier and more alien than water or earth, with no hope but to smother quickly. He could see Emrist, though thick glass seemed to be between them, and he noted that his friend's face looked white as death. If this spell succeeded, Trevyn remembered dully, he had promised to kill him. That would be the worst of promises to keep. But if his own strong body felt weakened under its magical load, how was Emrist to withstand it much longer?

As if moving in lead, Trevyn forced a hand to his tunic, drew from it a rolled parchment. With a wrenching effort of will, he made his tongue move, form speech. "Wael," he asked, "do you know anything of this?" He let the scroll fall open in his fingers.

The spell left as suddenly as a weight dropping from a snapped string. In the empty moment that followed, Trevyn thought he could sense Wael's startled fear.

"Give it to me!" Wael demanded sharply.

"I will trade it for a certain brooch," Trevyn replied.

Beside him, Emrist stood breathing deeply. "Freca," he whispered between gasps, "you must by no means let him have it. It is a very evil thing."

"I will do what I must," Trevyn told him obliquely, but with a covert wink.

"Come, come," said Wael, reverting to his caressing tones. "It is a paltry thing, of no importance except that I fancy it. . . . Why struggle for it? I will take it from you either way."

"The brooch, if you please," Trevyn answered evenly.

Wael pressed his lips to a line like a scar and extended his hand. The parchment in Trevyn's grasp sent sudden pain through him like a searing iron, burning hot. He managed to keep his grip, though agony twisted his face. "False fire!" he taunted, between clenched teeth. Wael's fire did not injure him, could not consume, if he wished to keep the parchment whole.

"And water of like sort," Emrist added. Trevyn felt his hand drenched in healing coolness, though nothing was wet. Wael wheeled away from him to face Emrist in consummate fury.

"Renegade sorcerer—" Wael spat out the words with choking emphasis. "How I wish I could deal with you at my leisure! I would make you into a thing a dog would pity! But it seems that I must dispose of you here and now, if I am to have my way with this young fool. . . ." Wael swept his hand across his body like a scythe, and Emrist slid to the floor with a gasp. Trevyn stood, feeling his knees turn to water as Wael confronted him. The old warlock was grining with triumph, his gaping teeth as jagged as fangs in his ancient jaws.

"And now for you," he breathed. "See the Wolf, Princeling? You shall be His tonight." Wael turned toward the gilded wolf of wood, but froze, thunderstruck, as it burst to splinters before his eyes. From the crumpled form on the floor a movement had come; a hoarded bolt of power had dearly spent itself. Wael spun with an inarticulate screech and struck the air with his clenched fists. Emrist moaned deeply, then lay still.

"Now, I will have that scroll!" Wael advanced on Trevyn with burning eyes. Trevyn let him come without a sign. All fear for himself had left him with Emrist's moan. Rage filled him, but he did not let it show—not yet. He stilled himself until the sorcerer was within two paces, within one pace, and then he sprang with lion force, silent as Fate. Knocked to the ground, Wael gasped and flailed the air with his hands, but to no avail. Trevyn tore the brooch from his clothing. The moment he seized it, Wael slithered from his encumbered grasp and made for the door. "Guard!" he shrieked. "Guard!" The ancient warlock scuttled away down the corridor, and Trevyn let him go. With brooch and parchment in hand, he knelt by Emrist, taking his head into his arms. Emrist opened his eyes and smiled.

"You have them both?" he murmured. "That is good, very good. We wore him out at last, it seems. But you must go now, Freca, quickly."

"Let me get you on my back, then." Trevyn spoke past the lump in his throat.

"Nay, I am done." Shouts and the sound of running feet echoed through the corridor, drew nearer. "Go, make haste."

"I cannot leave you here!" Trevyn blinked back stinging tears.

"By the mighty One," Emrist begged in the Old Language, "do not let me fail in this one last thing. Alberic, as you love me, think of your kingdom and your sire and go!"

The guards reached the door. Trevyn kissed Emrist once, the kiss of death's parting, and then ran. The door opened before him; he burst through the startled guards like a stag through the bushes. The stair by which he had come was blocked. He ran the other way, the guards hard after him, found the front stair and leaped down it, careless of his neck, half crazed. He sped down another corridor, almost toppling a lean, swarthy man in a crown. The guards lagged far behind him now, but the whole palace was acry for him. Leaping, half falling, he descended some more stairs, then paused, listening. Shouts closed in from every side. He did not know which way to turn.

A hand plucked his elbow, and he whirled. The old man, his fellow slave, beckoned, led him to a servant's door behind a curtain. From there they twisted through a maze of dark, narrow passages and rooms smelling of chamber pots and unwashed bodies: the slave quarters. The shouting faded away behind them. The old man went surely, though none too quickly, with Trevyn treading restively at his heels. Slaves gaped at them from doorways, scurried out of their path.

"You'll get worse than a drubbing for this, if any of those tell," Trevyn said tightly.

"Someone will tell. But I am an old man, and quite ready for death," the slave replied placidly. They came out at last to the back courtyard where Trevyn had found him before. The old man led the way to the postern gate, gripped the iron bars, and braced himself against them. "On my back," he directed tersely.

Trevyn kicked off his sandals and climbed up, one-handed, clutching the parchment and the brooch. Wriggling, he was able to squeeze out over the pikes and drop down outside the gate. "Good speed to ye," said the old slave, and stood watching as Trevyn silently saluted him and trotted away.

He had not left the shadow of the wall before the guards sighted him. The cry went up, and as he sped away he heard the call to horse. He ran aimlessly. The town gates would be closed against him, he knew. He and Emrist had not planned for this; hopeless as their confrontation of Wael had seemed, getting Trevyn and the brooch out of Tokar had been goals as distant as the stars. Now the tumult of his mind kept him from thinking. If only because it was easier on his tiring legs, he ran downhill. Between the houses and shops he could glimpse the gleam of the southern sea. Foolishness to go that way, where he would be trapped against the endless water. Yet some deep instinct of his elfin heritage called him to the sea, the longtime deliverer of his mother's people. He ran toward the shining deep.

He ran with aching heart and burning lungs. Folk scattered before him, caught sight of his straining, tear-streaked face, his eyes blazing with a fey green brilliance, and saw that face later in their dreams. Trevyn saw nothing except the sea. He scarcely heard the shouts of his pursuers over the pounding in his ears, but as he reached the harbor the ring of hooves on cobbles cut through the clamor of his desperation. He glanced back to see Rheged's mounted warriors scarcely a stone's throw behind him. Trevyn bit his lip, darting like a deer for some escape. He reached the tip of the farthest wharf, raised his arm to hurl his treasures into the sea. Then fishermen shouted, and he followed their gaze open-mouthed. A form of dark loveliness rippled the sunlit water. A slender elf-boat skimmed toward him faster than any dead craft of men could ever sail. She sped through the crowded harbor and touched dock at his feet. Trevyn stumbled on board and sank down just as the kingsmen came up to him. The elf-boat bounded off with him the moment she felt his weight. The kingsmen scrambled aboard a merchant vessel, but Trevyn did not even trouble himself to watch the pursuit. No power of sail or slaves could match the speed of this swimming thing.

He laid his face down on her friendly deck and wept. He grieved for Emrist, and for the old slave whose name he did not know, and perhaps for himself. He hoped against reason that the elf-boat was taking him home to Isle, to his father's strength and his mother's comfort and a chance of forgiveness from Meg. He had long since forgotten to dream of Elwestrand. He wept until he could weep no more, and then he slept. The parchment lay crumpled beneath him, where his body held it. But the brooch nestled in fingers slackened by exhaustion. And presently, and quite unknown to Trevyn, a gentle wave came up and took it from him.

Chapter Seven

Alan had hardly been his ardent self since Hal had turned his face to the west. And he had struggled with the slow gnawing of despair since the springtime day that Trevyn had left on a glittering ship that sailed east. But the sharp unrest that struck him one morning in late summer was a new sensation.

"It's like something tugging under my ribs," he told Lysse.

"Indigestion," she replied in wifely tones. "You'd better stay away from the seasonings for a while."

Alan agreed and tried to think of other things. But the pang did not leave him, and in a few days he realized that its focus lay to the east. "Something is pulling at me," he explained to Lysse. "I can't tell what, or whether for good or ill."

She searched his eyes lovingly, puzzling for a clue to his malaise. "I see no good to come of it," she finally said. "You must think of your people, my lord."

"It will do no harm to journey as far as Nemeton. It has been a long time since I've seen Cory. Perhaps something in those parts needs my attention."

Lysse stared at him with worry growing in her eyes. "It sounds fair," she exclaimed, "but I feel a foreboding—must you go?"

"Ay, I must go! I'll have no rest until I know the meaning of this—this force that wrenches at me."

"Then take me with you, Alan," she said earnestly, "for, by my troth, I am afraid to let you out of my sight."

"Why, Love? Do you not trust me?"

"My heart is heavy," she said, "and I think trust has nothing to do with it."

Alan shook his head, beleaguered. "But, Love, I need you to stay here and take command for me. I cannot depend on Ket these days; he is as addle-headed as a young gallant." Lysse had to smile at that. Ket courted Rosemary with dignity and gravest courtesy, but his joy in her had made him absentminded. "Perhaps they'll soon set the date and get back to business, so you can travel with me again," Alan continued. "But this time you must stay. . . . I am sorry."

Lysse regarded him with anxious exasperation. "Give me your word, then," she demanded at last.

"To what? Say what, and it is yours."

"I hardly know. . . ." Lysse frowned. "To take no rash course. To return to me straightway, and to your throne."

"Confound it, woman, did you think I'd do less? But certainly I'll give you my word."

Once he had decided on the journey, Alan wasted no time, reaching Nemeton with a group of retainers in only ten days. This was the easternmost town in Isle, and the closest to Tokar. At Nemeton the Eastern Invaders had landed their warships, and raised their infamous Tower, and ruled. Hal had been reared there; he had broken and burned the Tower when his time came, and he and Alan had moved their government to the gentler Laueroc, their father's holding. Now the place was held in fealty by Alan's former comrade, and the horror of its memory was gradually fading from folks' minds.

"Well met, Alan! But what brings you?" Corin asked when they had embraced.

"Whim," Alan replied. "Sheerest whim. Some wind of chance blows me this way."

Corin knew better. It had been years since Alan had taken time for carefree adventuring, and now that Hal was gone . . . Cory had not seen Alan since, but he guessed from long friendship the extent of Alan's burden in spirit and in duty. And the Prince mysteriously gone as well! Corin wished he knew what to say to Alan. He watched him and wondered as they feasted that night. He wondered the more when Alan rode out the next day to the Long Beaches, for Alan had never been a lover of the sea.

Alan went alone, without even a dog for company, and watched the sun blaze on the salt water, and loped his horse along the line of the tide. But he was not all alone on the deserted beach. Before noon he reached the point that projects to the east and found Gwern sitting there. Alan had not seen him since that day at the Bay of the Blessed, though he had sometimes heard report of him. Gwern was said to be living like a wild man on the fringes of Isle, eating fish and blackberries, traveling along the sandy southeastern coast. He did not turn to the sound of Alan's horse. He sat with his bare feet buried in the sand, staring out over the water, straight at the plains of Tokar, though Alan did not know that.

Alan vaulted off his horse and let it roam, walked over to Gwern, sat beside him on the gravel and seaweed left by high tide. Gwern scarcely glanced at him before his earth-brown eyes flicked back to the east. "King," he asked with his customary lack of ceremony, "what draws you here?"

"I wish I knew." Alan was not offended by Gwern's directness. In fact, he liked it somehow, though there was no comfort of warmth to be found in Gwern. Alan was used to the fellowship of his friends, but this youth who treated him as equal was neither friend nor enemy, he sensed. Gwern was supremely himself. Nothing he did or said could reflect on Alan in any way, and nothing Alan did could much affect him. His impersonal presence refreshed Alan's raw and burning mind like a cool breeze within.

Gwern said nothing. He never said anything unless there was something of essence to say. Alan frankly stared at him, knowing he would not mind. Gwern's clothing was in tatters, his body not filthy exactly, but definitely a stranger to soap. What could this dust-colored oddity have to do with Trevyn? And yet, *watch Gwern like a weathercock for Trevyn*, Lysse had said. Well, the weathercock pointed east.

"You have been following the shoreline." Alan broke silence. "Following Trevyn?"

"As closely as I can without leaving the land." Gwern dropped the words at his leisure, like pebbles into a pond, as if they were insignificant. But Alan felt his heart jump.

"Where is he, then? What do you see?"

"I see nothing; I do not have the Sight. I do nothing. I only feel." Gwern did not look at Alan as he talked, and his face, lit by the iridescence of the sea, was utterly expressionless.

"What do you feel, then?" pursued Alan, somewhat exasperated. "For I'm pickled if I can tell."

Gwern took breath to speak, then held it. "Hot," he finally said.

"What?" Alan almost shouted.

"Hot! He is hot. I can't help it." Gwern sullenly dug himself deeper into the sand.

Alan shared his lunch with Gwern, then left to go back to Nemeton, reluctantly; the eastward pull was strong on him. The next day he returned to the beach and found Gwern no more communicative than ever. They spent the day staring out over the waves. From time to time Gwern would rise and move southward a few feet, perhaps even a furlong. Once he smiled.

"What was that?" Alan asked.

"Love," Gwern replied without hesitation. "Longing and love." Later, his face subtly changed. "What?" Alan asked again. "Despair," answered Gwern.

Alan would not leave the shore that night, sleeping fitfully on the damp gravel. The next day Corin worriedly mustered some retainers and set out in search of him. He found him pacing the verge of the waves, wet to his knees. A bit farther along the strand sat an unkempt youth who neither moved nor spoke at his approach, but glared like a madman over the featureless water. Corin stared, then dismounted and fell into step beside Alan, asking him, as an old friend will, what troubled him. The answer made little sense. Alan seemed too distraught for sense.

"I gave her my word," he blurted disjointedly, "which she had never asked of me before, never. . . . I would be a villain to betray her. But if it were not for that, days ago I would have taken ship and set sail. It must be something to do with Trevyn. If he needs me, and calls me thus . . . I may never forgive myself. But I gave her my word. . . ."

Down the beach, Gwern stirred and made a strangled sound in his throat. Alan whirled. "What was that?" he demanded.

"Dread," Gwern replied.

Alan paced through the day with scarcely a rest or a bite to eat. The tug, like an invisible hook to his heart, had grown to a racking pain that threatened to tear him asunder. Gwern edged his way down the tideline, apparently in some distress of his own; his masklike face had gone hard and tight. Corin paced beside his liege, unable to help him. That night Alan lay tossing in restless exhaustion while Cory watched beside him. With daybreak he was up and pacing as before. Gwern emerged from the woodlot where he had disappeared for the night and stood at the strand's edge, blinking into the rising sun. Once it was well up, he settled into the sand and seemed to root himself, scarcely breathing, his clay-colored face intense with subterranean anguish. Trevyn had entered Wael's chamber at Kantukal.

Alan paced frenziedly, panting in pain, scarcely seeming aware anymore of his surroundings. Suddenly, in mid-morning, he cried out, a terrible cry of tormented defeat, and hurled himself into the waves. Cory caught hold of him, and struggled with him amid the froth, and with some retainers wrestled him to the sand where he lay groaning. Alan did not attempt to rise again, and Gwern sat still as a stump. An hour passed, perhaps more, as Alan lay sweating in agony while Corin and his men stood helplessly by. Then Gwern sighed, almost sobbed, and Alan sat up, blinking in bewilderment. His pain had left him all in a moment. "What in thunder?" he murmured.

Cory knelt by him. "Are you all right?" he whispered shakily.

"Hungry and in need of a wash. . . . Do I remember sleeping on this accursed beach?" Alan got slowly to his feet. Gwern sank his head into folded arms.

"What is it?" Alan asked numbly.

"Grief," Gwern moaned. "Death and grief, death and grief, grief. . . ."

Alan stared, motionless, his mind caught on a question that would not find its way to his lips. Cory tugged at his arm.

"Alan," he begged, "come away."

In a haze of weariness, Alan followed him back to the castle. Cory got him fed and couched at once, puzzled, but very much relieved to see him better. The next day they talked, and neither of them had any explanation for the other. So, hoping for a sign of some sort, Alan lingered on at Nemeton. From time to time he rode to the Beaches, scanning earth, sea, and sky for his answer. Gwern was gone, and after a while Cory learned not to fear for Alan, letting him go alone. So no one knew what Alan found.

The answer, or so he took it to be, came to him less than a fortnight after his narrow escape. In fact, it was on Trevyn's birth day, and that awareness played through Alan's mind as he rode gently along the fingertips of the reaching sea. A glow caught his eye, a golden shine among the pebbles of the beach, and he stopped to look—he felt as if a barbed shaft had pierced him to the heart. The rayed emblem of the rising sun glinted up at him, its spokes set with gems of many hues. As slowly as a man in a nightmare, Alan got down from his mount, picked it up, and turned it over and over in his hand. There was no mistaking the brooch, Hal's gift to him on this same day eighteen years before. Alan did not weep, but desolation settled over him like a black shroud, for he felt certain now that his son was dead.

He started back to Laueroc that very day. He did not show Lysse the brooch when he arrived, proud to spare her this grief, yet blaming her in his heart. He complained of nothing. But he ceased to be the loving husband Lysse had known, and as the weeks went by she grew sad, not knowing what to do for him.

Book Three

YLIM'S LOOM

Chapter One

Trevyn was never to remember anything of the voyage except sun and stars circling, the moon twirling between—all skimming through the movements of some inscrutable dance. Vaguely puzzling, he could not discern the pattern, so intricate was its phrasing, but he could feel its voiceless rhythm. He sensed that the elf-boat also moved in the dance, and so as not to interfere he lay very still on her deck, still and staring, with no thought of food or drink, twirl the moon as it might. If rain wet him he was not to recall it, or day's heat, or night's chill. Nor did he note his coming to shore. When awareness came back to him at last, it came with pain and reluctance of body and spirit, perhaps as keen as the pain of an infant in birth. But someone held him, cradled him as if he were a child, and the warmth of the embrace eased him. Trevyn knew those strong arms, he thought.

"Father?" he faltered.

"Nay, Trev." It was a well-beloved voice he heard, but for a moment he did not recognize it. He gazed up into the sea-lit face, blinking the darkness from his eyes.

"Uncle Hal," he murmured, and sank back into oblivion.

He sensed, distantly, that he was cared for. He felt the

warmth of a bath, the taste of a strengthening drink, soft
blankets, and a bed like an embrace. But his deeper awareness labored in the misery of Tokar. Vividly envisioning the
whips of the slavers, he found that he could no longer face
them; he flinched and struggled away from them, softly
weeping. Emrist lay dying under the whips of the slavers, and
he could not help him, not even by screaming. His grief bore
him down like a weight as massive as the world. His own
frailty struck him through with pity too deep even for tears.

Somehow a white stag flitted through the scarred texture of
his dreams, leading him away, though he knew he had not
moved. It took him to a forest of huge and knotted trees,
their branches woven together into a tapestry, forming
intricate pictures of ships with wings, and myriad shining
spheres, and leopards and dragons and black flowers. In the
midst of the forest grew a slender sapling, its branches terse as
winter, reaching. A cavalcade of alabaster ladies came and
gave it their jewels for leaves, seated themselves beneath the
young and growing tree. Trevyn followed the white hart. It
sped out of the forest, plunged into the sea, and swam away,
its silver antlers shining. Trevyn stood with his feet in the
water, yearning; he could not follow it there. By the shore a
man sat playing a silver harp.

Trevyn sat and listened. The music took him up winging,
carried him out of self, let him leap with the antelope and
glide with the eagles and fight by the side of the star-son
himself in a strange little land called Isle. . . . Trevyn
blinked, and looked again, and saw that the harper was his
Uncle Hal, playing his plinset by candlelight under a shelter
of golden cloth. Trevyn propped himself up in his warm bed.

"You have ransomed me with song," he said huskily, "as
you did for Father at Caerronan."

Hal set down his instrument to come to him, and one finger
caught a string, striking a single, rich note. A form spiraled
itself out of the vibrations; a bird flew up, ensouled by that
sound, a bird of the most ardent red Trevyn had ever seen,
red so true that it enthralled the eye. The bird circled the
confines of the tent, singing a phrase that swelled Trevyn's
heart, which he was never afterward quite able to remember.

Then Hal lifted the tent flap and the bird took its leave without fright, darting skyward.

"That was my love for you," Hal explained softly, sitting by Trevyn's bedside. "Things tend to become very real here. . . . Lad, you bear scars. I am very, very sorry it has been so hard for you."

"Family tradition." Trevyn grinned with moistened eyes as joy took hold of him. "I can't deny I've felt as beaten as an old rug. . . . But one good look at you heals me. You are . . ." Trevyn did not know how to finish.

"I am content," agreed Hal.

He was more than content; he was well and whole for the first time in all his tortuous life, and Trevyn was able to sense it quite surely. Hal's eyes glowed, and his body moved with certainty and ease. Moreover, he no longer seemed aloof and appraising to Trevyn; he had greeted him with the warmth of a friend and equal. As Trevyn gazed at him, smiling but lost for words, Hal rose with feral grace and pulled back the door flap, beckoning to someone outside. A boy, perhaps twelve years old, entered with a covered tray, set it down, bowed with youthful haste, and hurried out. Could it be that all people in this place were blessed? The boy was beautiful.

"One of your cousins," Hal explained.

Cousins! Trevyn's mind reeled. He had no cousins, no relations of any sort, except perhaps in . . .

"Then this is Elwestrand," he gulped.

"Of course."

Trevyn ate his food very slowly, as Hal cautioned him. He was caught in astonishment, and his flesh sat heavily on his unaccustomed spirit. He knew now that he had not filled his stomach for the months of the voyage—that thought alone stunned him. But the simple food, porridge and honey, soothed him with its familiarity. He slept peacefully afterward, and awoke later to the soft notes of Hal's plinset, and ate again. Then he dressed in the clothing Hal gave him: a tunic of finest wool, spring green—his mother's color—and light brown hose, and cloth boots, and a short leaf-gold cloak. "All right?" Hal asked. "Then let us go to see Adaoun. Your grandfather."

Once again Trevyn's mind was staggered. He had never had a grandfather, or expected to know one. Numbly, he followed Hal outside, to an air tremulous with sweetness. Tall, white, lilylike flowers grew wantonly as far as he could see; asphodel, he later learned they were called. Amid them clustered the rosy-purple amarinth, and amid . . . Trevyn stopped where he stood, scarcely a dozen paces from the tent. A unicorn raised its delicate, pearly-horned head from its grazing, met his gaze a moment with lilac eyes, then turned and whisked away at a floating run. Trevyn let out a long, shivering breath of delight. Hal gazed after the creature with sparkling eyes, even a smile.

"Everyone has a different notion of a unicorn," he remarked to Trevyn. "You'll see them all in time, and each one utterly beautiful, and each one true."

"You mean . . ."

"It is as I said; things become real here somehow. Thoughts. Dreams. Feelings, love and hate. All beautiful— even the darker ones, like that behind you. Look."

Trevyn whirled. A serpent confronted him, with scales like jet, a jeweled hood, blind eyes, and a crimson ribbon of tongue. Its head stood as tall, rearing, as Trevyn's waist. He took a step back.

"Is it—dangerous?" he asked edgily.

"Only if you want it to be. Sometimes men feel a need for danger."

"I feel no such need right now," Trevyn stated fervently.

"Well, come on, then." Hal turned his back on the serpent and walked away. Trevyn followed, and found that his fear ended after a few paces; he did not even look over his shoulder. Elwestrand entranced him, calling his eyes farther than he could see. He walked a curving footpath atop a gentle fold of land, watching the lush, random pattern of meadows and fragrant orchard and woven wilderness ripple away on either side. It took him a while to realize that no sun shone, that the sky, although clear, was not blue, but tender shades of peach and mauve, that the light, subtle and subdued, cast no shadows, only a kind of magenta haze. Hal seemed to read his thoughts. "We live in the afterglow here," he said.

"And is it always springtime?" The air was balmy, the land

luxurious with blossoms, many more kinds than he could name.

"Sometimes a bit hotter or colder, just for variety. Sometimes one of us dreams of snow and it falls—just for fun, I think. It quickly melts. The plants never wither, but there are seasons. I tell them by the flowers, and by the hills yonder. It is early winter in Isle."

Trevyn studied the distant, rolling hills that Hal pointed out, hills of the peculiar pinkish-gray of wintery woodland cloaked by neither leaves nor snow. "But . . ." Trevyn floundered. Hal glanced around, half laughing at him.

"The sea is wide. The voyage must have taken you three months, maybe four. It is nearly Winterfest."

"So I lay and stared all that time. All right. But if those trees are bare, there on those hills, why is it springtime here?"

Hal's smile broadened, and he sat down on a smooth-worn stone. "Now that is the marvel of all marvels here," he averred. "I believe those hills are there just for my benefit, to look at. You will never reach them by walking."

"Why not?" Trevyn sat also, glad of the rest, winded by just the small distance they had come. He wondered if Hal was teasing him on that account. But Hal seemed quite serious.

"You see that mountain—the rocky peak nearer than the hills? We call it Elundelei—Mount Sooth. Truth lives there, for those who are able to grasp it. And if you climbed to the top, you might be able to see that we are on an island far smaller than Isle, with the sea ringing it all around."

"But how can that be?" Trevyn protested. "It looks as if the land goes on forever."

"And there is room enough for everyone who comes here, and all their creations, and room to roam, and solitude for anyone who seeks it." Hal shrugged whimsically. "This is Elwestrand, Trevyn, and I dare say you will never understand it; no one does. Come, let us find Adaoun."

They walked along through wilderness interspersed with meadows, gardens, wheat fields, and occasional bright-colored canopies, graceful saillike shapes nestled into the curves of the land. Trevyn saw only a few folk, all comely even from a distance, raising hands in greeting, dressed in soft, rich-hued clothing like his own. "There is no need for crowns here," Hal declared, "and no need for settled dwellings. We move as the whim takes us. And there is no need of firewood except for cooking, praise be. You know how the elves hate to fell trees."

"Is it only elves who live here?"

"Nay, many others. Men of peace. Look, there is Adaoun."

Trevyn saw Adaoun's horse first, the splendid, blazing-white, gold-winged steed that had once flown over Welas. It grazed beside a placid stream. Beyond, on a gentle rise overlooking the meadow, a swan-white awning draped slender birch trees. On a couch beneath the awning, propped up by linen pillows, sat an old, old white-bearded man.

Trevyn approached by Hal's side, his mind clamoring. Ever since his earliest childhood, he had been told about Adaoun, father of the elves, first sung in the First Song of Aene at the beginning of time, ageless as the elements, sturdy as the mountains, visionary. . . . Surely this shrunken mortal could not be he! But the eyes that met Trevyn's plunged deep as wells, nearly drowning him in wonder. He sank to one knee beside the ancient patriarch and felt a withered hand touch his hair in the gesture of blessing.

"Alberic," said Adaoun in a voice soft and vibrant and powerful as the wind. "Welcome."

"Someone else has called me by that name," Trevyn whispered. "But I do not know why, Grandfather." He dared the old man's eyes again, and found that he could meet Adaoun's unfathomable gaze.

"Sometime you will know," Adaoun told him. "But for now I shall call you Grandson, if you like. I have grandchildren now, you know, by the hundreds, now that my children have chosen the lot of mortals and taken mortal mates. But you, whom I have never met, were the first. The years flit by like mayflies for a mortal. . . . You must be nearly of age."

"I am sev—nay, I am eighteen."

"Marvelous," Adaoun murmured. "How marvelous to be so young, and growing. . . . I remember quite well when the world was so young. But at last the One has blessed me with ending. Day by day my body grows weaker, and it will not be long now before I am gathered into death's embrace."

Trevyn flinched and lowered his eyes, for he was not himself on such good terms with death. But he had no need to respond. A young woman came toward them through the birch grove, walking with a sway like sea wind, carrying a tray of food. She brought it to Adaoun, her dress nearly as red as Hal's red bird, set it before him, and wordlessly stood by his side.

"This is Ylim." Adaoun introduced her as if her name told all about her.

"Time's weaver beyond time, whom I met in Isle once," Hal added with amusement. "Alan and I blundered into her valley where the elfin gold still flowered in spite of the blight of the evil kings—but I did not know how to read her web then, and I did not know her name, and certainly I did not know her in that form."

It was the form that made Trevyn stare. How could this lissome woman be the ancient seeress of Isle, the crone who had given her advice to Bevan? He could believe that she was ageless, for nothing about her suggested the tenderness of youth. But she was also lovely, and, he sensed, dangerous, if he so desired. Her skin, soft and lineless, glowed as white as lilies, as white as the belly of a white foal. Her hair, a ripple of wild mane, fell almost to her knees, golden—silver. . . . Trevyn blinked; it was of all colors, like a dream of horses, as changeable as the moon, as shining as the sea. Indigo eyes gazed back at him out of the full-lipped face, and something in Ylim's level look made Trevyn lower his own eyes. They caught on the high swell of her breasts, then closed in confusion. Suddenly he recognized her as the "princess" he had dreamed of in Isle.

"Well met, Alberic," said Ylim.

Her voice was husky, impersonal, not unfriendly. Trevyn could not reply. He heard her turn and take her leave, but he could not raise his eyes to look after her.

"You will get used to her presently," Adaoun remarked mildly. "Come, help me eat."

He meant eat with him. There was enough food for all, bread and mellow cheese and tangy fruits that Trevyn could not name; perhaps they had no names. Afterward, he and Hal followed the stream down to the seashore, where it spread into a lagoon. Tufted grasses edged it, and tall birds waded in the shallows, flashing blue or gray or green as they caught the shifting light. Hal and Trevyn sat down on a gravelly hummock to watch.

"So," blurted Trevyn, "am I dead?"

"Do you feel dead?" Hal asked dryly.

"How should I know? But Ylim is dead, I know that. Father found her slain by lordsmen, and laid her to rest beneath a willow tree—but she was an old woman then."

Hal puffed his lips. "Very true. But perhaps death need not kill. Most men are born squalling, and eat and sweat and brawl out their lives, and die, but there are some . . . Ylim is not of mortal sort anyway. And never was. Nor is she elf. I thing she is just—herself."

"But she has changed."

"Some are able to change—to go through the greatest of changes—and yet not change. I knew her at once when I met her here, though we had met only once before."

Trevyn swung his arms impatiently, batting away Hal's words as if they were bothersome insects. "Uncle," he asked doggedly, "am I going to be able to return to Isle? For return I must, and quickly. There is grave peril."

"I did not want to ask before you were ready. But I can see you have been in evil hands." Hal's eyes glinted angrily at the thought. "What is it? The warlords again out of the north?"

"Nay. Far worse. Tokar."

"Tokar! The Eastern Invaders wish to try again! But Alan will not let them land, Trevyn. They will be slaughtered as they set foot on shore."

"They will not come by ship," Trevyn replied heavily. "Or at least not at first. I think there are already invaders in Isle. They come by magic and take for their own the bodies of wolves." He stopped, expecting an argument, but Hal only turned to him with a face gone intensely still.

"Do not think I disbelieve you," said Hal after a long pause. "All things are possible. . . . But will you tell me what has happened to make you say this?"

So Trevyn told him about the wolves, and Meg, and the

gilded ship, and Emrist, and the confrontation with Wael. He ached, thinking of Meg, and sharper pangs went through him when he spoke of Emrist. Still, those events seemed a distant and puzzling pattern to him from the far shore of Elwestrand, and he recounted them as if telling about a sorrowful dream. And with those memories still floating like lacework in his mind, he absently picked up a handful of gravel, let it trickle through his fingers, then froze, stunned. Each rough fragment had turned to a gem like a tear, silky smooth, of dusky sweet and subtle colors, shot through with winks of moth-white light. Trevyn touched them shakily.

"In another hand, or at another time," Hal marveled, "they might have become crystals, or bits of colored glass, or nothing. Expect no more, Trev. Those are the purest of gifts, as random as rain."

Trevyn picked out one that glimmered plumply, like a tiny moon, autumn pink, with a pale shape like a spindle at its heart. "For Meg, if I am ever to see her again," he stated grimly. "Which you have not yet told me, Uncle."

Hal sighed. "Not even an elf-boat can weather the winter storms on that wide sea. You must wait until spring, at least. Spring in Isle, I mean."

Trevyn jumped up, startling the wading birds, though not into flight. "While my father and my people suffer under Wael's treachery. . . . Thunder!" He turned on Hal in sudden consternation. "Do you have the brooch and the parchment safe?"

"I have the parchment, to my dismay. It is written in the court language of old Nemeton. An ugly reminder. But the brooch was not on the boat."

"Tides and tempests!" Trevyn groaned. "If Wael has it again, then all is lost."

"I dare say the sea guards it well," Hal comforted.

"She guarded it ill before. Mother of mercy, why did I not kill Wael when I had the chance!"

"Mother of mercy, why didn't you?" Hal threw the question back at him.

"Aene knows," replied Trevyn bitterly.

"Very true. "You were sent to Tokar in good time to know your enemy, but still kept from Wael's grasp. So you took it into your head to be a mute—forsooth!—which chance brought you straightway to the rare man who could help you. And that the old slave should have come to Rheged's palace—most wonderful. Ay, Aene has been at work." Hal searched Trevyn's face, and his voice softened. "I know it was a hard journey, Trev. But you must accept your scars as I have learned to accept. Everyone bears scars."

"I reproach the One for Emrist's sake," Trevyn snapped, "not my own. If only he could have been spared. . . ."

"You loved him well," Hal said gently.

"Ay. I think I could scarcely have loved him better if I had known him a lifetime, and I would gladly have befriended him that long."

"Yet you say he was not unwilling to die."

"When I left him." Trevyn turned tormented eyes to meet Hal's. "I don't know what they did to him after I had gone."

"Someone so frail would have died quickly." Hal grasped Trevyn with his gaze. "For whom, really, is it that you mourn, Alberic? Is it not, in truth, for yourself?"

Trevyn clenched his fists, but Hal went on, gentle even in his relentless understanding. "Do not think I trifle with your grief. More than one brave man has died in torment on my account."

Wild white swans sailed down between the trees, fleeting and lovely as spirits, if spirits could be seen. They skimmed past, singing softly among themselves, and disappeared over the waves before Trevyn spoke. Truth had struck him out of Hal's words like a blow to the heart, and it was with trembling voice that he brought himself to admit it. "I—I shall be so much alone, Uncle. I shall never have another such friend. And Father shall leave me before long—" He stopped, shaken by his own sureness. Hal nodded.

"Ay. The Sight is strong in you, Alberic."

Trevyn settled wearily back to his place by Hal's side, feeling weak and not understanding why. "Even if I make it back to Isle, to Megan," he murmured, "and even if she still loves me, and forgives me, and will have me, I shall be alone. Though woman's love counts for much joy."

"Much joy," agreed Hal softly, looking straight out to sea. "Nearly every night I dream of my sweet Rosemary. . . .

How I hope Ket gives her a babe, Trev. She is Isle's nurturer, the Rowan Lady of the Forest; with an heir she will be fulfilled at last. And Alan should come to me, as you have said. Far better fortune than I deserve. I was always a coward in love. . . . Bold enough in body, but a coward in my heart. Nemeton taught me early how love can be used for a torment, and I suppose I never learned better. Coming here, I thought I could not bear the pain of parting from you all. So I stilled my love, and left the pain to others."

"We understood," Trevyn protested. Hal glanced at him with a tiny smile.

"Did you? I doubt it; not Alan, anyway. . . . He is too great of heart to understand, but perhaps he will forgive. How I wish I could tell him that I love him." Hal's voice shook.

"I will tell him," said Trevyn quietly. "But will you not be able to tell him yourself, Uncle, when he comes here?"

Hal could not, or would not, answer. They sat, the two of them, side by side, and watched the sun approach, a fiery wheel out of the azure east—the edge of the west to all the rest of the world. They watched Menwy's dark dragons come up out of the sea to meet it, shaking their sinuous necks, sending up plumes of regal gold and purple spray. They circled, and the blazing disc, its gentler back turned toward Elwestrand, went down in their midst with a mighty roar of water and a bronze glow and with clouds of violet steam. Elwestrand lay beyond the sunset, as Hal had often said. The dragons plunged and vanished in a fountain of amethyst roil; twilight spread. Elwestrand went misty and charcoal gray, but still softly lit by the glow from the depths of the sea.

"He must swim all the way back by dawn," Hal said, stirring at last.

"He does so every day," Trevyn complained, annoyed by Hal's evasions. "Uncle, will you still not tell me if I am going back to Isle?"

Hal studied the darkening, pale-crested waves. "I do not know."

"You call me Alberic," cried Trevyn querulously, "and you speak of the Sight, and you say you do not know?"

"The Sight is a guide, nothing more. It is like a dream,

which deeds must make real. You must live out your own
destiny, Trevyn. You must stay here, really stay, before you
will be able to go."

"Say you will help me go, at least."

"I cannot say even that."

Trevyn sat staring at his uncle in perplexity. Hal would not
return his gaze. Big, soft stars, like snowflakes, came out in
the charcoal sky while they waited. A slender crescent moon
took form atop Elundelei mountain.

"Why do you think you were brought here?" Hal broke
silence at last.

"I can't tell! There is no sense to it. So that you can read me
the parchment?" Trevyn laughed harshly. "That will not take
until spring."

"Ay, it is for your knowledge, but in greater part, I think, it
is for your healing." Hal turned to Trevyn at last, his voice
soft with pity. "You have supped too full of sorrows, Trevyn.
Put the cup from you a while. There is peace for you here.
Taste it."

"How can I," Trevyn shouted, "when you talk riddles and
will not meet my eyes? When you will give me no assurance?"

Hal sighed and wordlessly sent a flutter of plinset notes like
pale green moths into the night; his instrument never lay far
from his hand. A figure took form in the darkness of the
beach, walking toward them. The man came and joined
them, facing them, sitting cross-legged in the sand. An
unaccountable trembling took hold of Trevyn.

"Emrist!" he whispered, though the stranger bore scarcely
any resemblance to Emrist. He was slender, almost boyish,
with dark, straight hair and coal-black eyes burning out of his
fair face.

"Nay," he replied, "I am Bevan. I was in Emrist for a while
before he died." His was the sweetest voice Trevyn had ever
heard, manly and melodious, even lovelier than Hal's. "As I
have been in others from time to time," he added, with a
grave, moonlit smile at that other star-son, the Sunset King.

"I knew it!" Trevyn yelped. "Why—why would you not tell
me?"

"Emrist could not know. He was himself, as he told you,
and very brave. . . . I am not Emrist, Prince, though he is in

me as I was in him. . . . How well I remember his love for you." Trevyn felt the touch of dark eyes. "I, myself, do not love you, not yet, but I remember. And nay, he did not suffer much at the end."

"It seems to me," Trevyn grumbled distractedly, "that everyone knows the pattern of my life except myself."

"It is always thus." Bevan wryly smiled, remembering his own entangled life. "Trust the tides, Alberic."

"That is easy for you to say, who are immortal," Trevyn retorted. "But if the tide tosses me to my death, that is the end for me."

"Why? What makes you think you are different from me? Because you are a fool? Think nothing of it, Prince. I am the one who bequeathed my kingdom a shadowed sword, who doomed my mother's people by the breaking of the caldron, who left the fairest maiden in Isle and the dearest comrade to follow a gleam." Bevan's tone was whimsical. "You are here with me, are you not, Alberic?"

Trevyn could not answer; the implications stunned him.

"Take hold of peace, Trevyn, and it will all come plain," said Hal quietly. "Lie back and watch the Wheel."

Trevyn sprang up and strode away from them both. But he paused when he reached the stream, feeling weakness overtake him. Dappled deer had come to drink; they did not tremble at his approach, but only raised their delicate heads to meet his gaze, sprinkling silvery droplets from their soft mouths. Trevyn stood, yearning, as Hal walked up beside him.

"I am afraid," Trevyn breathed. "I fear this peace. All day I have been on the edge between Elwestrand and Isle; both are like dreams to me, and I ache for both. I float, like a craft without a mooring. If I turn my thoughts away from Isle, she may be lost to me forever. I may never wish to leave this place of wonders. I may forget. And what then, if Wael has his way and sends his minions on to Elwestrand?"

"Bevan and I will take care of them." Hal sounded amused, and Trevyn snapped his head up to look at him.

"There is something you are not telling me. I don't understand."

Hal sobered. "Perhaps you will understand sometime," he

said softly. "Perhaps you will never understand. Does it matter?"

Trevyn wanted to shout that it did, and yet he vaguely sensed that it did not. The brief wisp of realization shook him, dizzied him. He lowered his head, pressed cool palms against his burning eyes, felt Hal's arms around his shoulders. He laid his head on his uncle's shoulder for a moment, feeling that touch ease him.

"Too long a day," murmured Hal. "I'm sorry. Come on; it is not far to our tent."

They trudged down the beach, side by side. The legendary Prince of Eburacon sat and watched them disappear into the dusky night, then winked out like swordlight sheathed.

Chapter Two

It took a week for Trevyn to regain normal strength. During that time he met many of his cousins and found, somewhat to his dismay, that they were all at least as handsome as he, and fleeter of foot. The girls stunned him with their beauty; he would not have dreamed of touching any of them. The people who were native to the Strand, whom the elves had wed, were as fair, but somehow unmistakably mortal, almost sensuous. Most of them had been there since the Beginning, Hal said, untouched by the shadow that had blighted Isle for a while. They were peaceful folk.

During that time also, Trevyn watched Hal populate an entire meadow with dazzling butterflies from his plinset. He experienced at least fifteen kinds of unicorn, each of them mostly white and utterly lovely. He watched Ylim's high-crested horses careering over the insubstantial distant hills. And he slept a lot, those lazy, healing days. One day, Hal came to wake him with a smile starting at the corners of his chiseled mouth.

"Have you been dreaming of trees?"

Trevyn sat up groggily. "I don't think so. Why?"

"Because they've sprung up all around the tent. Hazel,

alder, birch, rowan, kerm-oak, big and beautiful. I thought perhaps you'd been planting a grove in your sleep."

Trevyn blinked. "No, actually"—he yawned—"I think I was dreaming of Gwern."

"Of Gwern? The wyrd? Well, dream of him more often. There is always room for more trees."

Hal wandered out, singing softly. Trevyn followed, stretching and admiring his new grove. He and Hal had made a reluctant pact to begin reading the parchment he had brought from Tokar, a thing and a task that seemed supremely out of place in Elwestrand. Still, during the next few days they deciphered it, sitting beneath the dream trees. It was in the court language of the Eastern Invaders, as Hal had said, which he had been obliged to learn as a child, and he approached it with distaste. After he and Trevyn understood the spell for the transferring of the living soul, as well as they could grasp anything so vicious, they devised exorcisms in both Wael's unlovely language and in the Ancient Tongue. But Hal felt dubious.

"I have learned a bit about magic since I have been here," he expounded, "enough to know that for every spell there is a counter, and no end to it. I don't think this will settle anything, Trev—though perhaps I am not the best judge. I had some power, in Isle, but it was prophesied that I was not to use magic because the Easterners had made it shameful. A King's power must reside in rightfulness. I spurned the Sword of Lyrdion for that reason, and I still wonder if—if it is fitting for a King to do magic."

"To make birds out of air and music?" Trevyn smiled.

"Ah—but I am no King, here. And I am not the one that does it. Aene, perhaps."

"Bevan did magic, and he was the greatest of the High Kings."

"Ay, but that was in the old days." A twinge crossed Hal's face. "Before the Children of Duv went to woe, before the Easterners brought blight and shadow—"

"Magic is in us all, nevertheless. And anyway," Trevyn added, before Hal could argue, "if I can learn Wael's true-name, I'll have no need of spells. I'll need no other power to vanquish him."

"Then take care he does not learn yours." Hal's eyes narrowed. "From what you have told me, he seems like such a warlock as would have been at home in the dark keep of Nemeton. My old foe Waverly, perhaps."

"Or perhaps Bevan's old foe Pel Blagden, Emrist said. Where is Bevan? I would like to speak to him again."

Hal shook his head. "He is as hard to find as those mysterious hills of mine. I have only seen him twice, and one of those times was with you."

"You invoked him, whether you know it or not," Trevyn declared, "with your music. Well, I need some answers, Uncle. I am off to the mountain."

Hal raised his brows. "To Elundelei? Alone?"

"Of course, quite alone. Did you not tell me I could find truth there?"

"Truth and peril, ay. There might be a price to pay."

Trevyn sighed. "Well, I must risk it. And it seems to me—perhaps I have already paid."

He baked himself a supply of bread and got some cheese from the herders. Food came without great labor in Elwestrand, and people shared it cheerfully. Trevyn left on his journey the next morning, afoot, munching fruit from the wayside trees as he went. It did not occur to him, in Elwestrand, to catch a horse, subject it to his will, and ride. He would not attempt to harness any dream in this land of dreams. He walked toward the high pasturelands, the foothills of Elundelei, pausing from time to time to admire the coursers he saw.

It took him three days to top Elundelei. He met with no one after the first day, after he passed the upper meadows. The second day he wound his way up the crags—a steep path, but not perilous. Rowan and columbine grew in the cracks of the rocks, and the ledges were dense with ferns; he slept among them without a twinge. The third day, late, he reached the top and found a graceful tree with fruit that shone like Ylim's hair, silver or gold; he could hardly tell in the magenta light. He took one and ate it, for he was hungry. It filled him like bread, yet delighted him like red wine; he thought he could eat a dozen, but found he could scarcely finish the one. As he ate, he stood atop the crags and looked around him. He had heard that no one had ever been able to circle the shoreline of Elwestrand; it always stretched endlessly ahead. Yet, plainly, he stood on a tiny island, a mere speck in the vastness of the sea, which stretched into shadowy infinity on all sides. Only at the farthest reach of the east could Trevyn see a horizon, a thin, bright line. He faced it, watching for the sun. Behind him, and beside the laden tree, a seemingly bottomless cavern serpentined down between the last two upright horns of crag. The home of the moon, Trevyn knew. He would not enter there. He seated himself on the grassy plot beneath the tree and looked on from afar as the sun flamed into view, plunged and sank, boiling, into the sea. Great eagles, as golden as the sun, called and circled over Elundelei. Among them all, Trevyn saw, the largest one shone white.

"Alys," he whispered. No uproar ensued, no trembling of the mountain beneath him. "Alys!" he repeated, more loudly. Only intense stillness answered him. Even the eagles seemed stilled. The silence prickled at him, and he called no more. He sat without a fire as the purple twilight deepened into velvety night, not quite black. The strange Strand stars came out, the big, mothlike stars that formed pictures he did not quite understand: the Griffin, the Spindle, the Silver Wheel. Trevyn stared at them, and after a while, almost without conscious decision, he lay down on the grass and slept.

He was awakened by a touch of something—not a hand, something within. He looked up to see Ylim standing over him, a white gown floating around her, the half-revealed flesh of her breasts palely shining, full as the globes on the tree. With stumbling haste, he sprang up and away from her.

"Nay!" he declared. "Not again, not while Meg lives. It was shameful enough with Maeve." But she laughed at him softly.

"Have no fear; that is not my function. Come, you called, did you not?"

"Are you Alys?" he whispered.

"In a way. I can speak for her, and for Aene. But if you wish to truly meet Alys, you must come within."

"Within," he murmured weakly.

"Come," she chided, "you ate of the fruit, did you not, and still are standing? I knew you when you were a fleck on the outer rim of the Wheel. And now you fall asleep on the doorstep of the Hub."

Her tender scorn reminded him somehow of his mother. Half stung, half comforted, he followed her into the obscurity of the narrow cavern. He felt his way along the walls as the floor dropped with dizzying steepness under his feet. Ylim threaded her way swiftly before him, seeming not to need a light, through darkness so deep that he could not see even the white sheen of her dress. The passageway twisted and burrowed into the heart of the mountain. Then, just as Trevyn thought the depth and darkness would crush him, it took a gentle upward turn and leveled. Trevyn blinked in a whisper of pearly light. He could not find the source or tell the limits of the chamber. Shadows stirred all around him. In a moment his confused eye picked out the figure of a woman who sat on a glimmering curve of crescent throne, encircled by the most delicate of light: Ylim—nay, Maeve—nay, Megan! He started toward her, then stopped and swallowed at his half-formed tears as the vision flickered away.

"I can only appear to you in forms you understand, or partly understand," said a voice both distant and loving, feminine and fierce. Between the horns of the throne there appeared a blue-eyed cat, then a white swan; a silver harp; a ghostly, graceful ship. Finally there appeared the hazy form of a mandorla, shape of mystic union, floating above the crescent but still within its circular aureole. "Welcome, my well-beloved son," said the voice of the goddess.

Trevyn stood awed, but rebellion flared in him at that. "Well-beloved son! Then why do I bear scars?" he retorted curtly.

"Suffering is the mark of a Very King. Though you will be something more. . . . I demand suffering of those to whom I give my favor. Still, do not blame me for your whip weals. You could have found ways to prevent them, if you had let yourself be less than you are. If you had contented yourself to be a twittering, fluttering thing, such as most men are, instead of an eagle, you would have been spared much. The choice was yours."

"I was not aware of any choice," stated Trevyn stiffly. But the goddess of many names laughed softly at him.

"There is always a choice. . . . And now you are here. Is this what you have come for? To scold me?"

Trevyn stood strangling on his anger, vexed the more by the goddess's imperturbable good humor. It was as if, in motherly style, she did not consider his wrath worth ruffling herself. With an effort, he kept himself from stamping like a child in response. "I came to ask you about Wael," he said flatly at last. "He is my enemy; is he yours?"

"He has taken my creature, the wolf, that worships me, and turned it into a horror." For the first time Trevyn discerned an edge in the goddess's disembodied voice, and he warmed to her anger. "Wael was born as one of my children; everything is. But he has willfully dishonored me. Ay, he is my enemy. But he is not the worst enemy you face, Alberic."

Trevyn ignored that. He did not want another such lecture as Emrist had given him. "Then tell me, Goddess," he asked more politely, "how am I to defeat him?"

"Where are the dragons of Lyrdion?" she riddled in return. The mandorla twirled like a spindle, shimmering above the throne. Trevyn kept precarious hold of his temper.

"I know of a magical sword that came from Lyrdion."

"But I said nothing of magic or a sword. When you find the dragons of Lyrdion, you will know how to deal with Wael."

Trevyn shook his head at this nonsense. "I will need magic to face him."

"What is magic? The tricks Wael does? There is more magic in a stunted sour-apple tree than in all his sorcery. Be that tree, Prince, root and branch, leaf and flower, and you will know how to deal with Wael. Be whole, and you will know how to deal with Wael. Watch." The mandorla glowed brighter, and Trevyn became aware of its continuation, its beyond, the circles that formed its segments on opposing sides. Silver and gold they shone, softly at first but then with a flaming, spinning glory that stunned him beyond taking note of his surroundings. The sharp-ended curve where they met blazed with unfathomable, unsearchable candescence. Essence of sun and moon were in it, essence of earth and sky. . . .

"Aene," Trevyn whispered, hiding his eyes.

"So, there are some things you recognize readily enough." The mandorla subsided to a dusky shimmer, and Trevyn was once again able to face it. "Still, you will never be able to think of me as something other than female"—the voice changed to deeper, manly tones—"or male."

"Adaoun?" Trevyn murmured confusedly.

"Call me Wael, if you like. He is in me too." Trevyn started badly at that. But then Emrist sat for a moment on the crescent throne, smiling at him in reassurance. Adaoun; his father; Hal; a figure he did not at first recognize: it was himself, with a wolf curled at his feet. He watched himself lean down to pat it. "And in you," the voice added.

"Wael?" Trevyn protested. "If I knew his true-name, I would banish him off the earth."

"I have already told you his true-name half a dozen times. When you really know your own sooth-name, you will remember his."

The mandorla expanded, engulfed him, disappeared into the darkness on all sides. He knew it still surrounded him. Perhaps it surrounded the world. But all he could see was a simple circle before him, a halo of pale light culminating in the crescent of the throne. On impulse, Trevyn walked over to it, wondering vaguely of what metal or material it was made that it gave off such a pearly glow. He laid a hand on it and felt nothing beneath the hand—only a shock that flung him back and sent him tumbling into oblivion before he thudded against the wall.

He awoke, hours later, to find himself still confronted by the same whispering, muted light. It came from Bevan, who sat beside him on the floor, his face sober but not overly concerned.

"That was a bit bold," he remarked, "even for a Prince of Laueroc."

Trevyn sat up, rubbing a lump where his head had apparently hit something. "Have you been here long?"

"In a sense, I am always here." At Trevyn's sharp glance, Bevan smiled. "All right, no more riddles."

"Are you real?" asked Trevyn sourly.

The star-son shrugged. "Feel me, if you like. But what is 'real,' Prince?—All right, all right! Let me lead you out." He got lithely to his feet and helped Trevyn up with a warm and glowing hand.

Bevan walked with him all through the three days' journey down the mountain, though Trevyn made poor company, not talking much, only muttering to himself from time to time. "Am I to return to Isle?" he asked Bevan abruptly at one point.

"That is entirely up to you," the other coolly replied.

"Everything is up to me, and nothing is up to me!" Trevyn shouted. "I don't understand!" Bevan cupped his graceful hands, a peculiarly soothing gesture, and Trevyn subsided.

"It's all very well for you, all this mystery, Star-Son," he added tartly after a while. "The moon is your mother. But I am the son of—of a Sun King and an elf." Trevyn winced; the words rang with the wrong effect, even to his ears. "What does—what does She have to do with me? The one whose name I am not going to mention, lest I fail to utter it with proper respect and have something thrown at my sore head."

Grave Bevan almost had to laugh at his petulance. "You are also a child of the ash-maiden, and of earth," he said, restraining his mirth. "And all things are in Alys and Aene, and both are one, and both are in you; how can you separate yourself from anything? You are a star-son, as much as I. You are the child of the round-bellied mother whom we call Celonwy, the full moon, who mothers forth all things of earth. You love the maiden Melidwen, who sails her crescent boat across the sky. And Menwy of the Sable Moon—you haven't met her yet, but you will. The sea is her domain."

"I've met the others?" Trevyn asked, startled.

"Of course you've met them. Even if you've never loved a woman, there is still the goddess within."

They made their way down through the shelving, flower-studded pastureland and across the lush meadows beyond to a grove of silver beech where a man sat playing a peculiar stringed instrument to a group of wide-eyed children. A young-looking man, Trevyn thought, though gray streaked his hair. It occurred to him that Hal could not have touched a scholarly tome since he had been in Elwestrand. The former King of Welas rose to meet them, greeting Bevan with a silent touch of the hand.

"What did you find for answers?" he asked Trevyn.

"More questions. Where are the dragons of Lyrdion, and what is the magic of a rowan tree. Bah!" Trevyn flopped down amid the staring children, they who were as beautiful as he, every one of them. Hal strummed his plinset thoughtfully, picked out a jangling tune.

> "What is the stuff of magic? Clay,
>   and boughs that bleed, and roots that bind:
>
> Ardent alder brown-tipped,
>   red of hue beneath the bark;
>
> Ruddy kerm the holly-like,
>   the terebinth, the oak-twin;
>
> Mountain rowan quick-beamed,
>   high-flying, horse-taming,
>
> Royal canna arrow-swift,
>   golden ivy spiral-twining,
>
> Birch for birthing, heather, and
>   the white bloom of the bean for breath."

"What tune is that?" Trevyn asked. "Not one of yours, surely."

"Nay, it's an old, old tune I brought with me from Isle." Hal smiled ruefully. "Not a very good one, either."

"No wonder I've never heard it. Bah! Uncle, I'm done."

"Done?" asked Hal quietly.

"Done with striving, done with questioning, done with even trying to understand. There is no place for Wael in this western land, praise be. Let him go. For the time. Though I still fear . . ."

"What?" Hal sat beside him. The children shyly scattered, and Bevan saluted and wandered away between the lustrous tree trunks.

"That I will not remember to return, or wish to, come spring."

"Trust, Trevyn. Trust yourself, or trust the tide. It's all the same."

The Prince sighed shakily, like a child who has just ceased to weep, and rolled onto his stomach and went to sleep in the grass, knowing that Hal would awaken him in time for supper. Hal sat beside him without a sound. And out of Trevyn's mingling dreams formed yet another unicorn, a graceful, deerlike one with azure eyes and a spiraling golden horn. Hal glimpsed an odd curve centered in the eyes, a spindle shape—he could not be certain. The creature gravely bowed its heavy horn to him, then turned and stepped softly away on delicate lapis hooves, away toward the salt-flavored grass by the sea, as Hal looked after.

Chapter Three

Far across that sea, Tokar's treacherous attack on Isle had finally been launched. Four months of peace had passed since Trevyn had left Kantukal; it had taken Wael that long to make his preparations, so much had he been weakened by his defeat. Isle's ordeal would have been much worse if part of Wael's power had not been splintered along with a gilded figurehead. But his most essential power resided in another leaping wolf, the emblem on the parchment that set forth the Wolf's favorite spell. The talisman's potency sustained that spell even from Elwestrand, enabling Wael to run with his minions in the wilds, harrowing Isle with a horror that left folk floundering and helpless. For generations afterward, Islenders were to speak of "the Winter of Shadows," and tell its tales to their children when the mood for fear was on them.

The terror began silently, slowly. Later, no one could say exactly when or where. Some thought the first victim must have been the woodcutter who was found one day in the Forest above Nemeton with his throat torn out and coarse gray hairs stuck to his bloodied ax. Others said it was the lad from Celydon who never came back from herding the cows in the farthest meadow. Or the three guards from Whitewater

who started through the Forest on horseback and never
finished their journey. Robbers, folk had concluded at the
time, though robbers had not troubled those parts for many
years. But then rumors began of shadows, of gray, stalking
forms seen amid the Forest trees at the approach of night,
glimpsed by the cottage wife as she stooped for fuel or
by the tenant gathering the rabbit from his snare. Fanciful
talk, many said, for wolves were not likely to show themselves so boldly early in the season, when food was still plentiful. But when Rafe of Lee heard the reports of wolves,
he frowned and arranged for extra patrols of the Forest
purlieus.

It was the patrol, Brock Woodsby said, that saved his
family and himself. Rafe's men heard the goodwife scream as
they rode near the cottage and rushed in to find Brock, torn
and bleeding, battling half a dozen gray brutes with the
poker. The goodwife, shrieking, flung brands from the fire,
and Megan wielded a table plank with a fierce abandon that
had kept her thus far untouched. Meg had not screamed; this
was the first time since Trevyn's departure that she had found
good reason to be violent, and she was rather enjoying
herself.

The wolves chose not to face swords. They scattered
quickly, bursting through the windows, streaking toward the
Forest. The patrollers could not follow; they were busy
stamping out the flaming firewood that threatened to burn
down the cottage. Moreover, their horses had bolted, and
they were obliged to make their way back to barracks on foot.
Brock left his family behind barred doors and went along, for
doctoring and to speak to his lord.

"It was the lass they wanted," he told Rafe. "Right in at
the door they came, and went for her with scarcely a glance at
the wife or me. By good chance, Meg had a pot of scalding
milk in her hand, and she threw it at them, kettle and all; that
blinded them for a bit. But then they went at her again as bad
as ever. They weren't starved wretches, my lord; they
were as sleek and strong as pit dogs fed for the fight. I don't
like it."

"Nor do I, no whit!" Rafe gulped. "Do you think the girl
would be safe here at the manor fortress?"

"I'll send her up at once. Thank 'ee." Brock departed, and Rafe went straight to his table to write to Alan.

> To my Dear Friend and Golden Protector, Alan, Liege King in Laueroc, Greeting,

the missive ran, for Rafe loved a courtly flourish.

> I sorely crave your presence and advice in this matter of the wolves, of which my young lord the Prince may have told you. They have become bolder now, even entering in at the cottage door, seeking to rend the maiden Megan, which must be on the Prince's account, whom she holds dear. My mind is at pains to know the meaning of this thing, of which question the Prince could offer no answer. Now others remark it; the land is rife with talk of the daring of the beasts; my men fear them, though they will not say it; and my heart is full of unreasoning distress, though I feel the fool even to write it! Pray commend me to your lady, and pray counsel me in this matter as swiftly as you may see fit. In love and service, Rafe, from Lee, the second week of December, the twentieth year of reign.

A messenger took this swiftly to Laueroc, to the King. Alan puzzled over it for some time before he heavily climbed the stairs to Lysse's sunlit tower chamber and handed it to her. "Did he say anything to you?" he asked her.

"Trevyn?" She wondered why he would not speak their son's name.

Alan only nodded.

"Nay, he said nothing to me of wolves," Lysse replied. "Rafe seems disconcerted."

"Ay, I must go to him, I suppose. Rafe was always one to shout at a pinprick, but still . . ." Alan eyed his wife, frowning. "You told me we would have hard times. Did you see any trouble of this kind?"

"Nay. And the Sight is lost to me these days; I cannot advise you, my lord." Lysse spoke without self-pity, and kept her eyes on her hands so as not to accuse him, for she knew quite well that the cause of her loss was that he withheld his love from her. Alan knew it also, and knew she would not judge him, and found himself irked by her fineness even as he longed to comfort her. The leaden lump that was his heart had no comfort to offer. After standing awhile and finding nothing to say, he turned and left her without a word.

Within the hour he took horse toward Lee and kissed her ceremoniously from the saddle. It was the first kiss she had received from him since his return from Nemeton. She wondered if she would ever see him again; her loss was so great that she could not tell. Still, she noted that the green Elfstone she had given him shone proudly on his chest. And as he turned from her, the rayed emblem at its heart blazed back at her with sudden brilliance. Lysse thankfully accepted this sign for her sustaining, and felt it warm her as she watched her husband ride away.

When Alan came to Lee, Rafe greeted him with fervent relief. There had been more attacks: a peddler dragged from his cart, a young wife torn as she searched for her cow. The wolves struck in the evening hours, and, except in Meg's case, in the open. The patrols saw them often, grinning from twilight shadows, but then darkness and the Forest would swallow them up. Hunts had been organized to no good effect; twice Rafe's men had located wolves, but their horses shied from the attack and their quarry mocked them.

"And Meg has gone off somewhere, confound the girl," Rafe added.

Megan had responded to her father's arrangements on her behalf with silence and a tense whiteness at the tip of her pointed nose. She had obediently gone to pack her things, then slipped out of the cottage and disappeared before her parents knew she was missing. Not for any peril would she be sent to the manor town, where people would stare at her and whisper behind her back! She had not been seen since. It was hard to believe that she would have been so foolhardy as to venture into the Forest, much as she loved it. And yet . . . Still, Alan could not say where the girl might be, and he was far more concerned with the wolves then.

"How many are there, do you think?" he asked.

"I cannot tell. We know there were six at goodman Brock's. My men see them in twos and threes. . . . Travelers say that folk are in fear of them as far north as the Waste. But I hope they may not be many, only roaming far afield. They run tirelessly, as fast as a horse."

"Many or few, they will not be easily come upon," Alan grumbled. "The Forest is large."

"Vast," Rafe agreed quietly, "and few know the inwardness of it as well as you, of the place or its creatures. I have heard there are strange things deep within."

"Haunts, and hot steams, and grottos, and moss-men, and soft voices in the night." Alan eyed Rafe pensively. "All that is wild and wonderful. But no such evil as this."

"Then you know nothing of it?" Rafe was crestfallen.

"Nothing. Not even as much as you. I had heard no news of wolves before I received your letter."

"What! The lad didn't tell you—"

"Not a whisper." Alan's face darkened, but he tried to make light of Trevyn's omission. "On account of the lass, I dare say."

Rafe grinned at that, then told the tale quickly enough. Alan heard it in heavy-hearted silence, envisioning a glittering ship with a leaping wolf for figurehead and a sunburst brooch lodged in the pebbles of the Long Beaches. "I must go to Nemeton," he said abruptly when Rafe was done.

"What!" Rafe was taken aback.

"It is there that the true peril will strike. From the east; I am sure of it. I must warn Corin. And I will send for Ket, though I know he will be sorry to leave Laueroc. Perhaps his woodsmanship can help you. And I will get you men to aid you in your patrols, and I will go myself to Whitewater, to see Craig. There is one who knows the Forest, Rafe, though I expect his old bones would rather bide by the fire."

"To Nemeton!" Rafe still floundered.

"Ay!" Alan clapped him on the shoulder, as if to awaken him. "But I will return within the month, if I can. Celydon also should increase the guard. If I write some orders, will you send them for me?"

"Of course," muttered Rafe, then burst out, "There is no Forest within miles of Nemeton!"

"Those creatures are in the Forest, but not of it. Nor do I judge that we can hunt them down, though of course we must try. . . . But for now, and unless Ket advises otherwise, I think you will do well enough if you just keep them within the Forest and your folk unharmed. Waste no men in pursuing them."

Alan went off to write his letters. The hardest was the one to Lysse, appointing her his second-in-command and telling her to send Ket to await him at Lee. He knew he had treated her badly, and his warrior spirit drove him to give her what he could, if only honesty. He wrote:

I feel a foreboding beyond all measure of reason that these wolves may put an end to us, Love. So if I do not see you again, shall you still know that I love you? It is true, my heart had gone as dead as a stone within me, but that changes nothing. The sun shines even when the clouds cover it; pray trust in that, as I must. Keep Rosemary by you there, to comfort you, and do not let her come to Celydon, as I know she will long to do; it is too perilous. Tell her that I charge her to stay with you. Now I must hasten to Nemeton, to warn Cory of a danger I can scarcely describe.

He traveled to Nemeton as fast as his retainers could follow him, skirting the Forest, though the precaution galled him. After spending only one evening with Corin he pressed onward, up the Eastern Way, to take counsel with Craig, former leader of all the outlaws in the southern Forest. Even as he traveled he heard rumors of wolves. They stalked the Forest's fringes in broad daylight now, folk said, and attacked children sent to gather sticks for the hearth. People were beginning to suffer for lack of fuel, for no one dared now to go near the Forest unless in the safety of a large group. When he came to Whitewater, Alan found that Craig had already organized patrols and expeditions for the gathering of wood. The old outlaw could not explain the strange behavior of the wolves. He had never seen anything like it, not in all the years he had dwelt in the wilds.

"Surely it cannot be *all* the wolves," Craig offered in his cautious way.

"It could be a dozen, perhaps a score, and those very industrious in their perversity, hah? But there will be more, and worse trouble to come, Craig; I feel it."

"For half my life I fought brutes in men's clothing," Craig shrugged. "It will be no worse to fight brutes that wear hair and go on all fours."

"That is very true," Alan murmured. "I have never met such brutes except in human form. . . . I must make the acquaintance of these wolves."

And the next day he rode straight into the Forest, though his retainers followed him nervously and Craig creased his brow in protest. They wound their way through the wilderness in the half-light of a gray winter's day, glancing over their shoulders at the gloomy distances beneath the trees. But it was not in a shadowy assault that Alan met his adversary. While the day was still young, the company came up against a big wolf sitting on its haunches squarely in the path, as indolent as a dog on a doorstep, with its long tongue lolling from its grinning mouth. Alan motioned his men to hold.

"What game is this, little brother?" he asked in the Old Language.

The wolf laughed, a shrill, yapping sound. "The sweetest game, O Crowned Head! Likely it will give you the soundest sleep you have ever known. Your heir has learned the game, O Fading Sun; ask him about it, when you see him! Where is the Princeling, O Majesty?"

Alan flushed hotly with inarticulate rage and signaled his men to the attack. But on the instant a dozen more wolves leaped to the side of the first, facing them with gleeful snarls. The horses reared back from the sight, plunging for escape, even the *elwedeyn* horse that Alan rode. He flung himself down from his unruly steed and snatched out his sword to attack the wolves on foot, heedless of his men's frightened cries. But his enemies turned away and trotted off into the Forest, insolent in their leisure. When they were gone, Alan's fury turned all at once into sick sorrow, making him so weak that he leaned on his sword for support with the blood of his son swirling before his eyes. Shed to death by tearing teeth, Alan thought.

"If these are creatures of the One," he groaned, "then we have all been betrayed." His wrath and despair hardened within him into a cold, helpless knot of resolve.

He left the Forest, leading his retainers back to Whitewater for the night, then northward the next day onto the barren, stony expanse of the Waste. He did not tell Craig his plan. Alan did not like to speak of deeds until he had done them. And Craig would not have heard of Hau Ferddas anyway, except perhaps as the dimmest kind of legend, a children's tale of a long-ago magical sword. Even scholars who had studied the ancient Great Books hardly knew more. But Alan had seen the magnificent golden sword one day of his youth, and Hal had touched it, and renounced it, and let it lie.

"Mine by right," Alan muttered as he rode, for he traced his lineage to the ancient house of Lyrdion.

He took his men for a hard journey, pressing the pace, riding long and late, sleeping short hours on the comfortless ground. Still, Winterfest had come and gone without their notice before they reached the place Alan remembered. A copse, a scar of brittle stone, a gentle rise, and a barrow on top ringed by man-size standing stones. Alan's retainers, pallid and trembling, pulled their horses to a stop without his command. They sensed the haunt, he knew.

"Wait for me here, then," he told them, and left his horse with them, and strode, businesslike, up the hill. But halfway to the barrow the fear of the unresting shades struck him in his turn, brought him up short with astonishment that almost topped the terror: he had not felt such fear of the wakeful dead since the day, years ago, that Hal had taken his hand and led him gently through their cordon. Hal's warm touch. . . . The memory, though mixed with pain, softened the fear somewhat, and he was able to push his way through it. Bent and panting, he reached the barrow. The fear left him at the circle of standing stones, but no warm welcome awaited him. He sensed the spirits' dismay tingling through their bodiless presence all around him.

"Elwyndas," spoke a deep voice, echoing through a void of

time and Otherness. The single word, Alan's elfin name, seemed to be neither greeting nor question, but rather a reminder—of what? Prophecies and destinies? Mireldeyn had left; those days were over now.

"Culean," Alan responded coolly. The last of the High Kings had been cut off in his youth, in the ruin of his realm, and by his own hand.

"You come here with anger and hatred in your heart," the low voice of the dead King stated. "Why? You have always been full of loyalty and love."

"I have enemies now," Alan grimly replied, "and my loyalties have betrayed me. Aene, brother, wife, and son— they have all betrayed me." He stooped and started tugging at the barrow stones, clawing himself an entrance.

"You come for the sword? But it was not offered to you, Elwyndas, worthy as you are of all our aid. We were told that an elf-man shall take it back to the sea. Your son, perhaps."

"You will wait long for him!" Alan shouted, stung by sudden pain. He grappled furiously with the stones, then crawled into the barrow. The dim interior was much as he remembered: bones, dust, weapons, shreds of ancient finery. Centered under the dome lay a slab supporting the remains of High King Culean, his blackened crown, and his mighty sword. Stepping over skulls, Alan made his way to the skeleton's side and reached for the sword, then hesitated with his hand poised to take it, feeling an eerie reluctance seize him.

"That sword could kill one whom you love," breathed the deep, unearthly voice of the departed monarch. "It killed me." But Alan felt stubborn resentment stir in him at the dead man's interference.

"What, am I to surrender Isle to the wolves, then?" he mumbled, and grasped the golden sword by its jewel-studded hilt, wrestled it from its place. The weapon hung heavily in his hand, its massive point dragging on the ground. With an effort, Alan swung it clear and carried it outside. Strange—it had not seemed so unwieldy when Hal had lifted it, and he remembered its fair golden sheen. But now the precious metal glared coppery red in the cold daylight and the jewels crouched sullenly, unblinking, on the hilt. Alan matched their stare for a moment, frowning, then suddenly pulled off his cloak and wrapped the sword in it, scorning the winter wind. Heaving Hau Ferddas up, he hoisted it with both hands, lancelike, and trudged back to the others. The reproachful presence of the spirits followed him far down the hill.

Chapter Four

"There was no scabbard," he told Rafe crossly, a week later. He had carried Hau Ferddas to Lee wrapped in his blanket, finding himself obliged to sleep with it, when he chose to sleep. He had set course straight through the Forest and kept good guard, with fully half his men standing awake at night. Alan took turns at guard himself, swinging his heavy weapon. But no wolves were to be seen, though the Forest often rang with their mocking wails, full of darkest meaning to Alan's ears. His whole being felt dragged down into that darkness when he reached Lee. And Rafe met him with a haggard face.

"I have not succeeded in doing even what you said. The patrols cannot contain them. They stalk the land now by bright light of day, and folk huddle within doors for fear of them. Only yesterday, my men found a graybeard and his goodwife dead in their home. They froze for want of fuel."

"The wolves are to blame, even so," declared Ket. He had come from Laueroc to join Alan, bringing him Rhyssiart, Trevyn's golden charger, and a missive from Lysse. He would have need of a war horse, she said. She had put out a call for volunteers, and when companies were formed she would send

169

them eastward. She longed to see him, even if only for a day, to talk with him. But there was no gainsaying the dread that lay over the land, a vague and shadowy fear that touched even the folk of Laueroc, who lived far from any forest. She would see him when the peril was past. Alan felt shamefully glad that he would not have to face her. For some reason he would not explain even to himself, he could not have showed her the sword.

He showed it to Ket and Rafe in private. Ket was dubious, Rafe awed and cheered by the sight of Hau Ferddas. "So that is the weapon of which Gwern sang!" he exclaimed, and Alan lifted his bent head to eye him fishily.

"Gwern sang? That must have been a treat! And how would he know of this sword?"

"What matter?" Rafe cried recklessly. "You have got yourself a magical sword to use against the wolves! Now, if only you could find a magical steed to put under it!"

Alan had ordered Rafe special troops from Laueroc, picked men mounted on horses of the elfin blood. But the news of their performance was disappointing.

"Ordinary horses flee from the wolves," Rafe reported bleakly. "The elwedeyn steeds flee sooner and more swiftly. They bolt at even the sound of a wolf."

"Marvelously sensible creatures," Alan grumbled. "If only we could all follow their example! But Isle is not big enough for that. Has Rhyssiart had a chance to prove himself, Ket?"

The lanky seneschal looked uncomfortable. "Ye know I'm no horseman, Alan. But the first time we spied a shadow in the Forest, he carried me clear back to the river before I could stop him."

"We must hunt the wolves afoot, then."

"That suits me," Ket drawled.

"My men have no stomach to face them afoot, not in the Forest," Rafe stated. "And I will not order them to do what I would not do myself." His fear showed frankly in his dark, ardent eyes.

"Rafe and the Forest," Alan sighed. "Will you never come to terms? Well, Ket and I are woodsmen, and we'll find some volunteers. What power will we need, do you think? How many wolves are seen these days?"

"As many as a dozen at a time!" Rafe burst out. "I've seen that many myself—and none have been slain! They will not come near a sword, though they mock a swordsman from a distance. Instead, they plague the poor folk who are helpless against them. They are clever, insolent cowards!"

"We must bait them, then, to entrap them." Alan's eyes glowed with a grim light that made Rafe stare.

"How?"

"Don't you think," Alan rejoined, "that they would like to catch themselves a King?"

Alan proposed to lure the wolves into battle, using himself as an enticement. But Ket and Rafe both opposed the plan, magical sword or no. With the Prince absent, Alan's peril also put the throne at stake. The three of them argued for hours. Rafe was so dismayed that he offered to go himself in Alan's stead. Rafe, who regarded the Forest with nightmare dread! Even in his despair, Alan was touched by such loyalty. But talk of Prince and kingdom meant nothing to him. For some reason beyond reason, he believed they were as good as lost. And he felt angrily compelled to thrust himself against his enemy. He silenced the protests at last by power of his royal command, and he and Ket laid their plans.

Alan was to venture into the Forest on horseback with a few retainers, few enough to tempt the wolves but still sufficient to provide some security. He would appear to hunt at random, but actually he would ride toward a fortified place known to him and to Ket, who had roamed these parts for years of outlawry. Ket would follow him after an hour or so with more men and with blankets and food, backpacked, in case the horses fled. Ket and Alan knew the Forest. It would take them no more than a day or two to return to Lee afoot—if they lived.

The following morning dawned gray, but clear of sky. Alan started out early with a company of half a dozen men, carrying his monstrous sword. The evening before, wolves had set upon a young tenant as he hauled water to his cottage. Alan and his men rode to the spot, then cantered into the Forest, following the tracks of their quarry. After a while they seemed to lose the trail and went on deeper into the vast woods, appearing to search aimlessly. The men glanced about them nervously, but followed their King without a murmur. Before midday the wail of the wolves arose from all sides. The men stiffened in their saddles and the horses shied, but Alan smiled grimly.

"Good," he said. "They are keeping their distance, and we will meet them as planned. Hold your pace."

They continued at the walk and heard the wolves draw gradually closer. But before long they came to the remains of what must once have been a circular tower. Twice man high at spots, it was at least waist high all around, except for the gaping doorway.

"What people could have built this, to abide here in this wilderness?" a man wondered aloud.

"A very ancient people," Alan answered him equably, "for I dare say the Forest has grown around it since. . . . Tether your horses off to one side there, and range yourselves within."

They dismounted and took positions with drawn swords. Alan himself took the door, with Hau Ferddas in hand. His eyes glinted and his nostrils pulsed at the thought of combat, a chance to vent his hatred and despair. He felt Hau Ferddas lighten in his hand, come alive. Roused, it sliced upward and poised itself, like a stooping hawk, at the level of Alan's face.

"Here they come," he told his men.

A rippling, flowing mass of gray, the wolves loped from among the trees. The horses shrieked, snapped their tethers, and bolted away. Within the moment, wolves as large as half-grown calves surrounded the ruined tower three deep, standing with trembling eagerness, jeering. Alan felt his hair prickle, for he understood their song, though he could not tell why they lusted for his blood. He recognized their leader at once: the wolf even bigger than the rest, seated apart. It was the same insolent brute he had encountered near White-water; he felt sure of it. This time Alan would not speak to it, but he studied it intently. Bristly gray snout and eyes of yellowish hue—where had he seen those bilious eyes before?

The jaundiced gaze met his, and for a moment Alan's body went as watery as tears. Hau Ferddas faltered in his hand, and he didn't notice; all he could see was Trevyn's fair form, torn and defiled by leering beasts. Then something rock-hard within him pushed the vision aside. Anger surged through him, the sword leaped in his hand, and his head snapped up, shaking off the haze of nightmare. In an instant the wolf leader yapped, and battle was joined.

Like so many arrows loosed from the same string, the wolves sprang. The sword in Alan's grasp whistled down at them of its own accord, rendered mighty by its own weight, breaking a lupine neck with its first blow. Chanting harshly, filled with a fierce, bitter joy, Alan raised a pile of dead wolves before him. But the living ones sprang again and again, gleefully, mindlessly, leaping over the bodies of their slain comrades as if they were so much grass.

Lost in the satisfaction of his own power and revenge, Alan did not notice at first that his men were tiring, flinching wide-eyed from the frenzy of the wolves. Then the man beside him gurgled and fell, borne down by the wolf that had leaped past his wearied stroke. Alan turned and smote, but the blow came too late; the beast had opened the man's throat.

"Courage!" Alan shouted to the others. "Ket should come soon." From his easy seat off to one side, the big wolf panted his pleasure. But in a moment his sneer faded, as Ket and his company burst into view.

Their horses plunged about and would not charge. So they dismounted and let the steeds bolt, forming a long line of attack on foot. Ket fought with the bow, his favorite weapon. His men used swords or cudgels. Even with swords to front and swords to back, the wolves lost none of their feverish zeal. But their numbers were lessened, and they were forced back. Hemmed in by the press, the leader rose from his place and circled, growling. "Get that one!" Alan shouted, pointing, and Ket aimed his shaft. Then he froze, stunned.

Wolves poured out of the Forest; wolves, so it seemed, by the hundred. Before Alan could stir his tongue to cry out, they engulfed Ket and his men, as sudden and deadly as a flood. Soldiers fell, screaming, and the few with Alan in the tower stood dumbfounded with shock. His own shield arm hung slack, his magical sword plummeted earthward, and before his very face loomed the grinning countenance of the yellow-eyed leader. Obstinate instinct still stirred in Alan, though hope was gone. Rallying, he cut at his bestial adversary and called on those from whom he had often received succor in the past: *"O lian elys liedendes, holme a on, il prier!"* ["Oh spirits of those who once lived, come to me, I pray!"] Then he shouted to his men, "Stand! Stand where you are, for your lives' sake!"

The presence of the spirits enveloped them instantly, and his command was lost in the uproar that resulted. Wolves and men shrieked, their screams mingling and their paths crossing as they fled into the Forest like demented things. Though the spirits came to Alan as friends in his time of need, the others felt them only as a mind-blackening terror of the unknown. The wolfish leader scuttled away from them like a kicked cur. Ket's face went as white as death, and he swayed as if he had been struck a mighty blow. "Ket! Stand!" Alan cried, dropped his sword and ran to him, leaping corpses. The spirits had already passed and gone their way. Alan held Ket until his trembling stopped and he raised his head, gasping for air like a drowning man.

"What wonder is this?" he demanded shakily. "The haunt is miles hence. Has it come to us?"

"I called the spirits, ay. Are you all right, Ket?"

"I'll live," he sighed.

"Come, help me, then." They turned their attention to the bodies that choked the place, checking them one by one. There were no survivors; the wolves had struck straight to the life's blood of each man. Alan and Ket would not meet each other's sickened eyes.

"What about the others?" Ket asked gruffly.

"We must try to round them up, I dare say. . . . But look, it is starting to snow."

Tiny, hard-edged flakes whizzed past thickly, harried by a biting wind. Already, as Alan spoke, the ground was sprinkled and the trees shrouded with white.

"The sky was clear this morning," Ket complained wearily. "Whence came this snow? And whence came those wolves, I wonder? There were none about as we rode; I would swear to that. It's as if someone conjured them up."

Alan shot him a startled glance, then shook off the thought; he did not like the notion of such a conjuror. And the present pressed harder. He and Ket loaded themselves with blankets and food from the dead men's packs. Alan fetched his sword. He regarded the massive, bloody brand in sudden distaste, cleaned it on the snowy ground, and swaddled it.

"I need a horse just to carry this thing," he grumbled, cradling it in both arms.

He and Ket plodded off into the Forest, toward Lee, for some of the men had run that way. They called for them as they walked, and got no answers. Trees looked like ghosts of trees in the snow, and an eerie silence brooded all around. After a while Ket and Alan let their shouts trail away. Ket peered into the wilderness, stopped, and for no reason set arrow to his bow.

"Do we need to fear those wolves, think ye?"

"I can't say." Alan frowned, bemused. "Animals should not fear the shades of dead men. . . . I can't even say why I summoned the spirits, except for sheer, desperate whim. Yet the wolves ran away with plentiful speed, Ket. I fear this snow more right now."

In fact, the two of them were already having trouble keeping their course toward Lee. The Forest had turned into a directionless fog of white. Occasional sounds echoed weirdly in the muffled silence. Ket and Alan blundered along blindly, watching for shelter, searching for their comrades, finding neither. The day drew on. They could not tell the hour by the pallid light, but they felt the pressure of time. They had to find a refuge before nightfall.

"It'll be a marvel if any of us make it back to Lee," said Alan starkly.

Ket gasped by way of answer and raised his bow. Something gray had moved in the dizzying whiteness not far before them. But Alan struck Ket's arrow into the air with his hand.

"There's no malice in that wolf," he exclaimed. "Look again."

She stood facing them not ten feet away, great-bellied with young, her gray fur fluffed softly by the wind, levelly meeting Alan's gaze. In a moment she came up to him and tugged at the hem of his tunic with her teeth, whining.

"*Galte faer; el rafte,*" Alan told her. ["Lead on; I'll follow."]

"What?" Ket demanded. He could not understand the Old Language.

"She wants us to follow her." Alan strode after the wolf that bounded away through the drifting snow, swift and supple in spite of her maternal girth.

"And what if she leads us into a trap?" Ket cried, hurrying after. "If she takes us to the pack?"

"Would you rather freeze to death in the snow?" Alan shot back over his shoulder. Ket silently panted along behind him, teeth clenched against a sharp reply. "She is a brave and generous creature," Alan added more gently after a bit. "She will lead us to no harm."

They stumbled along through the darkening day, numb from cold and fatigue, straining their dazed eyes for the quick, shadowy form of the female wolf beneath the creaking trees. Sometimes she would dash back and whimper at them, impatient at their slowness. As the light grew worse, she stayed closer to them, whining anxiously. They followed her more by sound than by sight. Night had almost fallen when Ket jerked to a standstill.

"The haunt," he whispered. "We're turned clear around, and gone beyond where we started. I feel the haunt ahead."

"I know. Come on!" Alan muttered, and reached out to tug at Ket's unresponsive arm. "It's the best of good fortune that she takes us to the haunt, Ket, don't you see? Nothing evil can reach us there."

Ket plunged on a few steps, then stopped, quivering, unable to move. The Forest had gone almost black; only vaguely looming forms could be seen amid the flutter of the snow. Ahead of Alan, the wolf barked sharply.

Alan obeyed that urgent summons. He dropped his bundled sword and seized Ket as quickly as he could, lifted him bodily, and slung him over his shoulders. Taken by surprise, Ket gave a startled shout, struggling in Alan's grasp.

"Hold still!" Alan wheezed, bent nearly double under his burden, struggling after the wolf. She led him now by walking, doglike, almost at his feet. Their course lay between ancient earthworks and barrows, he dimly sensed, though not with sight. He could feel the bodiless presence of the spirits and feel Ket's fear, a taut distress that somehow augmented the man's weight on his back. If only Ket would faint, or even scream. . . . Alan wondered how much farther he had to stagger.

Then: "Look," he whispered. "A light." Ket gave no answer, though Alan could tell he turned his head to see. Not far ahead, ruddy firelight flickered. The wolf streaked toward it. The haunt lay behind them now, an encircling barrier against any harm, and Ket went limp as a rag with relief. Alan lunged forward, banging against trees, and stumbled through an open doorway. The wolf sat, panting, by the fire, under a low, vaulted roof of unhewn stone. Alan dumped Ket on the ground and straightened himself painfully to look around.

Firelight showed him a small, musty stone chamber, circular in shape, evidently long disused. Smoke stung his eyes, finding its way reluctantly from the central hearth to window slits. Wreckage of a stone stair led to rubble where an upper room had once been. Snow blew in at the doorless entry. A jumble of deadwood for burning climbed halfway up the bare walls on all sides. Beyond the fire stood a figure, very still. . . . Alan felt an unexpected leap and tumble of heart. He saw a royal-blue cloak, and he recognized the brooch that fastened it—but the person looked far too small to be his son. A mere slip of a girl confronted him, huddled in the thick cloth. A name floated effortlessly to Alan's mind.

"Meg?" he blurted.

"Ay." She frowned up at him, as bold as a trapped mouse but not, somehow, uncourteous. "And who're ye that my friend has brought me instead of dinner?"

"I—I am Trevyn's father." Alan stammered out the name, amazed to find that he could not call himself King, not to her. And why would she believe him anyway? he asked himself hotly. Covered with snow as they were, he and Ket might as well have been a pair of brigands. But Meg gazed into his face and silently nodded.

"And this is Ket the Red," Alan added, going to kneel by his companion. "Ket, this is Meg."

The poor fellow was sitting up, looking perturbed, his face nearly as pale as the snow. Alan brushed him off, grumbling softly. "Sorry to have hauled you in here like that. I should have stunned you first, but there wasn't time."

Ket rolled his eyes. "I'm as glad not to have a lump on my head."

"Can I get ye something to eat?" Meg offered doubtfully. There was not a bit of food in sight. Ket looked at her in dry amusement.

"Ay, I'm famished. What's fer supper?"

"Only a bit of cold fish," she admitted. "I was expecting Flossie to bring me a rabbit for supper, and she brought me you two instead."

Ket and Alan both eyed the wolf. She lay curled by a tangle of firewood opposite the door, her plume of a tail covering her nose, her dark eyes shining over it. Lovely eyes, Alan thought. "We're grateful," he said suddenly. "Bring the fish, Meg, and we'll put something more with it."

He and Ket started digging in their packs, scattering blankets in the process. "Such beautiful blankets!" Meg breathed, though they were mostly plain brown. Then she gazed, wide-eyed, as food began to appear.

As it turned out, no one even touched the fish. They ate fresh bread lightly toasted by the fire, and bits of cheese, and dried apple snits, and sausage that they roasted on sticks until it dripped and sizzled. Alan and Ket fixed a blanket over the gaping doorway with arrows jammed between the stones. Meg sat by the fire, flushed pink from warmth and food and excitement. She had not felt so comfortable and full in weeks, and already she adored Alan, though she stood in awe of him. Her shy smile eased the taut angles of her face. Watching the quiet way her small head rode above her borrowed finery, Alan began to understand how Trevyn might have loved her. She moved with the unschooled poise of all the wild things.

Ket had heard about Meg and Trevyn at Lee. He felt ready to be fond of her, since she, a country person like himself, had likewise found herself entangled with these mysterious Lalerocs. He also regarded her with something of wonder. "So ye're Rafe's runaway!" he exclaimed, sitting at his ease. "And in the haunt! I roamed these parts for more years than I care to remember and never met a man who could brave this haunt, except a certain pair of rogues who became Kings. And now I've had to be carried into it. How'd ye ever come here, lass?"

"I can't say," she answered, puzzled. "I just didn't care, that's all. . . . I was cold and tired and disgusted, and I wasn't going to be tracked down and taken back to Lee, not for anything. People have been snickering at me ever since . . ." She stopped.

"Since my son left you," Alan put in quietly from his side of the fire.

"Ay. They envied us when we were together, and now they are glad to see me saddened. I would rather live among the beasts; they are kinder." Meg talked to the fire, but in a moment she straightened to meet Alan's eyes. "What news of Trevyn, Liege?"

"He's dead," said Alan harshly.

"What!" shouted Ket, and for no reason scrambled to his feet, utterly startled.

"He's dead, I say. I dream of his corpse at night." Alan turned away from them both, tired tears wetting his face. He could not say what had moved him to speak the truth as he perceived it. He had hurt the girl to no purpose, he berated himself. He could have let her hope yet a while. . . . Still, it felt good, the warm release of tears on his cheeks.

"Sire." Meg came to stand before him, facing him. "Have ye seen Gwern about this?"

"Nay." Alan found that he did not mind her steady-eyed presence. "Why, lass?"

"He will know where Trevyn is, or if he is really dead. I am sure of it."

Alan grimaced in exasperation. "Gwern, this and Gwern, that! Gwern eats of my food and sings of my sword. . . . Who is this Gwern, that he knows everything and does nothing?" The King waved his arms in a grand gesture of futility. "I can't go chasing after a barefoot weathercock, lass! I am likely to have a war to fight."

"I'll go." She returned sedately to her place by the fire.

"You'll go nowhere except back to Lee," Alan stated, suddenly annoyed. "Your folk are worried about you."

She glanced up in genuine surprise at his apparent lack of common sense. "Ye can tell them ye saw me."

Ket stiffened and sputtered into his flask, apparently choking on the liquor. Alan choked, too, on nothing but air, though he had not been above running errands in his time. "You have no business traipsing about Isle, putting yourself in danger," he flared at last. "These are perilous times, Megan! Get home, where you belong!"

"I belong here as much as anywhere," Megan flared back. "Who're ye to tell me where I may or may not go?"

Caught in another paroxysm, Ket expelled a wheeze that was indeterminate as to emotional color. Alan let out a harried bark, half laugh, half roar of rage.

"Your King, girl! Just your poor, old King, that's all. You should obey me, unquestioning!"

"Drag me to Laueroc, then. Put me in chains." She glared at him.

"Halt! Truce! *Hold!*" Ket jumped to his feet with such an air of desperate command that they both gaped at him. "Ye're not going anywhere for several days, neither of ye, if I read this storm aright. So take a breath! Alan, where is that big, bloody sword ye've latched onto?"

Alan stared at him a moment, thinking, then began to laugh soundlessly. "I let it drop when I jumped you. . . . Confound it, I can only just carry so much! Why do you ask, Ket? Do you think I should use it on her?"

"I asked," Ket replied pointedly, "to take yer mind off yer spleen. Anger is comfortless in these close quarters." He turned sternly to the girl. "Meg, tread more lightly, if ye please! We have watched brave men die today."

"I am sorry," she said with no cringing, only cleanest sympathy. "I didn't know. The wolves?"

"Ay." Alan sat down, surprised to find how suddenly and intensely he liked her. "Ket is right; I am out of sorts. I beg pardon for my manner, Meg. But I am still concerned for your safety."

"I must go to Gwern," she said softly, "as the salmon must go to the sea, or the stag to the meadow, safety or no safety. Can ye understand?"

"I understand many things I don't like. But I know Trevyn cared for you, as I am beginning to care for you myself. Give him something to return to. He may wish to wed you, for all I know. The young fool."

"You just told me he was dead!" Meg cried.

Alan blinked at her. "For a moment, just now, I thought he was alive," he whispered, and bowed his head as pain washed over him.

Ket got up and kicked ashes over the embers of the fire. "Sleep," he ordered with the succinct authority of the servant. He distributed blankets, giving Meg an extra one. The night was icy cold, even within walls. They lay with their feet to the fire, and close together, for warmth.

"What place is this?" Alan wondered aloud. A place that had already changed him, he sensed.

"A sort of a—a mighty ruin." Meg's voice floated through the darkness, hushed, like a moth. "The fish live in circular pools rimmed with stone," she added, after a long pause. "They lie right under the ice. There were a few apples still hanging from the trees when I first came."

"What place could it have been!" Alan murmured. Exhausted, he could not think, and in a moment he fell asleep. The she-wolf came and settled comfortably into the bony curve of Megan's side. Sleeping warmer than she had slept for many days, Meg dreamed of a white stag. But Alan, slumbering in a sentry tower of shattered Eburacon, dreamed of his son, and saw him laughing, whole, and well.

Chapter Five

It snowed, on and off, for five days, as Ket had predicted. When it didn't snow, it blew. So the odd threesome was stuck in their lodging for a week, seldom venturing out, and then hurriedly, ducking through a blur of white. By the fourth day, they had eaten all their sausage and were already growing tired of fish. Despite that, and despite occasional sparring between Alan and Meg, they got along well. They played countless guessing games to pass the time, and drew puzzles in the dirt. In the evenings they sat talking for hours, keeping the fire going as late as they could. Flossie, the wolf, would lie in her own place by the fire, gnawing at the ends of their scorned fish. She made no doglike displays of affection, encouraged no impudence, but joined their circle companionably—as an equal, they sensed.

The wolf had befriended her quite of its own accord, Meg explained. Her first, freezing night in the open, shivering under her ragged blanket, Meg had awakened to find the big, furry body pressed against hers. By morning, the two females were on familiar terms, and Meg had named her new comrade after her favorite childhood doll. Flossie had helped her evade the patrols Rafe had sent searching for her. Flossie had held back a skulking pack of unfriendly wolves with her snarls, leading Meg through a confusion of taunting howls to safety in the haunt. Awestruck, Alan and Ket stared at the placid creature.

"Wolves are beasts!" Alan protested in bewilderment. "They go their own ways like other beasts; they hunt, and run, and mate and fight and die, and pay little attention to men if they can help it. That they should take up war against us is—it is most unnatural. And that this one should protect you, Meg, is a happier chance, but no more fitting for a wolf. What can it mean? Her eyes—I have known wolves, lass. Their eyes shine yellow in moonlight, red in firelight, spectral as a cat's. But hers are the eyes of a lovely woman. Look."

Flossie gazed steadily back at them all, seemingly unperturbed. Her eyes were of a warm brown with a purplish tinge, deepening in the firelight to the color of violets. As Alan had said, they looked as if they should have been courted with candlelight and wine. He envisioned those eyes closing under smooth human lids, then shuddered.

"Countryfolk say that certain people are marked to turn to wolves," Ket said doubtfully. "Those who're born with teeth or with brows that meet over their noses—"

"Lying tales!" Alan retorted somewhat more violently than he had expected to. "I know I have not lived forever, Ket," he added more discreetly, "but I—we—roamed the wilderness for years and learned no great harm of wolves. Most of the time they paid us no mind. But I remember one night when—Hal felt sad and played it out on the plinset, and the wolves ringed the fire to listen." Alan swallowed. "We were not afraid."

"I have never been able to think too badly of wolves," Ket said quietly, "since the time they circled the rowan grove at my lady's feet and did homage to her."

The three of them had become very close, as people sometimes will when they are confined together. Shy Ket had found ways to speak of his longstanding love for the Queen. Meg had told with wry amusement of her dealings with Trevyn and Gwern. And Alan seemed more like himself than he had been for many months, Ket thought, gentler, more open—but still not happy. Ket longed for Alan's happiness.

"Hal—" Alan pronounced the name with difficulty. "Hal never placed credence in werewolves. He said that men fear wolves because they are so much like dogs. But dogs are friendly, and wolves are not, and they are cannibals, and rend each other from time to time. . . ." Alan gulped again. "That is their own business, but men think, what if dogs should act like that? Or what if my other friends, my fellowmen, my neighbors, should go wild, betray me, turn on me to rend me, bite off my outstretched hand. . . ." He paused to steady his voice, wondering at his own emotion. "Men fear themselves most. That is why they speak of werewolves. . . ."

"Dogs are famed for their faithfulness," Ket murmured.

Meg looked down at the wolf that lay unmoved at her side. "D'ye really think Flossie would turn on me t' rend me?" she challenged.

"Nay," Alan replied gruffly, "I cannot think that, even now. Even though . . ."

"Well, what?" Ket prodded gently, after a long pause.

"Even though," Alan blurted, not understanding why, "my own most faithful comrade has betrayed me, rent me to the heart, though not with teeth or steel." Alan hid his face in his hands, though his eyes remained dry and burning as coals. "How, how, could he leave me so, without a tear?"

Meg came around the fire to kneel before him, her hands light as leaves on his shoulders. In an instant he understood why he had spoken after all the silent months: healing stirred in her lightest touch. "D'ye mean King Hal, Liege?"

"Of course, Hal." He raised his twitching face to her scrutiny and smiled slowly, distraught as he was. "Trevyn gave me a tear or two."

"Ay, well, he didn't honor me with so much as a wish-ye-well." Meg smiled bitterly in her turn. "So, Liege, though I hadn't much claim on yer son, I can feel perhaps the tithe of what ye're feeling. And I know ye're angry enough to burst."

"Angry?" He drew back from her touch. "At Trevyn? But he's dead."

"He's not!" she snapped in exasperation. "And anyhow, I meant at Hal. So ye'll give him no tears, either?"

"I—" he sputtered, found he could not speak, and

scrambled to his feet. "I'm not angry!" he shouted at last. Ket snorted quietly from his place by the fire. Alan ignored him.

"Are ye made of flesh, then?" Meg inquired politely.

"Let be, lass." Ket spoke up unexpectedly. "Alan—"

"What?" the monarch muttered, face turned away.

"If ever ye're to see Hal again, what will ye do or say?"

For an instant, the question blazed through Alan. Shouts, blows, tears, an embrace; each flashed like fire across his mind, burned, and vanished. Nothing remained but a stark conviction and a black abyss of gloom.

"I am never to see him again," he mumbled.

"Why not?" Ket sensed that Alan needed hope. "Ye're as special as he was."

But Alan would talk no more about Hal. He refused to explain what he instinctively knew—that the Sword of Lyrdion had somehow cut him off from his brother. For all time.

The weather cleared during the night; the wind stopped and the clouds wandered away. At midnight, Flossie roused Megan with her firm, cool nose, and the girl silently slipped out, clutching her pack and her ragged blanket, leaving the others slumbering by the ashes of the fire. Even struggling through waist-high snow, she would be miles away by morning, well on her way southward to seek Gwern.

"Confound it!" Ket shouted when he awoke the next morning to find her gone. "There's another one that's left without a word. . . . The girl must be daft, Alan." He sounded aggrieved, but Alan seemed amused, even relieved. He smiled whimsically.

"Nay, she's a wise lass. She knew I could not really keep her from going her way, but she spared me the facing of it. So I still have some shreds of pride and honor left. . . . Well, we had better get back to Lee as quickly as we can. Rafe will be fit for a madhouse."

"But we have to find Meg," Ket protested incredulously. "She'll freeze, or—or something."

"Mothers, nay! I pity anything that tries to harm her with Flossie near. She'll be rocking at her ease when I'm turning to dust. Find some food, Ket."

They packed what they could and crawled out of their shelter, then stood motionless, blinking. Deep snow glinted in the wintry light, but that was not what took their breath. A vast, ghostly, snow-draped vista from out of the deep past confronted them. Battlements and broken towers, turrets and court and ruined keep, silent fountains and tumbled walls—all quiet, shrouded and overgrown.

"It must have been a city!" Ket gasped. "Here, in the midst of the Forest?"

"Eburacon," Alan murmured, suddenly understanding.

"I have heard that name when men talk around the hilltop fires of magic and the way Isle used to be. . . . That is a most ancient shrine of the Lady. But what is Meg, that she was able to come here all alone?"

"My son was an ass to leave her," Alan growled in oblique reply, and abruptly stalked away. "Come on!"

He led Ket back the way they had come, as near as he could reckon, and started searching for the giant sword of Lyrdion. It was difficult to find underneath the snow. Alan burrowed busily while Ket watched, frowning. "Is it within the ring of the barrows?" he asked suddenly.

"Just at the barrows. Where you lost your—ah—strength."

"I'll venture to say, then," Ket drawled, "that no one'll come near it. Let it lie, Alan."

"And get it later, you mean? There won't be time; I'll need it." Alan glanced up impatiently. "Come on, Ket; help me!"

"Alan, let it go." A trace of desperation tinged Ket's calm voice. "It's not worth the price, at any price. It has changed you. Thanks be, you've gained some healing here. . . ."

Alan paused, snow-caked and statuesque, half stooped, glaring. "Do you want me to give Isle over to the wolves, then?" he barked.

"What matter!" Ket cried, suddenly anguished. "You were as wolfish as any of them for a while." Alan met his wide eyes, looking as white and frozen as the snow. Ket saw a pang go through him. But then something else settled, hard and heavy.

"What price I have paid is already paid," Alan answered hollowly. "And I'll keep what I have bargained for, Ket. My mistress, if you will. All I have left. Here she lies." He strode with uncanny sureness to a spot a few yards away, reached into the snow and drew forth the sword. Hau Ferddas hung sullenly in his hand. Ket stared without moving, caught up in horror and mute appeal. Alan met his gaze with a flash of rage.

"To Lee," he ordered coldly, in tones he would formerly not have used to the balkiest of servitors.

They trudged through the snow to Lee without speaking for the two days of the journey. Alan glared blackly for most of that time, and Ket kept silence as much from sorrow as from hurt pride. Late the second day they met Rafe and a patrol near the fringes of the Forest. Rafe looked frenzied. "All gods be praised!" he exclaimed thankfully when he saw Alan. He vaulted down from his mount and ran toward him to embrace him. Then he noticed Alan's glowering face and offered his horse instead. He shepherded the two strays back to his fortress, sent the servants hustling with demands for warmth and food. Only when he had seen Ket and Alan fed and settled by a crackling fire did he speak again.

"Half a dozen of my men made it back," he stated quietly. "They've given me news of what happened. The wolves use horror as their weapon now, it seems."

"Nay, the fear was my weapon." Alan spoke thickly. "A double-edged blade. . . . It also worked against me. My men fled as well as the wolves. Only Ket stayed."

Ket stirred at that. "More may yet make it home," he offered.

"I doubt it." Rafe touched his forehead distractedly, wild-eyed from sleepless nights and comfortless days. "Nearly fifty men lost! What went wrong?"

Alan seemed not to hear. "Nothing," Ket told him at last, "except that there were more wolves than we expected. We slew a few score, and left eleven men dead."

Rafe gaped. "How many wolves?" he breathed at last.

"Hundreds," Alan answered flatly. "A forest's worth." Rafe looked into his hard, set face and found nothing to say to him.

"Perhaps the rising sun will shed a brighter light on it," he floundered at last. Rafe had never known the distress that warmth and food and sound sleep could not cure, though more than once he had felt the cold finger of death on his shoulder. "Come, both of you, your beds are warmed and turned for you." For Rafe did not understand that Alan was chilled by more than mere loss of life.

Alan went numbly and slept a sleep like death, though blood colored his dreams. He did not ride out the next day, or the next. In fact, he did not stir from his chamber. He accepted food with ill grace, light not at all, and warned away all visitors. Neither Rafe nor Ket could shake him out of the gloom that had taken hold of him like a sickness.

Alan had no way of knowing that Wael, cloaked in his lupine form, lay frightened, powerless, and exhausted in his own dark den. That enemy had paid dearly for his victory. There had been no wolves seen for the week since the battle; folk thanked the deep snow for that. And yet, so peculiar is the mind of man, they blamed the wolves for the deaths of the soldiers who did not return from the Forest. In fact, Wael and his legions lay through the storm with noses on paws and no thoughts of troubling the desperate wanderers in their wilderness domain. All strength of evil had gone out of them for the time.

Merest curiosity stirred Alan from his retreat at last, as the days ranked themselves into weeks and the wolves did not strike. Ket rode forth daily with Rafe's patrols, and every evening he reported to his liege, gravely oblivious to black stares and thunderous noises. His keen woodsman's eye had seen no sign of wolves, not the faintest pawprint, and that fact pricked Alan into action at last.

"No report of them at all?" he demanded one night.

"No one has even heard a howl." Ket masked his delight as he encouraged Alan into further response. "Folk devoutly hope that they are gone for good."

"Fools!" Alan exploded. "They have only moved on. . . . Any word from Celydon?"

"Ay, and all is well there. We hear nothing from Whitewater, though. No one dares to venture through the Forest."

"Least of all myself," Alan retorted sardonically. "If we are to check on Whitewater, it will be by way of Nemeton. But I have no doubt at all that we shall find them strewing bodies to the south and east."

"Are we to ride, then?" Ket spoke diffidently.

"Certainly!" Alan glared at him. "Did you think I would stay the winter in this hole? We'll ride tomorrow, early. See to it!"

Ket bowed and left the room without a word, saving his smile until he was well down the corridor.

They departed from Lee at sunrise, with scant courtesy from Alan, though Rafe saw him off with warm affection. It was three weeks before they came to Nemeton, for they swung wide of the Forest. When they arrived at last, in murky weather, Corin looked askance at Alan, wondering when he had lost his smile. He was thankful he had no ill news to report. Messengers from Whitewater had brought word of no new attacks in the past month or more. Troops from Laueroc had arrived and been billeted, but as yet there was no work for them. Lookouts posted at the seaside reported no hostile craft on the water. Patrols roaming the southern reaches of the Forest found no sign of wolves and nothing amiss.

"Do not slack your guard. The siege will come before long," said Alan, and with ill grace he settled himself to wait. Ruddy, swelling tree buds whispered of the coming spring when the air was still icy cold, and folk began to hope that the terror might be over. Who had ever heard of wolf attacks except in the starving season of winter? But Alan had not yet been at Nemeton a fortnight when the patrollers' horses came home riderless in the dusk. Alan and Ket and Cory rode out with a retinue the next day and found the men laid out, every one, with gaping gullets and vacant, staring eyes. They were not even within the Forest ways, but well out upon the wealds, with nothing but grass around them. Bodies of three wolves lay nearby.

"These were brave men," Cory whispered, sickened. "How could they fare so badly, here where nothing concealed their enemy?"

"If their steeds were as brave, they might have done better," Alan answered bitterly.

"Failing that," Ket suggested, "they might henceforth carry larger shields, and form their own fortress when their mounts desert them."

"Ay, let them carry shields to their toes, and cupboards

stocked with siege food!" railed Alan. "No wonder the wolves mock us."

Ket faced him steadily. "What do you propose, Sire?"

"Nothing," Alan retorted morosely. "I have no proposal." He would not meet their eyes. He turned away to ride back to Nemeton, and they followed him silently.

Scarcely a day followed thereafter that did not bring some news of grisly death: a hunter found slain before his huddled hounds, a priestess beset at her altar, a cottage family killed. Within a week, a carefully concerned missive arrived from Craig in Whitewater and a nearly panicky one from Rafe in Lee. Wolves roamed their demesnes once again, and they could not protect all who deserved their aid. Folk had been killed. Those who lived survived as if under siege, huddled within walls and already running low on food. Some had fled their lands altogether, seeking a place far from the Forest. Famine threatened, for tilling could be done only under guard. Trade had come to a halt. The land cowered under a shadow of terror like a chick beneath the hawk. What was to be done?

Alan had no answer, no hope to offer. There were not enough men in Isle, he knew, to subdue the Forest. Nor could he yet believe or understand that its creatures had turned against him: he, who had slept the nights of his youth fearlessly beneath its leafy shelter! His mind stumbled in darkness; his heart felt like a stony weight. Only obstinacy sustained him. He moved through the days numbly, riding out with the patrols, doing battle at times, viewing the dead, feeling as if he already lay among them. Ket stayed constantly beside him. After a while, Rafe and the others came and held council, laid plans, asked his approval. Alan nodded, hardly hearing what they were saying. One hand held to his mighty sword. These days, he hardly ever put it down.

Chapter Six

"I must soon be going back," Trevyn said to Hal when the first trace of springtime red tinged the distant hills.

"Stay a few more days," Hal replied, "and help us send your grandfather to his rest. Death will come soon for him; don't you feel it?"

He did, indeed, sense Adaoun's gradual departure. It seemed that all of life and death lay open now to the touch of his mind. They surrounded him like an ocean, in Elwestrand. Trevyn had flown higher than the eagles on the back of the immortal white winged horse; he had tangled his hands in the mane at first, and later learned to trust. He had bathed in the sunset sea with Menwy's jewel-black dragons, and he had walked beside the shy, sinuous leopards of Elundelei. He had slept fearlessly upon earth's bosom, wherever night found him. Elwestrand was a land to mother all lands, he decided: marvelous, relentless, and yet most gently healing. He looked into her indigo lakes and saw Meg there, lovelier than any elf-maiden in all the bright valleys of this paradise. Trevyn wondered why he had not perceived her so before.

So at the first faint signs of spring, Trevyn's heart bounded like a stag, thinking he might soon be on his way back to his beloved, to Meg. If he had not lost her. . . . He would not think that. No use to think that, with three months yet to spend on the ship, even if he left in the morning. And he no longer tried to hasten the circling years of his life. He, too, moved in the cosmic dance, Trevyn knew, and made up some small part of its beauty. Its rhythm would guide and sustain him for all time, if only he could heed its soundless motion.

"You will know when it is time to go," Hal agreed, reading his thoughts.

That evening there were new faces around the cooking fires, elves and elf-kin and fair folk of other lineage, drifting in and taking their places without a word of explanation, as floating leaves come to shore. All the next morning more came, until several thousand were gathered. They sat by the sea and watched their children run along the lapping waves. Trevyn sat with them and listened to the melody of their talk. After a while, something moved in him, and he got up and went to Adaoun.

The ancient elf lay on his couch beneath his snowy canopy, as he had lain since Trevyn had known him. At no great distance, Ylim sat beneath the birch trees, weaving white lace of delicate pattern on a hand loom. With a nod to her, Trevyn settled himself by Adaoun's bedside, taking a frail, dry hand into his own.

"Alberic," Adaoun greeted him, though his eyes could no longer see him. "Do you yet know the meaning of your name, lad?"

"Partly, Grandfather." Trevyn spoke softly, knowing that the patriarch understood him not so much through sound as through some soundless meeting of spirit with spirit. "It has something to do with unicorns, and white and gold. . . . They told me on Elundelei, and they told me the sooth-name of my enemy, but I cannot remember."

"You should be able to remember when the time comes. Enmity has small meaning here."

"I should be able to remember. For it seems to me," Trevyn added, after a long pause, "that the words of the goddess were words that my mother tried to tell me long ago."

"Ah, your mother!" Adaoun smiled, the labored smile of

great age. "I can see her in my mind's eye, all green and golden, spring leaves in sunshine. What was it she told you, lad?"

"That I am—all one." The words seemed lacking, and Trevyn's lips tightened as he spoke again. "That I am all alone. I am not sure why."

"The star-son in you." There was no trace of pity in Adaoun's tones, only mindful understanding. "You will always yearn for fellowship. Hal yearned, all his life. . . . Had he turned his back on the call that brought him here, it would have been like killing his veriest self. If your father cannot understand, it is because he has always been at one with anyone he befriends—but even he will need some healing here. The price of kingship is high."

"And I," Trevyn murmured, "will I ever return?"

"I cannot say. Ask Ylim."

"Nay, I don't want to ask her. I don't want to know what—what I already know." Trevyn's voice broke. "A person cannot expect to come twice to Elwestrand."

"Perhaps you are right. I dare not say. . . . But Elwestrand is in you now, lad, and you will carry it with you wherever you go. Something of it may come to you also in other ways. Be comforted, Grandson. . . ." The old elf's voice trailed away to a whisper like that of winter leaves.

"I will remember, Grandfather, and I thank you. But I am to blame for wearying you with talking. I had better go."

"Nay, stay a bit longer. It is not the talking that drains my strength; life wearies me. But I shall rest from it before long. They will send us off together, lad." Adaoun's smile broadened. "I also go to the sea, to Menwy's domain. My ashes will flow with the circling waters and ripple with the wind, touching many shores. . . . Take me out of here, Grandson, to a place where I may lie on the earth and feel the sky. I don't want to die under a roof."

The airy canopy was hardly to be called a roof, but to Adaoun, father of all elves, it was an irksome interruption of Aene's song. So Trevyn gathered him up, light as a bundle of dried kindling, and carried him out to a wooded slope where the wind sounded in the trees and eagles sang far overhead.

"Here," Adaoun whispered.

Trevyn laid him down on the bare earth, feeling a pang as he did it.

"Now go, Grandson." Adaoun spoke in words scarcely more than a movement. "I crave no company for dying. Farewell."

"Farewell, Grandfather," Trevyn murmured, then went down to the sea to wait with the others. He told no one what had passed. But they knew it nevertheless. As the descending sun approached the sea crests, tipping them with gold, and as the sea-drakes formed their escort, the elves raised their heads and hearkened as if to unseen wings. Then Hal and some others got up and went to the place where Adaoun lay, as surely as if they had seen. They returned to the seaside in soft twilight, bearing the leaf-light body on a litter between them, shoulder high. Adaoun lay with eyes bright and open, robed in white, with a purple cloak trailing over his feet. Evergreen ivy girdled him and garlanded his head; a curled frond encircled his right hand. His kindred surrounded him in awe too deep for words. These were not people who made much of death: the leaf greened and withered and returned to earth, as was just. But Adaoun was one who had been with them since the Beginning. His passing brought the elves to the fullness of all the circling ages they had known.

Trevyn had never expected to see the elves revel with fire. Trees, like all living things, were most precious to them, and they hated to cut them even to clear land for their crops. But on this night, they spent freely of all things, fire and food and selves. The ranged great pyres along the strand, and danced around them in solemn triumph, and sang to the music of Hal's instrument and many more. Between times they feasted, roasting nuts on the glowing coals, toasting bread over the flames. Feral eyes shone from the shadows at the reaches of the firelight: unicorns, and bright birds, and many other rare creatures stood there to watch this unaccustomed feast of fires. Huddled on the sand, blanket-wrapped children gazed wide-eyed at the leaping flames and at Adaoun, whose still form sometimes seemed to stir in the flickering light. When they dozed off at last, flames still leaped before their lidded eyes. The older elves did not sleep, nor did Trevyn. They exulted through the night on Adaoun's account, and when the sun blazed up at last, sending streamers of brightness over the sea, it seemed simply the just reflection of the glory on shore.

Dawn's light showed Trevyn a boat waiting restively in the shallows. Close by it floated a far smaller vessel, a mere platform of wood, almost flush with the water. The elves waded around it, stacking on it their precious stores of fuel, cord upon cord, until a couch of wood was formed. On this they laid Adaoun, folding his cloak beneath him, settling him tenderly. Then, scarcely speaking, they turned to Trevyn. Hal embraced him in farewell.

"I'll see Father off to you when it is time," Trevyn said.

"I know it. And yet, that is entirely up to him!" Hal smiled wryly. "Do you understand now? Destinies must discover themselves. . . . So I'll watch the sea and hope. You are going to light Adaoun's pyre for us?"

"If I may." Trevyn regarded his uncle lovingly. "A fitting time for the trying of power, is it not?"

"None better, since power is not to be used lightly. . . . I have put that parchment with your things. But have a care how you handle it!"

"If all goes well against Wael, I'll gladly destroy it. Though I may have to barter it to him yet. . . . But I must go; my heart cries in me to be gone." Trevyn cast a yearning glance at the marvels that lined the shore, the white swans, the subtle cats, the unicorns. . . . "My heart cries," he amended. "Let me go swiftly. Farewell, Uncle, and—many thanks."

"All blessing go with you," Hal said, and kissed him, and released him. The sun still clung to the sea as Trevyn climbed on board the elf-boat and threw away ladder and rope. The ship swirled away from shore with the still form of the departed patriarch following in its wake. Trevyn looked beyond and saw the hundreds of his friends and kindred raise their hands to him in silent salute. He gazed until he could no longer see their faces, then blinked as he turned to front the rising sun.

When he glanced back again, they were just dark posts on the rim of the water, so swiftly did the elf-boat swim. Trevyn waited until they had almost faded into his horizon. Then he spoke a soft command. *"Luppe,"* he said, "halt," and the

elf-boat eased to a stop, turning aside from Adaoun's trailing
bark. Trevyn loosed the rope that bound it to his ship, letting
it drop into the sea. Then he stretched out his hand.

"Alys," he whispered, "hear me. A fire for my grandfather, if you please. A bright blossom to adorn his going and
seed his remnants where it will." He moved his hand, and fire
burst from the bark, curving and cupping Adaoun and
cradling him in its glow. Sea birds circled overhead with
wondering cries, winged shapes of aching whiteness against
the sky. A far larger form circled above, blazing white and
gold: Wynnda, the immortal winged horse, bidding farewell
to his only master. For a moment, to the watchers on shore,
sun and ship, pyre and gold-pinioned steed converged. Then
the sun, streaming, tore loose of the sea, the ship sailed from
view, the steed wheeled away and the fire sank into the water
with only a plume of white smoke to mark its place: and that,
too, soon faded into oneness with the spinning wind, as
Adaoun's ashes drifted with the dance of the sea.

Trevyn watched the horse and the fire until his eyes could
bear no more beauty. Then he whispered, *"Switte, go on,"*
and the ship swirled away once more, quartering north of the
rising sun. Trevyn leaned on her prow and watched the waters
cleave, and would not look back. More than time and seas, he
knew, would sunder him from that place of peace. Star-sons
had sailed to Elwestrand, but none had ever returned. . . .
He did not know how Bevan stood looking after him on that
far shore, with his hands cupped to comfort Hal.

Book Four

MENWY
AND MAGIC

Chapter One

Trevyn did not lie and stare through this voyage; his body pulsed too full of eager life for that. He paced and pondered and studied sea and sky. The elf-ship was plentifully stocked with everything he needed, and some baubles besides, to amuse him. He ate provisions worthy of a King's son, and slept in bright blankets, and dressed in soft clothing embroidered as beautifully as a ballad. All in all, he stood the months of the voyage well. His dealings with the goddess had taught him a kind of wry serenity. Still, his heart jolted him to his feet when, one day as the sun neared its equinox, a gray seabird flew overhead and circled to meet him.

"How near lies Isle, little brother?" he hailed it.

"No more than a skim and a flitter," it cried cheerfully, "for you fly faster than I—phew!" The bird circled away as it fell behind. Trevyn scanned the horizon that day until his eyes burned. Disorderly thoughts crowded his mind—fleeting visions of his home and people there, sometimes people he scarcely knew; but mostly he thought of Meg. He stayed on deck that evening until full dark had fallen, and saw nothing. But the next morning the rocky headlands of Welas lay so close that he shouted and reached out as if to touch them. Cliffs soared from seaside to mountaintops; Trevyn could see every tree that clung to them, and he hugged the elf-boat's prow in wet-eyed delight.

Before midday she turned the point and entered the Bay of the Blessed. Trevyn gulped, for at the far end someone awaited him, a still figure beside a white horse. No ordinary person could be about; this was a forbidden place. . . . His mother, perhaps? Nay, he could see now, it was Gwern! Trevyn felt only faintly surprised by the warm surge of joy that went through him. In a moment the elf-boat slid to the shore by Gwern's bare feet, and he silently positioned the boarding plank for Trevyn to disembark. Gwern's brown face no longer seemed quite so unreadable; Trevyn saw him bite his lip to still it, and grinned in unsolicited reply. He shouldered his blanketroll and strode to shore, extended a hand, touched fingertips the color of earth. To his chagrin, his full eyes overflowed.

"I wasn't expecting anyone to meet me," he mumbled.

Gwern turned without comment and pulled the plank to shore. The elf-boat wheeled away and scudded out of the Bay. Trevyn stood watching her as one watches a departing friend, almost dismayed that she had spoken no word of farewell. Then he blinked and shook his head, as if to shake off foolishness.

"Did it hurt to leave Elwestrand?" Gwern asked in his curiously flat, husky voice.

"Ay. . . . And yet, I am so glad to be back, Gwern! This is home, after all." He breathed deeply, looking around at the land that somehow sang particularly to him. Then his glance caught on the white horse, and his breath stopped in his throat.

"For you," Gwern said stolidly. "You'll have need of a bold horse."

The stallion wore not a thread of trapping except a lunula of silver on its breast, held there by silklike scarlet cord. It was light and graceful of build, swan-necked, not thewed like a war horse but with something of unicorn fineness, Trevyn thought, and perhaps unicorn fierceness, if fierceness were called for. Bright azure eyes blazed down at him from the stallion's high-flung, bony head. It was these that stopped Trevyn's breath, for the pupils were spindle-shaped, like a cat's, and the strange, blue sheen was ringed with fey white. Trevyn found his voice only after a moment's sincere search.

"Where, in mercy—" he began, but Gwern interrupted him irritably.

"I don't know! I woke up one morning, and there he stood, moon mark and all. But he's yours, right enough. Find out for yourself."

"That's no *elwedeyn* horse," Trevyn protested. "That's more like one of Ylim's wild star-crossed steeds from the foothills of Elundelei."

The horse jerked down its head so that its azure gaze met his of opal green, and Trevyn felt its impatient command. "All right," he breathed, and moved to its side, vaulted onto its back, half expecting to be flung off headlong. But the horse stood taut and still for his mounting. Gwern handed up his blanketroll.

"Why does he serve me?" Trevyn demanded. "There's not a speck of love or loyalty in him."

Gwern shrugged, then whistled like a plover, calling an *elwedeyn* colt out of the woods for his own use. He had no gear, not so much as a cup to drink from, and his ragged clothing fluttered about him like brown, tattered leaves. Perhaps he smelled, also, but Trevyn either did not notice or did not mind. The two of them set off side by side at trot and canter toward Laueroc. The land was green and lovely, lush with early June rains, surpassingly beautiful even to Trevyn's elfin eyes.

"Have you seen Meg?" he asked before they had ridden very far.

"She has traveled with me all spring." Coming from Gwern, this statement sounded perfectly unremarkable, and meant not a nuance more than it said. "She left me a week ago, when I felt sure you were coming to land. She is bound eastward, to see your father."

Trevyn tried to muddle this through for a moment. "Is she—is she very angry with me?" he asked at last.

"She loves you." Gwern's tone did not even try to reassure; he spoke only simple fact. "But she has her qualms, and she is not likely to come to you. You'll have to seek her out."

"But I won't be able to, not for a while," said Trevyn painfully. "I mean . . ."

"The wolves, ay. All of Isle is under the shadow of them."

"And my father; what has he done about them? Where is he? Has battle been joined?"

Gwern grimaced uncomfortably. "I don't know. How should I know? Some things I can tell, but others . . . I know your father thinks you're dead. Meg said so."

"What!" Trevyn had never felt so alive, and he sputtered in astonishment that anyone, especially his father, could fail to feel his wellbeing. "Whatever gave him that idea?" he cried.

"I don't know. Meg's gone to tell him you're coming. But if we ride hard, we're likely to find him before she does."

They rode until deep dark, ate Trevyn's elfin viands, and were up by the following dawn. They rode rapidly and companionably through that day and the next. Trevyn could not understand why he had ever disliked Gwern. The brown youth's plainspoken presence cheered and soothed and excited him now; he felt some feeling both achingly lovely and as comfortable as old clothes. Gwern, like Trevyn, guided his unbridled steed with a touch and a word of the Elder Tongue. Gwern was someone as alone as himself, Trevyn understood now, and very much like himself. The glow he felt was more than comradeship. But for the time he would not give it any other name.

They made Laueroc on the fourth day. Trevyn noted, as they traversed the town, how still the streets seemed, how lacking in chatter and workaday bustle. Those few folk who were about gave him no salute except a stare. An air of dread and hopelessness brooded over the place, as palpable as a cloud of fog. Trevyn entered the castle grounds with foreboding. The courtyard was empty. He left Gwern there with the horses and ran into the keep, up the spiraling stairway toward the living quarters. Halfway up, he almost collided with Rosemary. She gasped at the sight of him.

"Hello, Aunt Ro." He kissed her hastily. "Wherever is everyone?"

"At the fighting, Trevyn," she answered softly, "or else fled."

He nodded, unsurprised. "Where is Mother?"

"Above." Trevyn turned to go, but Rosemary laid a hand on his arm. "Trev—she is not herself."

"How so?" He had not foreseen this.

"She is sad and troubled, even more than most of us. . . . But I hope your coming will cheer her."

"Aene be willing," he muttered, and plunged up the stairs.

Lysse was sitting at the loom in the large central chamber— only sitting, not weaving. She did not glance up as Trevyn entered, and he stopped for a moment to look at her, feeling the sight jab him like a knife. She was not so much changed; her dress was still soft green, her hair a flow of gold and her face rose-petal smooth. But her eyes were locked on pain like prison iron.

"Mother," he whispered, then went and took her by the shoulders. "Mother." She looked up at him and smiled, but the smile touched only the surface of her pain. He hugged her.

"Had you forgotten I was coming back?"

"Nay, not a bit." Her face did not change. "I am glad to see you, Trev. There is much work for you here."

"Mother," he queried very gently, "will you tell me what ails you?"

"Nay, that I will not." Her jaw hardened with the resolve. "But if you send your father back to me, perhaps we can cure it."

"Where is he?"

"In the midlands somewhere." She faced him, helpless to gauge the extent of his knowledge, now that her Sight was gone. "Have you heard about the wolves?"

"I have spoken to no one here except Gwern. But I have met those wolves already, here and in Tokar. How bad is it?"

"In loss of life, not really severe. . . . Perhaps some few hundred folk have fallen their prey. But the whole land quakes in terror of them. They roam at will, insolently bold.

Even within doors people do not feel safe from them. They have pulled an infant from a cradle at the mother's feet and torn a grandmother sitting by her fire. They spread nightmare like a pestilence. Strong men who have seen no more than a gray shadow have left cottage and land, thinking somehow to escape them. But the dread is everywhere."

"How far afield do they range?"

"I believe they have not yet ventured far into the south. . . . A few have come to Laueroc, and you have seen how the town has emptied on their account. In the east, the land is desolate."

"I must be off at once." Trevyn rose restively. "I don't have time to go hunting dragons. . . . Mother, where are the dragons of Lyrdion?"

"Long gone!" She peered at him, justly puzzled. "They have not been seen for years and years, not since Veran's time."

"Riddles," Trevyn grumbled. "There is no time for riddles. I must go, and . . . Mother, I know you must stay here; you are the governor, with Father gone. But shouldn't Aunt Rosemary be in Celydon?"

"I know she longs to go to her home. But Alan and Ket have both bid her stay by me, for her own safety and also to keep me company. Celydon is hard beset. What could she do there?"

"Do? Perhaps nothing." Trevyn gestured helplessly. "She is the gentle Lady of All Trees, Mother. The wolves worshiped her once at the Rowan grove. Her presence could—I don't know. Could stir the Forest back toward the old order."

Lysse gazed, vague and absorbed, as if a distant bell had rung. "Of course," she murmured. "A dark spell needs magic to combat it. But Isle has nearly forgotten the old magic. . . ."

"See if Aunt Ro can get to Celydon. I cannot take her there; I must go to Father. I'll send tidings when I can, Mother." He started out.

"Trevyn," she warned, "the horses will not face the wolves, not even Arundel, before he died in the winter."

"I knew old Arundel would not last long without Hal. But I

have a horse of a different sort." He paused a moment, bemused, thinking of that horse, then turned away again.

"Trevyn," Lysse called after him, "you'll need a sword."

"Indeed!" He grinned at her; she almost sounded like his mother again. "I lost mine when that gaudy ship went down. What do you suggest?"

"Take Hal's, then, and his shield and helm. And Trevyn," she called him back again, "take care."

"I will." He regarded her a moment, then said quite suddenly, "Mother, your father sends you his love and greeting. He is with the tide now."

"Ah!" Her face softened. "Then he is content. What is it like, that Elwestrand?"

"A gentle country, full of peace and enchantment and singing. I'll tell you when I return. . . . Farewell, Mother." He left her with light of Elwestrand in her eyes, and it eased his going.

Gwern had put some harness on the horses, Trevyn discovered when he clattered back to the courtyard. For his own part, he had armed himself and found Gwern a pack and some clothes. He instinctively knew better than to offer Gwern weapons. He had seen Gwern angry, even furious, but he could not envision him taking part in any ordered combat.

"I don't need those things," Gwern complained.

"Carry them for me, then. Come on." They took some food from the kitchen, then departed. It felt odd to ride out through the deserted courtyard, the nearly unmanned gates of the city. Trevyn looked about uneasily. Laueroc seemed ready to yield with scarcely a struggle to a Tokarian invasion, and much of the rest of Isle might be the same. The warships might already have landed.

It took Gwern and Trevyn a week of hard riding to reach the midlands, and another two days to locate Alan. Wolves and King and liegemen had joined battle on a grassy plain near the Black River, a plain that had seen battle before, and more than once. In evening light the fighters appeared as a dark, struggling mass, like gurgling mud. A coppery blaze shot through it, and Trevyn pulled up his fey white steed. "The sword!" he gasped, stricken, and they both stared. Even at the distance, they could hear Alan roaring and snarling like the wolves he smote. The sound was blood red and crushing, like the mighty weapon in his hand.

"By my troth," Trevyn breathed, "I'd as soon beard a dragon as handle that blade. The song you sang, Gwern . . ."

"Hal's song. I could always feel him singing, inside. . . . He felt the shadow of Hau Ferddas, and the prophecy."

"That it must be flung into the sea—"

"By a mortal of elfin kind. Your father is not the man, Prince."

They had come up behind the wolves, opposite Alan, and Gwern's steed had already started to plunge and buck at the lupine scent. Resigned, he dismounted and let the horse pound away. "Go on," he told Trevyn. "I'll join you later."

"To do what? I have no desire to kill wolves, poor things! And I'm not going to touch that bloody sword, either."

"Go on! Just go to your father. He needs you, and he certainly doesn't need to see me. Go on."

Trevyn bit his lip and nodded. He unsheathed his silver sword, a gesture only of defense, and put heels to white flanks. Without hesitation, the cat-eyed steed cantered forward.

Alan raised a sword that flew on wings of rage. The battle meant nothing to him except the release of rage; kingdom, family, friends, and folk had long since ceased to matter to him. His innermost will was locked into hatred, and he watched in bitter triumph as his sword beat back those who tried to slay him.

His men, and men from all the southern towns, and from Whitewater and Lee and as far north as Firth, followed him apprehensively. Perhaps their King was demented, but what choice was theirs? They hoped they kept the wolves from doing other harm, that they saved a few lives in Nemeton. Alan wanted to drive the wolves clear away from the Forest into the southern sea. It appeared as if he even thought he succeeded. But his men could see that every day the creatures made a mockery of their efforts, toyed with them gleefully, leaving them cheerfully at sundown to return as cheerfully in the morning. If Alan's army moved, it was because the wolves chivied them and harried them and herded them here and there, picking off panicky men who faced them only because they had found it was worse to run, to feel the shadowy horror panting behind. Only Alan seemed oblivious to dread of the wolves. He dreaded night worse. While his men took all too brief a respite, he paced, shutting out a nightmare he refused even to name. He strode to battle almost eagerly in the mornings, for then he could lose himself in the glory of his magical sword.

So when the setting sun blinded him one evening, blazing in his eyes, he cursed; he hated it. He hated to remember that Hal and Trevyn had passed beyond the sunset, to the uttermost west, whence there was no return. . . . What figure rode toward him, emerging out of the sunset, a form armed in silver but haloed in rays of gold? It shimmered before Alan's blinking eyes like a vision of the glorious past that he had nearly forgotten in the gory present. It was Hal! But it could not be Hal. . . . Hau Ferddas thudded to the ground, and Alan stood without noticing, watching the rider draw nearer. A shout sounded in his ears, someone seized him and tugged him back from the fray, but he only stared. The approaching horse was white, its forehead blazing white, on its breast a crescent of silver. It sprang fiercely, almost joyfully, into the midst of the wolves, scattering them with its hooves. The rider laid about him with the flat of his sword. Golden hair shone under the silver helm, and gray-green eyes flashed beneath. It was not Hal, then, but someone like him, a hero of elfin stature whom Alan did not know. He had spied the enemy leader now, the big wolf that always sat and grinned; he sent his horse lunging toward it. But the wolf shied away, yapped once, and all of the wolves loped off. The men cheered, but the rider sat his horse and watched the gray beasts go without pursuing them.

Alan pulled away from the arms that held him, walked forward without realizing he had taken a step. His bloody sword hung from his limp hand and dragged in the dirt as he stumbled around bodies of men and beasts. The rider heard him coming, glanced around, and snatched off his helm as he slid to the ground. "Father!" he exclaimed, coming toward him.

"Trevyn?" Alan whispered.

"Ay, to be sure!" The young man gripped him, for Alan swayed where he stood. "What, have you forgotten me already?"

"Nay, indeed. But you have changed." Alan looked as pale as if he had seen a ghost. "And I felt quite sure that you were dead of shipwreck."

"Why? Did I not tell you I would return?" Trevyn smiled, teasing, trying to rouse Alan to some touch of joy. But Alan only fumbled at an inner pocket and brought forth a jeweled brooch, a sunburst of gold.

"I picked this up along the shore," he explained dully.

"That brooch," said Trevyn with feeling, "has taken part in more mischief than I can fathom! Guard it carefully, and keep it away from the sea. By the tides, I shall tell you a tale of that brooch! But first I must tell you a tale of these wolves. Let us go where we can talk. . . . Father, you look spent. Take my horse."

Trevyn had to help him onto the cat-eyed steed. As they prepared to leave, Ket came up and merely glanced at Trevyn in greeting.

"Liege," he addressed Alan, "shall I have the men advance their position?"

"Do what you like," Alan told him numbly, and turned away. But Trevyn shook his head, and Ket silently acknowledged.

Trevyn walked off by Alan to the cottage where he had established his post of command, a mile away. Ket ordered the men to stay where they were for the time. Then, discreetly, he also made his way toward the cottage, to watch over Alan as he had done for many weeks, and to speak with Trevyn when he could.

Inside the cottage, Alan sank onto a seat without moving even to clean the blood from his hands. His clotted sword rested between his knees, naked under its coat of gore. Trevyn quietly found wine and poured his father a tumbler full, which he handed to him with some biscuit. He did the same for himself and found himself a bench along the wall.

"You will have heard by now that I met with these wolves before I left Isle."

Alan scarcely nodded. Dazed from weariness, Trevyn thought. He went on.

"I was a fool not to tell you of them. I hope I have gained better wisdom since then, but at least I can offer knowledge."

As briefly as he could, Trevyn recounted his adventures, speaking not so much of what he had done as of what he had learned. He brought forth the parchment that was headed by a leaping wolf and explained its meaning. Silence rang hollowly in the room after he finished. It was a long moment before Alan stirred and spoke.

"You have studied in sorcery?"

"After a fashion, ay." Trevyn frowned in puzzlement. His father hardly seemed to have heard him.

"Well, you'll use no sorcery here."

Trevyn gaped in astonishment, fighting to keep his composure. "You face a wizard," he said carefully. "How will you defeat him?"

"With a bright blade." Alan's hands twitched on the jeweled hilt they grasped.

"Do you plan to slay every wolf in Isle?" Trevyn protested. "They are victims of Wael's treachery as much as we ourselves!" But Alan exploded into sudden fury.

"You think I don't know my enemy!" he shouted. "By the Wheel, I will be King in my kingdom, and those that have shed my people's blood shall feel my wrath! And you, if you cross me! There shall be no sorcery, or talk of sorcery, in my land. Heed me well!"

"That is a sword full of ancient sorcery in your hand," Trevyn told him quietly.

With an inarticulate roar, Alan lifted the weapon and rushed against the bright figure of a brash youth who had threatened his power. His son was dead; nothing remained to him except his rage and his power. . . . *"Dounamir!"* Trevyn gasped. "Father!" But even the Old Language had no power on Alan's hearing anymore.

Frozen and incredulous, Trevyn watched him come. Though his own sword hung at his belt, he could not move to draw it, not against Alan. . . . He was too stunned to flee. But as the invincible blade of Lyrdion whistled toward his head, Ket burst in and caught Alan's descending arm. "Alan, ye're as mad as a mad dog!" he cried. "Look before ye! Who is it that ye smite!"

Startled, Alan looked, and saw anguish in the eyes of—his son! Shaking, he dropped Hau Ferddas clattering to the floor and sobbed into his bloody hands. Trevyn went to his father, motioning Ket away. Ket hesitated, then seized the sword and retreated.

Alan wept tears of blood, or at least so it seemed. They ran in red streaks down his face, as if they had been torn from his heart. Trevyn clutched him tightly. "It has been hard for you, far too hard," he faltered. "The whole land in shadow, and you most of all, being King. . . . And that accursed sword—"

"There is no excuse for me," Alan choked. "I was half lunatic before I ever touched the sword. Trev, I have wronged you—"

"Hush."

"And not only you." Words burst from Alan in a feverish torrent, like his red torrent of tears. "Your mother has had nothing from me these many months but hard looks. . . . And Rafe! He who stood by me all through this hellish business, dead days ago, with no thanks for his constancy but the rough side of my tongue—"

"Hush," said Trevyn more firmly, swallowing his own sorrow. "Rafe needed no thanks from you. . . . Father, of all people in Isle you have been hardest beset, and I must badger you yet again. In very truth, our fate depends on the morrow. May we speak of it once again?"

"Nay." Alan quieted and faced his son with desperate honesty. "Nay, there is no need. It is as Ket has said; I am unfit. The command is yours. If anyone questions your authority, send them to me. But I think they will all be glad enough to obey you."

Trevyn regarded him with aching heart, finding nothing to say. "Will you sleep now?" he asked at last.

"By my troth, ay!" Alan murmured in wonder. "Ay, I shall sleep well." He started toward his bed, but turned to stand before Trevyn a moment longer. "I believe I forgot to say welcome!" he told him, and grasped his shoulders and kissed him.

Chapter Two

"It's just as well," Ket said when Trevyn told him of the change of command. But Trevyn disagreed.

"It's not a bit well," he sighed. "But he shall be well, Ket, mark my words. . . . What have you done with that great, bloody sword?"

Ket looked at the ground. "I've hidden it—and I'll reveal it to no one, Prince. Not even t' ye." His brown eyes flashed up, pleading for understanding. Trevyn smiled wearily.

"You're wise," he acknowledged. "You know I'm no more proof against its spell than Father was. But what of yourself, Ket? How long do you think it will be before thoughts of the thing eat away your reason and contentment?"

"Better me than ye," Ket snapped unhappily. "I'll call council."

"Wait!" Trevyn exclaimed. A familiar form was approaching through the dusk. Gwern trudged up to stand by his elbow, raising his straight, shaggy brows in blank inquiry at the stares he was receiving from two sides.

"Gwern," Trevyn declared, "I believe you might finally become useful in your own peculiar way."

"Ay," Ket muttered. "Ay, it can't touch him; even a fish

can feel that." He disappeared into the gathering darkness and reappeared shortly with the sword, offering it to Gwern as if he could not wait to be rid of it. The weapon lay blanket-wrapped on his outstretched hands with the covering slipping away from the blade. Gwern stared as if he were confronted with something indecent.

"Take charge of the sword, Gwern," Trevyn instructed. "Don't let anyone have it, least of all my father. A deadly magic is in it."

"I'll bury it, then," said Gwern. "Earth is good for such ills."

"Nay, some fool will dig it up again. You must keep it by you."

Gwern shrugged and grasped it, not at the hilt but by the midpoint, as if it were a stick. He lifted it with a grunt and bundled it under one arm, blade backmost. Trevyn made fast the wrappings that hid the bright metal.

"What a nuisance," Gwern remarked, hefting the bulky thing.

"Guard it at all times," Trevyn charged him. "See to it, Gwern." The son of earth sighed and wandered off with his unwieldy burden.

Later that evening, Trevyn sat around a fire with Ket, and Craig, and Robin of Firth, and lords and captains of all the southern towns—far older men than Trevyn, all of them. Yet they looked to him for guidance.

"If there is any question of my right to command," Trevyn told them, "the King has said it must come to him. I hope there will be none, for he is sleeping."

"There shall be none," growled old Craig, glancing about him with a hint of menace. No one gainsaid him.

"Good," Trevyn stated. "Now, I shall not tell you how I came by certain knowledge, for it makes far too long a tale. But be assured of this: it is not beasts we fight here. By sorcery, the souls of brigands and murderers have been spirited into the bodies of the wolves. An ancient wizard named Wael has done this, to smooth the way for an invasion by his master, Rheged of Tokar. So it does not avail us to slay the wolves: when one is killed, it is a simple matter for Wael to transfer the captive soul to another. And if he lacked wolves, I dare say he could use another scheme."

"Lack wolves!" Ket exclaimed wryly. "Why, there are more wolves in Isle than men! The Westwood is full of them, and the mountains of Welas, and the Northern Barrens—"

"Exactly." Trevyn smiled at him.

"So what is to be done?" someone asked.

"I must confront Wael and strive to reverse the spell. Failing that, I might be able to strike a bargain with him. I have something he wants."

"Wael would be the big one," Robin said. "The laughing wolf."

"Ay. So far he has no more than trifled with you, waiting for the Tokarian fleet. But he knows me, and fears me a little. I expect him to strike with all his force in the morning. So draw the lines tight."

Throughout that night the captains roused tired men and instructed them to fall back toward Alan's position, forming a compact group in preparation for the morrow. When all was ready, a few hours before dawn, Ket and Craig and the others went to snatch a bit of sleep. But Trevyn wandered, fighting to keep the calm he had brought from Elwestrand, trying to dream himself back to a certain night on Elundelei. He settled at last on the roots of an elm, near the cottage where Alan slumbered, and looked for a legend in the moon and wandering stars.

At the first light of day the men stood ranked, tensely awaiting the attack. Trevyn rode the lines on his lithe white horse to steady them. But full day dawned, and no wolves came.

Alan awoke hours after sunrise to the same eerie silence. It did not seem odd to him at first. He smiled drowsily in the bright sunlight and turned to look for Lysse. He had embraced her in a dream, and for a moment he could not understand where she was, where he was, or why. When he remembered, he could not explain his own happiness. Hastily he washed his hands and face in the cold water that awaited him. Only when he reached for his sword and found it missing did Alan recall the events of the past evening. No wonder he had slept late; he would not be leading any battles now.

Slowly, ashamed in spite of his joy, he moved to his cottage door. The mass of his men stood ranked not far away, waiting. Even closer at hand lounged the lanky, red-haired form of Ket. It was no use going weaponless, Alan decided, with a battle forming. "Do you think I might have a sword?" he hailed him.

"I have your own sword here, my lord," Ket said quietly, not quite looking at him. He brought it over. It was the one with the lion's-head hilt, the one he had worn for years, and Ket must have spent half the night polishing it, Alan judged, when he should have been getting his rest. Alan peered at his seneschal. "Why are you my-lording me?" he asked.

"For the sake of respect, I was told." Ket studied Alan's face and smiled his slow, warm smile. "Ye don't remember!"

"I seem to remember being the worst kind of an ass," Alan sighed, "but the details are lost to me, praise be. Will you forget the respect now?"

"As you say," Ket drawled. There was little need for words between these two old friends. But the greatest of debts constrained Alan to speak.

"And for what you did last evening, Ket—a thousand thanks."

Ket flushed, and helped Alan into his helm without comment. Trevyn cantered up and dismounted, facing his father with grave affection. "Are you all right?" he asked.

"I'm as likely to be a dolt as ever, Trev." Alan grinned broadly. "Since my gladness is out of all proportion with the occasion. Would you look at that tree!"

"Why, what about that tree?" Ket gasped, staring at the muscular elm as if it might conceal a wolf.

"Look at the way it spreads deep and high, joining earth and sky. It has flesh and skin, flowing blood and reaching fingertips; it's as alive as I am. And it shall remain, it or its seed, long after we are gone."

Ket's face sobered at this strange talk, but Trevyn nodded. "Ay," he said softly, "and once you have hold on such truth, nothing can utterly destroy you."

"In regard to destruction," Alan rejoined lightly, "what am I to do today?"

"Keep clear of the fighting if you can; your reflexes are not likely to be at their best. Take this oddity of a horse, and lend your presence to the lines." Trevyn handed him the reins. "The men are anxious about you; it will hearten them to see you."

"And you? Should you not be mounted?"

"Nay. . . . Can you lend me that brooch, Father, the ill-fated one? Perhaps it'll give Wael a moment's pause."

Alan brought out the jeweled pin and watched Trevyn fasten it to his cloak. "Why, what are your plans?" he asked worriedly.

"I can't really plan for Wael. . . . Though I admit, I wish I could remember a—a certain name, as it was promised I would. But I have a spell or two to try on him. We'll spar at spells, that is all."

"Are you sure—" Alan began, but even as he spoke a shout went up. The wolves had appeared, running to the charge. "Take care, Father!" Trevyn cried, and sprinted to the battle line.

On a rise, a bit apart from the other wolves, the yellow-eyed leader sat. Trevyn strode out to face him, feeling very alone and yet not entirely alone; something shielded him, kept the snarling brutes he passed from snapping at him. Alys, perhaps? He hardly dared to hope it. He walked up to the big, gray wolf with his naked sword leveled at its chest, and it sat unmoved, grinning at him.

"Are you ready, Wael?" Trevyn asked curtly.

"Ready!" Lupine laughter curdled the air. "What readiness might I need for a pup like you!"

Trevyn's mind still darted in search of the elusive name. He fiercely constrained it to focus on the task at hand. Slowly, strongly, he began to recite the words that Hal had taught him, grim words of the old Eastern tongue, that would compel these wretched spirits back to their proper bodies: *"Zaichos Karben, arb ud Grezig. . . ."* Souls moved to obey; Trevyn could feel their stifling heaviness in the air around him. Behind him, the wolves faltered in their attack, and men cheered. But Wael's will strove with Trevyn's. His yellow eyes narrowed with strain and his borrowed body tightened beyond the sword's point. Forcing himself to concentrate on the struggle, hoping somehow to breach his enemy's power, if only for an instant, Trevyn brought forth the parchment from his tunic and fingered it as he continued with his counterspell. Crushing strength opposed him, and he felt the sway of the balance; he seemed neither to win nor lose.

"If you did not have that scroll you thieved from me," Wael panted, "your strength would be no equal to mine." Though he dreaded that Trevyn might try to turn the talisman's power to his own account, Wael hoped the Prince would value the parchment and preserve it with greatest care. But Trevyn glanced at the thing with loathing so sudden and intense that it drove all spellwords and strategy from his mind.

"I will take no power from a thing so evil," he grated. "Fire of Menwy have it!" His fingers flicked, and the parchment puffed into flame. Wael shrieked in despair, lunged to save it, but even as his lupine body leaped the scroll vanished, leaving only a shower of ash. Wael's self and his spell left Isle like smoke whisked away by a strong wind. Terrified and confused, the wolves sped toward their Forest home; they were only pitiful animals now.

The largest one lay impaled on Trevyn's sword, mutely suffering, its golden eyes bewildered. Beside it lay the Prince, as still as death, though not a mark showed on him. Alan reached him first, and killed the wolf, for mercy—it had been a long time since he had killed so gently. But he could not rouse his son.

Not long afterward, Gwern appeared anxiously at Alan's cottage door. Trevyn lay on the narrow bed, stripped to the waist, and Alan held him while Ket tried to give him wine. But the crimson liquid spilled over him, and he never moved. Alan was weeping.

"He's not dead," Gwern stated, a bit too loudly. "Why do you weep?"

"Have you seen these welts?" Alan choked.

Gwern looked at the whip scars and shuddered like a horse when the fly bites. His claylike face moved, and he turned away without a word. Alan railed on.

"I'd like to know who gave him those stripes. . . . I'd hunt them down and rip them apart with my fingers! Sweet

Mothers, all things gained, and then it seems all falls to ruin again. What ails him, Gwern? Wè can't help him."

Gwern came closer and studied the Prince. "Shadows," he said at last. "Years ago, you would have cured him with the little yellow flower."

"Veran's gold? None has bloomed hereabouts for hundreds of years. We had some in jars, but it all turned to dust when Hal went." Alan's face twisted with the pain of the memory. Then he stiffened, noticing for the first time the bundle that Gwern carried. "Mother of mercy!" he breathed. "Get that accursed sword away from me!"

"Trevyn told me to keep hold of it," Gwern said.

"Then do so, but keep it far from me! I feel it draw. . . ." Alan shook where he sat cradling his son in his arms. Only that inert form kept him seated, Ket sensed. "It cozens me like a woman, and I thought I was past such folly! It shames me. Get it away, Gwern!"

"I'm going." Gwern retreated a few paces. "May I borrow Trevyn's horse? I'll go get Meg."

"Meg?" Alan straightened, his fear suddenly gone. "Take any horse you like. How can you find her?"

"Easily enough." Gwern slouched out of the door and was on his way within the minute.

"Meg," Alan murmured. "There is healing in her lightest touch." He felt the almost forgotten stirrings of hope.

For the five days of Gwern's absence, Trevyn lay, and ate nothing, and drank scarcely anything, and never came to himself Sometimes he thrashed and moaned in black dreams, crying out against the wolves, or against the slavers, cursing them. Once he pleaded, "Let him be. . . ." Later he whispered, "Oh, my sorrow, what did they do to him after I had gone and left him?" Alan talked to him constantly, stroking his brow, calling to him, trying to calm him. If he succeeded, it was only to see Trevyn sink into a deeper stupor.

There had been no sign of the wolves, no messengers, no action of any kind. Alan's army camped at his feet and waited, almost breathlessly, for news of wolves, or war, or the Prince. Unmistakably, the shadow that had been on the land was gone. For the first time in months, the men really felt sunshine, felt it with a relief too deep for rejoicing, even if rejoicing had been fitting, with the Prince so ill. . . . Every man of the thousands gathered there longed to aid Alan in some way. Ket spent his time stumping in and out of the cottage, almost as sleepless as Alan. "Let me watch the lad for a while," he would say gruffly from time to time. But Alan would not yield his seat for long, not to anyone.

As Trevyn weakened for lack of food or rest, he began to call Meg. He would stare past his father, gazing at some insubstantial form of horror, and sob out her name as if he called on his god for succor. "Name of Aene, may she come soon," Alan breathed.

She came in the twilight of the fifth day, cantering through the staring soldiers without an answering glance, looking like a dark-cloaked queen of ancient legend with her pale face proudly raised over her moon-marked steed. She might have been as starved as Trevyn; her hair clung tremulously by her hollow cheek. But the sun brooch at her throat shone bright. Alan left his place at Trevyn's side to meet her, helped her from her horse with outstretched arms, and led her to his son.

The Prince tossed restlessly, moaning, "Meg—Meg— forgive—" Yet, he did not see her. The girl sank down beside him, grasping his faltering hands. "Sweet Prince, be whole!" she begged, but he looked past her without a sign.

"Call him, lass," Alan urged.

"Trev! 'Tis I, Meg!" she beseeched him, but to no avail. Trevyn flinched away from her touch, and sweat stood out on his face.

"He doesn't know you," Alan whispered.

"Trevyn!" Meg pleaded. But he turned away from her, hiding his face and cursing the slave pits of Tokar.

Alan felt as if, hope won and healing in sight, all his world had fallen to ruin yet once more. Groaning, he fell to his knees at the bedside, clenching his fists in fury and despair. If Trevyn should really die . . . The forbidden thought went through Alan with a force that laid open the deepest reaches of his soul.

He sprang to his feet, gripping the glimmering Elfstone that hung on his chest, his gift of hope from Lysse at their first parting. "Alberic!" he cried, though a moment before he had not known the name or its meaning. "By all that is beautiful, by all things that render you fealty, I charge you—govern yourself! *Pelle mir*—look at me, Alberic!"

Slowly and painfully, Trevyn focused his eyes on him. "My sire," he breathed.

"Trevyn," said Alan, quite gently, "you have a visitor. Welcome her."

Meg sat biting her lip in misery at her failure, stunned to silence by Alan's passion. But as Trevyn's eyes turned upon her, she instantly knew what she must do. Like dawn after shadows, her wan face lit with the smile she knew he loved. "Hello, Trev," she said.

He only stared at her with widening eyes and speechless mouth, and she accosted him tenderly but saucily. "What, fair Prince, d'ye not remember me? Me and my sister Molly, the one with the red hair?"

Trevyn could not quite find his voice. "Meg!" he whispered hoarsely, and reached out to her. She came and sat beside him on the bed, and he flung his arms about her. "Oh, Meg!" The cry was like a moan, and she bit her lip again, for he was weeping. "Hush, Trev; ye'll be all right," she faltered, and her hands came up to cradle his head.

Alan went out. An hour later, when he looked in again, Trevyn lay deeply asleep with his head on Megan's lap; she sat absently stroking his golden hair. Alan smiled shakily. "Meg, lass, you look spent," he whispered. "Come, let's find you some food and a place to rest." He gently placed Trevyn's head back on its pillow and took the girl out, an arm around her thin shoulders.

During the night, Gwern trudged stoically in, still toting his swaddled burden of sword. During the night also, Megan slipped out of her tent and away, to the confusion of the sentries, who had been given no orders concerning her. Alan slept until an hour or two after dawn, then heard the news with wholehearted vexation and dismay, in manner so much like his old, ardent self that Ket wept. When that was taken care of, they went to the cottage and found Gwern dozing by Trevyn, his bare, grimy feet planted on the bedframe. This time, somehow, Alan managed to ignore the sword. He and Ket sat companionably, waiting for Trevyn to awaken.

It was nearly noon before Trevyn rolled over and looked

around, confused. Alan went to him, his face still drawn and gray with strain in spite of his rest. "Go to bed," Trevyn told him promptly. "What day is it? How was I hurt?"

"It has been nearly a week." Alan smiled at him dryly. "You weren't wounded. I think Wael gave you some bad dreams."

"Thunder, ay!" Trevyn shuddered at the memory. "But something comforted me. . . ." Suddenly he sat bolt upright, nearly falling in his excitement. "Meg! Was she really here?"

"Ay, she was, Trev." Alan spoke unhappily. "But she's gone again. I can't imagine what ails the girl."

"I can." Trevyn settled back with a sigh and a frown, then caught sight of Gwern snoring beside him and smiled in spite of his disappointment. "Can't I even have a bed to myself?" he complained.

"You like him better than you used to," Alan asked, "don't you?"

"I—" Trevyn did not know how to admit that he loved Gwern like a brother. "Well, he went for Meg, did he not?" he barked at last.

"Ay."

"Let him sleep, then. What's to eat?"

But he was too weak to eat much, or even sit up for long. He dozed off again shortly, and awoke in late afternoon. Busy, clattering sounds drifted in from outside; the men were breaking camp. Alan stumped in to face his son with a worried frown.

"I've just had a messenger from Corin, Trev. Tokarian warships have been sighted off the Long Beaches; they may have landed by now. I must march my men eastward."

Trevyn gaped at him for a long moment, digesting this news, adjusting his sense of time; then he let out a shout that roused Gwern.

"Tides and tempests!" he cried. "Do you mean to tell me that all the time I've been lolling about, an army has been lolling about with me?"

"I did seem to remember something about a Tokarian invasion," Alan retorted stiffly, "and I sent Craig off with half the men. But now I must go, and quickly." Alan's tone softened. "I am sorry, Trev—we've scarcely had time to talk.

But I must go myself. I owe my people some kingship, after—after all my foolery. I'll leave a company with you—"

"Mothers, nay!" said Trevyn emphatically. "Take every man. Gwern and I will be fine by ourselves. I'll ride after you in a few days."

"You should rest for at least a week."

"I'm stronger already. Look." Trevyn slipped out of bed and stood, tottering. Alan eyed him doubtfully. But Gwern extended a hand to steady him, and unexpectedly spoke.

"I'll feed him well," he volunteered, "and he'll stay here till he's healed. He's never been able to get the best of me yet," Gwern added darkly.

"We'll see, in the morning," Alan hedged.

But in the morning Trevyn walked to the table to eat, and Alan made ready to march with all his men, muttering. He had called his son Alberic, King That Shall Be. But it was hard to let go of the little boy that once was. For his own part, Trevyn seemed as protective of his father.

"Be wary," he warned. "Rheged is full of treachery. And Wael is probably with him."

"I thought you dispatched him!" Alan exclaimed.

"Nay, I only slew his borrowed body, poor thing. . . . And I believe I did away with the transferring of living souls when I destroyed the parchment. But Wael still has plenty of tricks left."

"I don't mind any magic, now that that shadow's gone," Alan grumbled. "Trev, lad, be gentle with yourself. . . ." They embraced, and Alan strode to the golden charger Rhyssiart, took saddle. Trevyn stood on the doorstep and raised a hand in farewell as his father jingled off at the head of his army. The men saluted him as they passed, and Trevyn bit his lip, feeling his knees forsake him; he couldn't weaken now! Gwern slipped a casual hand under his elbow.

"Thanks," Trevyn hissed between clenched teeth.

They stood until the last of the troops had passed. Then Trevyn staggered inside and collapsed on his bed, groaning. "I must be out of my mind," he lamented. "Gwern, you are an execrable cook, and I know it."

"I'm no cook at all," Gwern stated in his factual way.

They ate cold food for three days, until Trevyn was well

enough to make himself some soup. Then they spent another three days in almost constant baking and roasting, preparing supplies for their journey. They had no way of knowing what was happening in Nemeton, but Trevyn felt sure there must be fighting. Peasants wandered by their windows in bewilderment, some fleeing the rumored invasion, some returning to their homes since the threat of the wolves had passed. The proper owners of their cottage came back to it and peeked timidly in.

"We'll leave in the morning," Trevyn assured them.

He and Gwern spent the evening packing. Trevyn worked silently, frowning in thought. "Meg is wandering somewhere in all this confusion," he said suddenly, when they were done. "How am I ever to find her, Gwern, since she won't come to me? How did you find her to bring her here?"

Gwern kept uneasy silence for a moment, moving his big hands, fumbling for words. "She is to the east, somewhere near Nemeton," he said finally. "I can feel the focus of her being in much the same way as I am always drawn to you, but—it is through your love for her that I sense her. When I see her, it is through your eyes."

"And you love her," Trevyn murmured.

"Through your heart."

Trevyn stood staring at him, afraid to put into words something unfathomable he had felt. "But you must be yourself, Gwern," he protested at last. "You always have been. Everyone is."

"I—I'm not sure."

Chapter Three

They left the cottage at dawn and rode toward Nemeton, with Trevyn on his strange, cat-eyed steed and Gwern on his colt. They rode all day, steadily but not hard, since Trevyn had still not regained his full strength. His own frailty troubled him, and starting the journey brought all his concerns to the fore.

"Confound it, Gwern," he grumbled by the campfire that evening, "do you know anything about the dragons of Lyrdion?"

"Nay."

"Confound it!" Trevyn exclaimed again. "How am I ever going to defeat Wael? I can't remember—I am nothing more than I was the last time I faced him and nearly died of it."

"But it was not Wael that hurt you the last time," Gwern remarked reasonably.

"It wasn't?" Trevyn whispered. "Then—Menwy? Why, that black—" With difficulty he restrained himself from applying the epithet of female dog to the goddess.

"She had to work through your hatred." Gwern neither reproved nor explained. That toneless voice calmed Trevyn.

"Well, if I can't use her—Gwern, the problem remains the

same. I am no match for Wael. And I must face him again, soon or late, whether he awaits me at Nemeton or not."

"Perhaps you will not have to face him alone," Gwern said. Trevyn turned to him curiously, sensing—what?

"What do you have in mind, Gwern?" he asked slowly. But Gwern shrugged and would not answer, sitting blank-faced by a hulking bundle of sword.

The next morning they traveled on. To make for easier fording of the Black River, they headed slightly north. Three days later they crossed the main river and reached the point of land between its arms at the southern fringe of the Forest. Trevyn tried to stun rabbits for their supper as they rode, but his stones all missed. Muttering, he wished out loud that he had a hunting bird like the one he had lost, some time back, fighting with Gwern.

"Look!" Gwern pointed. "An eagle."

The great golden raptor, shining like the sun, skimmed just over the treetops, its wings nearly five feet in span. "It must have come all the way from Veran's Mountain!" Trevyn exclaimed. *"Laifrita thae,* little brother, you have seen far; what news?" He held up an arm for the bird, calling it to him. But the eagle swooped past his outstretched wrist and on toward Gwern, striking with a screech at the base of his neck where it met the shoulder. Curved talons drew blood, and Gwern, utterly startled, fell off his horse with a thud. The eagle flapped heavily away, and Trevyn jumped down from his own mount, hurried to Gwern. The youth was sitting up, looking browner than ever with leaf mold and rubbing his head in surprise.

"I'm sorry!" Trevyn exclaimed. "I never in a thousand years would have expected that. . . . Are you all right?" He tried to examine Gwern's cuts, but Gwern pushed his hand away, gently enough.

"Scratches. I'm just stunned. Can Wael be setting the eagles against us now?"

"I hope not!" Trevyn shuddered. Gwern looked up thoughtfully.

"The eagles are the messengers of the goddess. But I can't think how I might have offended her."

"Still, I didn't smell any stench of Wael," Trevyn mused.

They rode on a little farther and camped in a Forest glade not too far from the river. They set a snare and had a rabbit for their supper. But in the morning Gwern groaned and struggled to rise from his bed. His face looked flushed under its habitual coat of grime. Trevyn pushed him back to his blanket, feeling the heat of his forehead with alarm. The cuts the eagle had given him looked swollen and raw.

Trevyn cursed. "By blood, Gwern, that's what you get for never washing!" he shouted in conclusion, and trudged to the river, grumbling. He returned with pans of water and bathed Gwern's cuts and face. They did not ride that day. Trevyn spent the time cooking soup, but Gwern hardly ate any. He drank water from time to time. Trevyn made trip after trip to the river, bringing cool water, laying a cool cloth on the infected cuts. He didn't sleep much that night, tending Gwern almost as frequently as he had during the day. But by the following morning Gwern no longer knew him. His wounds had swollen to double size, and he cried and moaned in delirious pain.

Trevyn tried the only crude treatment he knew. Braving Gwern's struggles and screams, he sliced the scabs open, squeezed out the pus, and seared the cuts with a hot blade. To do this, he had to sit on top of Gwern and pin down his flailing arms; later, he went off in the woods, and retched, and wept. Still later, in a sort of penance, he sat for hours by Gwern, patiently washing him, peeling away the tattered clothing that seemed to have adhered to his skin. Beneath the rags he found scars. It took him a while to realize that the marks were identical, line for line, with his own scars from the slave whips and the wolves. When he could no longer deny it, he wept again. That night, every time he tried to sleep, he seemed to hear Gwern's screams under his knife-wielding hand.

The searing did not help. Contagion crept down Gwern's arm and up his neck; Trevyn thought the skin would break with swelling, and half of Gwern's face turned a vivid puce, like a bruise; he looked as if he had been beaten. Whenever he moved, he shrieked with pain. Trevyn scarcely dared to touch him, even with the wet cloth. He no longer attempted to sleep. Exhaustion would take him for a few moments from time to time, and then he would wake with a start and try to comfort Gwern, if only with clumsy words.

By the time Trevyn lost count of days, Gwern no longer had strength to scream. He lay softly moaning, but Trevyn could tell that his pain had not abated. Then one day, near evening, Gwern suddenly quieted, lying limp and still. Filled with dread, Trevyn felt for his breath. But Gwern opened his eyes and fixed them on Trevyn's haggard face.

"The pain is gone," he whispered wonderingly.

Trevyn only swallowed, and Gwern looked thoughtful. "Not good," he added after a pause.

"Nay." Trevyn had heard about the respite that sometimes came just before death.

"Tell me," Gwern said.

"Your whole arm is purple with infection, and your shoulder down to your ribs, and your neck and face. . . ." For a moment, Trevyn closed his own burning eyes. "I can't help you. I've tried to help, and I've only hurt you."

"But I can't die," Gwern murmured incredulously. "I don't understand."

"That's what I keep saying," Trevyn groaned. "I don't understand. Sometimes I think I have been accursed since the day I was born. I had only just learned to—to love you, Gwern, and then this—"

"But I can't sicken! I am not mortal; I was never born," Gwern explained laboriously. "Alys made me, somehow, to embody your deepest being, the Prince you liked the least. She ensouled me with her own breath. So I am Alys and I am you; how can I die while either of you lives? I have wept when you wept, loved when you loved, kept that feeling safe and helped it bring you back to Isle. I am wyrd; how can I just end? I don't understand. . . ."

"You are more than friend, even more than brother," Trevyn whispered, shaking. "You are second self. . . ."

"I am your inner fate. I am the child you have tried to leave behind; I am the white hart, the wild thing, and I am the wilderness within. I have loved you when you would not love yourself."

"Yet, you are also yourself, Gwern," said Trevyn tightly, "to our sorrow."

"I am selfhead and godhead. So how have I become doomed to a mortal death. . . ." Weary, Gwern closed his eyes.

Still trembling, unable to speak, Trevyn took his good left hand and held it between his own, stroking it, warming it when it began to grow cold. He did not dare a larger embrace; he would not risk jostling Gwern and causing him pain when he lay so peacefully. He could hardly tell when Gwern ceased to breathe, but he saw the purple tinge creep all the way across his still face, felt the chill in his hand. Trevyn laid it down and edged away, sensing dark waters of hatred on all sides, welling up within him, drowning deep. He staggered to his feet, turned blindly and ran.

Within a few strides he surged into rage that he thought would destroy him, destroy the world; he didn't care. He careered against trees, punishing them and himself with all the strength in his body, smashing them with head and hands and knees, shrieking, but not with pain. He cursed with curses torn up from his reddest depths, cursed every person of the goddess, cursed Aene. Sometimes he stumbled and fell, ripping at earth with his bloodied hands. Sometimes he scrambled along, crashing through thickets like a hunted deer. He came up headlong against rocks, seized them and hurled them against the unresponsive earth, then plunged aimlessly onward. But he was too weak from fatigue and from his own recent illness to run mad for long. After a while he lay feebly thrashing, too exhausted to rise, too stubborn to weep. Later, eerily, he reached a calm even deeper than his hatred, and he knew quite surely that the goddess had not stirred for all his rage and all his grief. He felt her implacable love and understood that he would always be hers, always be alone. He bowed his head in acquiescence, laid his face in the dirt and slept.

Something awakened him before dawn, some internal pang. He stared at the shadowy Forest, and remembered, and groaned. Then, unsteadily, he rose, wondering how far he had come from his campsite and how he would bury his—his companion; he could not bear to think of a more fitting title.

He did not even know which direction would take him back to Gwern. But a faintly scornful snort sounded through the darkness and a white blur walked up to him: his wild-eyed horse. He crawled onto the beast, and it carried him off without a word of instruction through the gray dusk of dawn.

He found Gwern, no more than a lump in the dim light, and beyond him a bundle that had been impatiently pushed out of the way. Trevyn needed the massive sword of Lyrdion now. He pulled the weapon from its wrappings, took it and felt his way to the top of a slight rise beyond the glade. There he began to hack a hole in the ground for his wyrd.

He worked through bright dawn and sunrise. The hacking and scraping soothed him somehow. But even through the numbness of his grief he could feel the haunting tug of the sword. Culean had killed himself with that weapon, Trevyn grimly remembered, and with less cause than he had, he thought. . . . No matter. He dared say he put it to more fitting use. When he judged the grave was done, he went to get the body.

He reached the edge of the glade, stopped and reached shakily for a tree. Gwern lay where he had left him. But he looked like a graceful young god, lying there, like a woman's dream of her sleeping lover somehow caught in light and form. His rugged face and the bare rise of his chest caught the early sun and took on a golden glow; no trace of sickly purple remained. Trevyn walked over to him, knelt beside him and felt the movement of his ribs, felt the warm pulse of his neck, felt breath, scarcely daring to believe. Gwern stirred under his touch, blinked, then sat up and gaped at him.

"What on earth—" he exclaimed, as agitated as Trevyn had ever seen him. "What—Trev, what has happened? You're all blood and dirt; you're a mess! You look—like me!"

Trevyn felt for his voice; it came out a hoarse whisper. "And you look better than I can fathom." He raised a hand, and with the bruised fingertips he delicately traced the smooth line of Gwern's neck and shoulder. "Not so much as a scar on you," he marveled.

Gwern stiffened, stunned by memory. "I was dead!" he gulped. "Was—wasn't I dead?"

"Stark and cold." Trevyn shivered with horror and growing joy.

"I was dead, and now I am alive. . . . Sweet Mothers, Trev, what have you done? What—what ransom have you paid for me?"

"I think I have sacrificed nothing but my pride. By my wounds, Gwern, I'm glad you couldn't see me! I threw a fit." Trevyn collapsed beside Gwern with a tremulous laugh. "I railed like a child—and after a while I knew—I understood—and now I don't understand! Bah!" He sat up again. "Mother of mercy, is there to be no end of riddling?"

Gwern made a small sound that Trevyn could not identify, not until he saw the tears running down the gentle brown slopes of his counterpart's face. He had never seen Gwern weep, and at first he could not react or comprehend. "My Prince—" Gwern spoke huskily.

"Gwern, what—" Trevyn awkwardly reached out toward him, touching only one cupped hand.

"Trev, I love you; I owe you everything. Will you try not to leave me again? I want only to be at one with you for as long as the riddles shall last. Without end."

"Then come here," Trevyn breathed, stirred to his soul's depths. "Come here, my second self." He embraced the son of earth, drew him in with both arms, felt Gwern's answering embrace, warm head on his shoulder, hair by his cheek, bare, smooth chest against his heart, tears—all in an instant, and for the first time, he felt that, and then it vanished with an odd twinge. He held a bundle of blossoms and leafy sticks wrapped in vines and sealed with clay. Crying out, Trevyn leaped to his feet and flung it away, breaking the clay binding. "My curse on all your devices!" he wailed at the goddess, at the entire heedless world. Then he sank to the ground again and wept. "Oh, I have destroyed him!" he choked to no listener. "He loved me, and I have destroyed him!"

He wept for hours, sometimes pacing in circles, sometimes quieting only to begin again. When the sun neared its zenith, he calmed somewhat at last and sat staring dully at white bean blossoms, ruddy tips of rowan and fragrant purple heather, all fresh and thriving. For no reason, his eyes glanced beyond the strewn sticks to where a wolf sat at the foot of a tall oak tree, gazing back at him. A wolf with lovely, violet eyes. . . .

"Alys?" he whispered.

"Nay, it is Maeve. I am only one small speck in Alys." The wolf trotted up to sit gravely beside him, laid a paw on his knee in a gesture not so much doglike as human: for his comforting, he knew. He could barely speak.

"Wael transformed you?" he faltered.

"Nay, I came of my own accord. There was need of—of some balance. But the Lady has returned to the Forest now, and my task will soon be done. . . . Freca, why do you grieve? The earth-son is not gone. He is at one with you, just as he wished."

Trevyn had sensed this truth even before she spoke. He knew where the dragons of Lyrdion were: in honeycomb depths of earth, his to loose as he had loosed his rage, for he was at one with that earth now. He could feel the song of a rowan's root. He knew Wael's sooth-name: it was the obverse of his own, encompassing his own despair and death. Gwern had given him all knowledge in making him whole. He comprehended mysteries of all realms, whether sky, sea, Isle or twilit Elwestrand—all stations of the sun, all phases of the changing moon. And all pain; he stiffened stubbornly against that knowledge.

"I don't care," he grumbled. "Gwern was himself, as well as me, and now he's dead."

"Changed, Alberic, only changed," she said gently. She nosed at the disorderly array of sticks and blossoms that had been the wyrd. "Plant these in that trail of tears you've left, and you'll have a grove that will be the glory of Isle in years to come, and better than any monument to his memory."

Even tired as he was, he obeyed her, thrusting the leafy shoots into the ground, spacing them in a sort of outward spiral. He surveyed his finished work sourly.

"A poor substitute for a warm and gentle touch," he stated.

"Come with me now," she told him, and led him to the tall oak tree at the edge of the glade. Nestled between its roots lay a wolf pup, soft, bright-eyed, still in its first fur. It gazed up at him with mingled valor and distress, wriggling. Automatically, Trevyn sat down so that his size would not frighten it, reached out to caress it. The little thing ran onto his lap and nuzzled under his chin, pressing against him, sending a spasm of longing through him.

"Your son," Maeve said.

"What?" he whispered.

"Your son, and his destiny is far stranger than yours. Being born a wolf may be the least of it." She gazed at him out of dusky damson eyes. "Take him with you, to comfort you, and to grieve you when it is time."

He stood, cradling the wolf cub against his chest, where it lay contentedly. "But Maeve," he faltered, "won't you miss him?"

"The babe is weaned," she answered, then stood grinning toothily at him. "Prince, you know I am a creature of the wilds! Get on to Nemeton; they have need of you there." She turned and trotted across the glade, between the newly planted trees. At the edge she faced around. "Look above you," she added, then disappeared into the Forest.

Trevyn looked. The eagle perched on a limb of the oak, staring down at him with hard, topaz eyes. Trevyn sighed, put out an arm, and the bird glided down to him, landing gently just above his wrist. He held it at a level with his face, and it regarded him steadily.

"So you did only what you had to do," he acceded. "What the goddess told you to do. All right. Will you get me something to eat, little brother, if you please? Or I am likely to starve before I ever reach Nemeton."

He put the golden sword of Lyrdion in Gwern's grave, pushed earth over it with his hands, planted heather and white blossoms of bean to mark the place. He knew he would have to come back for it, but he would not take it where it might cause his father pain. Later, he rode away on a fey white horse, with a belly full of half-cooked rabbit, holding a wolf cub on the saddle before him. An eagle flew close overhead. It was only a few hours until dusk, but Trevyn would not stay another night in the place where he had so painfully become whole. He rode through twilight, deep into night, noticing to his vague surprise that his horse's forehead shone with a clear, faint light, white on white, like a star. It had not done so before.

"A quaint sight I make," he muttered, "looking like a wild man, riding to face a sorcerer, all two of me, on a mad mystery of a horse, with a baby werewolf in my arms and an eagle almost bigger than I am thumping down on me from time to time. . . . Rheged may run when he sees me, but Wael is likely to laugh himself into oblivion."

Chapter Four

After three days of hard riding, not even taking time to wash, he approached Alan's encampment outside the walls of Nemeton. Alan blinked, watching him. "Gwern?" he queried, and then, as the rider drew closer, incredulously, "Trevyn?"

"I think I shall be, mostly, when I'm bathed." Trevyn dismounted, letting the wolf sit in the saddle. He had named the little one Dair, a word of strong comfort. Already Dair balanced expertly on the horse, in company with the eagle, which fed him scraps of raw meat. Alan glanced, open-mouthed, from the odd trio to his son's thin, hollow-eyed face.

"What in mercy has been going on?"

"Gwern took ill and died—or seemed to die. . . ." Trevyn sat limply on the ground beneath his horse's nose. "Father, I can't begin to tell you half of what's been happening to me. But Maeve—someone told me I was needed here."

"I'm relieved to see you; I've been expecting you for a week. But what you can do, I'm not sure." Alan sat beside his son. "We've wiped the countryside clear of the invaders at last. It's been grim work, but my men fight well now that the shadow of the wolves is gone and now—now that you are back and I am better. We've scuttled their clumsy ships. But on the day that I arrived some of the enemy took Nemeton, and they're holed up there yet. It would be no trouble to starve them out, but Corin is in there, and some others who were too stubborn to flee. . . ."

"Meg among them," Trevyn murmured. He had felt her presence long since, with all of Gwern's sureness.

"Ay." Alan's face showed his distress. "She got caught up in the confusion, it seems, and took refuge there. . . . But how did you know, lad?"

"I just know. . . . She's come to no harm so far, Father. I'd feel it if she had."

"And Cory? And the others?" Alan leaned forward eagerly.

"I can't tell about them," Trevyn admitted, hating to disappoint him. "I can only tell that Meg is all right. And I seem to catch a whiff of Wael."

"Ay, he's there, I think. Talk has it that a particularly villainous-looking, yellow-eyed old devil landed with Rheged. But you must have drawn his fangs, Trev. He's given us no trouble."

"I doubt it," Trevyn said. "He's just waiting for a time that suits his fancy. Wael is peculiar that way. And he hates me worse than poison. You'll see some fireworks yet. We must strike quickly, Father, before—"

Before Wael harmed Meg, Alan knew, though Trevyn could not say it. "As quickly as may be," he gruffly replied. "I have men at work up by the Forest constructing siege towers."

"No need. I can open the gates for you with a touch. I have the ancient powers of Bevan now, Father. Watch." Trevyn indicated his blanketroll, scarcely moving his finger, and it undid itself from his saddle, floated gently through the air, and settled at his feet. The wolf cub jumped down, pattered over, and curled up in his lap.

"What—what have you bargained away for this power?" Alan breathed, startled and dismayed. "What have you sacrificed, Trevyn?"

"Gwern is gone." Trevyn could not still the spasm of pain

that crossed his face. "But there was no bargaining done, Father, believe me. I would far rather . . ." For a moment he could not go on. "I even think it might have been Gwern's idea," he finally said.

"You don't look strong enough to break a biscuit," Alan told him roughly, to temper his concern.

"I'm as weak as a kitten," Trevyn acknowledged. "But in a way I'm stronger than I ever was before. And I won't be able to sleep until this is settled—until I see Meg safe. Tomorrow, Father. Please."

Alan hesitated, measuring his stature and his need. "Only if I am never far from your side," he said at last.

"I'll be glad of your shield."

"All right, then. . . . Where did you get the wolf?"

Trevyn lifted the creature to his face, rested his taut cheek for a moment in its warm fur. "From the All-Mother," he answered after a pause, "and he's dearer to me than life, Father. Will you guard him, too?"

"Of course. Trevyn, will I ever understand?"

"When this is over, I'll sleep for a month. Then we'll talk for a year."

In the morning a messenger arrived whose news sent Alan stamping in circles with anxiety. "A second wave of invaders has landed," he told Trevyn. "They're marching on us across deserted countryside. My men are faithful, but they have been fighting for months; those who live are worn to the bone. They can't take much more of this."

"All the more reason to regain Nemeton quickly," said Trevyn. Alan nodded and called his army into battle readiness.

He and Trevyn reached the main gate under cover provided by Craig's expert archers. Still, rocks and hot lead hailed down upon them as they stood before the iron-sheathed doors. Holding a cowhide over himself and his son, Alan waited patiently while Trevyn ran questing fingers along the timbers, spoke a soft command. Nothing happened, and the Prince frowned.

"Wael has put a locking spell on these gates," he explained. "So we can't afford to be delicate. . . ." A quiet light flickered through his sea-green eyes. He judged that he had power now to call on the dark goddess once more. He need not possess strength of body; Emrist had showed him that. He need only assent completely to her aid. "Here goes," he muttered, and struck the gates once, lightly, with clenched fist. "Break them, Menwy, break them!"

The huge portals burst inward, hurling splinters and metal shards for a hundred feet. The portcullis that stood just beyond them writhed apart and flew through the air like nightmare snakes. Even the stones of the gatehouse flew. Within an instant, Alan found himself staring through a clean, open passageway into the main street of Nemeton, where a troop of Tokarians stood at muster. Luckily, the enemy soldiers were even more startled than he, and some were already mortally wounded. Hastily, Alan pulled Trevyn aside and bellowed for the charge.

Half of the Tokarians were trapped on the walls, demoralized by the sudden change in their circumstances. Alan's army swirled in and took them from behind, quickly dispatching them. Others of the enemy were hunted through the streets and deserted houses of the town; this was slow, nerve-racking work. Ket spotted a glimpse of golden crown and was pleased to take Rheged his prisoner. Alan didn't know. As soon as he could, he set a company to barricading the blasted gates, saw Trevyn onto his weird white steed, gathered some mounted retainers, and led on to Corin's keep. There another set of barred and guarded doors awaited them.

The Tokarians within the keep saw them coming and met them with a shower of arrows and rocks. Sensing doom, they fought feverishly, hurling anything they could think of to hold vengeance at a distance. But Trevyn drew rein just beyond the range of their fire and flung up one arm. The gates toppled as if pushed by a strong wind, and he galloped over them, ducking, a wolf cub sheltered against his chest. The Tokarians scattered, and Alan's liegemen began stoically to hunt them down.

"The dungeons," Alan said.

"Meg's on the roof," Trevyn murmured, peering up. He could see nothing but his eagle, high overhead.

"There are enemies on the stairs. Let the men take care of them. The dungeons, first."

Robin of Firth, Corin's foster brother, was also intent on reaching the dungeons. He sped down the dark stairs ahead of them and greeted Cory with a shout of joyful relief. The lord of Nemeton and his followers sat fettered to their cell walls, looking somewhat starved and rather bewildered by the explosive noises they had been hearing. "No use breaking up the place," Alan remarked as Trevyn reached for a lock. "We might need it."

"You're right," Trevyn sighed. "Find the keys, Father; I'm tired." He collapsed onto a dank stone step, laid his head against the rough-cut doorjamb, and closed his eyes. Robin had already found the keys and was opening cells, unlocking fetters. Alan glanced worriedly at his son, then looked up sharply as Ket brought his royal prisoner clattering down the stairs. Cory hugged Robin and came over to speak to Alan, rubbing his sore wrists.

"The girl, Meg," he asked, "where might she be? Tokar's sinister old spellbinder came down here a short while ago and took her."

"Just like Wael," Rheged snarled, "to shelter behind a wench, saving his own ancient hide, while brave men suffer—"

"Silence!" Alan roared at him. Trevyn stood up, arrow swift, arrow straight, but pale beneath his grime. Ket put the captured king in a cell.

"Witch's whelp," Rheged sneered at Trevyn from behind the bars. "Pretty warlock, Wael will put an end to you yet. He was deathless and strong before you were born."

Trevyn gave him not even a glance for reply. "Upstairs," he ordered the others, and began toiling up the tower steps. Several times he had to stop to gather strength, cursing at his own slowness. Alan followed him closely. Corin, Robin, and some retainers puffed along behind. The way out onto the platform was by a trapdoor; Alan insisted on going first, but no one was waiting to knock off their heads. Wael stood at the opposite extreme of the circular space, very close to the edge, with Megan arranged before him like a shield, her arms twisted behind her back. Trevyn knew that Wael did not have much physical strength in his withered, clawlike hands, but he also knew his power to terrify and deceive. Meg looked frozen; she might as well have been held in a vise.

"By my troth," Alan exclaimed, "it's Waverly!"

"Hal thought as much," Trevyn remarked.

"I am flattered, Laueroc!" hissed the chamberlain of the late and evil Iscovar. "That you should remember me after all these years! Though of course I remember you well. You drove me forth from this very court, set my old bones to wandering the weary seas, you and your bastard brother, a pair of pups! So I set my course toward revenge. But all has gone against me: the bastard has escaped me, and this elf-sprout has thwarted and defied me at every turn." Wael glared venomously at Trevyn. "At last he robbed and destroyed the ancient thing that sustained me. Yet I will have my revenge at last, and you will both learn to hate the day you ever crossed me!" He twitched Megan nearer to the edge, where a smooth wall dropped hundreds of feet to the cobbled courtyard below.

"As I recall it," Alan said, courteously enough, "you were asked only to obey Hal as heir to the throne. Instead, you slipped away and took ship of your own accord."

"Do not speak to me of obedience!" shrieked Wael. "If I were in strength, you would all bow down to me and beg to know my will! Dogs! Sons of she-dogs! You would grovel before the Wolf as the jackal before the lion!"

"By thunder," Alan grated, "here is one lion that would willingly tame your wolf!" He drew his sword with the golden lion on the hilt. Wael's eyes glittered, and one hand flicked out to send the weapon flying with an invisible bolt. But at that instant, Trevyn quietly spoke a single word.

"Melidwen."

Megan came out of her pallid trance with a blaze of fury. "Filthy old man! Let go!" she cried, kicking back at Wael's knee. He yelped, and she broke lightly away from him, sped toward Trevyn. But at the last moment she seemed to remember that she was angry with him, swerved aside, and darted toward the stairs.

"Father!" Trevyn called. "Catch her!"

"Got her," Alan tersely replied.

"Don't let her go," Trevyn panted between clenched teeth. "I want to talk to her!" He tensed himself against pain. Wael was hopping about on his end of the platform, frenzied and gibbering with rage, raining invisible blows on the Prince. "Stop that!" Trevyn shouted. "Stop it! Begone, you—you Crebla!" He spoke the sooth-name.

Wael vanished. Without even a gesture or a puff of smoke, he disappeared. A tall, cloaked figure stood on the platform in his stead, very still, very silent, unfathomably black, with only the black vortex of a hood for face. All of Isle seemed to stop, simply stop. Even the distant clatter of soldiers in the courtyard ceased, and the slight, random movement of clouds in the sky.

"Pel Blagden," Trevyn breathed, and took a single step back.

"Nay," said a sweet, dusky woman's voice, "it is I." Then Trevyn noticed that tiny silver bells hung from the points of the apparition's empty sleeves. He went down on one knee, not in worship so much as in limp relief.

"Menwy," he whispered. "Dark lady, thank you. But why are you faceless, like the mantled lord?"

"Because he is in me, as Wael is in me now. I must appear to you in forms you can understand." Looming, she stalked over to Trevyn, stooped and extended to him the black cavern of her sleeve. Alan could not have aided his son, then, if both their lives had depended on it. He could not move even to retreat. But Trevyn reached up, grasped the invisible hand, and rose lightly to his feet. The lovely Black Virgin faced him now, with pearls draped over her shimmering forehead. Corin moaned and hid his eyes. He who had faced the faceless one could not withstand that beauty. But she looked up to Trevyn like a lover.

"Where are the dragons of Lyrdion, Alberic?" she asked him.

He had to clear his throat. "Within. Bound in the depths," he answered huskily. "Until now, by all that is dark and beautiful." He raised a hand, pointed eastward, and the others looked, stood rigid. Beyond the walls and turrets of

Nemeton they could plainly see, from their height, the grasslands that rolled away toward the sea—on which came the newly landed Tokarian army, marching.

But the earth of the plain moved like so much water, bubbled and burst. And the dragons arose through the rippling, parting grass, loosed by Trevyn's gesture, scores and hundreds of them, with flashing, scaly flanks of ruddy gold, red-crested, black-clawed, launching themselves against the invaders with a flick of their fluted wings, letting out brazen cries that seemed to echo across the world. Trevyn was never to forget the sound of that fierce, nasal battle chant.

Everyone on the tower stood staring, agape. Even Menwy watched as the dragons drove off the Tokarians with tail-lashing leaps and puffs of fiery breath. The scene worked itself out within that middle distance where everything looks suspended, very solid but not quite real. They could not hear the cries of the enemy soldiers, but they could see them fall. The men could not flee fast enough to evade the dragons; they were trampled, crushed, and burned. The dragons trumpeted in triumph. Only one of them had fallen, killed by a lucky arrow to the eye. The others intently pursued their human prey.

"Bloodthirsty," Trevyn blurted, sickened. "Too bloodthirsty! Why can't they just drive them back to the ships?"

"Mercy is not in the nature of dragons," Menwy replied, though Trevyn had not really expected any reply.

The dragons and the fleeing remnants of the army topped a rise and disappeared toward the Long Beaches. Nothing remained of the strange tableau except a lumpy expanse of strewn bodies. Trevyn looked away from them, faced the goddess again.

"Why does it trouble you?" she asked. "You have saved many of your father's liegemen, perhaps even saved your land."

"Because—I know those dragons are mine. They are in me."

"So you were able to loose them to good effect. And if you have gained the victory over Wael, Prince, it is because you no longer hate the shadowy deeps, the realm of the sable moon. My workings are not all for ill, Alberic. Even a villain such as Wael cannot help but do some good. In a sense, he brought you two together, Prince and Maiden."

With his eyes still on Menwy's subtle, sculpted face, Trevyn held out an arm and felt Meg move to fill it. The slender girl pressed against him, took the wolf cub from his cupped hand, and cradled it by her own small breasts.

"Without darkness, there would be no dawn," Menwy added.

"So you, who flung me into the hands of slavers, who stole my father's brooch to make mischief with, now choose to aid me." Trevyn sounded merely whimsical, not bitter, just then. "Why, ancient lady?"

"Because you are fair; no better reason."

Trevyn risked a glance at Meg, felt with a shock her fine-drawn loveliness, saw Dair, his baby son, lay a searching muzzle along her neck.

"And I will give the Tokarians fair winds home, those who live, as I have given them foul winds hither," added Menwy, with a hint of jealous edge to her voice. "Still, I am no one's servant. So, lest you lose all respect for me, Prince—feel this!"

A shock sent Trevyn staggering. Meg screamed; Menwy loomed taller and ever taller, in form of the fearsome horned god, her head a skull with the antlers of a stag.

"Farewell, Prince of Isle," she sang, before he had recovered, and engulfed him. In an instant the tower was only a fleck caught in the hem of her cloak, in a black and roaring, directionless blackness darker than a thousand nights. Trevyn clutched at Meg, hid his face in her hair; Robin moaned, and Alan flung an arm over his eyes. Then they all looked up at bright sky and blinked. Voices sounded from the courtyard; Trevyn's eagle swooped down to perch on a parapet. The day moved on apace.

"Are ye hurt!" Megan demanded. Trevyn held on to her for support with one hand, and the other held on to his head.

"I think I'm going to swoon," he said plaintively. "Be here when I wake up, Meg. Promise!"

"All right, I promise!" She peered up at him anxiously. "Trev—"

"Is it really all over?" Alan exclaimed incredulously, gazing down at the quiet town, the empty battle plain. "Is it really done?"

"I'm done in," Trevyn murmured. "Meg, take good care of that wolf."

"Of course."

"It's my son," he explained, lucidly.

"Of course. Trevyn, will ye sit down before ye fall and hurt yerself?"

"Not until I've kissed you." But he missed his aim, lurching.

"Later," she told him, and shouted at the others, "Dolts, will ye help me with this big oaf!"

They were all still dazed, gaping like Alan. "Can it really be all over?" he marveled again. "After all these hellish months?"

"My dream has just begun," Trevyn protested softly, and folded onto the paving stones.

Chapter Five

They got him into a bed presently, and he slept for a full day, then awoke to ravenously gulp a meal, then slept again. He kept it up, not for the month he had promised, but for a week. A few times the servants roused him and ordered him into a tub, soaking grime and brown, caked blood out of his golden hair. But no one had leisure to really nurse him, in the aftermath of war, and it was plain to see that he was well and content. The servants took to leaving food on a table by the bedside, fruit and bread and cheese and cold cooked meat. Trevyn would wake at odd hours, eat, drink water, and instantly doze off again. As he slept, he dreamed—pleasant dreams, mostly. Even when not sleeping, he dreamed with open eyes. Of Isle, and Elwestrand, and love, and Maeve, and, the seventh day, of Melidwen—

Meg burst into his room that day; Dair pattered after her and jumped up on the bed. "Trevyn, what d'ye mean!" Meg cried. "What can ye be thinking of! I can't wear this!"

He gazed at her, breathless, and not only because of the furry, gray weight on top of him. She looked like a princess— nay, some being that was freer and more magical than a princess. She looked like someone Emrist might have invoked, spirit of starlight and daisy field and white winter lacework of birch. Soft, sparkling cloth enfolded her like an embrace, patterned white on white, floating richly around her bare, smooth feet. Her sparrow-brown hair flew as airily as the gown. She tolerated his stare for a moment, then stamped impatiently.

"It'll take washing every blessed day," she complained. "And everyone who saw me thinks I'm putting on airs. And how d'ye expect me to go walking that precious son of yers in this?"

Clutching his blankets, Trevyn wriggled out from under the wolf in question. "Take it off, if you don't like it," he gasped.

"I adore it." Her pointed face softened into a smile. "But it's too grand, Trev. Dream me a few that are a bit more practical."

"I don't direct my dreams," he whispered, and reached out to touch her fingertips, drew her down to him by her warm fingertips, nothing more. Her flower of a mouth touched his; he parted it tenderly, probed with consummate tenderness, felt a sweet ache grow. Rosebuds and dew. . . . His fingers entwined her hair, found the warm nape of her neck, followed her tresses to the startled tip of her young breast under the magical cloth. . . . Meg placed her hands on his, dropped her head to his bare shoulder.

"Love me," he begged.

"I do."

"I know—I should have always known. I'd have known how I loved you, if I'd paid heed. But love me now, Meg. That is your wedding gown."

"Then let us ride to where the wedding party awaits us," she told him reasonably. "At the sacred grove."

"What?"

"At the Forest' southern skirt, where the two rivers join. Gwern's grove."

That sobered him. He let her go and sat to face her. "How did you know?"

"I—some things I just know—like I know that Dair really is yer son somehow—and I know that Gwern gave ye himself. He had to, for ye to be so whole now."

"Ay. I feel like my life has just begun, Meg. As if you've just woken me to a new world. All that's happened since—since a young fool left you at Lee—hardly seems to count."

"It counts." She grinned wickedly at him. "But ye're right about the new world. Or a new Isle, anyway. Wonders are springing up all over. The whole land's taken on a new sheen; everyone notices it."

He stared at her. "The magic is coming back," he breathed.

"Ye've dreamed it back. Ye've even made me a touch on the pretty side somehow. Won't ye go back to sleep now, like a good prince, and dream me a few more dresses?"

"Great goddess, nay," he exclaimed. "I've slept long enough. Where's Father?"

"Sped to his love."

Alan had long since gone to Lysse, as fast as horse could take him. All along the path of his swift journey he saw magic springing up. Tiny yellow flowers winked from the grass, each one a radiant coronet. Veran's crown, the Elfin Gold, had come back to Isle, and all the land glowed with intangible luster by virtue of its presence.

Lysse met Alan on the road, far outside the gates. Sight and heart had returned to her together, and she sensed his coming long before he arrived. She greeted him smiling, but he wept in her embrace. "Even at my worst, I knew you would forgive me," he told her when he could speak, "and that is a fearful knowledge."

"Hal thought the same of you."

"I know. Trevyn has told me a little. . . . My brother sends me his love, from Elwestrand. He wept to speak of me. . . . Well, I am no longer so proud that I can afford to think ill of him, Lissy." He grinned wryly. "And I can somewhat account for the change in me; but what is to account for the marvels abroad in the land?"

"A turn of the great tide. Aene is claiming back what was lost for a while." Lysse smiled dreamily. "Isle might soon be as magical as Elwestrand, I believe. But Hal and my people cannot return."

"I know. When do we sail?"

"In the spring. There will be a ship at the Bay."

"Far better fortune than I deserve," Alan said softly, "if Hal awaits me. But Lysse, when I took the wrong path, when I laid hold of that great, bloody sword, I felt sure it severed me from him. For all time. How can I feel so sure now that I shall see him again?"

"Mother of mercy," she chided, "can't you tell? Isle is like a clean-washed stone, like a bright leaf after rain, and your small transgressions are gone in the tide of time, like all others. Alan, the haunts are gone from the land."

"What?" he whispered.

"The shades have gone to rest, even the stubborn shades by the Blessed Bay. All penances are done. And the dragons have left their gloomy lairs."

"Ay, Trevyn seems to be in charge of them now. I wish I understood. . . . Love, glad as I shall be to sail to Elwestrand, I am glad we need not go soon. I would like to get to know my son."

After Trevyn was up and about for a few days, he and Meg took horse toward the place she had named. Liegemen and a few maids rode with them, for decorum's sake, and Corin, out of friendly curiosity, and Ket. Craig and Robin and the other lords had long since sped back to their demesnes. There was a tremendous amount of work to be done; unguarded cottages had been robbed, repairs had been neglected, and spring planting had gone almost entirely undone in the eastern half of the realm. Already Alan had sent messengers to Tokar demanding ransom for Rheged, not in treasure, but in food, to avert famine. And the very day of the final battle he had sent patrols throughout Isle to prevent plundering and to spread news of peace. But there was little need of such reassurance. Folk sensed comfort as if it were a fragrance in the air and returned quickly to their homes. Even Trevyn's dragons, blundering northward along the eastern shore, did not seriously upset them. All along the road to their rendezvous, the Prince and his retainers were greeted by happy folk. It seemed to awe them that he carried a young wolf in his arms.

They rode gently, in easy stages, letting Trevyn regain his

strength. Late on the seventh day they neared the river crossing, and Trevyn peered ahead with a faint frown. Against the glowing sunset sky he could see the figure of an eagle, his eagle, perched atop a tall tree, or group of trees, that he felt certain had not been there before.

"What the—" he muttered.

"Gwern's grove," Megan replied from her palfrey beside him. She rode in her lovely white dress, the only one she presently owned, though she had Trevyn's promise of more from a certain Gypsy seamstress. She had found her fears mistaken; the gown did not need daily washing. In fact, dirt did not seem to touch it at all. The paradoxical fabric, floating and crisp, seemed no more prone to mundane soil than a cloud wisp or the caught light of the moon.

The company splashed through the river branch, through water well above the horses' knees. Afterward, drops sprinkled down like strings of pearls from Meg's hem, and stayed there. A few fell to the ground and lay glimmering. Trevyn looked at them in mild surprise and let them be. Meg already wore another such magical jewel, the pink moonstone he had brought her from Elwestrand, with the mandorla at its heart. But Corin and the others picked up the gems with gasps of wonder.

"Magic!" Corin breathed. Then no one said more, not even the irrepressible Meg. They had entered under the woven shade of the Wyrdwood.

They rode through sheerest stillness. No underbrush rustled against their saddles; no branches scraped. The trees towered immensely, in form like the pillars of earth, the trunks smooth and unbranched to thirty feet above their heads. Hooves fell soundlessly on the leaf loam of a hundred seasons, so it seemed. Within a moment, the riders were swallowed by soft, random spaces like the honeycomb caverns of deep earth where dragons used to dwell, like the shadowy roots of the sea where the sun swims back to the east. Birds sang somewhere in the pinpoint foliage far above. Trevyn signaled a stop, looking all about him, to depths and heights, with eager, straining face.

"We're likely never to come out of here," Corin blurted, breaking silence. He had looked behind him and seen no trace of the way he had come; now he held the reins with sweaty hands. But Trevyn scarcely heard him, lost in longing and awe.

"By the Mothers, he's here! I can feel him. . . ." Trevyn bit back a sob. Silent tears ran down his face. "Gwern . . ."

"The place suits him," Meg said softly.

"Ay, it's a god's grove. And Gwern has invited his fellows, it seems. I feel Bevan here as well." Trevyn struggled to compose himself. Memories gripped him and made him feel weak, memories of Emrist and of Elwestrand.

"Trev," Ket burst out, "please. We're frightened."

Surprised, he scanned their pale faces. Meg sat serenely, but a couple of the maids had started to whimper.

"We're not lost!" Trevyn exclaimed. "Why, we're nearer to heart's home than we've been since birth. . . . All right, follow me. There is always a pattern. This way." He led off through the motionless dance of the trees.

He took them in a sweeping spiral, gradually closing in on an unseen vortex at the center of the hushed grove. They rounded the last gentle curve and arrived. Sunlight streamed down into a clearing amid the giants. There a single sapling grew, its leaves translucent jewels that sent flakes of color skimming like dragonflies across the grass. Resting in the sun-dappled shade sat a pair of wedding guests, Alan and Lysse. Beside them, at the sunlit base of the slender tree, lay a unicorn, moon-white, with a golden horn.

"Is that beastie yours, too, lad?" Alan asked Trevyn when they had embraced.

"Mine and everyone's." He took Meg by the hand and led her to meet his mother.

They all camped there that night, feasting on plain food that tasted better than it had any right to, talking beneath the light of a swelling moon, answering innumerable questions. Trevyn heard about Megan's travels and her lupine friend. Lysse found that she liked the girl better by the moment. Alan heard at last the full history of his jeweled brooch, and he learned that he had sworn a spell upon his green Elfstone.

"Things that show the sun crest are your talisman, as the parchment with the wolf emblem was Wael's," Trevyn explained "And your gem is magical in its own right, mightily so. . . . Only a King could have managed it. But I think nothing less could have woken me."

"I'm no sorcerer," Alan protested.

"But you've always been great in power, you and Hal. You never used your magic, that's all. . . . And you called me by my sooth-name. That was prettily done."

"It should have been done far sooner," Alan grumbled. "But it was hard for me to know you as the Very King who shall succeed me. . . . What is your talisman to be, Alberic?"

By way of answer, the unicorn came and laid its head in his lap.

They all sat half drunk with wine of magic and love. By dawn they lay drowsily, but still softly talking. At first light, Trevyn regretfully left the others and went off by himself.

By closing his eyes, he quickly found Gwern's grave, hidden under a blanket of luxuriant flowers. Though he hated to do it, he upended them with his dagger and dug away industriously, muttering at the mess he was making of himself. But he found the sword of Lyrdion before too long and lifted it, intending to hide it among his gear until he had a chance to take it to the sea. . . . A flash like the blaze of the rising sun went up from the weapon, and everyone in the grove came running.

"Bevan, you nuisance," Trevyn quietly rebuked the air, "why did you do that?"

His family and friends gathered around, absorbing the scene. "I thought Gwern lay there!" Alan exclaimed, looking at the open grave.

"Nay, Gwern lies nowhere, except—everywhere, here. All powers of loveliness seem to be met here today." Obeying an impulse, Trevyn lifted the great sword skyward. Hau Ferddas shone like a fair, golden bird, effortlessly soaring, as warm in his hand as a living thing. The gems on the hilt were pools, were eyes, were magic mirrors. The metal of the blade shimmered like a silken gown.

"What, more marvels now?" Alan breathed. "Suddenly that sword has become as fair as sunshine, a token of all honor and goodness, in your grasp."

"Bevan's doing," Trevyn said. "So that we should see it as it was for him, and understand."

"And this is the weapon you must take to the sea?" Alan murmured incredulously.

"Ay, that I must. At another place or time, it could yet become a horror." He scowled at the invisible spirit of the star-son. "And this has not made it any easier!" He swaddled the sword in its fabric bonds.

They all seemed to realize at once that they were exhausted. Of one accord they trooped back to their campsite and quickly fell asleep. But they only slept for a few hours; in late morning they were awakened by the approach of more riders. Rosemary appeared, looking lovely in cloth of russet and cream. Two countryfolk followed her. Ket ran to meet her, and Megan ran to embrace the others; they were her mother and father. Goodman Brock had earned fame for his courage and tenacity in holding his land and helping his neighbors throughout the siege of wolves. But he looked uncomfortable on horseback, and stunned to see his daughter in such finery. He scrambled down from his mount and gave her a cautious kiss, then stood disconsolately while his wife went off, chattering, with the other women. Because he felt out of place, he glowered when Trevyn greeted him.

"Whew!" Trevyn whistled. "I believe you're remembering a cocky young fool—"

Brock had to smile at that. "Why, nay, I recall no foolishness," he declared. "But I have heard much talk of a certain marvelous Prince." He gulped, and lost his smile again. "Is that a unicorn?"

"It's quite peaceable," Trevyn assured him. "Come, meet my father."

As it turned out, Brock had business with Alan. "Folk have gotten together and named me a sort of steward at Lee," he explained gruffly, "to do for them until ye can name a new lord, Sire, since Rafe left no heir. So I'm to report t' ye."

"So you're the people's chosen leader!" Alan said thoughtfully. "Why don't you just stay on, then, Goodman? Be lord yourself."

"I!" Brock protested. "I'll make no velvet-clad lord, Sire. I've no manners, no learning—"

"I'll send you a scribe. The velvet's not required. But stay a steward, then, if you don't want the title. The work's the same." Alan beckoned at him. "Come and help me with these kettles." The King was hungry, and trying to hurry along breakfast.

They all ate, finally, porridge and honey and a few boiled eggs, and in the process of dealing with the sticky meal everyone became well acquainted. Brock no longer felt out of place by the time they were done. "Now, then," Alan asked, "since we're all here, will someone tell me how these weddings are to take place?"

"By the old style, I suppose, of consent," Trevyn answered. "Or you could marry us by royal decree."

"Wait a bit," Rosemary told them. "I believe there's one person yet to come." She was the Rowan Lady, and she sensed whatever moved within the Forest. So they waited.

"Here I am, dears," a voice said after a while, and with one accord they all rose, though they had seen no one. Then, walking straight and strong, a very old woman came toward them out of the grove.

"Ylim!" Trevyn exclaimed, though he had never seen her in that form. Alan stared; he had raised a cairn over that body, but he had never known her name.

"In this place, I am Alys." She stood, not smiling and yet not unkind, folding her gnarled hands on her muslin apron. "But I must come to you in a form you understand, or partly understand."

"In the valley beyond Celydon," said Rosemary softly, "you would be the ancient seeress, the weaver."

"Ay. You are wise, Lady. Ylim is only a servant of Alys. . . . But here I am all, or nearly all. This is a place of power, my own power and power of my son. . . . The best of all places for these weddings."

"And will you stay now?" Trevyn asked. "Are you truly back in Isle?"

"Ylim will stay." She smiled at that, mostly with her deep and glowing eyes. "Alys was never gone."

Without much talk or need for thought, all was made ready for the nuptials. In a few minutes, Trevyn and Meg stood paired before the goddess beneath the young and growing tree, he in the whitest tunic the elves had given him, she in her dream dress with a spray of rare white heather in her hand. Ket and Rosemary stood behind them, more soberly clad, but arm in arm. Young Dair lay quietly in Alan's arms.

"There's small need for words," Ylim said. "Symbols show more." From her apron pockets she drew yards of lace—of her own weaving, Trevyn knew, and of pattern as intricate as all creation, simple as love, white as the unicorn. With a length of this she encircled Megan's brow, crowning her like a blossom, then sent a streamer over to Trevyn, weaving her to him.

She worked quickly, scarcely moving, directing the lacework by gesture rather than touch. When she had finished, Trevyn stood at the center of a pattern that spread to include the jeweled tree, and a stag that wandered by, and everyone present; even the unicorn held a loop of lace with its horn. For his own part, Trevyn felt once again captured and tied, even more entangled now than he had been in Tokar. But Meg stood tranquilly.

"The bonds will remain only in your mind," Ylim said. "Kiss your bride, Alberic." He felt as if he could scarcely move, but he leaned over to comply. His lips met Meg's smoothly. And as they kissed, the lace parted into bits, fell like snowflakes to the ground. Ever afterward, the most delicate of flowers grew there, flowers found nowhere else in Isle. But Trevyn could never remember what pattern the lace had made; he had forgotten to look. And those who had looked, when he asked, each gave a different answer.

"All blessings on you, Meg and Trevyn, Ket and Rosemary," said Ylim the ancient seeress, and turned, and left. Trevyn still stood kissing Meg. Moments after Ylim had gone, he raised his head with a start. "Wait!" he exclaimed, but silence answered him.

"I forgot to ask her about anything," he complained. "About Maeve, about Dair!"

"Wait and see. . . ." The voice of Alys floated back.

Epilogue

On a bright day of the following May, the twenty-first anniversary of Alan's coronation, all the lords in Isle and Welas gathered at the gentle summit near Laueroc where Adaoun had marked the beginning and ending of an Age by wedding and crowning the Sunrise and Sunset Kings. It was not so many years before, Alan mused, that he had taken Lysse to wife on that spot and Hal had wed Rosemary. But the weight of those years had slowed him, nevertheless, and made him glad of promised rest. He brought the great crown of Veran from the treasure room, the rayed crown like the sunburst emblem of the Elfstone. He took it to the appointed place and waited for his son.

In the presence of the watching multitude, Trevyn came before his father, scorning heavy robes, clad free as the wind in a soft linen tunic and deerskin boots. He dropped to one knee, and Alan placed the ceremonial burden on his head. Then he rose, and Alan girded him with his own newly forged sword, silver of hue, with a running unicorn for hilt. He presented his son to the assembled lords.

"Here is your King now," he told them, "and I am King no more."

A great, golden bird circled overhead, scattering the meadowlarks. The lords took up the omen with a shout. "Hail, Eagle King!" they cried. "Hail, Liege King of Laueroc!" They lifted clasped hands in salute.

"You're far more than that," Alan murmured to his son.

"Ay," Trevyn agreed without a trace of hesitation. "I might just as well be called Unicorn King."

"You're silver and gold, as Hal foresaw."

Four rode out the next day: Alan, Lysse, Trevyn, and Meg on a round little mare she called Bess. The weather was fine, and they went at a leisurely pace, taking four days to pass the settled land. Meg was thrilled by the wilderness beyond. Riding through a changing pattern of slope and rocky tor, thick-woven forest and silky meadow, sunlight and shade and shadow, she drew in beauty with every breath, nourishing the budding life she carried within her—for Meg was with child.

On the seventh day of their journey, the four came to the Bay of the Blessed, a place of deepest green shade and silvery water, a place meant for moonlight. A boat swam like a dusky swan in the shallows. Alan tethered it and found the plank to board it. Then he and Lysse turned to face their son and daughter-in-law.

"How do you want to manage this matter of the sword?" Alan asked quietly.

Trevyn brought the magical weapon out of the wrappings it had worn all winter. It shone as fair as the first flower of spring. Impulsively, he offered it to his father. "You've had the most sorrow from it. Will you hurl it away?"

"Trevyn," Alan chided. "All you've been through, and you still try to meddle with fate? I don't dare to touch it. Do you want to borrow my boat?"

Trevyn shook his head. He knew what a pang of longing it would send through him to stand on the deck of an elf-ship. He stood thinking for a moment, then nodded, and pointed at a precise spot on the taut surface of the Bay. "There," he said.

The lustrous water broke like a veil, fell apart in fragments. From the rent a sea-drake with scales of dark crimson raised its dripping head, glaring out of flat carnelian eyes. Meg gulped and took a step back.

"One of Menwy's people," Trevyn explained, and he flung the sword with all his strength, sent it spinning through the air like a shining wheel. Fearlessly the dragon caught the weapon in its great mouth, held it as a dog holds a bone, and dove. The watchers on shore saw ripples trail it into the western sea.

"I hope we don't encounter such creatures on the way," Alan breathed, somewhat shaken.

"You'll never know," Trevyn answered. "You'll remember nothing but peace. Go joyfully, and regret nothing." He embraced Alan and then his mother, kissing them. Alan gripped his hand.

"I regret many things in my life," he told his son, meeting his eyes, "and some of those you know, Trev. . . . But this is not one of them. Farewell, Megan; keep him in charge. Come, Love, let us go." Alan put an arm around his Elf-Queen, and together they boarded the waiting ship.

"Go with all blessing," whispered Meg.

Trevyn lifted the plank. The quickening ship swam away from the shore. Lysse and Alan settled themselves on the deck, waving in farewell. Trevyn returned the gesture with desolation in his heart. The elf-boat carried away his only kindred in Isle except for the son that stood, four-legged, at his feet. . . . Trevyn watched the lovely boat until it rounded the headland, then turned to Meg, laid his face in her hair, and wept. His love of this woman was part of the pattern; it was very good. But in spite of her love, hers and others', Trevyn knew himself to be alone at his core, a naked thing joining earth and sky. Perhaps all men were so at the core. Being so alone, he had no way of knowing.

"Even that weird white horse," he muttered.

The moon-marked steed had left him without a backward glance, once the journey was done, leaping craggy rocks and skimming the grass between, ineffably alone, like a swift spirit blown from the far, dark places between the stars. Trevyn shook his head ruefully at the memory, and Dair sprang up, placed massive forepaws on his chest. Trevyn caressed the smooth hollow between his eyes.

"Very true, you're still here," he said. "And you'll yet be yourself in human form, Dair; mark it." He had seen that truth on an ancient woman's loom in a valley above Celydon. A startling, regal face had looked back at him from Ylim's web, a face with wide-set, feral, amethyst eyes, brows that met, nostrils that faintly pulsed—yet unmistakably the face of Dair, his son. But how would that youth come to him? When?

"Trust the tides," answered Meg, sensing his thoughts.

Trevyn and his bride spent the night on the shore, clinging together for warmth of more than body. In the morning they started back toward Laueroc, where liegemen and vassals awaited their King. Glancing behind him for one last look at the Bay, Trevyn noted a shimmer of white beneath the deepest green shadows of the firs. A unicorn stood there, watching him go.

I am the son.
I am the steadfast son,
I am the son of earth.
I am hazel roots,
I am red dragons,
I am robin and wren,
I am strong magic.

I am the eagle,
I am the soaring son,
I am the son of sky.
I am wings of wind,
I am a golden wheel,
I am a warrior,
I am the circle dance,
I am the song.

I am the swan,
I am the wandering son,
I am the son of sea.
I am changing eyes,
I am green shadow,
I am between the stars,
I am the stars.
I am the star-son.
I am the son.

Glossary of Names

ADAOUN: father of all the elves, creation of the First Song of Aene.

AENE: not, strictly speaking, a name, but the elfin term translatable as "the One": a power neither good nor evil, female nor male, but all of each.

ALAN: Sunrise King, Hal's brother and longtime companion, Trevyn's father.

ALBERIC: Trevyn's true-name or elfin name, meaning "a ruler of elfin blood," but comprising many opposites.

ALYS: the most inclusive name of the Goddess of Many Names, the earth-mother, moon-mother, maiden, and hag.

ARUNDEL: Hal's horse, who harked from the Eagle Valley of the elves.

BAY OF THE BLESSED: the estuary of the Gleaming River, where Bevan set sail for Elwestrand and Veran landed; where the elves took ship, and Hal, the last of Veran's line.

BEVAN: son of Celonwy, the moon goddess, and Byve, High King in Eburacon before the sack of that city. A star-son.

CELONWY: the moon-mother or Argent Moon, one phase of the great goddess. Within the history of Isle, Bevan's mother.

CELYDON: the Forest Island of Many Trees. Rosemary's home.

CORIN: in the wandering days, Alan's comrade. Later, lord of Nemeton.

CRAIG THE GRIM: onetime outlaw, later lord of Whitewater.

CREBLA: Wael's true-name, an anagram of Trevyn's own.

CUERT: Prince of Laueroc who fled with Veran to Welas.

CUIN: Alan's distant ancestor, Bevan's comrade, first High King of Laueroc.

CULEAN: the last High King of Laueroc. Killed himself with Hau Ferddas at the time of the Eastern invasion.

DAIR: an elfin name referring to the oak, for strength. Trevyn's son.

DEONA: Alan's great-great-grandmother, reared in Welden, through whom the blood of the Cuin found its way back to Laueroc. Cuert's granddaughter.

DOL SOLDEN: elfin for *The Book of Suns*, Veran's account of the prophecies of Aene.

DUV: an ancient name of the great mother, the goddess.

EAGLE VALLEY: inaccessible valley where Hal and Alan found the elves, on Veran's Mountain.

EBURACON: the ruined city of Bevan and Byve, surrounded by Forest and haunt.

ELUNDELEI: moon mountain, mountain of eagle vision, Mount Sooth. On Elwestrand.

ELWESTRAND: the elves' strand or the western land, a magical island beyond the sunset.

ELWYNDAS: Alan's elfin name, meaning elf brother, spirit brother, Elf-Friend.

EMRIST: a Tokarian magician.

FRECA: the name Trevyn was given in Tokar, elfin for "Brave One."

GWERN: alder-son and son of earth; Trevyn's wyrd.

HAL: Sunset King, Very King, healer, bard and seer, Alan's brother and fellow ruler at Laueroc.

HAU FERDDAS: elfin for Mighty Protector, Peace-Friend. The magical sword of Lyrdion, dangerous in its own right and darkened through the ages by the deeds of the men who used it.

HERNE: first of the Eastern Kings; invader of Isle.

ISCOVAR: Hal's purported father, the last of the hated Eastern kings who ruled at Nemeton.

ISLE: a water-ringed land that stands as a rampart between Elwestrand and the shadowed east.

KET THE RED: onetime outlaw, later seneschal of Laueroc.

LAUEROC: originally, Laveroc—that is to say, City of Meadowlarks. Founded by Cuin; longtime home of the High Kings. Later, court city of the Sun Kings.

LEUIN: seventh lord of Laueroc under the Eastern kings. Alan's father; Hal's actual father.

LYRDION: an isolated ruin along the northwest coast of Isle, once home of a dragon-king and his dragon-lords.

LYSSE: Alan's wife, Trevyn's mother. An elf and a seeress.

MAEVE: Emrist's sister; also an aspect of the goddess.

MARROK: Herne's sorcerer.

MEGAN: Trevyn's beloved; also, the maidenly aspect of the goddess.

MELIDWEN: a name for the Goddess of Many Names, applied to her aspect as maiden and crescent moon.

MENWY: Goddess of the Sable Moon, better known as the Black Virgin of the Gypsies.

MIRELDEYN: Hal's elfin name, meaning "Elf-Man, Elf-Master."

NEMETON: a city near the mouth of the Black River where the Eastern Kings, the invaders, ruled.

PEL BLAGDEN: the Mantled God, Lord of the Dead, whom Bevan vanquished.

RAFE: Hal's friend and captain, later lord of Lee.

RHEGED: king of Tokar.

ROBIN: Hal's companion and Corin's foster brother, later lord of Firth.

ROSEMARY: Hal's wife, the Lady of Celydon.

TOKAR: a country to the eastward of Isle, separated from it by the southern sea.

TREVYN: Alan's son, Prince of Isle and Welas, heir of the Sun Kings.

VERAN: a scion of Bevan, called back to Isle from Elwestrand; the first of the Blessed Kings of Welas.

VERAN'S MOUNTAIN: the tallest mountain in Welas, on top of which nestles the Eagle Valley, where the elves lived.

WAEL: a sorcerer, high priest of the Wolf cult, enemy of Isle. Formerly Waverly.

WAVERLY: Iscovar's sorcerer and chamberlain.

WELAS: the western portion of Isle, beyond the Gleaming River, where a different language is spoken.

WELDEN: the Elde Castle, founded by Veran upon the Gleaming River; court city of the Blessed Kings.

WYNNDA: the immortal white winged horse that served Adaoun.

YLIM: an immortal weaving seeress.

Glossary of Terms

Amaranth: a reddish-purple flower that never dies.

Asphodel: a white, lilylike flower that grows only in magical climes.

Athane: the black-handled sword used by sorcerers for sacrifice and for tracing the mystic circle.

Elf-ship: a graceful, gray, sailless boat made of living wood, moving swiftly and of its own volition, homing to Elwestrand. Attributed to elves, but actually first created and ridden by Bevan.

Elwedeyn: an adjective describing something of the old order—loosely, elfin.

Hollow hills: the raths where the gods lived after they gave up the sunlit lands to the Mothers of men and before they followed Bevan to the Blessed Bay, where they became shades.

Laifrita thae: elfin for "sweet peace to thee"; a greeting.

Mandorla: the mystic almond, the shape where two circles overlap. An emblem of the union of opposites.

Mothers: the mortal women who succeeded the Mother Goddess Duv and her children, the gods.

Plinset: a Welandais stringed musical instrument.

Sister-son: in the old style of reckoning descent through the woman, a man's heir.

Star-son: a wanderer from Otherness; a stranger in the midst of men who later leaves them.

Veran's crown: a healing flower, very rare after the Eastern invasion. Also called Elfin Gold, Veran's Balm.

Wyrd: the fate within, the dark twin, the rival.

Festivals

Old Style—Feasts of Fires

1 November—for repose of dead
2 February—in honor of the Mothers
1 May—for purification
2 August—for harvest

New Style—Festivals of the Sun
(Eastern reckoning)

21 December—Winterfest, a gifting time in honor of the Sacred
    Son
22 March—Glainfest, a vernal observance
24 June—Bowerfest, for the Oak King
22 September—Cornfest, for threshing

Eastern Kings

Herne
Hervyn
Heinin
Hent
Iuchar
Idno
Iscovar

Iscovar's supposed son, Hervoyel,
later reigned as Hal of Laueroc

A Brief Genealogy of the Sun Kings Based on "The Book of Suns"*

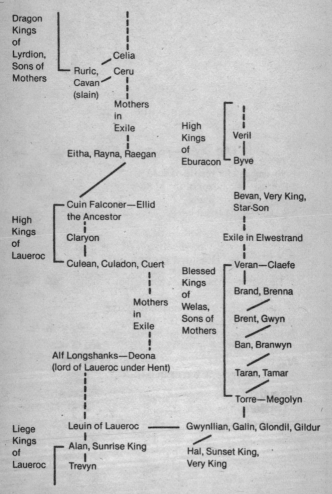

Dragon Kings of Lyrdion, Sons of Mothers

Celia
Ruric, Ceru
Cavan (slain)

Mothers in Exile

Eitha, Rayna, Raegan

High Kings of Eburacon

Veril
Byve

Bevan, Very King, Star-Son

High Kings of Laueroc

Cuin Falconer—Ellid the Ancestor
Claryon
Culean, Culadon, Cuert

Exile in Elwestrand

Veran—Claefe

Brand, Brenna

Blessed Kings of Welas, Sons of Mothers

Mothers in Exile

Brent, Gwyn

Ban, Branwyn

Alf Longshanks—Deona (lord of Laueroc under Hent)

Taran, Tamar

Torre—Megolyn

Liege Kings of Laueroc

Leuin of Laueroc ——— Gwynllian, Galin, Glondil, Gildur

Alan, Sunrise King

Hal, Sunset King, Very King

Trevyn

*Diagonal lines signify descent through the female, in the old fashion. The mother of the king is the sister of his predecessor. The sibling relationship is indicated by a comma; wives are indicated by a dash.